THE LOVE STORY OF PINKY WOLLERMAN

BY ED COLE

Published by:
River Rock Books
P.O. Box 19730
Sacramento, CA 95819

ISBN: 978-0-9994385-5-8

Cover illustration and book design: Angela Tannehill, ThinkstockPhotos.com

Author photograph: Dick Schmidt

This book is a work of fiction. Names, characters, incidents and some places are either products of the author's imagination or are used fictitiously. Any resemblance to actual events or locales or persons, living or dead, is entirely coincidental.

PART ONE

ONE

The day before the burial, Logan, working alone, dug the grave in the rocky ground with nothing but a digging bar and a shovel, each strain and tug of his muscle and tendon a tribute to Pinky Wollerman, the man he called father.

The following day, as a small group of neighbors and friends gathered at the hilltop gravesite, their eyes were irresistibly drawn from the October greening of the wild grasses at their feet up through the rolling, oak-spotted foothills of the Once Wide Valley, up farther into the juniper and pine of the rising mountain slopes, and on to the distant horizon formed by the rugged granite crest of the high Sierra Nevada. Seeing their spirits captured by this breathtaking expanse, Logan chose to open the service with a discernment of Pinky's.

"Open space," Logan said. "It's a good thing." Then he waved his hand across the sprawling terrain as Pinky would have, and added, "Just because it's open don't mean it's empty."

When the minister's customary and heartfelt service came to a close, Logan turned back toward the mountains and quietly said, "Wait."

Everyone at the service had watched Logan grow from a boy into a man, tall, with a powerful build, rugged good looks and the unusual common sense of a much older man. Perhaps it was Logan's strong presence, or perhaps it was the solemnity of the moment, or perhaps the spirit of the place itself, but no one moved.

In the tranquil silence Logan recited lines from a legend of the ancient peoples who had once lived in the surrounding mountains and valleys.

"Our people came to this place with a wandering spirit leading them upstream, uphill and into the pockets formed by stone and tree and water, came with the spirit of the migratory clouds, curious of the secrets horizons hold, came with honor for the land alive beneath their feet. So favored were our people that the valley swallowed them up. And since that time our people have been of the land as the spark is of the flint."

With a nod toward the polished pine casket draped with a wreath of wild rose and pine boughs, Logan repeated, "of the land as the spark is of the flint," then added, "That was…that is, Pinky Wollerman."

After the mourners left, Logan silently read the inscription engraved on the slab of grey granite stone.

> I am only the dust on my Lover's path
> and from dust I will rise and turn into a flower.

Those who knew Pinky as a survivor of the Depression and the Dust Bowl and as a hardened foothill cattle rancher were puzzled by his choice of such a poignant poem. Perhaps, they thought, it recalled the days of love with his now-estranged wife.

Logan knew otherwise.

In the evening Logan walked beyond the barn to be with the land, under the stars. The legend from which he had spoken at Pinky's service haunted him. It was old, as old as the coming together of the tribe, the gathering of the favored ones. It was a story passed down by Logan's great-grandmother, whose people inhabited the Valley of the Once Wide Creek for centuries before the Europeans arrived.

The stories of the ancestors say there is a range of mountains so long and so high it divides the east from the west. Low on the sunset side of these mountains is an old valley, a place that knows the passage of years, but as a creature of endless cycles does not know the start or end of any single year.

Storms as large as many days pass by, laying down their waters to grow the grasses that feed herds of deer and warrens of squirrels and rabbits, in turn to feed the loping, lanky wolf, the shy bobcat, and the seldom seen lion.

High above the place, in thin air, granite crags collect snow and pack it away for the dry times when shimmering heat wallows in from western lowlands. The mountains flush the melt as rushing waters through steep canyons, and release a slow seep through cracks deep inside the earth to springs that feed creeks whose bottomlands harbor the tasseled wild onion, the fuzzy-stalked milkweed and the large-leafed sycamore.

Great oaks with clouds of midnight leaves stand wide apart with room for sun and air, yet weave themselves together as a layer of forest between the desert valley sage and the highland pines, and birds with wings as wide as grandmother's blanket soar through skies as fresh as morning.

———·———

It was handwritten on yellowed and wrinkled paper and salvaged from a sagging trunk of moldering papers, and Logan knew there had been tinkering as well as translation, but whether fiction or legend, it stirred a set of memories he hadn't known he had, which, oddly enough, left him feeling comfortably at home anywhere in the valley.

———·———

"It took a hundred years to turn them into a memory," Pinky had said. "A hundred years seems like a long time, but it's a knife edge on the thousands of years they were here. Most were killed outright by force or disease, some were pushed onto lesser lands or 'integrated' to live as white people. But there were others, Logan. Forgotten. Those who stayed on the land and died for lack of a place. Don't underestimate the lack of a place, Logan. The land holds a people's history, their sense of time, their ideas about God, reason for living. Change the face of the land, they get sick. Body *and* soul. Whole peoples can die off. It's a damned shame, Logan, but it happened here. This land has ghosts."

———·———

Logan stared into the darkness, overwhelmed by the eons of life upon the land. Did the spirit of the ancient ones still wander here? He surveyed the weathered and worn barn. Over 100 years had passed since his great-great-grandfather Cyrus Wilson had settled the ranch and built the barn, and though periodically renovated, it showed hard use and age. How long could it last? He envisioned the long-lived cedar studs and oak beams meeting their match in ten thousand storms and dozens of quakes and finally giving way to splintering and rot. After a few hundred years of nature's abuse the only thing left would be the stone perimeter foundation nearly hidden in the grass of a distant summer and in the duff of many trees yet to live and die in the time to come.

The foundation blocks were naturally formed stones that Cyrus Wilson hauled into place with two yoked oxen, a strong back, and a conviction he was taming the land and building something to last. Logan knew it could not. Like all such efforts, in any place, in any time, the ranch would someday be buried within the ancient and relentless land.

TWO
1853–1936

Escaping a family he was born into for no other reason than another ranch hand was needed, Cyrus was the first Wilson to come west. In 1853, searching for a place of his own, he rode a tall bay roan from the Territories to the high desert at the eastern base of the Sierra Nevada where he talked options for mountain crossings with the Paiutes. He waited for most of the snow to melt, climbed through steep, boulder-strewn passes, then wandered southwest across a high table land the Paiutes called the Shagoopah because a respected chief by that name had chosen it as his place to die. Cyrus did not know whether he might meet the man's ghost there, as an old Paiute said he would. But he did not. His fate was not to engage with the spirit of man, nor had he traveled sufficiently west for his appointed spiritual bequest, but he did pause at the western edge of Shagoopah's plateau, looked back, and wondered.

Beyond the plateau he followed an incline thinly covered by wind-scoured snow past several barren lakes and dropped into a valley once used as a place for trading goods and relatives between the Paiutes and the Yokuts.

When Cyrus entered the abandoned valley, he saw a place of stark beauty, dimpled with tall pines and stunted aspens standing in segregated islands stranded between avalanche runs. White granite peaks gave the place its high and craggy horizon, a saw-toothed silhouette against a sky of such deep blue as to hint of an infinite darkness holding purchase on all that lay beyond. It was a place of eccentric weather where, even in summer, a clear-sky sun could, in less time than it took to remove a too-warm coat, fold itself behind a gentle shower, then as quickly shift to blowing snow and winter cold. In the midst of awe he paused, wondered if this was where he was to meet up with the spirit of Shagoopah, and then wondered why such nonsense crossed his mind.

The rugged ground to the west of the valley—having been churned since the creation by earthquakes, and graded, raked and distributed by several glacial periods and by the persistent rains and snows—gave birth many miles downslope to a spreading and gentle foothill area that held the Valley of the Once Wide Creek, which was where Cyrus ended his journey. He was struck by the pastoral beauty of this solitary watershed valley, and his roan, for his own animal reasons, picked a place to stop and survey the valley where the two sat in pleasant appreciation for quite some time. And it was there a spirit, primitive and gentle, welcomed Cyrus. As he took the valley in through his eyes and ears and skin, he sensed a giant presence— silent but for a whisper—like the steady searching of wind through a thousand acres of tall grass. He was not sure if it was flowing out across the valley before him, or moving across a landscape within, but it infused him with a sense of welcome, as if he were engulfed in ancient hospitality. The presence of God came to mind, but he never had held such a belief. Being unaccustomed to such a nonsensical feeling, he willed it out of his recollection. Even in his old age, as he passed the stories of his mountain crossing to his grandchildren, he never once mentioned the oddness of that day, though it was what some part of him had searched for during the whole of his crossing.

———•———

The Once Wide clan of the Gawia Yokuts had lived for centuries in the valley where Cyrus settled. Their ancestors, according to oral history, found the valley rich, unoccupied and awaiting their pleasure, as it had been since the time of the creation. The Gawia and other Yokuts were mostly killed or chased off by the government-sponsored and vigilante Indian wars, so when Cyrus arrived in the valley, it seemed full with possibility and expanse, and he could not believe his good fortune and opportunity to find such a place so fertile and yet unoccupied. He stopped there and fashioned the wild space into a ranch, and in the process developed an intense sense of ownership, followed by its scion, the naturalized tyranny of inheritance.

Cyrus also left behind legendary stories and an image to match. The two surviving photographs showed an imposing man, tall, wide shouldered, lean and muscular, dressed in the iconic blue jeans and Stetson hat of the Old West cattle rancher, perhaps good-looking underneath the heavy weathering of a life lived outside in all seasons.

Some stories had Cyrus, wielding a six-shooter and a .44 Henry lever action rifle, bravely fighting off any number of scoundrels who would have taken the land. And he killed some of them, which was necessary, the stories said, to keep the ranch.

But the numerous scoundrels Cyrus was supposed to have shot amounted to one boy, and that was by pure accident.

A small band of Indians had settled in the mountains on the high side of the ranch. Cyrus rode to their camp to make sure their stay was temporary. They ran when they saw him, and Cyrus decided to shoot into the branches over their heads just to make a point. In their haste one of them stepped on a dead limb that broke with a loud crack, and another kicked a rock that rolled and smacked into other rocks. The noise and movement skittered Cyrus' normally staid horse, and Cyrus pulled the shot and hit one of the fleeing band.

Cyrus had seen no sign of weapons; nevertheless, he rode cautiously up the hillside. He followed a trail of blood into a stand of scrub oak and found the man sprawled on the ground, his back propped against a boulder to face his attacker. Cyrus was surprised to see that he was little more than a boy, maybe in his teens. He wore threadbare jeans and a red, long sleeved canvas shirt, both equally soiled, and carried a wool blanket, rolled and wrapped tight with a frayed rope that looped over his shoulder. As soon as he saw the gore at the boy's midsection, Cyrus knew the wound was fatal. As he approached the boy, Cyrus heard a rock roll on the hill above and saw the others, still running, as they crossed over the ridge. All were smaller than this one, and Cyrus wondered how old they were.

Cyrus turned to the boy, and sickened by what he had done, pointed to the kid's midsection. "I did not mean this," he said. He didn't know if the kid spoke English, but he didn't look able to talk, so Cyrus said no more. He lifted the strap of his canteen from the saddle horn and offered the kid a drink. The kid shook his head, so Cyrus sat on his heel a few feet away and waited. The kid was strong and took the better part of an hour to die. During that hour Cyrus could think of nothing except that he'd killed a kid who had done him no harm, and the realization started to pick raw spots on his mind and heart. He'd wanted to kill at times, out of anger, but he hadn't. And he realized he had never anticipated what he might feel like after the anger and after the killing.

The kid made no fuss. He sat motionless and stared at Cyrus with no sign of malice. Then he died. Cyrus had worked on through broken arms and ribs, and one winter, through frost-bitten toes. He had put up with all variety of painful ailments in his gut—one that nearly killed him. But he knew he fell short of this kid's grit.

Fall had ushered in a cold storm and, in the high mountains to the east of the ranch, summer's bald granite peaks were draped with white capes of snow. The storm had blown through, but Cyrus could still see a few dark clouds trying to hang onto the jagged southern peaks as the northwest wind insistently pushed them over and through the high passes of the Sierra crest. The western sky was clear, but with the wind the late afternoon sun failed to warm, and Cyrus pulled his oiled canvas coat closed.

Most of the local Indians who survived disease and starvation and the '56 Indian War had ended up on the Tule River Farm down by Porterville, but it was the custom of some to spend the summers in the cool of the high country and move back down to the lowland oak-covered foothills barely ahead of the snows of winter. Jesse Stills, one of the younger hired hands, had found the small band of the Gawia River Yokuts encamped above Homer's Nose Summit. "Living by the old ways," he said. Apparently the early storm had taken them by surprise, so they scampered down to escape the cold and had landed on Cyrus' place.

Stills, a somewhat excitable boy, had arrived at the Stone Corrals with his horse in a lather and his eyes big. He had seen the Indians, he said, "camped smack in the middle of the ranch, where the Sycamore Spring runs into Alder Creek." Jesse had looked around at the other ranch hands and added, "They looked like a pack of wet dogs left outside in a hard rain."

Cyrus had noticed the smirk and heard the scorn in the young man's voice. Cyrus was a man with no use for bravado, which he thought was often a cover for cowardice. Cyrus asked Jesse why he hadn't chased them off, and Jesse had looked back up the valley where he'd come upon the little band and answered that he hadn't known how Cyrus would have wanted the situation handled. Then, after a considerable silence in the conversation with Cyrus staring at the boy and the boy studying the backdrop of the hills, Jesse cautiously offered to go back up and do the job. Cyrus had waited another uncomfortable minute before he said he'd handle it himself, and he continued to watch the humiliated boy while the color returned to his face.

Watching the Indian boy die, Cyrus wished he'd sent Jesse. Though it could have turned out much worse.

Occasionally a justification for the murder would try to surface in Cyrus' mind. The problem with the Indians was they had no respect for property rights. He had heard of other ranches nearly taken over when they allowed trespassers to hang around. Like the big rancher up north who lost nearly 100 acres of his best grazing land along the Sacramento River to gold field hobos because they squatted on his land, and he hadn't kicked them off quick enough. But Cyrus' heart would not let him get by with blaming the boy's death on his refusal to abide by the rule of ownership, for it was a rule that had gained allegiance only after the tribal owners had been chased from the land.

After the kid's body went slack and his eyes took on that glazed look that Cyrus knew meant that whatever it was about living things that made them alive had left him, Cyrus took in several deep breaths to settle his gorge. He went over in his mind what had happened, and went over it again and again, unable to accept the final outcome. Late in the afternoon his knees started to pain him, and he realized he was still kneeling beside the boy. As he stood, he felt the cold that had crept into his body nearly as deeply as it had the corpse.

The only thing left to do was to bury the boy. Cyrus owed him that, though the sum of this debt could never be repaid.

It did not occur to Cyrus what a task it would be without a pick and shovel to bury someone in ground that was full of small stones in a landscape nearly devoid of rocks big enough to cover and protect a body but small enough to carry. Nor did it occur to him not to do it.

He gouged a shallow trough in the ground with a broken tree limb and by dark had collected enough rocks to barely cover the body. He did not notice his bloodied fingers and bruised hands. He did notice a small rat making dashes toward the body, and he shooed it away, then collected a pile of pebbles, spread the saddle blanket over the rocks of the grave, pulled his bedroll around his shoulders, and sat on a rough boulder where he could fend off the surprisingly insistent night creatures. He did not sleep that night.

At first light, Cyrus went in search of more rocks, carrying some for nearly a quarter of a mile. By noon a substantial mound of earth and rocks covered the boy's body, and though knowing it would never be enough, Cyrus stopped. He stood by the rock rubble tomb, silently asked forgiveness, and gave over the body to the earth, then was surprised to hear his stomach growl, acknowledging the insistence of life.

Cyrus saddled his horse and picked a path down the hillside.

On the way he worried about preparing the ranch for winter, but it was not enough to shunt aside the ever-present remorse. He felt odd inside his chest and belly and heard a voice cussing him: "Goddamn you, Cyrus Wilson."

"You're a killer," the voice accused.

It was his own voice, but there was no one to hear but the ground squirrels, a scrub jay and his horse. "Damn it!" he yelled. The exclamation caused his horse to break into a run, and Cyrus reined him in. A horse running through rough country with squirrel holes could break a leg, and he sure as hell did not want to shoot another living thing.

Cyrus moved his rant inside. It would not do for others to hear the disturbance of his soul.

Cyrus made it to the main trail running down Once Wide Creek by mid-afternoon. With more confident footing, he gave the sorrel his head and let him find his own way downstream, even letting him break into a trot when he felt like it.

The early fall storm had caught him by surprise as well as the Indians, and it was now going to be a race with the weather to get the hay at the lower end of the ranch cut, dried and stacked in the barn. And there were 50 head of cattle needing to be rounded up and brought down. On a cattle ranch if it wasn't one damned thing, it was another. This was his ranch, so it was always up to him to make sure what needed done was done. The more he thought about the ranch, the less he thought about the boy.

The trail looped up away from the creek and over a grassy knoll where Cyrus could see the home place in the distance. He slowed the gelding to a walk, noticing the details of the homestead—the ranch house and bunkhouse, the windmill and barn, and the stacked black stone of the corrals—flattening in dark relief as dusk began to settle into the valley. In the distance he could see the three hired hands pause in their evening chores to watch his approach. Cyrus snorted. He seldom laughed, but seeing the boys still at their chores this late in a long day reminded him of his reputation for working his hired hands hard, and any other day might have brought out a smile. Word from a neighbor was that Joseph, a wiry young man from Kansas and the best worker of the three, told a story at a church meeting that everyone working for Cyrus J. Wilson was given a lantern the day they hired on so they would never have an excuse to stop work only because it got dark.

As Cyrus came through the gate, still a good distance from the men, he saw they were still watching him and slowly gathering at the corral, and he felt his jaw clench. He knew they must be wondering what had happened, but it was none of their damned business. There was work to be done, and if they were still standing around when he got to the corral, he was going to put his boot up somebody's backside. Even as he felt this anger, he knew it was fueled by the killing, but he couldn't help the whelming of it. He loosed the reins and kicked the big gelding in the flanks, guiding him in a full gallop straight for the knot of idle men. The gelding wasn't much to look at, but Cyrus was a big man and had chosen a big horse, weighing in at upwards of 1,000 pounds. Coming straight at you, head down, nostrils flared, stretched out in a full run, that gelding could be damned scary.

As the men scattered, Cyrus pulled the blowing horse to a stop. "This!" He paused and stabbed a finger downward. "Is a working ranch!" His voice was forceful, but he wasn't yelling, and he put a strong emphasis on the word "working."

"You girls want to stand around gawking..." The excited mount whirled in a circle, and Cyrus reined him in. "...there's a street corner." He jabbed his hand, fingers extended and tight together, pointing into the western twilight. "Down in the town."

Satisfied that everyone had gotten back to work, he took his own advice and headed the gelding for the barn to water, feed and brush him. He had worked him hard over the past few days, so Cyrus thought he might leave him in the stables for a day's rest and try out the new mare tomorrow. Getting the boys back to work and caring for the horse somehow helped his insides. But only a little.

Mentioning the town had reminded Cyrus of something he had to do before next fall. Ruth had moved down to Visalia with their boy a year ago last winter. Cyrus often thought that he shouldn't have married Ruth. She was the prettiest woman he had ever seen, but anyone could see she wasn't strong enough for ranch life. Her kind of beauty was like a weak fire—promising with flame, but without near enough heat for the hard nights. No matter—he missed her company sometimes. But whether Ruth came along or not, he wanted the boy back on the ranch before he turned 5. Most of the ranchers had three or four boys, a missus and a few girls to help out. Cyrus only had Adam, and, given Ruth's feeble condition, he wasn't likely to have any more. And the kid had a lot to learn. More than how to work a ranch, and more than how to run a ranch. What the kid needed to learn was what it took to own a ranch and keep it. That was a much bigger undertaking, and Cyrus figured he couldn't start too early in the kid's life exposing him to the right kinds of lessons. Lessons that Cyrus wanted to last for all the generations to come.

Cyrus picked up an armload of firewood on his way up to the little white house he'd built for Ruth, reminded yet again that the house was not close enough to the barn. But Ruth had wanted it there, on the gentle slope of a grass-covered hill with a view of Once Wide Creek meandering westward through the widening valley. So that's where it was, and would be, for longer than he expected to live. And now she was down in the town.

Walking carefully through the growing darkness, Cyrus looked up toward the new moon and wished to God that none of little Adam's lessons in ownership would involve killing. Startled, Cyrus wondered if he had said that out loud and looked back over his shoulder, relaxing as he saw a lantern light up in the bunkhouse and the forms of all three boys through the south window. No need to let them know he'd ever asked for anything — not even from God.

———··———

Three days after Cyrus killed the boy, he was in a sad state. He couldn't sleep more than an hour at a time and hadn't been able to keep anything in his stomach but boiled potatoes. He couldn't let the hired hands see him this way, so he told Joseph to let Jesse and the Swede know he was going up to the high country to round up the steers scattered by the storm.

Joseph knew he wasn't to question Cyrus, but he looked sideways at him as he nodded assent, hoping for an explanation, which did not come. Cyrus was not in the habit of explaining himself, and Joseph had grown to accept that sometimes Cyrus' reasoning would become clear later on, and sometimes he would simply never know.

Joseph also knew there was a good deal of serious work wanting to be done in the vicinity of the home place, and knew it must be weighing heavy on Cyrus' mind, so Joseph told Cyrus he'd make sure the hay got put up while Cyrus was gone.

Cyrus seemed a little surprised and thanked Joseph, which set Joseph to worrying because that was two things he'd never seen on his boss' face: surprise and gratitude. What the hell, he wondered, had happened up country with the Indians?

Cyrus saddled the sorrel gelding. He was a strong horse and smart on the trail and experienced with both Cyrus and cattle. Cyrus didn't know for sure how long he was going to be out. Long enough to get himself together, however long that took. He packed a cast iron skillet, an oiled canvas tarp, two wool blankets, an unopened red netting sack of Idaho spuds, two big onions with mildew spots and questionable durability, and a sorely worried chunk of salt pork he filched from the bunk house while the boys were out. There was an unbothered slab of the same in the spring house if anyone cared enough to look.

It would have been normal for Cyrus to tie on the brown leather saddle scabbard containing his .44 Henry, but the heft of it caused a vivid memory of the boy to flash through his mind and make his stomach roll.

The last thing he packed represented what was high in his mind. It was a black leather-bound King James Bible that belonged to Ruth. As terrible as it was, killing the kid was an accident, and he didn't think he'd be held accountable for it, but he wanted to look for some comfort in that little book. Hell, he thought, they killed whole nations back in the old days. The good book said that God Himself had done that. But for Cyrus it wasn't about a nation of people; it was about the one kid he had killed, and he wasn't God.

Cyrus knew he would have to return with the stranded cattle in tow, but he also knew he had something else that needed to be done, so he headed toward the spot where the ribbon of water from the Sycamore Spring joined with Alder Creek a half-mile above the Once Wide Creek. There was a patch of ground there with a lot of blood on it, and asleep or awake, it was what he had to look across to see anything else.

———··———

The day Cyrus left the stone holding corrals near his ranch house was a day that changed both his heart and his heritage. He left in the early afternoon so he would be in that place he wanted to be when it was time to set up camp. As he approached the place, the sun had set and the air was still, that moment between the rise of the day's warmth up the slope and the sinking of evening's cool, gently settling down toward the valley. Cyrus reined in the sorrel gelding a little before the bend in the trail that opened out onto the place he couldn't get out of his mind. He asked once more for either forgiveness or comfort. Both requests felt honest, he just didn't know how to address his plea. Was he talking to the boy, as though he might hear? God, as though there was one? Or was he dealing with his own conscience?

While Cyrus was in his reverie, the sorrel took his head, picked his way carefully along the stony trail and delivered Cyrus to his destination. When he came to himself and his vision focused, the sorrel had stopped.

Standing in the trail before him was a small girl, perhaps 5 or 6 years old, wearing a midnight blue skirt and light blue denim jacket, both soiled to the point their colors nearly blended. Her black hair was long, straight, and held a smattering of twigs and leaves. She had a smear of dirt on her left cheek and scowled at Cyrus through her dark eyebrows. Cyrus quickly scanned the area around them, but seeing no one, and noticing the sorrel's ears and eyes were focused fully on the girl, decided she was alone. He asked anyway, but she said nothing, did not move, and continued to scowl. Perhaps she did not speak English.

The sorrel extended his head and nuzzled the girl's cheek. She giggled and slapped his nose gently. The sorrel bobbed his head up and down, and then looked back at Cyrus.

"Well, all right," he said, dismounted, and sat on a rock beside the girl.

"Do you speak English?" he asked again, but slower and louder, enunciating each word. The scowl returned and again she did not speak.

The horse turned sideways in the trail and the girl's nostrils flared and she pointed her chin toward the saddle bag. Cyrus followed her eyes and saw the top of the red netting of the bag of potatoes sticking out and became aware of the onion smell.

"Are you hungry?" he asked.

Again she did not respond

Cyrus led the sorrel to the creek and removed the saddle and bridle to let him graze. He collected wood and fried a potato with some onion. The girl watched intently and, still standing, hastily ate all of it when offered.

"Would you like more?" he asked.

The girl nodded yes. Cyrus reached for a potato, then paused and looked at the girl, knowing now she did speak English but wondering how much. Her scowl was gone, but she was far from smiling.

He heard a scrub jay off to his left scolding an intruder and wondered if he and the girl were the focus of his displeasure, or if perhaps they were not alone. "Are you with others?" he asked. She shook her head no. Cyrus wondered if she had been with those he saw running away after he'd shot the boy. She didn't seem to recognize him if she was. But what explanation could there be for her to be here alone?

Cyrus sat, looking into her eyes, so dark brown they looked black in the evening light. He listened to the breathing of his horse and the clatter of dry leaves rising and falling as the first gust of night wind passed among the trees. He heard the gentle splash of the creek a few feet away where the high country water was taking its time getting over a log on its early fall journey down in to the valley. He felt the wind move the hair on the back of his hand, felt his pulse in his temples, felt the ache in his lower back from too much riding, and the pressure of the emptiness that had filled his gut for the past three days. He heard and felt everything around him and within him, but the only thing he saw was the life in the girl's eyes.

When the girl had eaten another potato, Cyrus offered her his saddle blanket as bedding. The girl turned and ran a few feet into the trees where she retrieved a wool blanket and a bandana. She pulled a piece of dried meat from the bandana and offered it to him.

———··———

The following morning, as the sun lightened the undersides of high clouds, Cyrus decided it was time to take care of the business he had come for. He retrieved the Bible from his saddle bags, pointed across the hillside toward the grave, then walked slowly toward it. After a few steps he looked back. The girl stood by their morning fire watching him walk away. She glanced at the horse, now tethered to a picket, and perhaps, he thought, decided he was not leaving for good. He didn't hear her following, but when he arrived at the grave, she was right behind him. He stopped, looked up to the sky, and then knelt. She walked past him to where she could see his face. She looked puzzled. Either she did not know about the boy or had not been with his small band. Either way, he felt relief. He wasn't sure he had the words to explain what had happened even if she spoke excellent English.

Cyrus knew little about a funeral service for someone of the Christian faith and was totally lost for how to proceed with the boy. Then he decided the service was as much for himself as for the boy and opened the Bible at random and read aloud. He did this three times. The reading took an hour. He had no idea if anything he read meant anything to God. It didn't to him. But when he was through, he felt as though an obligation had been fulfilled.

The Indian girl sat on a boulder on the hillside above him, and did not interrupt. Did she understand and respect something of the religious rite he had performed? More likely she was showing a child's patience with yet another thing adults did that she did not understand.

It caught him by surprise when he blurted out, "I'm not a killer. Not by nature. And I've had more than enough of it for this lifetime." He turned and made sure he had caught her eye. "So, if you are with your family or others, I'll not hurt them. You can call them in."

The scowl returned for a moment, and then she cocked her head to the side, looked puzzled, and shrugged. Cyrus also shrugged and headed back to their camp.

At noon he saddled the horse, and to his surprise she grabbed the mane, mounted with surprising agility and rode away. He was starting to wonder if he'd met a horse thief when he heard the hoofbeats returning. She dismounted and let Cyrus climb in the saddle, and then, again without stirrups, hopped onto a nearby log, grabbed the cantle, and vaulted over the croup, settling in behind him. Cyrus was impressed. And he decided she was older than 6.

"I can't keep calling you Girl, so what's your name?" When there was no response, he put his hand to his chest and said, "Call me Cyrus." Slapping his chest again, he said, "Cyrus."

She responded immediately with something that sounded to Cyrus as We Ah Mah, but after trying it out a couple of times, Cyrus said, "How about Wilma?"

The girl scowled, but she was behind him and he couldn't see, so that was what he called her.

Cyrus stayed near their camp for another day to see if anyone came for her, and when no one did, figured he'd best get back to finding the strays. He would check back when they were finished to see if anyone had come by, thinking he was a good enough tracker to follow them if they did. So he pointed to the high country and said simply, "Stranded cattle." She looked to the mountains, nodded, and off they went with Cyrus still wondering exactly how much the girl understood.

Cyrus had carried a serious load of guilt into the mountains with him. Now, riding into the upcountry and smelling the pine forests, he felt glad to be alive. It was early fall, but something about the day reminded him of spring. The events of the past few days were so strange he hardly recognized himself, and he wondered if perhaps he had died and was working his way through some form of an afterlife. He knew he was not in heaven because he was on a cattle ranch, but his path on this day seemed a long way from the hell he'd experienced since killing the boy.

Together they found the cattle. Cyrus thought himself to be a decent tracker, but Wilma saw signs that he missed, and when she did, admonished him with a shake of her head. And when he ran the gelding to head off a particularly feisty yearling intending to go its own way, she had whooped. It was a joyful sound, and one he believed she could not have made without smiling, though he couldn't make it out. But he smiled, for he also enjoyed moving swiftly on horseback through a beautiful landscape.

Once, after snacking on jerky in a meadow surrounded by aspen, Cyrus noticed Wilma staring at the Sierra skyline. He asked if her people were there. She shook her head and went to fetch the horse. Cyrus wondered if he ever would know how or why she was where she was. Maybe, if she stayed, she would someday remember, or learn enough English words to explain.

Unclear about what brought the two of them together, and uncertain for how long, each accepted their fate, collected the wayward cattle, and herded them back to the stone corrals. Cyrus wondered what life she had led that made her content to ride horseback 10 hours each day, eat only potatoes and onions, and herd cantankerous cattle.

A little girl couldn't live with the boys in the bunkhouse, so Cyrus set up a place for her in the barn until he could build something more suitable. His definition of suitable wasn't much more than a lean-to shack on the side of the barn. By the time he had it built, he had found a widow woman from down in Exeter to come up and be a momma to the girl. Sarah was her name, and she knew how to live on a ranch and how to raise kids, and she turned the lean-to into a respectable living space. Sarah and Wilma made themselves a part of the ranch, gardening and helping with cattle, as well as some sorely needed but seldom noticed housecleaning.

In October, soon after a storm, when the high mountains wore their first white winter coat, Ruth died while having their second baby. The baby died, too.

Cyrus buried Ruth on a hill above the ranch with a grand view of the Once Wide Valley. But he didn't feel like he had time for grief. Cyrus moved Adam to the ranch, and Sarah now had two kids to raise. Then Cyrus dove into his work and didn't let up for four years. The hired hands had trouble keeping up. He fired them when they didn't.

Joseph lasted. The others didn't. Joseph looked a little peaked by the end of the fourth year. But he knew he was born to work cattle, so he stayed with it.

In the winter of '69, Sarah died of a nasty infection from a snake bite.

Adam, 11, and Wilma, somewhere in her teens, were on their own, because Cyrus never allowed another woman to live on the ranch.

———··———

Wilma went to high school in Visalia and then to San Francisco for nurse's training, and Adam, who stayed on the ranch with Cyrus, lost track of her. He remembered her as having long, straight, black hair, dark brown eyes, a muted, but biting sense of humor, and a softness she seemed only to show when it was just the two of them. At times he felt uncomfortable with how attractive he remembered her to be.

The year Adam turned 30, Wilma came back to the ranch for a visit. Two months later, Adam visited Wilma in San Francisco. They returned to the ranch married and over the following five years had three healthy kids—Bradford, Lawrence and Sally. Cyrus died in 1890, attended lovingly by Adam and Wilma.

In 1920, Bradford, son of Adam, grandson of Cyrus, had a boy and named him Charles. In the following five years Bradford and Charlene had two more children, David and Julie. Charlie was quite large for his age, so everyone called him "Buck."

When Buck was 6, his Aunt Sally brushed his straight black hair out of his blue eyes and told him stories of what she had been told and what she believed must have been left out. Stories about how his great-grandfather Cyrus fought to keep his ranch, even killed a few interlopers when he had to. She thought they were good stories. So did Buck, who, in the way of children, counted them as true.

Bradford turned out to be a no-account, given to heavy drink and gambling. Sally figured if the youngster had to look past his own daddy to have someone to look up to, it might as well be someone similar to the now legendary cattle rancher, Cyrus J. Wilson. It was through these slanted biographical stories of his great-grandfather that Buck learned what it meant to be tough. And he learned one lesson well: Do what you need to do to keep the land. Kill if you have to, like Cyrus had to. But keep the land.

———··———

Buck was 16 when his father did the unthinkable. Bradford got drunk on a Saturday night, and in a game of pinochle lost a third of the ranch land.

Although Buck would never say it to anyone because he thought it far too strange, he firmly believed that his father's unthinkable act was in some way linked to his horribly gruesome death.

———··———

On a Saturday night during a two-day drinking binge, Bradford Cyrus Wilson was chasing a losing streak in a poker game and ran out of cash. His competitor, Dalford Hobson, known around the Orange Blossom Bar and Pool Hall as Dally, was a skinny dry goods sales clerk with a face that reminded Bradford of a weasel. Bradford considered the man to be a ne'er-do-well with little ambition, limited intelligence, and a body unlikely to last through half a hard day of real work. Bradford had played pinochle and poker with Dally nearly every Friday night of the previous two months and knew Dally was prone to streaks of winning followed by streaks of bad luck, whining and foul language. The man was a poor loser, but he was a certain loser, and the best strategy was to keep playing until Dally's bad luck took over. It irked Bradford to ask his opponent for credit from the pile of cash on the table that he knew was mostly his own. But the bank was closed, and there were no friends there that night who could or would lend him money. And the thought of the look on Dally's peaked face when he raked it all back in egged Bradford on, so he asked for a temporary loan. And he thought Dally a fool when he gave it to him.

Bradford subsequently asked Dally for credit for more hands than he had planned, and it was given to him each time he asked. And then the weasel-faced clerk proposed that Bradford put up a few acres of the ranch to cover the debt incurred. Bradford not only agreed, but when he lost those acres, he suggested throwing in a few more to keep the game going for a couple more hands. His offer was accepted. He lost those hands. With the desperate optimism of a drunk, Bradford firmly believed his luck absolutely had to change, so he raised the stakes, offered more land on the table, and demanded they play one last hand. Dally said, "Remember the Alamo, huh?" He bought Bradford yet another drink and agreed to one last hand. Bradford should have been surprised at how knowledgeable this dry goods clerk was of the landmarks that defined the acreage included in each of the agreements that were drawn up in writing for each advance of credit. He should have been suspicious of the careful inclusion of mineral and water rights. But his eyes were on winning, and he did not notice. And he should have noticed that each successive agreement included more and more valuable land. But Bradford had so little respect for the clerk that he did not consider the possibility there might be a design at work.

When the dust settled that night, Bradford had lost 8,320 acres — nearly one third of the ranch, and as would be talked about for years to come, exactly 13 square miles. Bradford didn't appreciate fully how disastrous the loss was until a couple of days had passed, and he sobered up and got past his hangover. Then his family helped him to realize the lost parcel was the heart of the ranch. It stretched from the center of his formerly 40-square-mile ranch up into the low mountain meadows, it had half of the farmable land, a long stretch of access to the creek, and a workable balance of summer and winter pasture.

But the worst of the loss came in the following days while Bradford was in the process of arranging loans from his bank and his neighbors and his family so he could buy the parcel back. Dally sold it.

Not wanting to sell the unlucky 13 square miles as one parcel, Dally split it into a 320-acre parcel and an 8,000-acre parcel, and found two cash buyers before Bradford knew what was happening. Both buyers had plans for the land and rebuffed Bradford's offers to buy their newly acquired land at a profit. Both said the land was more important to them than the money, a sentiment the now sober Bradford understood.

Bradford, normally a boisterous man, became morose, seldom spoke and never smiled. People who only knew of him found something to laugh about in Bradford's bad luck and sullen disposition. People who knew him well were worried and found there was no consoling him. Though only 16, Buck recognized the magnitude of the loss, knew he would live with the aftereffects of his father's poor judgment for a very long time, and had no inclination to offer consolation.

Six months after the sale and three months after Bradford had given up hope of buying the land back, as he was tilling one of his remaining fields in preparation to plant field corn, Bradford had a fatal accident. The local papers either referred to it as a "farming accident" or more precisely as a "tractor accident." Of course, everyone knew these to be the euphemisms for "he fell off his tractor and was run over by two 10-foot-wide sets of steel discs secured a foot apart and effectively designed for the first set to slice into the top half foot of hard soil and turn it over one way and then the second set to slice it again and turn it back the other way." It was no surprise to anyone that the funeral service did not include an open casket viewing.

———·———

By the time he was 16, Buck was as big as any full-grown man in the county. He was intelligent and as driven as a badger, and he took over the management and, when his schooling allowed, the operation of the ranch.

When Aunt Sally asked him what he wanted for his 17th birthday Buck replied, "The piece of the valley Dad lost in the card game."

Sally said, "Well, son, that might be a little difficult to arrange."

"I'll get it," was all he said.

———·———

That was the year Dalford Hobson was believed to have left town. Dally's banker, curious why he hadn't seen one of his best-heeled customers in the bank for some months, asked around about Dally but was met mostly with unconcerned shrugs. The old cowboy on the corner gave it some thought and remembered he had seen Dally in the back room of the Orange Blossom Bar playing poker on a weekend, Saturday maybe, and late in the night, midnight maybe, he drew a decent hand, full house maybe, and broke even for the night. Cowboy said Dally collected his chips, and sauntered out the back door. Consistent with his sullen nature, Dally said nothing to anyone when he left. Honoring Dally's privacy, or perhaps finding it forgettable that Dally was not around, his banker waited three years before mentioning to the police chief that Dally's sizeable bank account had not been touched during that time. The chief, not knowing where to start on such a problem that might not be a problem and if it was, was an old problem, suggested they wait to see if he might call for it in the future.

'THREE
1902-1950

In January 1902, in the Territory of Oklahoma, five years before it became a state, a small baby boy was born to the shunned, but landed, Miss Nola Joy Westerman. She named him Roland.

Young Roland had a few things going against him. As his growth did not keep up with the other kids, some called him Runt. And, since his father absented himself as soon as he found out about the pregnancy, some called him Dogie, which had a similar meaning but was less harsh sounding than Bastard. But, perhaps fortunately, it was his pale complexion that reddened even in the faint winter sun that gave him the nickname that stuck: Pinky.

When he was 10, a stepfather joined the household who valued work over schooling and worked him hard, seven days a week. Baxter Wollerman, sheriff of the hardscrabble ranching county of Chickasaw, gave Pinky what help, respect and encouragement the boy had. He made sure Pinky went to school, and when he was 13 and all the able-bodied men had gone off to war, put Pinky to work on his cattle ranch. Later, Sheriff Wollerman allowed Pinky to live by himself in a line shack in the hill country which gave him some escape from his stepfather's demands. Pinky had a horse and a dog to care for and talk to, and thanks to Mrs. Wollerman, had a wall full of books to befriend his imagination.

At 16, though still small, Pinky had grown broad-shouldered and strong, and was, in Sheriff Wollerman's words, "Earning his keep, and near as good as any of the old hands."

The war ended on a Monday, Pinky's dog died on Tuesday, and on Wednesday Pinky sold his horse to another ranch hand he trusted with his friend.

Pinky didn't go home, but directly to the bus station where he gave his name as Pinky Wollerman, a name he believed held more respect than his own, but which raised the clerk's eyebrows as she had always known him as a Westerman. Pinky was, of course, unaware that his choice of name initiated whispered rumors regarding the sheriff's private life. Pinky then asked for a ticket to the most westerly stop the bus made. His intention was not to travel toward any given place nor was it exactly to wander. He believed he would find his direction as he traveled, and in the end, as Sheriff Wollerman said, his place in the world.

His large hat, which he wore against the sun, was sweat-stained and hard-used so people recognized him right away as a cowboy. His calloused hands identified him as a working man, so, along with his weathered face and neck, people thought him to be older than he was.

The clothes he wore and the one change he carried rolled in a wool blanket consisted of grey chambray work shirts and khaki pants. Pinky found the khakis more comfortable for riding than the riveted canvas blue jeans worn by the cowboys out west.

His boots, called clodhoppers, as they were the choice of most farmers, were adequate for the stirrup and much easier on his feet when he had to walk than were the high-heeled boots he saw on the cowboys with the blue jeans.

Though small in stature, the sum of his looks presented him as a man capable of most any kind of hard labor, and he seldom had trouble finding work, so Pinky drifted through Colorado, Nevada and California, working on farms and ranches, but never finding his "place."

Then, in the mid-'30s, when the dust had begun to choke the life out of the Midwest, Pinky's stepfather left his mother on the farm to fend for herself and disappeared as completely as his father had. So Pinky re-assumed the Westerman name and went home to take care of his mother and the farm. Some people's lungs became so coated with dust they died. And so it was with Sheriff Baxter Wollerman and with Pinky's mother. Between the Depression and the Dust Bowl, life was hard and bleak, but the farm was now his, and Pinky was too stubborn to leave.

Even in the good years making a living on a farm wasn't easy, but folks could get by if they worked at it. Old Henry Standridge had called it working from can till cain't, which sometimes meant from first light to full dark and other times meant from when he got up out of bed until he dropped from exhaustion.

With that hard work farmers could at least put food on the table, but there were a nasty few years during the Dust Bowl when the weather didn't cooperate, and it was hard to grow anything, even a kitchen garden. There was so little rain Pinky couldn't dry farm. The high well went dry, and he couldn't shift water over the whole farm from the low well.

Most of his cattle starved, and in the end the handful he had left were taken away by the government men and shot in the head with a .30 caliber rifle and buried in a big pit with quick lime. Pinky cursed Roosevelt for saying it would increase the market price for the cattle that were left, because that didn't help him one damned bit.

The slaughter was a big operation, but Pinky remembered two men while he forgot the others. One was a young Montana cowboy who just kept shooting, reloading and shooting again, without flinching. He used two rifles so the barrels wouldn't get too hot, and he seldom had to shoot the same animal twice. Pinky wondered how the young man could kill so much and still sleep. The other fellow was a government man. It wasn't his clothes that made him memorable, although in his pressed pants and shined shoes he didn't seem dressed for the work at hand. And it wasn't his hands either, though they appeared never to have seen a hard day's work. It was his smile.

Though the newspapers later said ranchers had been paid at least $14 a head, the government man gave Pinky $10 for each of his slaughtered cattle, smiling as though he'd done him a big damned favor. And as he was taking the money, Pinky felt a little sick in his stomach and wondered about such waste when he knew there were people going hungry. People who couldn't have afforded beef at any price.

Over the years leading up to that terrible time every danged farmer in that part of the country decided to grow wheat, bought a tractor and churned up the prairie soil as though God didn't know what He was doing when He plunked down the big rooted tall prairie grasses there.

Those farmers paid for their arrogance by watching their land blow away on the incessant winds. But everybody else paid, too. Pinky couldn't raise hay, and he couldn't graze his cattle on grass that was buried under a foot of dust.

As worse years followed bad years, most of the merchants folded for lack of business. In the end lots of folks went hungry. Not the comfortable grumbling in the stomach felt right before a meal, but the headache, weak, dizzy, sick kind of hunger that a body knows deep inside, down in the bones and organs.

The worst part of that kind of hunger isn't the physical pain. The worst is a sense of helplessness and dread from not knowing how to end it or even if it will end.

Oklahoma farmers were, for the most part, a common sense bunch. And they were also blind optimists when it came to trusting in nature's patterns. But during that time of the dust, the weather was so unusual it frustrated the best of common sense, forcing farmers to fall back on a desperate optimism. Everybody was certain that the year that had just passed had to be the end of the drought because it had gone on so long. So every year they tried again to plant a crop. When that strategy left them flat broke, they mortgaged their farms to the bank and tried one more time, which left them homeless as well as broke and starving, casualties of something as simple as dust.

Most Dust Bowl farmers hadn't had any other option but to hunker down and keep at it until they died or the bank took their places for unpaid debts. But Pinky didn't have a family to worry over, and he didn't like debt, so he let his farm go fallow and got by on the few dollars he had stashed away and whatever survived in the garden against the wind and the bugs. The keys to a garden seemed to be to not plant everything at the same time or in the same place and to not be too proud to eat whatever was available. Pinky heard about folks eating pickled tumbleweed and figured it probably kept them alive, but it was a damned poor way to live.

In the end it was a good thing he didn't go into debt because his mother's childhood friends, Troy and Hazel Erlewine, who had no children of their own, left him their ranch. Both of them died the same spring, 15 years after settling out west. It was a terrible blow to

Pinky because they had been the last people alive who felt like family to him. Their deaths made him feel as though he'd been set down in the middle of nowhere without any idea which direction home was. But stubbornness has its limits, and not owing anything to anyone and not having much of anything left in Oklahoma, he was able to board up his house and turn his back on what had become nothing but a dust farm. Though he understood why many did so, he would not have been able to walk away if he'd owed somebody money. He was glad he didn't have to make that choice.

Pinky walked away from his Oklahoma farm in April 1940, a few days before a rainstorm would drop over eight inches of water and usher in the end of the drought. Even if Pinky had known of the coming rains, he likely would not have stayed on the Oklahoma farm, for he had already released his spirit to another place.

———·——

Relieved to be free of the dust, Pinky took a meandering route west, enjoying the western lands he knew partially from his previous travels. A wheel came off his car in Montana. The car was wrecked beyond use, but Pinky survived with only scratches and bruises. It was a pleasant day in early June when the Greyhound bus dropped him in the small town of Exeter, California. Pinky, prepared to walk the last few miles, asked directions to the Once Wide Valley.

A deliveryman for the farm supply warehouse in Exeter came upon Pinky walking the dusty road and offered him a ride. The flatbed truck was mounded high with farm supplies. When asked his name, he replied, "Pinky," then with a tone of finality, "Wollerman."

"They call me Hodge," the driver said.

Pinky asked about orchards of trees they passed, and Hodge told him some were oranges and some lemons. Other than naming trees, both men seemed happy with the quiet. Pinky didn't say he was going to the Once Wide Valley, but the driver didn't need to ask. There was only one road.

When they reached a swooping saddle south of a rock-covered hill named Rocky Hill, the driver stopped and Pinky hopped off the wagon to take in the view of the valley that held his inherited ranch.

The Once Wide Valley was neither vast nor cozy. The land, grass and water were in a workable configuration for a cattle ranch, a beautiful cattle ranch. The east end was beyond Pinky's view, hidden in the folds of the Sierra Nevada. The western and lower part of the valley bumped up to the base of the hill where he stood. He was looking at an in-between land, a loose chain of foothills coursing through an area belonging neither to the towering Sierra nor the great valley of the Tule Basin.

Hodge explained that his service area was large and he needed to keep moving, but Pinky could not take his eyes off of the scene before them, so nodded and told the man, "Thanks for the ride. I'll walk from here."

Hodge started to leave, and then whistled to get Pinky's attention. "You best stick to the road if you're going through that valley. Most of it belongs to Buck Wilson, and he don't care much for strangers trespassing on his land."

Pinky walked a deeply rutted dirt road along the saddle and climbed a high, round-topped rock with a view of it all. Looking into the valley Pinky was pulled instantly within this place, and it changed forever how he understood the word *beauty*. The floor of the valley was a half-mile-wide swath of grasses, tall and thick, making a patchwork pattern in every shade of green and providing a gentle, textured canvas through which was drawn a small ribbon of water meandering through wide curves. Along the creek's bed grey-green-barked sycamores provided shade with maple-like leaves as big as pie tins. As the edges of the valley started to rise, the grasses thinned and turned the color of summer straw. The oaks began here, shadowy green and sprinkled across the foothills. Hodge had called them valley oaks. Their canopies were nearly round, and some were 50 to 60 feet in diameter. East and above the valley Pinky saw dark evergreen forests, giving way in the distance to the magnificent skyline of the western front of the great Sierra Nevada, with a ragged stone spine as though borrowed from the blade of a logger's saw.

———·———

Pinky could see three ranches in the valley. A small house with a barn lay downstream about a mile; a very large house a couple of miles up and on the north side of the valley with two barns, several corrals, and what might be a bunkhouse, and a similarly arranged but more modest house perched on a hill near the valley's east end. Pinky had no idea which was his, so he headed toward the first, ignoring the driver's advice and cutting across the range land rather than following the road. Consequently, he arrived at the house not by the gravel drive but from around the corner of the barn.

A woman throwing chicken scratch startled him with a scream and ran into the house. The curtains moved slightly in the only window so, though he could see no one, he addressed the window.

"No need to be afraid. My name is Pinky Wollerman, and I'm looking for the Erlewine ranch. Which I have inherited. And am walking there now. But don't know which ranch it is."

Pinky didn't recognize how poorly he had planned his arrival until he heard his own words.

A voice from the window said, "It's the second ranch up the valley. There's only two, so you can't miss it." The words were followed by the metallic sounds of a rifle either being made safe or loaded. Pinky didn't know which so turned immediately and left, tense as a banjo string for the first hundred steps, and thinking Hodge should have warned him that everyone in the valley was hissy as a startled snake, not just Buck Wilson.

It was a long walk to the second ranch, but entering the valley that first day Pinky knew he was in a special place. It might have been the absence of the dust and incessant wind, but the place seemed to Pinky to have more color. The sky was so dark blue it looked almost thick. The grass was a deep and healthy green, rippling in the waves of the morning breeze. And the clouds looked like giant cotton balls. To him, the valley was a crisper place in terms of how things looked and sounded. A flock of more than 100 red-winged blackbirds were scattered through the willows in the distant creek bottom, making such a beautiful sound he stopped walking to listen. It was as though the valley itself had put on a show just to welcome him home, even before he ever set eyes on his ranch house.

Pinky was amazed at what he found on the ranch. It had both farm land and pasture land and lay in the rolling, oak-studded foothills around the small drainage area of Once Wide Creek. It had a good barn and corrals and a well-built house with a view toward the high granite Sierra. It had four wells and several springs, nearly 8,000 acres of natural pasture and upwards of 200 acres of rich farm land along the creek to the south.

Like the Oklahoma farm, the ranch was clearly a place where only hard work would get a body by, but compared to the places he'd seen up to then, it was heaven. Going there from the farms of the midlands after their losing fight with nature, Pinky felt like he was walking out of hell and into the loving presence of The Creator.

————

Pinky's timing was perfect. It took him a few years to build up the herd on the ranch, and by the time the inevitable next war was well underway and beef prices skyrocketed, he was ready to supply a hungry army. Pinky was in his 40s, too old to be conscripted into the military. And the warriors were pleased that he would stay at home and raise beef, which he did for a number of years, putting money aside for the lean times that always come to those who work with the land.

FOUR

FALL 1952

On a cool day in early fall the sun was low when Pinky Wollerman came in from the field to work in his barn until twilight fell and the chores were finished. He went into his house, built a fire and warmed his hands by the black potbelly stove, thinking how he'd never before liked a cat or disliked a neighbor, but it had come to that. He relaxed his overworked body into a faded blue wooden kitchen chair while his eyes adjusted to the dimming light. At 50 he was feeling pains in new places every year.

He wished Squatty Nelson hadn't left him when he did because after almost a year of working the place, Squatty had just about learned all the ins and outs. But Squatty was an Oklahoma drifter helping on whichever ranch suited him, and when he heard about work at a big cattle outfit over by Santa Barbara, he did what drifters do. The ranch was said to be paying $300 a month and found, so Squatty couldn't be blamed. But on that evening after a hard day working the ranch without help, even the simple hard chair felt good to Pinky. He sat and hoped he could find someone like Squatty soon because he couldn't much longer rely on inexperienced workers from the town and the goodwill of neighboring ranchers.

The foothill ranch could get nearly as hot in summer as the San Joaquin River Valley stretching out below, but that fall before September's heat had given way to October's cool, there had been several days of gentle rain with an occasional day of tepid sunshine, and the landscape of straw white summer grass had been transformed into a bright blanket of new green. The barely October days were in the mid 60s and the nights in the low 40s. Pinky liked to say that fall was a perfect time of year for the hard work of ranching because the temperature was neither too hot nor too cold and the days were neither too short nor too long. But the expected fall weather lasted only a few days that year, and then a bitter cold settled in. Surging on a mean-spirited north wind, sleet scoured all that stood in the open, and at night the stock watering troughs froze thick with ice. Pinky hurried through his fall checklist as winter's sharp elbows shoved aside the welcome moderation of fall and denied the customary offer of a season for preparation.

Sitting beside the stove, Pinky cocked an ear toward a low, yowling sound like an undertone of the wind flowing around the corners and under the eaves. He recognized it as the raspy mewing of the old grey and brindle cat that had come around two summers back.

At first the cat had been afraid and would streak away at the faintest sound or slightest movement to peek back from hiding places behind boards and between hay bales. Pinky knew what it felt like to be skittish around people, one reason he stayed mostly on the ranch—that and the constant work.

The moaning of the wind reminded Pinky of the first time he saw the pitiful critter out near the barn, a flash of molting dark fur streaking across the corral and around the weathered slats on the corner of the abandoned chicken coop.

The cat and the old boards on the chicken coop were about the same color—mostly dark brown with a grainy undertone showing up as streaks of black blending into a light grey that caught the light as silver. As a whole neither the chicken coop nor the cat was anything to look at. Later on when he looked closer, Pinky noticed complexities of patterns in the cat's fur and a mix of colors that Pinky found pleasing. But at that first sighting "mangy" was the word that came to mind.

The cat was awfully thin and left behind clumps of fur when he rubbed up against anything. Pinky saw him leap from his hiding place to swat down and swallow a moth and wondered where the cat had come from and what he had been through that left him hungry and feral.

Pinky remembered all too clearly those last couple of years in Oklahoma when he'd gotten awfully hungry. He remembered how the hunger hurt and how it scared him. Which was why in the middle of all the work he had waiting for him on the ranch, he had taken notice of the starving cat.

So right after the cat arrived at the ranch on that evening in the middle of June, the first thing he did the next day, even though he believed a cat could eat most anything, was drive down to the feed store and buy a 50-pound sack of cat food. Most cats fed themselves with birds and mice and those that didn't ate table scraps, so Pinky wouldn't have been able to explain why he did what he did and fortunately nobody asked. Fifty pounds was a lot, but if the cat didn't like it, Pinky figured he could feed it to the hog. Truth be known, it likely was hog feed but with a cat food label, so it could sell for a few more pennies. The food was dry, which was a good thing because it wasn't clear to Pinky how long it would sit out before the old cat worked himself up to being more concerned about his hunger than he was about his distrust. He was a strongly distrustful cat.

There was something about the cat Pinky couldn't quite explain. He felt a tenderness toward that cat he never could feel toward the farm animals, but he didn't feel like that toward his pets either. He seldom felt that brand of tenderness at all. He liked his dog and considered him a friend. He liked dogs in general more than he liked cats. He could tell what they were thinking and enjoyed their company more. What he felt for the cat was different because the poor damned cat just looked so hungry, and as far as Pinky was concerned no creature, no matter what its lot in life, should ever go hungry, really hurting hungry.

So Pinky mixed the dry food with some kitchen scraps in an old beat-up tin pan and took it about 40 steps out behind the house so the dog that slept on the front porch wouldn't chase the cat every time he tried to eat. He threaded a piece of bailing wire through a nail hole under the top lip of the pan and set it on a corner rail of the fence up out of reach of the hog, wrapping the wire around the end post to keep it there.

For the first couple of days the food was still there. Every morning after that it was gone. Pinky hoped the cat was getting it and that he hadn't simply started to pamper some coon or possum with store-bought food. Then late one evening he saw the cat up on the fence rail eating, so the next time he filled the pan he added a splash of cream.

A couple of weeks later he propped open the screen door to the back porch just wide enough for the cat and moved the pan in there. Three days passed before he found the pan empty. Eventually the cat would show up when Pinky rattled the feed sack, but the cat still kept some distance until he was sure Pinky had left the porch. The cat's coat started looking better, and Pinky wondered if it was merely hopeful thinking or if it was true that some of the wildness was gone from his eyes. The cat didn't seem quite so frantic when he ran, slowing up a bit and looking over his shoulder right before reaching cover. Pinky didn't think he was ever going to be like the preacher's wife's cat that you'd trip over in the kitchen. Truth is, if he turned into that kind of cat, Pinky thought he'd have to give him to someone else.

Sitting by the fire listening to the howling of the wind and the mewing of the cat, Pinky thought someday maybe, if he kept feeding it while sufficiently ignoring it, the cat might come up on the porch to eat while he was there. And that visit would be important to him, even if he wasn't entirely partial to cats.

Though he hadn't named him, Pinky had an odd sense the cat had a name. He ached his way up from the wooden chair and went out on the porch, shivering in his shirt sleeves and, looking into the cold, black expanse of a landscape void of even a single moonbeam, he knew that cat was out there somewhere. And even if he couldn't see the cat, he knew the cat was seeing whatever needed to be seen by the wispy light of the stars. He didn't know why the name came to him. It came slowly, as though a memory returning piece by piece or a secret slowly unveiled. But once the name was fully in his consciousness, it was clearly the right name. "Your name is Henry," he spoke into the dark. He waited and shivered, and the cat didn't say anything, and Pinky wondered why he thought he might, and why he felt so confident that he could if he wanted to.

Gently Pinky said his name again: "Henry."

Pinky felt it was a good thing to have the chance to feed the stray. He figured kindly gestures had probably brought together stranger creatures than him and that cat, and he hoped, but with a large dose of doubt, that someday such simple kindness might bring him a little closer with his neighbors.

FIVE
WINTER 1952

Fall should not have been finished when winter secured its place that year. On Pinky's porch the dog's water bowl was more ice than water. It seemed odd to Pinky that the cold had come unaccompanied by a storm, but then, he had never seen a normal year of weather.

Certain things always happen in the Sierra foothills. The fraudulent summer clouds, puffed up and showy but delivering little rain, give way to the serious workhorse clouds of winter. The sun isn't out as much. The oak trees lose their leaves, unveiling their halos of lacy twigs arching high above massive trunks and spreading limbs. The sun-bleached yellow of the summer grasses turns green in the fall rains, then straw grey with the first heavy frost. The creeks run higher. The ground gets softer, even muddy at times, except when it freezes hard. The birds hide out or go south. The number of deer increases as the high-country herds move down from the snow-covered peaks. And, of course, there is wind and rain and snow and ice and colder and colder days.

But each year, in an attempt to avoid being normal, these things happen at different times and take unpredictable turns happening in the extremes. Crops and livestock do better under certain conditions, and the variations in the seasons, especially at the extremes, make the rancher's job harder. Pinky had liked the change of seasons, not because he enjoyed more or less heat or cold or rain or sun, but because it changed how he worked. In the game of chance called ranching, the only hand the rancher has to play is the one dealt by God. And Pinky was, by the choice he had made to be there, anteed up and all in every year. Pinky worked with what came to him, grew accustomed to the unpredictable weather, and for years and years was challenged by it and enjoyed succeeding in spite of it. But as that winter came and went, with its early freeze, low and heavy snows, and late retreat, Pinky, for the first time since he had arrived in the valley, came to see it as just another winter of working with a temperamental God.

SIX
SPRING 1953

Spring was far enough along for the days to be warming, but not enough to banish the last bit of winter's cool. The light gusts of a breeze blowing up from the valley made the sky feel as clean and clear as it looked. Horizon to horizon it was blue as the mountain jay sitting high up in a bent old sycamore squawking about Pinky riding by, because jays do not acknowledge a man's claim to ownership of the land.

Two weeks had passed since the storm, but there was still mud in the low places that Pinky's pickup could not navigate, so he had been riding fence on horseback, clearing brush, restringing barbed wire, and generally patching things up. Where the fence approached Once Wide Creek, the water had receded enough to cross, so Pinky decided to see how Bill Jenkins, his neighbor on the other side, had fared. Bill hadn't been seen much since his wife, Constance, died, and people had begun to talk, wondering if he still had all his faculties. But Pinky suspected those people likely said the same about him because there really weren't enough hours in the day to run a ranch without regular help, and when you were too busy and weren't seen for a long stretch, people made assumptions. Pinky didn't know if Bill had anyone to check in on him, and figured it would be a neighborly thing to do to see if he needed anything.

Pinky was dumbfounded by how much the storm had rearranged the lay of the land. It was as though the wind and rain had aimed its fury directly at Bill's place and worked its worst before moving on. Entire hillsides had soaked through to the point they sloughed off like wet pudding. And there was a wide swath of devastation about a half-mile long where the trees were uprooted that went through where Bill's home had been. The barn and corrals were still intact, but the house had been spread out to look like an exclamation point with the bare rock foundation forming the period, and a streak of boards and tarpaper strewn up the hillside a couple of hundred yards forming the vertical slash.

Riding apprehensively toward the foundation, Pinky heard a voice coming from up by the barn. A figure came into view around the corner of the barn, and Pinky reined his horse to a stop. Maybe they were right about Bill losing his mind. He was standing in the swale between two hills, next to the remnants of a dead oak, looking skyward. His right hand was up in the air as though trying to get someone's attention.

The breeze changed, blowing his way, and Pinky could hear the conversation clearly.

"... so, God, if you and Constance can hear me now, I want you both to know that I'm hopin' there's not a whole lot more stones for me to dig through before I get to the water."

Pinky relaxed. He didn't understand the prayer, but he could see the man wasn't crazy. He was simply praying aloud. To respect his privacy, Pinky turned his horse to leave when Bill abandoned his conversation with the sky and scanned the jumbled landscape. Seeing Pinky, Bill called down the hill, "Hello there, Pilgrim."

"Hello, Bill." As Pinky's horse plodded up the hill, he added, "I just stopped over to see if you needed anything after the storm."

Both men surveyed the damage surrounding them. But Bill was silent, seeming not to know where to start with an answer to Pinky's offer. Suddenly, he seemed to remember something. "Is that West Texas cowboy still workin' your place?"

"Squatty? Naw. He left to work a horse ranch for some movie star and get rich. Been gone a while now."

"I hear them movie stars got money to burn," Bill said.

Pinky thought a minute. "I think it might have been a little more than that, though. Squatty fancied himself a peeler, and I was down to four horses at my place. They were all four broke, so I knew when he showed up that he wouldn't stay put for the long run. Besides, Squatty had a notion of how big a ranch was supposed to be, and there isn't a ranch that size in all of California. Not all in one piece anyway. Hell, there probably isn't any that big back in Texas anymore either. Australia's got 'em. Maybe some down in Argentina or Brazil. But not up here."

The two of them scanned the valley.

"I think I'd go down to Argentina if I was younger," Bill said.

Pinky nodded, imagining the vast ranches of other places. "There is something appealing about big spreads."

Both men were quiet again, wondering what it might be like elsewhere.

"Anyway," Pinky said, "Squatty heard there was work over by Santa Barbara and went on down there. I don't know if they had horses to break in Santa Barbara, and I doubt they had a place with the space he was yearning for. It's a way of life that's gone. But they were said to be paying a decent month's wage plus room and board, so that's what he said he was going for, and I couldn't blame him either way."

After another few minutes of enjoying the quiet, Bill said, "I'll bet you could use some help to clean up after the storm, Pinky."

Pinky looked up the valley and shrugged. "My place wasn't hit as hard as yours, Bill." He flung his hand out toward the devastation. "This here's awful."

"Yeah, but your place is 20 times the size of mine, Pinky." Bill looked at his feet and started again. "I may be old, but I know how to work a ranch." After another pause, but now looking out across the rolling foothill grassland, he added, "And I could use the work." Both men were now gazing down Once Wide Creek toward the distant San Joaquin valley when Bill said, "Do you suppose you might want to hire me on for a spell?"

Pinky was surprised that Bill had been so direct. He knew the man needed work and was sorry he had waited until after Bill had made a plea. So Pinky offered him a trade. "Well, it's for sure you could use some help around here, too, Bill. How about we exchange hours helping each other? Then if you work more hours at my place than I work at yours, I'll pay you for them."

Bill's shoulders squared. "Sounds fair."

Pinky knew he'd said the right thing. "It's still too wet to get the pickup in a lot of places, and you'll probably want to use your own horse, so why don't you saddle up and ride him over to my barn? I'll fix us some supper and we can talk out what needs to be done."

"Sold my horse to Buck Wilson yesterday."

Pinky looked closely at Bill's face but couldn't read it. Buck owned the big ranch that nearly encircled both of their ranches, and he wasn't always a good neighbor. "How'd that come about?"

"Buck came by again to see if I wanted to sell out to him." Bill was looking at his flattened barn, trying to sound matter of fact. "He's been pestering me about that for some time now. A while back he made me a generous offer for my farmable land—enough to pay off my debt and build up the ranch. I told him no thanks. He could see I was in bad shape after the storm, so he wasn't so generous this time. I told him no again. Then he offered me $90 for my horse. I don't have no cattle left, and I could sure use the money, Pinky, so I went and got the horse. When I led him out of the barn on a hackamore, Buck asked where the tack was. I said that wasn't included in the price, and he turned and started away. I guess I panicked a bit and yelled after him. He stopped. I went in the barn and came back with the bridle and then he said the $90 was for the saddle, too. I was beat, Pinky, and he knew it, so he left with all of it."

"That's a good bit less than half what all that's worth." As soon as the words were out, Pinky realized how embarrassed Bill must be to admit to such a skinning, and looked away with a shrug of his shoulders and a flip of his hand.

"I know, Pinky, but I haven't got much left. I figure if I can keep body and soul together, I can get by with a garden and the hog and a few chickens, but I need money for seed and a couple dollars now and then for flour and sugar and such." Bill looked down at the damp earth. "Worse thing, Pinky, I found where he'd left the hackamore on a fencepost down by the road. He didn't even want it. And wanted me to know he didn't. I never met such a son-of-a-bitch in my whole life."

Pinky recognized the look on Bill's face. He'd seen it too often during the Depression. Bill was too beat to even be mad. "I reckon he'll just buy my place one piece at a time, until he has it all."

Pinky looked up at the darkening evening sky and nodded, "But it don't have to happen that way." After another minute of silence, perhaps to allow his faint optimism to catch on, Pinky reached down to Bill with a weathered, calloused hand. "No need to worry about this mess any more tonight. Hop up, and let's go see what's for supper over at my place."

———··———

Bill rode on the horse's rump behind the saddle. He felt better having someone to talk to, someone who also knew Buck. As they approached Once Wide Creek he said, "We got to do somethin' about that Buck Wilson."

The horse's hooves were still splashing wet spots after crossing the creek when Pinky softly responded. "Forget Buck for now. We'll get you back on your feet."

In the late evening light Bill saw the sweat-stained Stetson in front of him bob quickly just once, and heard Pinky add, "Then we'll think of somethin'." Bill heard a determination that propped up his spirits with a little hope.

———··———

Bill Jenkins and Pinky Wollerman sat quietly at Pinky's table and ate a supper of fried eggs and fried bacon and fried bread. It had been a while since Bill's life had gone anything but poorly, and he had some things to say, but living alone, he hadn't had anyone to say it to. Pinky seemed to understand, because when Bill started talking, Pinky sat back and listened.

———··———

Who was to say if Bill was out of his right mind, Pinky thought, or barely succeeding at staying within it? Whichever it was, his story came out clear enough.

Bill looked out Pinky's window as though seeing what was there, but there was only the darkness that had settled over the land. "It was an odd time in the wrong season for such a bad storm." He paused, and then with a wave of his hand and an abrupt chuckle that didn't seem to fit with what he was saying, he went on. "'Course, I never had any luck predicting storms much before the clouds showed up on the horizon."

Bill sat forward in the wooden chair with his elbows on his knees and held out his thick, muscular hands and studied the tops with the scrapes and blood bruises and turned them over and looked at the palms with the rough calluses that were once blisters. He studied his hands as though he was looking for something or reading something. Maybe, Pinky thought, he was remembering storms.

————·————

"The old cowboy that hangs out on the corner by the drugstore down in Lindsay?" Bill said.

Pinky nodded. "Everybody calls him Cowboy, but for all I know he may just be a fruit picker with a weathered, sweat-stained old Stetson and nothin' to do on Sundays."

Bill relaxed into his chair and began telling the story he'd been carrying all wadded up inside of himself.

"Anyway, the Cowboy, he says his left leg starts to ache a couple days before a rain." Bill paused to look out the window again. "And Louise Donald? You know Ian and Louise who have that egg ranch south of town?"

"I know 'em," Pinky said. "She died of the ague last spring."

"That's her," Bill said. "She was too damned young for that, if you ask me. It's sad, Pinky, but there's a new way Ian sounds when he talks about Louise nowadays. He seems to remember things about her I never heard him mention before. I don't think I acted like that when Constance died last year. Ian seems to have changed somehow, gets all weepy for no reason. So I don't stop by his place as much as I used to."

"It seems to be awful hard on a man to lose a woman he's been with nearly his whole life," Pinky said.

"Yes, sir. I know that for a fact." Bill slumped for a moment, then straightened and went on. "But, anyway, Louise always said her wavy hair would curl up a little tighter right before a thunderstorm. Ian swears Louise would have saw that storm comin'. And if you was to go into town today and talk to the Cowboy, he'd tell you he saw it comin'. I sure as hell didn't. Way I see it though, the only way to handle a storm is hard work gittin' ready before it comes, and hard work cleanin' up after it's gone. It's not that storms don't do no good, bringin' rain and all, but there are times they sure do make you work for it."

Bill looked out the window and through the darkness, in his mind seeing the rubble that was once his house. He extended an arm in that direction, pointing with his upturned palm, offering it up in his memory as evidence for this last truth.

"Now, how we came by the ranch... that's a story within a story." Bill paused for a good laugh. "I have a good hand for cards. Came by it naturally.

"You know how the men from the ranches, the owners, cowboys, field hands, all kinds of people, will head in to Exeter to the Orange Blossom Pool Hall to play pinochle on Saturday night? Well, they did it back then, too. Some enjoyed playing the game, some thought they were going to get rich, and others simply wanted to hang out with the men. They'd start a game and then drink a bit, and then drink a little more as the evening wore on. I'd get a beer and nurse it 'cause I was there to play cards, not to drink. Constance thought I was out drinkin' with the boys on those nights and would turn away from me in bed when I got home.

"It took me the better part of six years, but I put together enough winnings to buy that little spread across the creek. Constance softened up to my evenings down in the town when I surprised her with the place.

"I bought it from a widow woman whose husband was killed in a hunting accident of some kind a year or so before. It's an irregular patch of ground with as much rock as grass, but it's 320 acres, Pinky. That's more ground that I ever thought I'd own.

"I heard that Buck Wilson was mad as hell when he found out the widow Thompson had sold the place to me. But you don't get to pick your neighbors.

"Now listen to this wrinkle. That piece I bought — Buck Wilson's daddy lost it in a card game at the same place I won the money to buy it with. Ain't that somethin'?

"You know it ain't the best grazing land, and it ain't the best farm land, but Constance and me were excited by havin' our own place, and we figured if we worked it hard, and a good market price lined up with a good stretch of weather once in a while, we might do okay. Hell, you got to try.

"I kept my seasonal job at the lemon packing shed, and the work on the ranch fit around that pretty good most of the time. We got a few head of cattle and made a couple of dollars off 'em from year to year. We tried turkeys for five years, but they are a sorry bunch of birds to care for, and we finally had had enough. At least there's some pride in the work you do while you're goin' broke raisin' cattle. The egg farm lasted a little longer and actually made us the most money of the bunch. And when the competition made us give that up, at least there were some feral chickens scattered around the ranch that we could pot for dinner once in a while.

"Over the years we were able to put a little money away and had over $2,000 in the rainy day jar by the time the bottom fell out of beef and eggs. The same year, the lemon packing shed changed hands, and the foreman and I got laid off so the new owner could put his two young sons in there. Can't blame him. If I'd had a boy, I'd have kept him over anyone else.

"The rainy day fund lasted a while, and then we borrowed a bit from the bank to keep the ranch going. We had a couple of 'hang on by your nails' years, then a good one, and paid the bank back.

"We'd built the rainy day jar back up to a couple hundred dollars when Constance died. Doc Boles down in Exeter said she died of a failed heart." Bill rubbed his face with both hands. "I don't know if he really knew, but it doesn't much matter to me what the details were. Though I doubt it was a weak heart.

"The thing is, Pinky, you don't always end up where you want. Whether you stepped out on hope alone, or you didn't make a move until you had things all mapped out and drawn up, you just never know when you head out west with your lover. Even if you find that natural other half of your brace, and that far away place that suits the two of you, and you are blessed with bodies that can work hard—you don't know—because storms are such a natural part of the way things are."

———·———

In spite of the way it had ended for Bill, Pinky felt a twinge of regret that he'd never known a woman who might have wanted to share the adventures and problems of life, but, as he had done for years, he pushed it to the back of his mind, thinking such luck didn't seem to happen for everyone.

———·———

"Somehow, I figured to have a little better set-up for my years in old age, having my own place and all." Bill shook his head and looked out the window where there was nothing but darkness. "But it's harder than it seems to make a place work."

"Ever since that storm I been asking God fairly regular to ease up on me a bit." Bill hung his head for a minute and then looked through the darkened window again. "But damned if he didn't just send me Buck Wilson.

"You know what Buck did last summer, Pinky?" Bill looked at Pinky and snorted in disgust. "He was moving his harvester from one of his fields to another, and when he came by my place, he just drove into my corn and harvested the rows all the way across the road front side."

Pinky squinted at him. "That could get a man shot, Bill."

"I got more reasons than a few ears of corn to shoot the bastard. And from what I hear, a lot of people do. But I doubt killing him is the right way to handle it."

"I suppose you're right, Bill. That was a careless thing for me to say. But it ain't right and Buck ought to be ashamed."

"He ought to be," Bill said. "But I heard him laughing about it with some of the men downtown. He made sure I heard." Bill was looking out the darkened window again when he added, "I hate that bastard. It ain't Christian. But I hate that bastard."

"Why's he doing it, Bill?"

"Because he wants my place, Pinky." Bill looked around at Pinky and added, "And he wants yours, too, because it was the other piece his daddy lost at the card table in the Orange Blossom Pool Hall. He says this whole valley is his legacy."

"He can't be serious about that," Pinky said, standing and collecting the supper dishes and piling them in the dishpan. "Buck has asked me a couple of times about buying my place. I told him it wasn't for sale, and he hasn't said anything more about it. Buck's not the easiest man to get along with, and I can't say he's the ideal neighbor, but he wouldn't steal another man's place out from under him."

Bill followed Pinky with his eyes. "Do you honestly believe Buck Wilson's not a serious threat to the two of us? When we crossed the creek on the way here, you said we'd think of some way to deal with Buck. It sounded like you meant it. Don't you understand what we're up against?"

Pinky shrugged and filled the sink with water. "It's not that bad, Bill. I'll wash and you dry."

Bill shook his head, but stood and picked up the dish towel. "If we don't do somethin', we won't have a square inch of land to our names."

Pinky was afraid there was a chance Bill might be right, but he wasn't ready to believe it yet, and certainly not to say it. Not about a neighbor. Not even a bad neighbor.

SEVEN
SUMMER 1953

It was mid-summer when, with a quarter hour to spare, Pinky Wollerman nosed his dust-covered black pickup into the curb around the corner from Bessie's Orange Blossom Café, where the old Ivanhoe Road dead-ends into Main. He could understand why a widow woman as fussily concerned about her reputation as Ruby Thomas might not want to come by a bachelor's ranch, but he wasn't sure why she hadn't simply told him what was on her mind last Sunday at the church potluck. Her request to meet at the café seemed a little too much like a date, and even the faint possibility of Bessie or one of her customers thinking such a thing made him squirm on the canvas seat.

Pinky knew that six days a week and all year long Bessie Henshaw arrived at the café at 5 a.m. so that by 6 a.m. the place could be cleaned up and ready for her to hang her friendly sign in the front window facing Main Street:

Orange Blossom Café
<u>Open for You</u>

At times it seemed the food was merely a good excuse to see Bessie, who could talk to anyone, man or woman, child or adult, rich or poor, smart or not. Everyone was made to feel welcome and comfortable at the Orange Blossom Café.

Bessie took the friendly café sign down at 5:30 p.m. when her husband, Jackson, arrived to remove the black-and-white checked tablecloths, put on slick squares of thick orange oilcloth, remove the curtain that covered the wall of liquor bottles, and open up the back room. When Jackson flipped on the neon sign on the back side of the place, the side facing the wide alley with space for seven cars to park anonymously, the Orange Blossom Café was transformed into the Orange Blossom Bar and Pool Hall.

The bar, originally the Rocky Hill Bar, had been in place since before Exeter was a town and beyond every living person's memory. Consequently, it had landmark status and was regularly used as a starting point for directions to such places as the pharmacy, the dry goods store, the police station and any number of churches. Men came from every small town within a 20-mile radius to play pool, drink and play cards. It was the latter that earned the Orange Blossom Bar and Pool Hall its legendary historical standing as it was the site of many high stakes games, some fair, and some outright fleecings. On most nights of the year the Orange Blossom Bar and Pool Hall was a place for the modestly exciting entertainment of the patrons engaging in mostly friendly games and enjoying no more than one fistfight over a weekend.

But there were rare but memorable occasions when the stars glittered strangely and the misshapen moon had lost the joy of fullness, and a dry harsh wind would blow up from the ancient desert to the west, and the threesome would conspire to set the teeth of life on edge. And two arrogant men who had awakened brash in the morning thinking it was their day to howl would, in the evening, come together over a card table butting heads like two rutting rams. And sometime in the night one would tragically and spectacularly lose, and one would win as in a dream, and those men would exchange places in the community, the rich with the poor and the poor with the rich. And those disturbances of the status quo provided an exhilaration lasting for months or even years and were why there were more men who chose the risky path of coming back than those who sensibly did not.

Pinky stopped in at the café when he was in town to enjoy a good meal and be in the presence of Bessie Henshaw, but considered the bar a foolish waste of time and Jackson an agent of recklessness.

At the previous Methodist Women's Sunday Potluck, the barber's sister, Ruby Thomas, approached Pinky and asked for a glass of his Kool-Aid. Ruby had always been nice to Pinky, but she had never before shown an interest in Kool-Aid, and although normally an uncomfortably talkative woman, she stood silently, looking deeply into her cup. Then she asked in a guarded whisper if Pinky could meet her on Tuesday over at the Orange Blossom to talk about Buck Wilson. Pinky had paused a minute, hoping Ruby wasn't asking for a drinking date with him at Jackson's place because he didn't want a date with Ruby and because he felt uneasy in the bar and with the way Jackson always looked at him sideways and from on high. He also paused because he was curious why Ruby was acting like she was not talking to him when she was, and he was feeling some guilt at the prospect of talking behind Buck Wilson's back because he was a fellow parishioner and a neighbor. All that thinking and feeling took long enough that Ruby put the Kool-Aid down and started to walk away, forcing Pinky to say a little louder than he would have liked, "How about 4:30?" That was early enough to mean coffee at Bessie's rather than a drink at Jackson's.

Ruby came back for the Kool-Aid, "Okay, then," she said, still speaking to the cup.

So on Tuesday Pinky pulled open the screen door of the Orange Blossom Cafe and hoped that whatever Ruby had to say wouldn't take nearly an hour, and they'd be gone well before Jackson arrived and the bar was uncovered.

Bessie didn't disappoint him when he walked through the front door. "Hot out there?" she asked.

That wasn't exactly an intimate greeting, but Pinky was seeing Bessie's tidy, baby-blue, fitted waitress outfit, her nearly black and neatly waved hair atop her 5-foot-11 frame, and, feeling the friendliness of her unusually resonant voice, he was pleased. As Pinky plopped down in a chair at a table for two, he suddenly realized how the drenching summer sweat on his back, chest and arms had given his chambray work shirt a pinto look in lighter and darker shades of blue, with white salt deposits here and there. He wished he'd opted for morning coffee and blushed at the thought that he might not smell agreeable to townspeople who might be enjoying a little something extra by going out to eat.

Bessie must have read his blush and lack for words. "Looks like you've been doing some honest work, honey."

Bessie called all the single men "honey," as well as all the married women, but it made Pinky feel accepted. He had started to relax when the not-so-gentle giant, Jackson Henshaw, lumbered in from the back a full hour early. He paused to take in Pinky's dusty boots, well-worked pants and sweat-soaked shirt, stared for a moment at Bessie, and then came to Pinky's table to tower over him.

"Well, if it isn't Pinky Wollerman," Jackson said. "How are you and your neighbor Buck Wilson getting along these days?"

Pinky cocked his head to the side and said, "Just fine," wondering why his relationship with Buck was of any concern to Jackson and noticing the curious coincidence that his reason for being there was to talk to Ruby about Buck Wilson.

Jackson snorted and shook his head. "You think so, huh?" When Pinky didn't respond, he added, "Why don't you stick around for some cards with the men this evening, Pinky?"

Pinky noticed that Jackson had sarcastically emphasized "the men."

"No, thanks, Jackson. I've got a ranch to take care of. No time for such nonsense."

Jackson did the snort and head shake again, then returned to the pool hall. He had greeted Pinky with the same once-over every time he saw him, and there was something about the encounter that made Pinky feel even shorter than he was. He looked down at his boots and pants, and when he looked up, Bessie was smiling at him. Suddenly nothing about Jackson's treatment of him bothered him, and he smiled without knowing it, and Bessie laughed that deep bass viola laugh of hers that made his 5-foot-8 frame resonate in tune with the wind in the aspens and made his insides smile.

Pinky ate an order of meatloaf and mashed potatoes and sipped occasionally at his Coca-Cola while the ice melted as he watched a stuttering stream of customers wander in from the street and drink coffee or Coca-Cola, eat apple pie or peach pie or some combination of coffee or soda and pie, then wander back out. A man dressed like a banker came in with three kids and ordered two of the meatloaf specials and had the whole brood fed and back on the street in less than 15 minutes. Pinky marveled at the man's child-herding skills. It was remarkable to be able to feed so many in so few minutes. But they were noisy minutes, and Pinky appreciated the quiet when they stacked their dishes together in the middle of the table and left. He didn't mind big kids, but he was not willing to go through the problem of having little kids in order to get them. Not that he had ever been given the choice. He had at times wondered if it might be nice to have a wife, but the dating that was necessary to get that far had always seemed far too troublesome.

Shortly before 5:30 Bessie swooped by without saying a word and clunked a small ceramic plate with apple pie in front of him. Pinky ate it but couldn't enjoy the pie because of how he hated the waiting.

A half hour after the friendly sign had been removed and the bar and pool hall began to take shape, Pinky gave up on Ruby and went to his truck. As Pinky reached to put the truck in gear, Ruby poked her head through the window.

"I'm in a hurry, Pinky. But listen up because this is important."

"Good to see you, Ruby. And don't worry about being late. I didn't have anything to do this afternoon."

Ruby didn't smile, apologize or offer a greeting. "Buck Wilson is obsessed with getting your place. He's talked about it from the time he was a teenager. You're a private man and probably haven't heard the talk around town, but a lot of people think he had something to do with Dally's disappearance."

"Who?" Pinky furrowed his brow.

"The gambler who won a big piece of the Wilson ranch from Buck's father. Anyway, there's also talk that he means to get your place. 'One way or the other,' is what they say."

Pinky shook his head in disagreement. "Buck is full of himself, Ruby, but I don't believe he'd do anything underhanded or illegal."

"Of course, you don't, Pinky. Which is why I wanted to warn you. You be careful of Buck Wilson. I'd hate to see you caught by surprise."

With that, Ruby turned on her heel and walked away, leaving Pinky a little confused, and a little uneasy.

Could Bill Jenkins have been right?

'EIGHT
SUMMER 1953

It was Emily Robin Macadam's turn to prepare supper. She sat on a wooden milk stool with once-painted legs worn bare and darkened from years of handling. She picked a potato from a half-full gunnysack and swiftly removed the skin with a paring knife, its blade narrowed and shorted from recurrent sharpening. She sang a hymn she had known since earliest memory:

> See the morning sun ascending,
> radiant in the eastern sky;
> hear the angel voices blending
> in their praise to God on high.

She let the peelings fall to the galvanized metal slop bucket between her knees and plunked the potato into the water of another bucket at her side, noticing the splashed droplets forming pellets of brown mud in the powdery dust of the Poor Farm's central yard. Emily Robin sang hymns because that was what she knew. The words were her way to get musical notes out into the air and were no more to be confused with an act of worship than the song of a radiant morning was to be mistaken as a description of the hellishly hot and muggy summer afternoon through which she labored.

A flash of light caught her attention, and she looked the half-mile across the alfalfa field toward the mailbox at the glare of a windshield leading a billowing fog of dust. She fell silent, stretched her back and shifted her buttocks against the hardness of the stool on which she had sat hunched and peeling potatoes for the past half hour. She plucked at the front of her bodice, rippling the fabric between her breasts to momentarily fan the late afternoon heat away from her sweating torso and complained to herself that she could never be in this place long enough to be comfortable with a San Joaquin Valley

July. Then she quickly conceded to her more positive side and said in the direction of the cotton field, "But the heat certainly does make the cotton grow." And, she thought, following the progress of the emerging trail of dust, it does make it easy to tell when someone is coming to visit.

She nodded to the approaching truck and said in the crisp fashion of a formal greeting that emphasized her native New Zealand accent, "Good of you to announce your arrival." Then she added in the direction of the potato sack, "Almost civilized."

In her soul it seemed she had lived in the other world of this place for a lifetime, but Logan was born a month after she arrived at the farm, so she could never forget how long they had been here. "Seven years and nine months," she murmured and then looked around to make sure she was alone. Some of the older women talked regularly to themselves. At 26, Emily Robin didn't yet want to be known for that oddness, even though she knew she talked to herself more often than she talked to any of the other eight women. So Emily Robin clenched her jaw to confine her thoughts within her mind and scanned the farm, its sounds muffled by the oppressive heat.

Emily Robin sat with the potatoes in the large circular area created by the kitchen, sleeping quarters, milk house, barn and implement shed. Logan was in the kitchen behind her getting a drink of water. Betty, the one woman at the Poor Farm who was close to Emily Robin in age and came closest to being accepted as a friend, had complained of cramps and had gone to lie down. All the other women were working in the fields, the three older children were in school, and the youngest was taking a nap. A shadow passed slowly across the courtyard and folded over the corral fence, giving away a buzzard floating high above in the pale summer sky. A half dozen Rhode Island Reds placidly scratched and dusted themselves out by the implement shed.

Emily Robin could see yellow beneath the glare of the flat windshield. The vehicle was clearly moving faster than a delivery truck. She wondered if it could be the yellow pickup that was at the farm last week. She had been in the south quarter section weeding cotton and had not seen the man who drove it. Betty told her he was a big bear of a man, a wealthy rancher, and very handsome. Two men had delivered a well-used, but serviceable, hay baler to the farm as a gift from the Methodist Church on the other side of Rocky Hill. A couple of hours after those two left, the big man had arrived with two large wooden crates filled with spare parts for the baler. Betty had absently brushed at her cheek as she recalled how this man had easily lifted the heavy crates from the bed of his truck and carried them to the barn.

Emily Robin had never been over Rocky Hill and reflected how it seemed all the good places—the high and cool mountains, the country churches, the places proper people gathered—were over that hill and, therefore, out of sight and out of reach. Apparently that's where the handsome men were, too.

But handsome men could be dangerous. It was a handsome man who had left her alone, waiting and in love in New Zealand. It was a handsome man who caused her to flee in the disgrace of unwed pregnancy to the opposite side of the world from her loving parents. Emily Robin knew she couldn't judge all the world's handsome men by that one. But she also knew that getting past him had hard-tempered her heart near to brittleness; she was certain that when she found the wretch, she would find a way to deal him justice. When she cursed him, she never called him bastard. There had been a number of those with their mothers on the farm, and they were far too sweet.

She was grateful for the Poor Farm. It kept her and Logan from starving. And being out of the way, it was a safer and gentler place to raise a bastard child. Making a living on the farm was hard work, but the work kept her from wallowing in self pity. There wasn't the time. The women agreed that the endless work had a way of dampening the pain and fear they carried along with their healing bodies, broken spirits and other reasons the place was known locally as the Wit's End Farm.

Logan burst outside from the kitchen and began spelling recently learned words in the dirt with a stick, pronouncing each letter loudly. The area served as a parking area and turnaround for visitors so, as the truck approached, Emily Robin called to him, "Logan, come over on the porch with your mother and give the truck some room."

Logan ran to her, jumped up on the porch with a two-legged

flatfooted stomp, slapping the railing with his free hand and then putting the porch post en garde with his stick. Emily Robin smiled at her son's happy exuberance and noted with pride that he was tall for his age and quite sturdy. As she turned toward the courtyard, the yellow truck pulled up in front of the sleeping quarters. Anxious to see this handsome man Betty told her about, and to find out why he had returned, Emily Robin stabbed her knife into a potato, intending to go out and meet the handsome stranger. But when Betty ran out from the sleeping quarters and climbed into passenger's side of the cab, Emily Robin realized that Betty had feigned her cramps.

Logan stared curiously at the truck and took a hesitant step in that direction. But Emily Robin saw the face of the handsome man and knew instantly it was the handsome man she had known in New Zealand. Logan's father. Buck Wilson. A hot soup of emotions hollowed her insides and weakened her knees, and an aura of memories muted her vision. In reflex she grabbed for Logan and, finding his wrist, pulled him toward the door of the tenant quarters.

Logan saw the scowl on his mother's face and asked, "What's wrong, Mother? Is that a mean man?"

"I don't know, honey. I don't think so," she said. When they were through the door, she said, "No. He won't hurt you. But he's here to see Betty." She wondered when Betty and Buck might have had the opportunity to get to know each other so well that Betty would run to him and climb in his truck. Emily Robin leaned down, swiped the sweat-soaked hair out of Logan's eyes, and added, "We should let them talk alone."

A minute of conversation later, Betty waved in Emily Robin's direction from the cab of the yellow truck as it left the rough huddle of the Poor Farm's buildings. Emily Robin did not return the wave, and, as she watched the tailgate disappear into a cloud of dust, she thought perhaps she should fear for her friend.

Logan broke into her thoughts. "Why do I have to stay inside?"

Emily Robin consciously relaxed her throat and said, "You can go outside now, honey. And play."

Emily Robin could hear Logan dragging a stick across the wire of the chicken coop at the far end of the barn and she began to shake.

She willed herself not to burst into tears, grabbed up a heavy ceramic cup sitting on the kitchen counter and slammed it back down. The dishes in the cupboard above the counter rattled. She did not curse and she did not scream. She stood at the kitchen window looking over the baking field of cotton and willed herself to stop shaking. Then she went back to the potatoes with precise vengeance. By the time supper was prepared, Emily Robin looked perfectly normal. The change had been internal.

After the table was cleared and the dishes cleaned and put away, Emily Robin Macadam put Logan Wilson Macadam to bed and read him a story until he fell asleep. She tucked him in and kissed him lightly on the forehead. Then she took a light shawl and a cup of tea to the wooden rocker on the porch and sat in the twilight summer evening with her memories of her New Zealand home during the years of the war and the day her sleeping son had been fathered.

———·———

Emily Robin remembered being in church every Sunday of her life because her father required her to be there. Mr. Macadam, as Emily Robin and her five sisters addressed their father, repaired musical instruments. The variety of work in his shop involved piano tunings and the refurbishing of brass instruments, but the greater of his time and nearly the entirety of his heart was devoted to violin repair. When not working, which was precious little, he spent time enough with his family to affirm that family life was important business, but much of family time was also church time devoted to a variety of midweek meetings and the worship service on the Sabbath. If you were to ask Mr. Macadam, his practiced answer was that God was first, his family second and his business third. He never mentioned his avocation, his love, or perhaps it was lust, for the perfect note from the perfect violin.

Emily Robin met Logan's father in the New Zealand First Presbyterian Church her father had helped to build. Emily Robin remembered how the spring sun filtering through the etched glass of the sanctuary had germinated within her a most unlady-like yearning. She remembered hearing the preacher say an occasional thee and thou. A subdued amen floated by from an indefinite place in the crowded sanctuary. New blue jeans crackled as the Simpson twins squirmed in the pew behind her. But she was primarily aware of the soldier, Buck Wilson, sitting in the pew in front of her. He was with the U.S. Marine Logistics Group that had arrived in Wellington the previous winter.

The Americans had been everywhere. Most of them, like Buck, were stationed at the depot where supplies were collected to be sent forward to the various theatres of battle. But some of them came to New Zealand to escape the constant pressure of the war so they wouldn't go crazy. Some of these men were scary, and Emily Robin, for the first time in her life, felt afraid to walk the streets of Wellington after dark.

Buck wasn't one of the scary ones. He could have been. At six-and-a-half feet tall with muscles bulging on his arms and neck, he could have been scary. Instead she found his size and good looks magnetic. His presence made her aware of her posture. She kept her back straight and shoulders back, which she knew accentuated her slender frame and large breasts. He was quiet and slow and handsome and seemed so gentle.

Once they were introduced, she sensed he was always aware of her without paying direct attention to her. When he attended church, he would sit in the pew in front of her, which she came to believe was no accident. Her suspicion was affirmed when later she found out he was Methodist and had only come to the Presbyterian Church because he had seen her standing out in front one Sunday morning. His body required the pew space of two of her bodies. She could see the bulk of his shoulders and arms through the khaki uniform shirt. She liked the way he sat, the way he stood, and the way he walked. When he sat in front of her, she thought very un-churchlike thoughts about him. With a "thou shalt not" ringing in her ears she imagined his back, and more, without the khaki. They talked after church, and then dated, going to various dances on the base and in town and, of course, going regularly to church.

Emily Robin was not unaware of her desirability and knew about men and lust. When her teenaged body had fully blossomed, she went swimming with a boy who was a year older and lived near her aunt's farm. He had shown an unusual interest in the fit of her swimsuit and developed a bulge that aroused her curiosity. She had led him to a nearly sheltered spot behind thin shrubbery lining a pasture. Ignoring his possible exposure to anyone working the sheep, he pulled the leg of his trunks up, exposing himself. She found the hardness remarkable. He guided the movement of her hand, and in only a few seconds she was surprised and fascinated by his climax. Then his knees almost gave way, and he put a hand on her shoulder and leaned against her, appearing exhausted and happy. A few seconds later he tensed and looked nervously around, checking for any observers, saw his father's dog working the sheep on the other side of the pasture, and quickly covered himself.

With little effort, Emily Robin saw that she had provided the boy with not only a pleasant experience, but one he craved past the point of caution and self control. She had been so intrigued by the experience that she had experimented with a classmate who was her own age, and later with his older, and married, brother. Remarkably, she observed, the three began to lose self control when she used her body to flirt with them, and they lost every shred of control in the moment she held them in her hand. For months afterward the effect had been the same with the two boys: They followed her around like pets when she was anywhere in their vicinity. The older brother was more discreet, and though she never touched him again, he remained hopeful and often found ways to be alone with her. She was aware of having discovered the useful power of her desirability and the weakness named lust.

———·———

But Buck wanted much more than her hand, and she found his wanting both compelling and awful. Frighteningly aware of a lifetime of admonitions to wait until marriage, she nevertheless felt herself opening to him. In the haze of her own lust, she decided an engagement would be an adequate foundation for making love, and when she asked him if they were going to get married, he said, "Sure." Since Buck was a man of little pretense, she did not doubt the sincerity of his agreement, if not proposal, to marry.

In spite of Buck's preference, she could not keep the wonderful news from her mother, who then talked to the minister, and, though both congratulated Buck in private, they also agreed to keep the secret until the couple made a public announcement.

Then, on a summer evening in January 1945, as the war was approaching an unexpected end, while her father's hands and heart were busy tuning a violin in his shop downtown, and while her mother was clapping her hands for two of her younger children at the community playhouse, Emily Robin imagined more vividly what her heart and body wanted... and invited it to happen.

While they lay on the bed caressing and kissing, she found she had started a thing she could not stop, even if she had wanted to. He was so far stronger that she had simply complied as he removed her clothes. She was embarrassed by her eagerness, a part of her wishing he would stop and another part craving him. In the end she held him tightly as he pushed into her.

———·———

Though more than 8 years old, these memories of Buck created a tingle below Emily Robin's navel, which irritated her, and she cursed, shook her head and gulped the last of her tea. Her mature self that sat on the San Joaquin Poor Farm — barely making a living for her son — remembered Buck's thoughtlessness and hated him for the callous lack of intimacy.

———·———

That evening in New Zealand, her yesterday self with a young girl's heart had noticed when his body relaxed, and she had asked, "Did you?" She had been surprised at his answer.

"Wow. That felt great. You Kiwis are something else."

Buck had rolled off her, sat on the edge of the bed, and pulled his pants on. She took a deep breath, realizing how hard it had been to breathe with his weight on her chest. With the release of pressure, it was as though her insides dissolved like a carelessly dropped summer melon, and it took all her willpower not to cry.

She felt a wetness creeping slowly down her buttocks, not knowing if it was blood or semen, but knowing for certain she was no longer a virgin and fearing possibly that she was pregnant.

"I'll see you tomorrow," Buck had said.

She had expected a kiss or a caress that did not come, and said, "We should plan our wedding."

"Yeah." Buck stood up, slipped into his shoes and headed toward the door.

"Let's get married this fall, before it gets too cold...." Her proposal had been cut off by the slam of the door. She had glimpsed the twilight summer night behind the open door and felt as though it had stayed with her for all the years since that door banged shut.

———··———

Emily Robin lost her virginity to her "fiancé" on a Wednesday. He wasn't in church on the following Sunday, and by Wednesday of the following week, she began to fret that his busy schedule would keep them from making love again, which was something she wanted very much. Emily Robin remembered thinking that she could be better for him the next time they made love, and years later, every time she remembered being so naïve as to think such a thing, she was a little more disgusted with herself.

He did not call on her for a week, and she began to worry he may have decided not to see her because, as she had been warned by her father, he might think she was a loose woman.

She had to find Buck and tell him that he was her first and only. It took her another week and a half to work up the nerve to go to the U.S. military base. A very young and formal soldier in a khaki uniform met her at the gate. She explained she was there to see her fiancé, Mr. Buck Wilson. The gate guard asked if Mr. Wilson was Army or Navy. She didn't know how to tell the difference and said that he was a Marine. Buck had given her a photograph, but in the photo he was in civilian work clothes, standing next to a corral, his arm around the neck of a horse. The young gate guard didn't recognize him, but he checked two rosters and informed her there was no one at the base by the name of Buck Wilson. She insisted that Buck had asked her to marry him and was an American soldier. The gate guard placed a call on a heavy black telephone and then informed her that the only Wilson on the base, a Captain Charles Wilson, U.S. Marine Corps, had shipped out three weeks earlier for the final assault and occupation of Japan. Emily Robin wondered if Buck's real name was Charles. She realized the day he left New Zealand was the day after they had made love, and a tightness gripped her chest that turned the simple act of breathing into a deliberate, anxious effort.

———··———

Other girls Emily Robin had known had married American GIs during the war, and when the war was over were assigned to sail on decommissioned troop transport ships for the three-week journey to Hawaii and on to the United States. Emily Robin had wondered many times since arriving at the Poor Farm why it had worked so perfectly for them and not for her.

———··———

At the time she had wanted to believe Buck was forced to leave without notice and did not know how to contact her, so she set about to convince the American authorities to allow her to emigrate. She knew Buck lived in California, and, having no concept of the size of a U.S. state, was confident she could find him and they would be reunited. She pulled in the minister of the Presbyterian Church to verify that she and Buck were engaged. She asked her parents to testify that Buck had spent his free time over the past several months with Emily Robin in their family home.

Ultimately, she lied to the emigration officer that she was six months pregnant. The number impressed him, but as a young, unmarried and inexperienced man, he was ill-equipped to correlate Emily Robin's size to the passage of time. He found her attractive in the way of his younger sister, liked her, was compelled to help her, and initiated the emigration process.

No one knew she was pregnant except the emigration officer

who had authorized her entry to the U.S., and she decided it best to keep her secret. The day she left New Zealand, a friend of Buck's told her what she did not want to believe—that he was married. She decided to let her family continue to believe she was "going abroad" with her fiancé.

Emily Robin wasn't sure what she would do when she reached California. She had cried most of every day during the trip. But then she dried her tears and began to work on surviving in a strange land with no money and no family except the one growing within her. The kindness of a woman in San Francisco who saw that no one met her when Emily Robin disembarked eventually led her to the San Joaquin Poor Farm. It was better than having no place to go, but the work never let up and survival bent her back and forced her head down.

———·———

Emily Robin placed her empty teacup on the porch railing and pulled the shawl around her shoulders. When she had arrived in California and found out how big it was, she had lost hope of finding Buck Wilson, but by some act of fate, he was not far from the Poor Farm. She wondered if perhaps finding Buck was a chance to make things right for Logan. It wasn't in her nature to second guess the past for long, so she settled into a soothing, slow rhythm with the rocking chair and tried to imagine what set of circumstances would be considered justice for the illegitimate son of a well-to-do man. And what might be considered justice for the man.

Betty returned before the next morning, and as she went about her chores, Emily Robin noticed that Betty seemed on edge and worked as though certain movements hurt. Emily Robin said nothing to Betty about Buck Wilson.

NINE
1946-1953

There are many ways a farmer can fail. The weather can take his crops at any stage of growth or harvest. The insects and other pests can eat their way to his ruin. And there are times, strange times, when a farmer's neighbors can put him off his land. The government of the people is a powerful neighbor. Mostly that has been a good thing for most people. But not for all. And not for Kazuko Nakamura.

Kazuko's folks had owned the Eldridge farm before the war but lost it when they were sent off to a detention center. The story was that the Eldridges bought the farm from the county for little more than back taxes. When Kazuko came back after the war, he had no home, and Leon and Birdie Eldridge, though hardly making a living for themselves, took him in. Kazuko helped them run the farm, and they paid him what they could when they could and let him live in the equipment shed. Amazingly, the arrangement seemed to work well for both parties.

Over the years, on his drives up to the mountains to fish the streams and rivers, Kazuko had seen Pinky in his fields and stopped to talk crops and weather. Sometimes he stopped by on his way back and dropped off a couple of trout.

Pinky enjoyed Kazuko's visits. He seemed an intelligent man, and once he found out Pinky had books, he borrowed one each time he came by, returning it on the next trip, sometimes weeks later.

―――

By its end, the summer of 1953 had had a lot of practice being hot, and Pinky was straining with a six-foot digging bar to pry a big rear tractor tire off its rim. He paused when he heard an engine down at the paved road a quarter-mile away, and he looked up to see Leon Eldridge's old grey Dodge turning up his drive. As the pickup and the clatter and the dust grew near, Pinky could see through the dirt-marbled windshield well enough to make out a form on the passenger side. He assumed it was Kazuko Nakamura as he often saw the two of them together at the feed store and around town. And every time he saw them, he was reminded that forgiveness and grace of a remarkable nature was not relegated to the divine, but could indeed happen at the human level.

Pinky appreciated that Leon slowed the pickup to a crawl as he approached the implement shed, trying not to stir up too much dust.

Pinky's hands were black with grease and oil, his arms and face were the dull brown of the dust and streaked darker brown where sweat had run, dripped and puddled.

Leon poked his head out through the pickup window, saw Pinky's labored condition and said, "What are you doin' lazing the day away here in the shade when there's real work waitin' out there in the fields?"

Pinky laughed, waved the two men over and went to the well where he cleaned up and then pumped a bucket of fresh cold water, which he offered up with a tin cup and a ladle.

After the customary pleasantries about the weather and cotton and beef prices, Leon asked Kazuko to excuse them for a few minutes. Kazuko went to the house and sat on the porch and entertained Pinky's overly friendly dog, Wilbur, with a fetching stick and a scratch behind the ears. As soon as Kazuko was out of good hearing, Leon folded his arms over his chest and said, "Pinky, I heard that old Texas boy who was helping you here drifted on down to Santa Barbara and that you could use a hand here on the ranch."

Pinky glanced over at the cantankerous tire. His mind swirled around the half dozen things he had intended to get done before it went flat, and he had to walk back to the barn and get the truck and fetch the thing, which was a chore because the big tire and wheel weighed over 100 pounds. The tire was split, so there was nothing to do but drive in to town and buy another. John Jessup at the tire shop had pointed out the tread on the old tire was nearly worn out and advised Pinky that if he didn't replace both rear tires, he'd be riding ski-jawed with the new tire a good three or four inches higher than the old one. By the time Pinky had changed both tires, he'd have wasted all morning and half the afternoon, and his list of things to do would be longer than it was at the beginning of the day. After Squatty had left, he and Bill Jenkins had traded help for a while. But Bill's place needed a lot of attention, and he hadn't been able to help Pinky recently, so Pinky's list of things to do had grown steadily. The idea of an extra hand sounded sensible so he said, "What's on your mind, Leon?"

Leon jerked his head toward the house where Kazuko sat on the porch scratching Wilbur's ears. "That there's the hardest working man you ever saw," he said, "though he may know very little about ranching."

"He may know more than you think, Leon," Pinky said, remembering all the times Kazuko had stopped by and realizing that Leon did not know that Kazuko had learned to ride on this ranch and that he had ridden the better part of it with Pinky. "But does he want to work here?"

Leon looked at the dust at his feet. "At this point it don't matter if he does or not. Birdie and I can't afford three mouths anymore. Time was you could make a living on 40 acres of cotton. But the price isn't there anymore." Leon looked out over the foothill grasslands, bleached from the sun of a long summer. "Thing is, I feel like we owe Kaz something. He's not only a hard worker, he's a friend. And a good man. We can't keep him on, but we can't just turn him out without a place to go, Pinky. He's already been kicked off that farm once. I understand why it happened, but it wasn't fair to him. He was as good an American boy as anybody else. The miracle is... he still is. After all that. He still is."

Knowing Kaz would be a tremendous help if he decided to be a ranch hand, Pinky said, "I'll offer him a job. And gladly. And I hope he accepts. But he's got several generations of farming in his blood, and farmers don't always want to work a ranch." Pinky scooped another cup of water from the bucket, poured it over his head, and shook the water off. "We'll have to see what he says."

———··———

The war ended in the spring of 1946, and a U.S. Army captain went to the bachelor's quarters of the Tule Lake Detention Center and told

Kazuko Nakamura it was his time to leave. Kazuko asked where he was to go. The officer said he was to go home. The captain paused a moment and then, sounding kindly when he said it, told Kazuko that it could be dangerous to go anywhere else. So for Kazuko Nakamura, home was the only place to go. But going home filled him with dread.

He had no choice but to leave home when the war started. And now that the war was over, he had no choice to go anywhere but home. He had nearly finished college when he had been labeled a troublemaker and sent to Tule Lake, but his parents were sent to Manzanar. For two years, ten months and three days he had experienced the heartless indifference of mistrust in a detention center, and now he was afraid what form that mistrust might have taken when it visited his home. But he accepted this order in the same dignified manner he had accepted every order since the one that sent him to the detention center.

The captain gave Kazuko a U.S. Government voucher for a one-way bus ticket home and ordered him to leave the internment camp. Kazuko nodded, gave the man a spare bow, thanked him and collected his things in a small satchel.

"One more thing," the captain said as Kazuko neared the exit of the compound. "This came for you in today's mail." He handed Kazuko a manila envelope with his name above the words "Tule Lake (probably)," The return address said only, "Manzanar." Kazuko looked inquiringly at the captain who shrugged and turned away.

Enough of Kazuko's life had happened within the Tule Lake compound that he didn't want to spend even a minute more of it there. He put the envelope into his satchel and started his walk toward the bus station in Newell.

At the bus station the agent was familiar with the voucher, exchanging it for a ticket without looking at him, and did not notice Kazuko's respectful bow.

Kazuko Nakamura stood outside the Newell, California, bus terminal in the early morning twilight with a rare spring snowstorm blowing flakes in circles around his head, and waited for two and a half hours with his ticket in an inside pocket where it would remain reasonably dry.

The southbound bus arrived, and Kazuko stared at the slushy

tire tracks on the snow-splattered road while the other passengers boarded. Then he approached the driver and respectfully handed over his damp ticket. The bus driver paused from putting the other passenger's baggage in a bin under the bus, pointed toward the rear of the big orange bus with the brown stripe, and without looking directly at Kazuko told him to settle himself on a seat toward the back and hold his bag in his lap.

Kazuko overheard a passenger saying it would take a little over 17 hours to get from the Tule Lake to Exeter, and the only stop of more than 10 minutes would be in Sacramento. In Sacramento, he was allowed, after politely asking, to use the toilet while waiting for the next bus. The two minutes in the stall was the only time during the 17 hours that not one of the passengers was looking directly at him. Two elderly men who certainly had not been soldiers in this war were waiting to continue watching when he came out. Kazuko wondered if they had some place to go or were only riding the bus thinking they were performing a civic duty as watchers. After Tule Lake he was not at all intimidated by being watched, and while in the camp had learned that if he did not notice the watchers, they seemed less agitated than if he watched back. So Kazuko pretended not to notice the watchers on the bus.

As the bus arrived in Exeter, the driver announced the time, 10:20 p.m. There was some sleepy grumbling and bag toting, and then within 15 minutes of arrival all the other passengers were gone. Ten minutes later the station operator turned out the lights, put a padlock on the door, and left for the night, as though it was customary to leave a man standing in the dark with his bag in the middle of the graveled parking area. Kazuko was not offended, but he was saddened. He thought it odd to be watched so closely for 17 hours and then ignored when a sentence or two and a finger lifted toward a desired direction might have helped him. He didn't need the help. But the ticket agent did not know that and did not have the courtesy to ask.

Kazuko's family farm was at the edge of the foothills, 7 miles to the southeast of Exeter. He took a long drink of water from a faucet at the side of the bus station and started walking. The March night was clear and cold, and the waning moon offered little light. Finding his footing was often an act of faith even after his eyes adjusted to the darkness. The paved country roads were narrow and straight with intersections a mile apart. When he heard a car coming, he would step away from the road to conceal himself within the crop he was passing. At times he stood behind the thick leaves of orange trees standing like giant licorice gumdrops in the darkness. In the pear and peach orchards, with their lacy silhouettes of leafless limbs covered in plump buds, he stood two rows back looking like one of the gnarled and shadowed trunks. In the open fields he simply moved several steps farther off the road and sat on his heels, blending into the night. As the headlights passed, he looked away and kept his eyes closed and noticed the musty odor of the damp fertile soil of the San Joaquin Valley.

Nearing the end of his journey he found a rare stand of native sycamore somehow still standing in the midst of the relentlessly cleared and cultivated patchwork of farms, and he settled into the leaves and duff at their center to sleep. There was no need to arrive home in the middle of the night and disturb or frighten his elderly parents. And if the worst had happened and someone else now lived on the farm, it could be dangerous to arrive unannounced in the night.

He was warm from walking, but the late night was cold and, as he lay at rest, the ground soaked the heat from his body, his back and leg muscles cramped, and so he soon moved on.

———··———

Kazuko arrived at the farm as dawn was breaking. In the way of places that for a long while have been seen only as memory, it was not the same place. The palms lining the quarter-mile driveway were still in place but had grown bushy toward the top, apparently having gone quite some time without pruning. The drive had a new gravel cover added to the raised arch of its bed. The foot-high concrete irrigation pipes with their domino-sized tin valve covers stood as before in an orderly line along the driveway bordering the 50-acre field next to the house. But ragged stocks of the past summer's cotton crop stood on the ridges of the furrowed field rather than the low, sprawling strawberry plants that were there when he left. And a clean, perhaps new, blue and grey tractor with red wheel hubs was parked by the implement shed.

Kazuko was certain he was at the right place, but was not sure it was home. He stopped and waited and watched the house, his house, the home where he was born and raised, the home where he lived until he went to college in Berkeley and got swept away to Tule Lake.

...Now he was home.

Only a minute passed before a man in bib overalls came out of the house, walking swiftly toward the implement shed. He had both arms in a quilted canvas jacket and was shrugging the jacket onto his back when he saw Kazuko and stopped abruptly.

Keeping his eyes on Kazuko, he backed toward the door of the house and said something over his shoulder. Immediately a long gun was passed through the door to the man. It disturbed Kazuko to realize these people kept a gun near the door. The man worked the rifle's lever action halfway and glanced down to verify that a shell was coming from the magazine, then worked the lever back to seat the shell in the chamber. No movement or sounds suggested the gun had been placed on safety, and the man walked slowly toward Kazuko.

Kazuko knew about guns. Contrary to his parents' wishes, he had joined the ROTC while at UC Berkeley. He thought it a good way to affirm his place as an American citizen. One of their activities was a competition rifle team. Kazuko had learned to shoot and was one of the better shots on the team. His "good American citizen" strategy had backfired. When everyone of Japanese ancestry was being rounded up for the detention centers, those considered to be more troublesome or more of a threat were sent to Tule Lake. He would have been sent to Manzanar with his parents and others considered harmless except for their heritage, but someone had pointed out his military background and his skill with a weapon, and under a cloud of fear and suspicion he had been sent to Tule Lake.

Kazuko was never sure who had sounded the suspicion. As he was looking out of the window of the bus that hauled him away, one of his fellow ROTC students had pointed at him the way little kids did when they mimicked shooting someone with a pistol. In the ROTC circles the man was known as Midshipman Wilson. The other students called him Buck. It might have been Wilson who raised the question of

Kazuko's loyalty and caused him to be sent to Tule Lake, but in those fearful times it could have been anyone.

Kazuko was startled by how widely his mind wandered while a gun was pointed at him. And he was very afraid. But he could not leave the farm without knowing if his parents had come back. He stood his ground with his arms at his sides and tried to ignore his suddenly overwhelming need to pee.

The man with the long gun stopped 10 steps away from him and aimed it toward Kazuko's chest.

Hoping he would not be shot, he said, "My name is Kazuko Nakamura. This is the farm of my parents—the Nakamura farm." He could not bring himself to use his parents' names, Yoshi and Hiyori.

"Not anymore," the man said. "I—me and Birdie—bought this farm from the county. It's ours now." The man paused and started to lower the gun, then raised it again. "This is the Eldridge farm now." He lowered the gun halfway and then made a scooting motion with the barrel. "You best get on down the road."

Kazuko scanned the farm from west to east and then looked skyward at a puff of cloud overhead brightening into a brilliant textured linen pillowcase as the sun rose over the eastern mountains. As the morning light advanced the shadows peeled away to reveal greater and greater detail and color, and the birds began moving out into the furrowed crops from the windrow trees along the north end of the field. Kazuko did not know where his parents were and thought it quite possible he would be shot. But this mystical vision of the new day surrounding him trimmed the ragged edges from his fear, his anguish, and his anger. "Where are the Nakamuras?" he asked.

Leon Eldridge was surprised by how calm the man looked and sounded and felt his own sense of calm return. "Sheriff might be able to tell you. I don't know."

Kazuko picked up his bag and wondered when he had dropped it. He turned intending to walk back down the driveway and then to the paved road, intending to go... someplace.

"I'm sorry your folks lost their farm."

Kazuko turned back. The sentiment sounded honest. "They didn't lose it. It was taken because they were born in Japan." The men looked at each other, neither knowing what to say. Kazuko looked at the fallow field on his left and broke the silence. "It's a good place. Rich soil. Plenty of sweet water. Please care for it."

A red-winged blackbird warbled a melodious greeting in the cool air, reminding Kazuko of the Presbyterian hymn that then uncontrollably sung itself through his abandoned soul:

> Morning has broken,
> like the first morning.
> Blackbird has spoken,
> like the first bird..."

The man shrugged, turned the rifle toward the field with the cotton and lowered the hammer into the safety position. "We're good farmers." He looked around, apparently seeing the place as he did so, seeing beyond the long shadows of the farm in this morning's sun, Kazuko thought, seeing seasons, seeing years. "You grew up on this place?"

"Yes."

After a long moment of quiet the man said, "You had your breakfast?"

"No."

"Birdie!" The man waited until the door to his house — to Kazuko's house — opened. "We got company. Put on another pot of coffee. And if we still got some eggs, that might be good."

Kazuko's stomach growled over the stillness of the morning, and the man laughed. Kazuko thought the laugh to be a little too loud, but it was laughter.

———··———

Leon Eldridge and Kazuko built an outhouse behind the implement shed so that Kazuko could live in the shed while he helped on the farm.

Leon knew enough people around the county to piece together what had happened to the Nakamuras. Late in the spring of '42, Yoshi and Hiyori were bused to the internment camp at Manzanar in the high desert at the eastern base of the harsh Sierra Nevada. During the first months of internment the residents lived in tents while they constructed their own quarters. The board walls, though solidly built, were without insulation, and while sufficient for the hardy, were inadequate for the elderly. Yoshi died of an unknown illness. The guess was Valley Fever, contracted before his arrival at the center. Hirori died soon after, also from an unnamed illness, perhaps a broken heart. Kazuko would forever feel guilt because of their death. He would have been with them if he had not joined ROTC against their wishes. They would not have died if he had been there to care for them.

The Nakamura home had been boarded up, but as an abandoned place far out in the country it had become the target of thieves. Everything of value, from the new oil stove to the gold leaf scrolls that had been in the Nakamura family for hundreds of years, were stolen. Even the electric pump for the fields was stolen.

When the county assessor was informed of the Nakamuras' death, she ignored the existence of an heir who was obviously a troublemaker, or he would not be at Tule Lake. She declared their farm an abandoned property, and a legal notice was placed in the newspaper. After the required waiting period, the place was sold at auction. Whether her actions were precisely legal, they were ignored by anyone who could have said otherwise. There were back taxes to be paid, and no one to pay them.

Other family farms had fared better when neighbors had joined together to watch after the homes, maintain the orchards and keep the tax collector at bay. The Nakamura farm was entirely row crops, so the land didn't need attention, and nobody wanted—nor was it easy with the shortages caused by the war—to replace the pump so the fallow land could be farmed. Their closest neighbor was an Italian couple in their 60s who lived a half-mile to the north in the middle of an orange grove where they could see nothing of the Nakamura place. He spoke limited English; she spoke none. And during the war they had their own nationalistic issues to deal with, so it was wise of them to stay hunkered down. The Eldridges got the farm at a reasonable price but hadn't stepped into a fully equipped and well-maintained place. It had taken quite a lot of work and money to bring it back to its current state of productivity. Kazuko admired the difficulty of that accomplishment.

Working his family's former fields with Leon Eldridge was a way for Kazuko to live. There was very little money in it and scant joy. But there was less pain than moving on would surely have brought. And he didn't need money.

Kazuko couldn't explain why he had waited so long to open the envelope given him when he left the Tule Lake detention center. Perhaps it was dread of finding out something he didn't want to know. But when he had finally opened the envelope there was a note from a Manzanar administrator saying, "These are yours now," and a sheaf of U.S. Savings Bonds. His parents had put their life savings into war bonds, over $27,000.

Kazuko cashed in $500 worth to be sure they could be, and to have money for what might be needed. When the time came to buy his own place, he would have enough... by cashing in war bonds. The irony was disturbing, but having his own land was important for Kazuko, for he was truly the son of the farmers, Yoshi and Hiyori Nakamura.

———·———

Birdie could drive, but she didn't like it much. One of her weekly chores was to drive over Rocky Hill to a small farm at the lower end of Once Wide Valley for milk and eggs and an occasional fryer. When she found out that Kazuko could drive, she asked him to make the trip. That suited Kazuko just fine because it got him away from the everyday labor.

Several times in the summer and fall, Kazuko took advantage of the milk and egg run to drive up into the mountains beyond Once Wide Valley to fish the streams for trout. On these treks he saw a few of the ranchers and hired hands on the cattle ranches in the valley. He always stopped to talk. Not all would talk to him, but most would. One was a quiet, odd little man with a constant sunburn. His name was Pinky Wollerman, but a wooden sign reading "Erlewine Cattle Co." hung at the gate to the gravel road leading to his house. Kazuko invited Pinky to go fishing once, and the little man snorted and said he didn't have time. But after a slow moment he had added, seemingly sincerely, that he'd like to do it another time. Kazuko wasn't sure, so didn't ask again.

Then, on a bright day the following February, during a couple of weeks of false spring, Kazuko stopped to talk, and Pinky asked a thing that surprised both of them. He asked Kazuko if he wanted to see the ranch. When Kazuko agreed, he had no idea what he was in for because the first thing Pinky said after that was, "Then you'll have to learn how to ride."

Kazuko could only spend one day a week at the ranch, so it took him a month to finally get into the saddle. First, Pinky said, he had to learn horses, how to approach them, how to touch them, how to talk to them, and how to feed them. When he could hold the hackamore and lead the horse and back into the horse to pick up a hoof, then he learned how to put on the blanket and the saddle and how to cinch it tight and make sure the horse wasn't holding its breath to keep it loose. Kazuko kidded Pinky about having to break the horse before he could ride it, but Pinky didn't understand the humor. Learning to ride wasn't a one-day event of getting on and pulling the reins this way and that. There was that, but there was also the care of the horse before, during and after, and there was the whole retraining of his body to fit the horse and to ride it for more than a few minutes, to ride it on rough ground with its need for caution, and ride it on a windy day with its fluttering world. Kazuko felt that Pinky could hear a horse think, and knew he was not able to do that. But he didn't dismiss it as impossible.

Spring was on the threshold of summer when Pinky thought Kazuko was ready. Pinky and Kazuko left the barn well before noon, and Kazuko was almost as easy as Pinky on the ride. They reached the highest point on the ranch in late afternoon, and sat the horses, and Kazuko looked out across the land thinking of the land—not of the horse, not of his butt on the saddle or his feet in the stirrups or the breathing of the horse—but only of the land.

It was that afternoon when a slow, invisible breeze blew over them, making waves in the tall grasses, the oaks whispered among themselves, a flock of a half dozen buzzards caught the currents, gliding back and forth and up and down the hillsides searching for a meal of something dead, two red-winged hawks soared and hovered looking for a meal of something alive. And the sky from west to overhead looked like the surface of a deep-blue well while the eastern sky billowed big thunderheads up over the Sierra crest, and thunder rolled in the distance. It was that afternoon—with ground squirrels scampering from grassy knoll to dust-mounded burrow and quail clucking and bobbling their top knots in and out of the wild berry vines and with his own chest more at rest than he could ever remember—that Kazuko first saw the ranch with Pinky Wollerman. And he finally knew what Pinky had asked the day he asked if Kazuko wanted to see the ranch.

———·———

One spring day Birdie Eldridge told Kazuko that she was going with him on his weekly trip to Once Wide Valley for eggs. Nothing was said until they crested Rocky Hill when Mrs. Eldridge said for him to pull off to the side of the road where they could see the valley. After a few minutes of sitting quietly, Kazuko climbed his way to the top of a rock outcropping to enjoy the morning view. Mrs. Eldridge walked to the base of the boulder where he was standing.

"Kaz?"

She sounded anxious, so Kazuko turned his gaze and attention to her and waited. She said nothing, so he said, "It is a nice view, isn't it?"

Mrs. Eldridge glanced his way with a furrowed brow and said, "What chance do you think we have of making a go of the farm?"

Kazuko didn't know why the question was coming now or why it was coming from Birdie rather than Leon, but he had been thinking the answer for three years, so he took a deep breath and asked, "Straight from the shoulder?"

"This is too important not to be," she replied.

"OK, but the answer is a little rough."

Birdie circled impatiently with her hand, then folded her arms tightly and looked out across the valley.

"The farm is too small," Kazuko said, "to make a go of it with cotton. There are farms working themselves out over on the west side with nearly free water from the federal government that will turn desert into cropland and are going to be 50 to 100 sections in size. Even with the allotment they'll plant thousands upon thousands of acres to cotton. They'll make it in cotton. Your 40-acre farm won't. The only way to make it with a small place is to do a truck farm. Grow strawberries or vegetables that are timed exactly right to the market. Cotton has become a commodity. You can't make it in cotton."

Mrs. Eldridge's gaze remained steady on the pastoral setting before them, but Kazuko noticed her shoulders slump slightly.

"Kaz, you know Leon don't have the back for a truck farm. The Romans had a saying. 'Plough the more, hoe the less.' Men with bad backs say the same thing. We built our farm on that saying. Neither of us can do the work of a strawberry farm."

The two of them stood at the saddle of Rocky Hill for several minutes maybe seeing the green valley, maybe feeling the wind in their hair, maybe feeling the sun on their skin, maybe hearing voices, maybe seeing dreams fade into blue sky, but neither of them spoke.

Then Kazuko Nakamura said to Birdie Eldridge, "I know you can't make it while you're supporting me. There isn't enough profit. I hope you can make it without me. But it will be a hard thing to do." He waited for what seemed like a full five minutes, and when she didn't move or speak, he said, "If you ever get to the place you don't want to go on, let me know. I can keep it going. I'll keep the farm going."

Birdie looked at him with a weary smile and said, "I know you will, Kaz. That's why I brought it up." She watched a car pass south through the valley coming down from Highway 198 and then turn right and start up the east side of Rocky Hill toward them. "I don't know when, Kaz. But we'll sell the place. And I want you to be in a position to buy it when we do."

Kazuko knew he had been given the gift of fair warning. Soon he would be asked to leave. Then, at some future time, when his prediction came to pass and Leon and Birdie gave up, he knew he would be offered the right of first refusal to buy back his family's farm. That would be a bittersweet moment.

And so it was in the summer of '53 that Leon asked Kazuko to drive with him up to visit Pinky Wollerman and, after the offer of a drink of cold well water from a bucket and the exchange of a few pleasantries, had asked Kazuko to give him a chance to talk business with Pinky.

From the porch of the ranch house Kazuko could see Leon talking intensely to Pinky, but couldn't hear what was said. After a few minutes, Pinky came up to the house while Leon remained by the well. Without preamble, Pinky offered Kazuko a job on his ranch at $120 a month and a place to bunk and cook. Kazuko looked at Leon, but Leon had turned his back to them. He looked around the ranch, accepted the offer, and shook hands with Pinky.

Kazuko knew the Eldridges had helped him long enough and well beyond their means, but Leon didn't offer any discussion on the ride home, so Kazuko told Leon that he was going to miss the farm. He meant he was going to miss Leon and Birdie as well as his parents' legacy, his childhood home. Perhaps Leon knew what Kazuko really meant, but all he said was, "You're one of the hardest working men I ever saw." The only other thing said on the trip home was Kazuko telling Leon that he looked forward to working with Pinky. And with that both men had said all they were going to.

———··———

Within one week of the offer, Kazuko was living in Pinky Wollerman's bunkhouse. As plain as it was, it was a move up from the Eldridge's tool shed in both comfort and convenience. He learned how to mend fence, feed cattle, milk a cow, and any number of things he was physically well-prepared-for but, as a flat land row crop farmer, had never done. He missed Leon and Birdie, but he liked the openness of Pinky's place and liked the work, and it was obvious that Pinky needed the help. Kazuko wondered if Pinky had had a premonition and had taught him to ride and to see the place precisely for this reason.

TEN
SUMMER 1953

Casually working on the caped client in his barber chair, Ralph Thomas paused in the middle of a serious observation about the weather and greeted Pinky in a voice calculated to exceed the clatter of the electric clippers and to suit his poor hearing. "Mornin', Pinky."

Pinky waved, nodded, and in his usual soft voice said, "Hello, Ralph."

"What's that?" Ralph yelled.

Remembering Ralph's hearing problem, Pinky yelled, "I said, 'Hello, Ralph.'"

"Oh. Hello. Shorty Waters got here ahead of you, but he went down by Tienken's Drug to shoot the breeze until his turn. It'll be another half hour afore I get to you." Ralph made an "oooheee" sound and laughed. "Seems like all you ranchers come down from the hills on the same day." He made the oooheee sound and laughed again. "You got some kind of telegraph system that says, 'Let's all of us go to town this Saturday and get a haircut?'"

Pinky was used to Deaf Ralph yelling, but he didn't understand why he was laughing while he was asking his question. He answered anyway, remembering to talk loudly, "No, Ralph. We come in for the cattle auction and use the trip to take care of other business."

The rapid clacking of the clippers in Ralph's left hand went silent for a second while he furrowed his brow, took on a confused appearance, and looked over the top of his spectacles at Pinky. He waved the coarse-toothed black comb in his right hand back and forth a couple of times as though he was going to say something more, then raised his eyebrows and turned back to the work of shearing his current customer down to the pale grey skin of his scalp.

After a minute's pause to see if the conversation was over, Pinky added, "I'll go wait with the boys on the corner."

Ralph drew out a long "uh huh," without looking up. "I'll be here when you get back."

As he turned to leave the barbershop, Pinky saw a picture on a magazine cover. It was a black man, dusty in the way of someone who lived outside in a dry place. He'd seen that look on people after the third or fourth year of the drought back in Oklahoma — people who had collected far more than one day's worth of dust from working the fields or the cattle. People who had barely enough water to drink, much less to wash. People who seemed to have given in and melded with the land.

The man had a large shock of black, curly hair and was sitting cross-legged in front of a wall of sheer rock, apparently applying color from a chalk-like stone to a picture of what might have been a lizard, except for the blue, red, and yellow polka-dots that formed the outline of the creature, and the unlikely size of the thing, dwarfing a human figure standing to the side and looking skyward with open arms. The human was an overly endowed male with diagonal lines across the face, torso and legs that gave the otherwise simple outline of the body structure and heft.

Pinky picked up the magazine. The title was "True Ranch Stories" and the subtitle was "Real Men and Real Adventures." In bold red letters an article title read, *Australia's Outback, the Land and People.* Pinky eased himself down on a chair of tubular chrome with a yellow plastic seat and legs that didn't all reach the floor until he sat, then flipped through the slick, glossy pages of the cover article. He thought what an odd place the Outback must be, collecting a variety of characters, including a man in worn-out short britches with a shirt unbuttoned at the chest, a broad-brimmed leather hat somewhat like a Stetson, and a face that looked like it had been fashioned from the same leather. After he returned from the world war, the article said, the man built a cement kangaroo nearly 30 feet high, with room for a seven-seat tavern where the pouch would have been. He painted the giant beast bright blue and served only beer brewed in the town of Adelaide, several hundred kilometers to the south. His was one of only two "civilized" stops along the road to Alice Springs, although he defined "civilized" to mean he served beer brewed in Adelaide, so there may have been other stops. He seemed able to make a living in what appeared on the map to be a long way in any direction from anywhere else. The man's pride in his accomplishment showed in his jovial face.

The article said the Outback was mostly "bush," which looked an awful lot like a desert, and there were black men called Aborigines who would go on "walkabouts" for months at a time, carrying nothing more than a stick. And they could find their way across a continent bigger than the United States simply by remembering songs they had learned when they came of age — songs taught by the old men of their clan, which Pinky thought must be somewhat like a tribe.

Pinky read and then re-read about the people, the strange animals that weren't mammals like he knew, but were "marsupials," the treacherous and poisonous plants and reptiles, and the vastness. He couldn't get his mind around the sheer size and emptiness of the place.

Ralph finished up the third of the Saturday haircut ranchers who had arrived at the barbershop after Pinky but were waved ahead because Pinky was so engrossed in reading. Pinky would read for a while and then stare unblinking out the window, his pale blue eyes apparently not noticing the world passing by in the street, then slowly turn to another page.

When all the other men had left, Ralph said, "OK, Pinky. It's time." When Pinky didn't look up, Ralph raised his voice, which for Deaf Ralph was pretty loud. "Get your butt up here, Pinky."

Pinky jumped, and his chrome-legged chair squeaked loudly.

"I want to git on home and get my supper afore the missus throws it out for the dog," Ralph yelled.

Pinky put down the magazine and stood up.

———·———

No wonder he lives alone, Ralph thought. Ralph's sister, Ruby, who went to the same church Pinky did, felt sorry for the little man, and was always trying to think of someone to get him attached to, but Ralph wasn't sure there even was such a thing as a good match for Pinky Wollerman.

On the other hand, Ralph admired Pinky's backbone. Because he got all the local news from his barber chair, he knew that Buck Wilson had been talking for some time about Pinky's place as though it was his. He also knew that Buck caught Pinky at the Methodist Church and told him he wanted to buy his place, and Pinky had calmly told him no thanks, which Ralph thought was a brave stance to take. As the story was told, Buck had steeled up and towered over Pinky and told him it was just a matter of time before he sold his place to Buck. Nearly every rancher in town could quote some variation of Pinky's response. "I appreciate your interest, Buck, but it's not for sale." So Ralph thought that Pinky was either very brave or else he was too simpleminded to know how dangerous a game Buck was playing with him.

"You want me to get those whiskers while I got you here?"

"No, thanks, Ralph. It's nearly Sunday. I'll get 'em then."

"Suit yourself," Ralph said, thinking that Pinky's hair was so pale he could hardly see the week's worth of stubble on his sun-reddened face.

———·———

For some the barber chair is a podium and for others a confessional. Pinky observed that the custom was for either the customer or Ralph to talk almost non-stop about anything and everything while Ralph cut their hair. So he had been trying to think of something to say since he climbed in the chair.

As Ralph wrapped a sheet-like bib cut from mattress ticking around his neck, Pinky decided not to talk about Australia because almost everything he knew was in the magazine a few feet away on Ralph's little round table, and Ralph had probably already read it. And the three men before him had worn out the subjects of weather and livestock prices. So he chose the other big thing on his mind.

"Hey, Ralph."

"Yeah, Pinky."

"I got a cat now." When Ralph didn't respond, Pinky offered, "Just a stray." And, after another pause, trying his best to keep the conversation going, added, "He showed up out of nowhere a while back." After an even longer period when Ralph said nothing, Pinky added, "Named him Henry."

"Uhh huhh," Ralph said, stretching his back as though the long day of bending over the barber chair had pained it. Then with a burst of interest he said, "How are you getting along with your next door neighbor these days?

"Who's that?

"You only got two. I mean Buck Wilson. How are you and Buck getting along?"

Here was yet another question about how he and Buck were getting along, and Pinky was starting to wonder why people seemed so interested in something that was none of their business. As far as Pinky was concerned, people only needed to know that Buck had expressed an interest in buying his place and he had told him no, so he answered, "Real good, I guess... as far as it goes. I hardly ever see the man except across the room at church."

Ralph said, "Is that so?" and then settled in to the work before him.

Pinky didn't know what to say to that, so he said nothing.

Ralph realized he wasn't going to get much news from Pinky on that topic, so he said nothing.

The two men maintained their silence until the haircut was done. As he was removing the cape from Pinky's neck Ralph said, "That'll be a dollar even, Pinky."

"He don't eat much," Pinky said, pulling a dog-eared, sweat-darkened leather wallet from his back pocket.

"Who don't eat much?"

"Henry." Pinky said, placing a dollar bill on the stainless steel tray where Ralph's clippers and combs sat. Ralph stared at him with an open mouth and a quizzical expression. Thinking Ralph must not be in the mood for conversation so late in the day, Pinky pushed open the screen door and crossed the sidewalk to his truck. When he looked back, Ralph was still holding the barber cape and staring after him. Pinky shrugged, wondering what Ralph might have on his mind that left him looking so perplexed.

Pinky reached through the open window of his pickup and scratched Wilbur behind the ears. The old white lab's tail started to pound the canvas-covered bench seat and stirred up a small cloud of dust inside the cab that almost choked Pinky as he climbed in.

"Well, that's done," Pinky coughed as he shoved the dog far enough over in the seat that he could sit behind the wheel. "Let's go home and get some supper." Wilbur expressed his approval by slobbering the length of the forearm of Pinky's grey work shirt. The two then drove out of Exeter and toward the foothills, discussing the events of the day in the way of old friends. Pinky was particularly animated when he told Wilbur about Australia, and Wilbur was so fascinated he failed to notice Pinky's new haircut.

Heading up into Once Wide Valley always put the two of them into a good mood. Being there was as about as close to feeling at home as Pinky could get, and Wilbur must have sensed they were going home because he put his front paws on the dashboard and began wagging his tail.

"I wonder what Henry's up to," Pinky said aloud. He was eager to see the cat doing whatever it was he did while hanging out around the barn. Henry wasn't much company because he seldom hung around with them, but as a cat he had a contagious mysteriousness that he somehow managed to scatter around the place like chicken scratch. "You have to admit, Wilbur," Pinky said, "the place has been a lot more interesting since Henry arrived."

———·———

The week after his haircut Pinky had a dream. In the midst of the dream, he became aware he was in a dream, and he knew it was a good one. He remembered hoping, while still dreaming, that he wouldn't wake up too soon.

He was on a series of trains for many days and, though watching intently, he saw no sign of a church. Nevertheless, his sense of the spiritual grew steadily as he bobbed and floated through his dream on one clattering, wheezing vehicle after another, following a gravity-fed current cascading towards the center of some vast place, an ocean or a desert.

Then he was standing in front of a train station. A curly-haired smiling Aborigine was extending a hand to him. He liked the sense of calm confidence of this thin, tall man. He reached out and grabbed the offered hand and allowed himself to be pulled up on the station's rustic waiting platform.

He stood shoulder to shoulder with the Aborigine, noticing the musty odor of layered perspiration and dust, a smell that reminded him of his own summer self. Looking outward at the expanse of brown and rust-red rocks and dirt surrounding the two small buildings of the station, he knew nothing green had graced this land for all the millions of years it had been here. The desolation stretched to the horizon in every direction, and while Pinky scanned it for any sign of life, a voice told him that it was honest land, land that would not lie.

He turned toward the sound of the voice and saw an odd creature looking like a cross between a 20-pound jack rabbit and a rat making its way across a shallow dry gulch about 50 yards away. He turned back to his newfound companion to ask about the creature, only to find the manform trotting silently and gracefully through the desolate Outback. He was already a good distance away, but in the flatness of this expanse he wouldn't be out of sight for quite a long time. He — "Bobbie," said a whisper — moved purposefully, as though he had some place to go, some place in mind.

Suddenly Pinky was certain there were people living in the desolate landscape, only a handful, and not visible. There was no water or greenery and darned few animals. But he sensed an abundance in this lack that would meet his needs, and he felt a calm confidence overpower feelings of never having done enough or having done the wrong things. With only a vast, cloudless sky, Pinky felt wholly at ease, perfectly at home.

Then Henry hopped off the train platform. Pinky was sure it was Henry. The cat ran a hundred feet or so in the direction the Aborigine had gone, stopped to look back at Pinky, then sat yowling and waiting for Pinky to follow along.

Pinky wasn't ready to wake up when he heard the cat loudly meowing outside. Damned cat, he thought, pressing his eyelids together in the hope of restarting the dream. Then the dog was barking at the cat. It was too late — he was awake. He yelled, "Dang you, Henry!" and threw off the covers. "You, too, Wilbur!" He jumped out of bed and dressed quickly, thinking of the dream. The particulars had already faded, but he did remember a vague image of a train station accompanied by an odd sense of desolation mixed with promise. Desolation mixed with promise. The dream had left him with a sense of comfort at the thought of absences and nothingness, and he continued to feel it even as he took in the real-life abundance around him.

It came back to him that in his dream the land was honest, and he thought it strange to think of land as though it was willful. He believed land to be indifferent to people, neither honest nor dishonest. If land could be dishonest, then he had known the biggest liar of all in the Oklahoma farm land that had promised fertility and then snatched it away during the Dust Bowl.

But it was only a dream, and Pinky had work to do. So he shook his head, put a match to the kindling in the cook stove and headed for the outhouse, giving Wilbur a scratch behind the ears as he crossed the porch. "Danged cat," Pinky said, and Wilbur looked toward the barn where no cat was to be seen.

Even as he did his chores, the dream nagged at Pinky, and he couldn't help trying again to bring it into focus. But the effort caused the memory of the dream to scamper this way and that as though it were repelled by the brightening morning. Only fragments of it lingered. He remembered the man's name was Bobbie, a name given to him for the convenience of those around him. He also had an ancestral name, with deeper meaning and connection to a powerful heritage of some sort. Pinky did not know the man's ancestral name and was intrigued by the prospect he wouldn't be allowed to know — even if he was to go there and meet the man.

In a final fragment of dream memory, Pinky saw the man standing passively in the powerful vastness that was so comforting to Pinky, but the land below the man's feet was dissolving into nothingness.

ᴱLEVEN
SUMMER 1953

A Sunday rite of the Once Wide Valley's Methodist Women's Society was a potluck. When Pinky first came to the little country church, he felt obliged to contribute something if he was going to eat, so he got up early and made biscuits. After a couple of Sundays, Inus, the perpetual organizer of the Methodist Women's Sunday potluck, suggested in a motherly way, "Sweetie, why don't you bring some milk to maybe soften the biscuits?"

A couple of Sundays later, she suggested he bring Kool-Aid instead of biscuits and milk. So that's what Pinky had done in the years since then; he emptied packages of Kool-Aid in water, added sugar and stirred. It was a better match for his kitchen skills, and the Kool-Aid did seem to be more popular than the biscuits, and not only with the kids.

One summer Sunday as Pinky was stirring four packages of grape Kool-Aid and two cups of sugar into a gallon of water, he overheard Bob Burns and Larry Johnson, two farmers from down in the valley, talking casually about Buck Wilson.

"You know what Buck Wilson did now?" Bob leaned back, laughed. "He got Bill Jenkins' horse and saddle and tack all for $90."

Larry replied, "Yeah, I heard about that. Got his corn last summer, now his horse. Don't that beat all. And I know Bill's horse well 'cause it was sired by one of my stallions. It's a fine horse and by itself worth more than twice what Buck paid for the whole kit and caboodle."

Both men laughed as if they had heard the funniest joke of the year. Pinky didn't understand what these men found so funny. He had heard men stand around in bunches swapping stories and knew they would laugh about such things as awful as two dogs chasing down and tearing up a cat, but Pinky didn't understand it. The misfortune of another wasn't funny, and he wondered if they would laugh if Buck took advantage of them while they were down.

As they went on, Pinky learned that Buck had also got into it with Arturo Hernandez. One of Arturo's old tractors had broken down out at his ranch near Woodlake. Not able to easily get the needed parts, he hadn't gotten around to fixing it for a few months. Buck declared Arturo's tractor abandoned, hauled it off while Arturo wasn't around, patched it with parts from one of his own old tractors, and started using it. Buck allowed that not only was the tractor broken down and abandoned, but a Mexican had more business with a shovel and hoe than with a complicated piece of machinery.

The two men laughed until their eyes watered, then they looked more seriously at each other as Bob said, "That didn't set too well with Arturo. Buck said that a few days ago Arturo and two of his boys caught up with him at the end of a long day on that borrowed tractor. Each one had a section of lead pipe for a club, and old Buck said they looked mad as hell and twice as mean. Arturo and one of the boys faced Buck down while the other boy got on the tractor and drove it off. Buck knew he was outgunned, so he let them go without a fight."

"He wouldn't be telling the story now if he hadn't," Larry snorted.

Bob nodded big. "You got that right." Then he added with a thoughtful look, "But truth be told, I think he kind of admired Art for standing up to him when nobody else would, even if it did take the whole bunch. I bet the whole thing could have blown over except that before they drove off, that damned Arturo thanked him for fixing up his tractor. 'Course that really pissed old Buck off." Both men broke into laughter again.

Larry pursed his lips and shook his head before adding, "There's bad blood between Buck and Arturo, and I expect that grudge will likely go another couple of rounds."

Both Bob and Larry, talking casually at the Methodist Women's Sunday Potluck, scowled at the floor, mounded their plates from the tables covered with delicious homemade dishes, carried them to a table in the middle of the hall, and then came back, stepping around Pinky to fill their glasses with grape Kool-Aid. Not once did they acknowledge his presence.

Having heard some things he maybe shouldn't have, Pinky was a little embarrassed, but he also was feeling a newfound disrespect for Bob and Larry. He was surprised by a growing anger he held toward Buck Wilson because anger of this dark nature was a sin, even if the man was a damned bully. And he wondered about men who not only tolerated such bullying but laughed about it.

TWELVE

FALL 1953

The second week of October, when the crops were in, the land had been put to bed for the winter, and summer rallied late for a warm spell, Emily Robin asked Betty if she wanted to go for an outing the next day—a picnic perhaps. Betty wanted to go anywhere at all, but when Emily Robin suggested driving up Once Wide Creek, Betty, not normally one to take the initiative when extra work was involved, boiled potatoes for a salad with onions and pickles and mustard, and packed it in a basket with bread and jam and cheese. Emily Robin would have laughed at Betty's enthusiasm if she hadn't understood the hopelessness behind it. Instead, she worried for her friend's heart and wondered if inviting her had been a bad idea. Everyone at the farm who was aware of their outing believed that it was Betty's idea, and that was useful to Emily Robin since she wanted no one to know or even suspect that she knew Buck.

Emily Robin had overheard the wife of the minister who ran the Poor Farm telling Betty that the man in the yellow truck had a ranch in Once Wide Valley and was named Charlie Wilson, but that everyone called him Buck. Emily Robin wanted to get a closer look at Buck and his place, and the first leg of that journey of discovery was to drive over Rocky Hill into the valley of the Once Wide Creek. The picnic was a good excuse for going over that hill.

The morning of the picnic, Emily Robin was awakened by Betty at dawn and rose to see that Betty had added cold tea and honey and freshly baked biscuits to the picnic basket. Emily Robin wondered if Betty had slept at all. She wondered what they would see in the valley, where exactly Buck lived, and how she could find him without him noticing her.

"Wake up, Emily Robin! We're going for a picnic!" Betty's voice roused Emily Robin from her reverie, and she found herself fully dressed, standing in the kitchen holding her tea and staring at her porridge. Blessed routine, she thought to herself. With breakfast over and the dishes done, she made a bed of folded blankets in the back seat of the car borrowed from the reverend. She carefully plucked the sleeping Logan from his bed, carried him to the car, and tucked him in. The tenderness of the effort was wasted, because Logan was as excited about the trip as Betty and was wide awake as soon as the car started to move.

Emily Robin tried to calm the youngster down, but it seemed appropriate that he should be excited since this was the day he would perhaps see his birthright.

The sun barely crested the Sierra when the three picnickers in the white Chevy sedan made their way down the long dirt drive to the paved road. The summer morning sun would evaporate the dew in short order, but for now the dewdrops on the grasses caught the light as though thousands of diamonds had been scattered across the fields, making a heartbreakingly beautiful promise to the two young women.

A half hour later, at the crest of Rocky Hill, Betty pulled the car off the pavement to watch the spectacle of morning unfolding across the sky. A cloud bank hanging on the Sierra peaks muted the blazing white sun to a pale buttercup yellow. A line of pebble clouds, like a stone path suspended in a translucent blue pool, turned from grey-topped white to ripe peach orange.

But in the land of the Sierra Nevada, nothing is static for long. There is wind, and the turn of the earth, and there is the saturation of one's senses. So as they sat watching, the sun rose a little higher in the sky, the clouds floated slowly northward, and Betty and Emily Robin averted their eyes from what might have been sacred and what both had prayed to for answers to the questions that now stood top heavy in their lives.

It was a whisper of hope in a fragment of time. Then it was over. The morning was not a promise of anything other than the beginning of yet another day. The sky was the same pale blue it was nearly every morning back at the farm. And the wistful clouds hinted at nothing more than a pleasant day for a picnic.

"Let's go!" Logan's impatient exclamation firmly ended the remnant of the spell.

Betty put the car in gear and pulled back on to the single lane blacktop track leading down the back side of Rocky Hill and into Once Wide Valley.

———·———

In both February and October this place enjoys a week or more of false spring. The sun is gentle and warm. The sky becomes a cleaner lens, showing the landscape in crisp relief. A healthy, vibrant green splashes across the rolling hills. To the observer's eye, both times are the same; both are like spring. But both are false. February's springtime is premature, though a harbinger of the true spring awakening. October's springtime is a last gasp before sinking into the bleakness of winter. Likewise, the two women drove into the Once Wide Valley October spring with different expectations. Betty felt the fertile glow of spring coursing within her body and so deluded herself into believing the false spring of October was real. Emily Robin knew it was October, knew and feared the descent toward a hard winter, but also willed herself to keep deep within the soil of her heart a seed of hope for the new growth of an honest spring in a future year.

———·———

Although Betty had been to the top of Rocky Hill once and had seen the lower part of Once Wide Valley, neither woman had been into the valley, so Betty drove slowly, stopping often to see if there might be a nice spot for a picnic. Logan was like a young puppy, on his knees in the back seat with his head and arms out through the window, taking in every sight and scent they passed. Each time Betty pulled over, Emily Robin had to stop Logan from bolting from the car to explore.

About a half hour after entering the valley, the road began to rise away from the creek, following the steep inclination of the terrain, away from the valley oaks and rangeland grasses and into the scrub oak, manzanita and pine of the middle ranges above. Betty suddenly announced she wanted to save the high country for another day and found a place to turn around. Truth be told, they had passed three houses, all on cattle ranches, and Emily Robin figured that Betty knew

Buck's must be one of them and didn't want to get too far afield of her target. A short distance back, past a dozen metal pipes imbedded across the road as a cattle guard, Betty found a turnout where the creek was visible below as it meandered through the fresh green of early fall on its way from the world of the Once Wide toward the Kaweah River and the great valley of the San Joaquin.

"This looks as good a place as any." Betty turned off the key and with a hefty pull, ratcheted the noisy parking brake into service. Logan exploded from the back, slamming the door behind him, running down the hillside toward the creek, slipping, falling on his bottom, sliding a couple of feet, then bouncing up and running on as though impervious to the pain of skidding over hard ground and gravel. He'll feel that later, Emily Robin thought, then yelled after him, "Watch out for rattlesnakes!"

Betty joined in, "And stay out of the creek." She laughed and raised her eyebrows. "As though that will do any good."

The two women grabbed the picnic basket and blankets and followed, although far more carefully, Logan's broken trail down to the creek. It was a perfect spot for a picnic. Under a barn-sized area of shade created by several ancient and gnarled sycamores, the creek bent around a bar of sand and decomposed granite left by higher water. A blue jay sat high in the sycamore farthest upstream, periodically scolding them for invading his territory. Otherwise, the only noise was the scampering of Logan's exploration. After the road noise of the car and its engine, the quiet provided a relief like cold water on a hot day. The creek was shallow and wide and flowing so slowly that only a dandelion puff floating past gave its movement away.

Emily Robin and Betty each took two corners of an army surplus wool blanket, pulled it tight and were lowering it on the grassy bank at the edge of the sandbar when a shrill buzz split their ears and the peaceful air. Betty froze, her face rigid with fear. Emily Robin felt a fear she did not know from her lifetime, but was recognized by that part of her brain at the base of her skull, an ancient fear from ancient times. With the instincts of a mother, she whirled to locate Logan.

Logan, over 30 yards upstream, stood in the creek looking up toward a series of shoulder-high, lichen-covered dark granite boulders seven or eight feet in front him. He was eye to eye with a large and irritated rattlesnake. The snake was as big around as the skinny little boy's arms, and coiled like a spring with the bottom half of its body resting on the ground and the upper half rising and falling as though building up tension within the coil for a powerful strike. The snake's tongue whipped the air. The tip of its tail was a blur, creating the hideous buzz that paralyzed the boy with fear and fascination and compressed time for Emily Robin in a way that a fraction of a second seemed slower than a summer sunset.

Emily Robin, knowing she didn't have time to reach the boy, snatched a river rock from the sand and hurled it, intending it to go over the snake's head, to distract him with a noise from behind.

The dandelion fluff had traveled a couple of feet, the scolding jay had flown halfway to a fence post on the hillside above Logan, and the rock was passing the apex of its arc through the air when Emily Robin was deafened by a clap of thunder.

Reacting to the sound, Emily Robin's eyes involuntarily blinked hard, and upon opening, Logan had not moved, Betty was falling backward onto the hillside beside the stream with her mouth open in a silent scream, the dandelion puff was caught on a rock, the now-fleeing blue jay had chosen not to stop at the fencepost, and the rock was landing with a thump 10 feet beyond where the snake had been on the boulder. But the snake was nowhere to be seen.

Emily Robin splashed in a run through the ankle-deep water to Logan, wrapped him in her arms and had him back to the sandbar before slowing even a bit. She heard a metallic sound, a slide and a click, and looked upstream to the other side of the creek where a small man with a wide-brimmed cowboy hat was working a lever on a short rifle to eject a shell casing. Her nostrils flared at the sharp scent of burnt gunpowder. The man was dressed in blue jeans and a grey chambray work shirt, like the cowboys she had seen in town. But as he moved toward her, she noticed he was wearing farmer-style work boots, known derisively as clod-hoppers, rather than cowboy boots, and he was only slightly taller than she.

Emily Robin became aware of Logan struggling to escape her clutch, so she looked around quickly, then put him down on the forgotten blanket. He immediately jumped up and ran toward where the snake had been. Before she could catch him, the small man intercepted him, scooping him up with the arm that wasn't holding the rifle.

"Hold up there, young man."

The man's voice was deeper than she expected, and Logan didn't struggle against the restraint, but allowed himself to be carried back to the blanket.

"You'd best let me take a look before you go running up there. If it's safe and your momma says it's okay, you can come look in a minute."

Emily Robin grabbed Logan's hand and held on tight as the man walked up toward the boulders, slowing with caution as he approached. A couple of steps behind the place the snake was last seen, he stopped, leaned the rifle against a boulder, and picked up a large flat rock. He adjusted his stance and dropped the rock with an obvious attempt at precision. Then he turned and motioned for them to come up.

"It's safe now," he said. "Come on up if you want to see a rattlesnake close up—and dead."

"Are you going up there?" It was Betty, finally no longer speechless.

"Sure. Why wouldn't we? The man says it's safe." Emily Robin wanted to sound calm, but wasn't sure she did.

"You don't know him." Betty replied.

"I know he's the man who just saved Logan from snakebite," Emily Robin said, certain now she sounded strong.

"Come on, Mother!" Logan was tugging Emily Robin's hand with both of his, almost pulling her off balance.

"Only if you calm down and keep a hold on my hand," Emily Robin replied, resisting the tugging just enough so the two of them started moving slowly upstream.

As they reached the man, he pointed to the large rock he had dropped. "Don't move that rock," he said looking at Logan, his face serious. "The head is under there, and it still has fangs, and the fangs still have poison in them. So you don't want to scratch yourself on those."

The body of the snake writhed, and Emily Robin jumped

backward a long step, pulling Logan with her, nearly dislocating his shoulder. Logan started to cry, but was too fascinated by the snake and was quickly distracted from his discomfort.

"The body will work like that for several hours," the man said. "The muscles seem to have a mind of their own. But it's dead."

"Can I see the fangs?" Logan asked.

The man looked at Emily Robin who shrugged, so he pointed to a spot on the ground in front of Logan's toes, looked at Logan, and said, "Don't come closer than that." When Logan nodded, he lifted the rock.

"Wow" was all Logan could say for a minute, then, "Look, Mother."

Emily Robin saw the flattened snake's head with the needle sharp fangs extended and decided the inspection was complete. "Let's get away from here," she said as calmly as she could. She guided Logan back to the sandbar to a somber and disheveled version of the Betty who had packed their picnic basket earlier that morning

The man walked upstream several feet from the dead snake, picked up a baseball-sized rock, then followed Emily Robin back. Betty helped Emily Robin re-spread the blankets. The man dropped the rock at the edge of the water, cleared the chamber of his rifle, and leaned it against a tree. "Name's Pinky Wollerman," he said, touching the front brim of his hat. Noticing Logan's interest in the rifle, he leaned down to the boy and added, "If you leave that alone, I'll show it to you after your momma and I talk, if she says it's OK."

Feeling the need for some formality to offset the unplanned adventure, Emily Robin introduced herself with her full name. "Pleased to meet you, Mr. Wollerman. My name is Emily Robin Macadam. This is my son, Logan. And this is Miss Betty Wilkerson." When Pinky didn't say anything, she added, "We drove up here for a picnic. We are most grateful for your help with that snake and would like for you to join us." Emily Robin's stomach was still tight, and she was not the least bit hungry, but it seemed the polite thing to make the offer.

"Well, sure," Pinky said, removing his hat, and looking at the basket with what Emily Robin thought might be the curiosity of a hungry man used to his own cooking.

"Can I see your hat?" Logan asked.

"Logan!" Emily Robin said sternly.

"It's okay," Pinky said, but as he saw the disgust on Emily Robin's face, he held onto the hat. It was wet beneath the sweat band, sweat-stained from many summer days, discolored with dust, spotted on one side with cattle muck, and the crown had been crushed and reshaped some number of times.

Pinky looked at the hat as though noticing it for the first time, and after a careful inspection, put it back on his head, saying, "It must be about time for a new hat."

But Logan had lost interest and was down the creek a few feet throwing rocks in the water.

When his hat was off, Emily Robin noticed that Pinky Wollerman had hair so blond it was nearly white. He had eyebrows to match and the palest blue eyes Emily Robin had ever seen. His hands, face and neck, the only parts of him not covered by clothing, were red and rough as though perpetually exposed to wind and sun. She thought that "Pinky" was probably one of those descriptive nicknames cowboys used for each other. He was small but had broad shoulders, a thick chest, and large, calloused hands. He had moved gracefully over the rough terrain in the creek bed, and now he sat on one heel in the way of men who spend their lives outside without chairs. There was a scratch on his left cheekbone where, as though not noticed, the blood had flowed slightly, then coagulated without having been wiped away. He smelled of sweat and saddle soap and tinker's oil with a slight whiff of burnt gunpowder. She knew that Pinky Wollerman was a working man, a cowman.

"That was quite a shot, Mr. Wollerman," Betty said, looking from where he had been standing to where the snake had been coiled.

"And that was quite a throw," Pinky said, looking at Emily Robin, who looked puzzled, so Pinky stood, picked up the rock he had dropped, and handed it to her. "I'd like to see you do it again." Emily Robin took the heavy rock and held it in both hands, but still didn't know how to respond, so Pinky added. "That's the rock you picked up and threw a good 40 yards upstream." Pinky said pointing toward the snake's boulders. "I'd like to see you do it again. And, if you can, there's a women's baseball league down in Visalia looking for players."

Emily Robin noticed Pinky was smiling, if ever so slightly, and felt herself blush.

"Do you have a horse?" Logan yelled as he hopped on one foot from shadow to shadow on a downstream gravel bar. It was an obvious question to a cowboy and came scarcely in time to save Emily Robin from her embarrassment.

"Up beyond those trees," Pinky said, pointing up the hill and smiling at the youngster.

This could be a good day after all, Emily Robin thought, catching Betty's eye and raising her eyebrows. Then she remembered why she came, felt a hard sensation creep across her heart, and felt a possibility die.

Emily Robin had intended to simply enjoy the picnic for a few minutes, and then find out a little more about their guest, but before the first spoonful of potato salad was halfway toward Mr. Wollerman's mouth, Betty blurted out, "Do you know Buck Wilson?" Emily Robin wasn't sure what went on in Pinky's mind, but his hand paused ever so slightly before delivering the goods into his mouth. His eyes closed and he let out a long, appreciative "ummm."

When Pinky opened his eyes, he put the spoon down, and looked downstream toward the last bend in the lazy creek. "Well, yes, I do know Buck Wilson." Pinky picked up a pebble and tossed it in the creek. When the rings reached the shore, he went on, "He's my neighbor. A prominent rancher. And he owns most of this valley. The Wilsons are a pioneer family who have been here since the mid-1800s and Buck inherited the place and took over the management of it when he got back from the war. Buck don't live on good fortune alone. He knows how to run a ranch, and he works as hard as anybody around here."

Emily Robin noticed the neutral tone Mr. Wollerman maintained throughout his description of Buck, and though his words conveyed a certain respect, she could not discern Pinky's like or dislike for the man.

But when Pinky added, "For better or worse, Buck pretty much does what he wants and figures it's what's best for the world," Emily Robin reflexively smirked and nodded her head in agreement. She saw Pinky tilt his head slightly, his eyes briefly searching her face. Emily Robin started to blush at perhaps having given away her knowledge of Buck, but then she saw Betty's face locked in a wide smile, and her blush turned to a wince at the thought that Betty believed she had found her man. And, poor thing, she was no longer pained and angry with him.

Pinky picked up the spoon, commented on how wonderfully skilled the cook was, and resumed his consumption of the potato salad, punctuated by an occasional appreciative grunt.

Emily Robin learned the land they were on was Pinky's. It was a large ranch by California standards, but Buck's place was bigger still and nearly surrounded Pinky's place. Across the creek from Pinky's place was a ranch owned by a widower named Bill Jenkins. Bill's place was surrounded on the three remaining sides by Buck's place. Pinky didn't use the word, but Emily Robin realized that Buck was the "king" of the valley. Pinky then proceeded to ask so many questions about the three of them that they found out very little more about him, but by the end of the afternoon they knew he was a bachelor, spoke with an odd accent due to his Okie upbringing, was a Methodist on Sundays, and seemed to be well-read. And she and Logan had an open invitation to visit his ranch at which time he would teach Logan to ride, if it was acceptable to Emily Robin. She accepted the open-ended invitation and then suggested the following Sunday afternoon as a possibility.

Pinky agreed, said his goodbyes to the three, and disappeared up the hill.

On the way back to the ranch, Pinky was feeling good about the encounter with people who seemed interesting and nice. He thought that Sunday would be a good choice for their visit because Kazuko went fishing on Sundays and likely would be happy to fix a trout dinner for everyone. Pinky thought he might even pick up a new hat for the occasion. Then he panicked, wondering if Kazuko might not be around, which would leave him to be the sole host and conversationalist, not easy things for him to be, and he wondered why he had so casually offered the invitation.

One of the things Kazuko liked about working at the ranch was that he could take off most Sunday mornings or afternoons. His usual routine was to grab his fishing tackle, borrow a book from the bookshelf in the main house, and drive up to Balch Park to pursue his two favorite pastimes.

When he had been at the ranch for about two months, Pinky asked Kazuko if he might be willing to fix a fish dinner for a woman and a boy he had met having a picnic on the ranch down by the creek. Kazuko agreed.

The following Sunday Kazuko returned from his fishing trip to find a woman and a young boy standing on the porch with Pinky. Pinky wore a wide smile and said, "Kaz, this is Emily Robin and Logan."

Kazuko noticed that the woman was plainly dressed, and her hands were chafed and strong, clearly working hands. Her face had the natural rouge of wind and sun, the look of one who worked outside. Yet she had a stately bearing and was quite attractive. At one time or another he had at least seen, if not met, most of the people living in the vicinity of the valley, so he wondered where Emily Robin and Logan lived.

"I told them you fix a great trout dinner," Pinky said, still beaming. "So I hope the fish were biting today."

Kazuko nodded and bowed slightly toward the woman and the boy, "Pleased to meet you." He held up a string of over a dozen trout from a bucket in the back of the pickup and, seeing an absence of the awkwardness Pinky normally displayed with women, wondered if something in the cultural fabric of the ranch was about to change.

"If you will make some of your famous hush puppies, Pinky, we should eat well tonight."

Kazuko turned away with the fish, then turned back. "How old are you, young man?"

"Eight," Logan said, standing straight. "Next week."

Kazuko nodded seriously. "How would you like to help me clean these fish?"

Logan looked up at his mother who smiled and told him not to get too wet. Kazuko put his hand on the boy's shoulder, and as they walked toward the pump he glanced back at the woman, nodded, and realized he was hopeful she might become a part of the fabric of the ranch.

THIRTEEN
1953-1954

Emily Robin's visits to the ranch became more and more frequent, and she began to help out with chores and, for the sake of variety, cooking. Towards the end of 1953, Pinky invited the two to periodically stay over in a living space he added on the bunkhouse. He said it was more practical than driving back and forth to the Poor Farm.

During the following summer, still pursuing the theme of practicality, Pinky noted how helpful Emily Robin was at the ranch and suggested she hire on. He was afraid she might be offended by the offer, but he made it anyway. Emily Robin, afraid Pinky may have noticed that it had become her intention to move to the ranch, hesitantly agreed to the practicality of the suggestion and accepted. Logan did not notice the undercurrents of the exchange, nor did he understand the practicalities being discussed, but he was ecstatic at the move.

Soon after, Pinky approached Emily Robin. "I didn't want to propose this while Logan was around, because this is your decision and it shouldn't be made with any pressure, but I'd like to give Logan a horse of his own."

Emily Robin looked out the window to where her son was playing catch with himself by throwing a rock in the air. "Isn't he somewhat young to be responsible for a horse?"

"He's quite tall for his age, and strong enough to do the work." Pinky said. "And he loves horses, and an 8-year-old can, given the right incentive, become very responsible. Caring for an animal can be a strong incentive."

Emily Robin watched her son for another moment, then turned to Pinky and said, "I suppose you are right, Pinky. I'm willing to give it a try. But let's see how it goes. If it seems dangerous or if Logan doesn't fully take care of the animal, we will need to make some adjustments."

That evening she followed Pinky and Logan to the back side of the barn. The waiting mare was tied by a rope looped loosely around her neck and circled twice around the top board of the corral near the gate. Though young, the horse had a weathered appearance, mottled grey with veins standing, like wind-blown waves upon a lake. Logan and the horse, like the evening air, were perfectly still, except the eyes of the horse had gone from sleepy half-lidded glaze to full round and glistening bright at the boy's approach.

At first Logan approached the mare as just another horse. But when Pinky said the horse was his, he looked quickly to his mother, who nodded, then he walked slowly up to the horse with a sense of awe, and then, as he began to understand that he would have his own horse to ride, his enthusiasm took over in a string of questions. "When can I ride her? Can I ride bareback? How fast is she? Can I sleep in the stable tonight?"

Pinky and Emily Robin laughed at Logan's eagerness, and Pinky told him, "You have much to learn, Logan. You can't just hop on. First you need to learn about how to care for your horse, and then I'll teach you to ride."

Then Pinky turned to Emily Robin and said, "The thing he needs most to learn — and I can't teach him, but the horse will — is patience."

———··———

A few days later, Pinky watched as Logan was to halter his horse for the first time. "Stay on her left," Pinky said quietly, and the boy said, "Okay. I remember." And he did, but then stopped, looked back at Pinky and cocked his head.

"Why, though? Does a horse know left from right?"

"You bet she does." Pinky realized it was a good question, getting at the nature of a horse. "I don't know if horses are calmer when a thing approaches it from the left because something in their brain makes it that way, or if it's just that we all train them that way and they know we usually come up on that side — sort of like we all drive on the right side of the road so everybody will know what to expect. It might even be both."

Over the time since they had met, Logan had come to appreciate how Pinky would hear his questions, and the boy nodded and reached up to rub the big black nose, again marveling at how soft it was on the palm of his hand. He pressed down on the nose and the horse lowered her head, expecting the halter the boy held in his hand, and the boy smiled. Then, as Pinky had shown him a half dozen times while he had half-watched with impatience because he thought it an easy thing he already knew how to do, he reached up and slipped the nose band on the smooth muzzle, and both the boy and the horse were still for a moment. Then the boy slid the crown up toward the horse's ears and pushed the ears down backward so the crown would pass over them. The horse tossed her head, the nose band slipped off, and the halter fell to the ground. The boy said, "Come on," and bent quickly to pick up the halter, and the horse shied away from him. Logan looked back at Pinky, frustrated, and shrugged.

Pinky didn't step forward to help. "Logan," he said quietly. "If you move fast and she doesn't expect it, like when you picked up the halter, she will shy away from you. And she doesn't like her ears to be pushed backward. It hurts. If you have to move them, move them forward. But the best way is to undo the buckle on the crown, slip the crown behind her ears, then re-buckle it."

"Horses are sure particular," Logan said.

"You're going to ask her to do a lot for you when you start riding. It won't hurt to let her be particular about a few small things."

———··———

During his time of getting to know his horse, Logan came to appreciate both how much Pinky knew about horses and how clearly he understood them. Logan learned how to listen more closely to what was shown and said and to use the memory of his body as well as his mind to first watch how and then to halter, bridle, saddle, ride, brush, feed and water the mare. And as he appreciated the horse more and was more attentive to what the horse wanted, the horse gave back in like manner. Logan named her Lady.

———··———

When Logan came to fully appreciate the horse and to appreciate there was yet more to understand, Pinky talked to him about getting a dog. When they talked, Logan saw in his mind a soft-furred puppy with floppy ears and big eyes, a round belly and all cuddles and licking tongue. But boys don't always know what they want and the following week, while riding with Pinky along the upper creek, they found a dog.

Logan's eyes had been drawn to an owl disturbed by a screeching hawk. The owl dropped off his perch on a sycamore limb, stocky and oval, gliding silent down the canyon. Logan saw a feather fall and was concerned, for wouldn't birds need all their feathers? He would ask Pinky later. Following the feather groundward to the winter grey grass, Logan saw the dog where he sat watching from near the Cross Rock Spring. Logan whistled, and when the dog came to him, he saw this dog was lean, wiry hair spotted black on dirty white, mud to the stifle, and eyes not big and round and soft brown but each one half clear marble and half speckled brown as though his momma couldn't make up her mind. Logan couldn't tell how old the dog was, but he was no puppy. It was not the dog Logan wanted, nor did keeping the dog cross his mind.

Expecting the dog was on his way to somewhere else, Logan and Pinky rode on and did not call to the dog to follow. And when he did follow, they did not acknowledge his presence, but watched him indirectly like a shadow lurking at the edge of the conscious mind that could not be acknowledged for fear of making it real and allowing it in where it should not be. But the dog heeled behind Logan's mare, and she walked with the dog in a way that seemed to Logan that the two had known each other before this meeting.

The dog took to Logan and went to him whenever he dismounted and seemed to have good manners and training. He watched the boy and acted as though he was Logan's dog. Logan wondered if the horse and dog had talked it over and decided the dog would be his as the horse was his.

In a few days it was as though the dog and the mare and boy had always been partners. Logan named him Jack because of his eagerness for chasing the lanky rabbits inhabiting the foothills.

———·———

In the mare, the dog, and himself, Logan had all the tools he needed to begin working the ranch. So Pinky started him working the livestock in the corrals and on the range. Logan, Jack and Lady worked with Pinky every minute Logan was not in school or helping his mother, who found things for him to do because, though it was useful to her for the man and the boy to bond, she did not want to lose him entirely to the man she had decided would be his future father.

------.------

Pinky saw that Logan knew the domesticated animals and understood how they saw their world and so next acquainted him with the animals that lived wild in the oak-spattered foothills along the Once Wide Creek and higher in the Jeffrey and Ponderosa pines of the Sierra Nevada—deer, badger, fox, lion, condor, hawk and a dozen others.

"Each animal has a different way of being in the world," Pinky explained. "And seeing each one as it sees itself is seeing a different world than your own and is a worthwhile way of being human."

As young boys do, in the winter Logan complained of the cold, and in the springtime of the wind, and in the summer of the heat, and each time he complained, Pinky told him these things were good. On a day in June, his face red and sweat soaking his clothes and stinging his eyes, Logan asked Pinky what good he found in such discomfort.

"The weather belongs here as much as we do," Pinky said. "This place is not just a way station where the seasons pass by and are gone, but this is home to the wind and the sun and the clouds. The land welcomes the weather even when it seems to us to be misbehaving, like a mother and father welcome their children home even when they are rowdy and rough."

Logan wasn't convinced, but he remembered.

Early one day, when the morning was still cool and crisp, Pinky pointed east, and Logan saw the moon was white and wide and hung on the high granite of the horizon, a jagged line at first seeming to separate all that was beyond from the mountain ranch, parting the sky of Shagoopah from the land of Shagoopah.

"But," Pinky said, "such divisions do not acknowledge the wholeness of the place."

As Pinky worked with Logan and Logan gained Pinky's understanding of the domestic animals and wild animals and of the land and the ranch, the two were brought together in the way of father and son. The bond was below the awareness of either Pinky or Logan. Like gravity, it was a natural force that influenced each, but so obvious as to be unnoticed in the time of its formation.

FOURTEEN
SPRING 1954

Emily Robin browsed the boys' shoes section of the dry goods store, checking sizes and price tags when a man's voice startled her from behind.

"Good to see you again, Miss Macadam."

She could not mistake the voice, and her stomach dropped even as she whirled. There stood the man she hadn't seen since the door had slammed shut behind him nine years before while she lay naked under a sheet: Buck Wilson.

The anger of abandonment fought with an unexpected flash of the attraction she felt for the man she had loved in New Zealand. His arresting good looks hadn't changed much, but, clearly, his intentions had. Hands on hips, he towered over her, breath smelling of whisky, mocking the properness of her New Zealand accent. Her cheeks flamed and she moved to ensure the display of shoes separated her from him.

"From what Betty tells me," he rumbled, "we have a son."

Her anger flared and she found her tongue. "Oh, and you are here because you are now ready to do what is right and marry me and take care of your obligations as a father?"

Buck shook his head. "Not exactly," he said. "I'm already married." He gave her a once-over, and announced as a cold fact, "And she's a keeper."

"If I am not a 'keeper,' it is because of you, Mr. Wilson." As many times as she had imagined this confrontation, she had never envisioned such a pitiful utterance.

He smirked. "You were a willing participant. An eager participant, as I recall." He then leered at her hips and let his gaze slowly climb past her waist, over her breasts, as though remembering her without clothes. When he reached her face, his eyes hardened. "But what's done is done," he said. "Now I want the boy."

Emily Robin felt her insides grow cold. Images of Logan growing into a loving child over the past eight years tumbled through her mind.

"You must have lied to get to the States," he said, "so we should end the pleasant reminiscing and talk about your options." Before Emily Robin could speak, he said, "How long since you've been home to visit your folks?"

Emily Robin was more frightened by the thought of losing Logan than of anything she could remember. But the thought that Buck Wilson could again turn her world upside down made her as angry as she was afraid, and anger was the emotion that surfaced both hot and cold on her face, braced her body inside and out with a hardness she had been tempering in the fires of hatred, and swirled out of her mouth like a swarm of hornets: "Leave us alone, or I'll kill you." She felt no shame in saying it.

Buck was not fazed. "Tough talk, little woman. But you don't mean it. And even if you do, you can't do anything about it. You're barely off the Poor Farm where you raised the boy with a bunch of strays and fallen women. Now you're an unmarried woman living with the bachelor Pinky Wollerman, which most proper folks would take to mean you're either a housemaid or a concubine. Neither one sounds impressive compared to the fact that I could give the boy a 25,000-acre ranch and a good home — with both a mother and a father. The court will think about that. You should, too. Don't you want the boy to have a better life than you're going to be able to give him? Hell, you might even be better off back in New Zealand. Couldn't be any worse off."

Emily Robin decided to play her strongest card. "Does your wife know about your illegitimate son? Conceived while you were married to her?"

Buck folded his arms across his chest and, with a look and voice that gave Emily Robin a chill, said, "Now it's my turn to make threats." He looked around the store. No other customers were there, and the owner was working on the window display. Buck leaned over the shoe display and slowly but forcefully pushed a strong finger into her breast bone, pushing her slightly off balance, and said with cool confidence, "And I can carry them off."

Emily Robin stood frozen, unwanted tears welling up.

Buck started to walk away, then turned back. "When it's time, I'll tell Mindy what she needs to know. In the meantime, you should be thinking of how much your son's well-being is worth to you."

"You think you can buy him?" Her words were lost against Buck's back, mirroring the day Logan had been conceived.

———··———

Some weeks later, Emily Robin sat on the porch of Pinky's ranch house, thinking. Sitting without working on some task was a thing she seldom did. She was thinking about justice for Buck Wilson. Now that she had time to consider her situation, she was no longer afraid.

Emily Robin had boxed up her fears, but what she kept out of the box was an intention, a purposeful force that filled her entire being. In the beginning, when she first realized she had been used and abandoned, that force had burst out as the anxious noise of the injured, but over the years it had quieted itself deep inside her being, and in that settled place had grown relentlessly into a willful thing, shrewd and fiercely strong. After Buck landed back in her life, she became aware that her deep-seated intention was fed as much by possibilities and the future as it was by revenge and the past. She glimpsed her father's reflection in her obsession to fix what was broken, to return damaged beauty to its former self. There was a perfect note to be played, which she did not yet know, but she knew that she was the instrument and the musician driven to play it. Logan would receive what was rightfully his, and Buck would receive justice.

FIFTEEN
SPRING 1954

Emily Robin, in her ordered fashion, decided to deal with one goal at a time. Buck Wilson wasn't going anywhere. Since the incident at the dry goods store she had been more watchful in town and avoided places like the church where he might see her. He had made no more attempts to contact her and made no more threats. Logan's claim to the Wilson ranch could wait. She focused on Pinky Wollerman.

————

The easy winter's light snow was mostly gone from the high pastures by the end of March, and Logan and Pinky went there on a breezy Saturday to check fences. They came back to the ranch house in the evening, cleaned up, and ate dinner while enthusiastically recounting the challenges of the day to Emily Robin. At bedtime Logan asked yet again about the cat, Henry. Pinky patiently retold the story of the stray, and Logan fell asleep during the telling. When Pinky was sure the boy was asleep, he got up from his bedside and met Emily Robin at the door. She surprised him by taking his hand, and then she led him to the porch and hugged him tightly.

"Pinky," she said, "I have a lot to be thankful for. But the one thing I am most thankful for is how well you and Logan get along with each other. And the reason I am thankful is because I love Logan. And I love you."

Pinky nodded, for he had come to admit that he did love the boy and he was thankful Emily Robin had brought him to the ranch and seemed herself to be happy there. Emily Robin released her hug and stood back to see Pinky's face, and when Pinky did nothing more than nod, she held his face in her hands then slipped her arms around his neck and pulled him into a kiss, heightening it by pressing into him with her whole body.

"Pinky, did you hear me say I love you?"

Pinky had wondered about love, but with each passing year had unconsciously increased his belief in the odds against love being available to him, so he was a little flustered by Emily Robin's proclamation of love. Since he had no experience in such matters, he did not recognize what was happening to him. For at the sight of a beautiful woman and the feel of her lips and the pressure of her body against his, he was moved into an altered state where his body began to order his mind and heart about what to think and feel, and the voice that wanted to express this new way of being welled up inside of him and wanted to say, "I love you, too, Emily Robin." But his years of practicing reserve and reticence kept him from saying anything but "thank you."

Emily Robin started for her room, saying over her shoulder, "Sometimes, Pinky, there's a better way than words to say 'thank you.'"

She turned back toward him and unbuttoned the top button on her blouse before entering her room, and Pinky understood what she meant but did not follow.

Emily Robin had a plan, and she hated waiting for it to develop. Having made it clear to Pinky how useful she could be on the ranch and what enjoyable companions they made, she now impatiently teased Pinky toward the muddle-headedness of lust with innocently suggestive words, careless and intimate touches, and even an occasional missing button so he could glimpse parts of her body she normally so modestly kept covered.

But still Pinky wondered. He wondered why Emily Robin would be attracted to him. He was much older than she, although that did not always make a difference. But it seemed to him that attractive people are attracted to attractive people. He knew Emily Robin was, and he was not. And he knew his opinion of her beauty was not his alone, springing from their friendship. He had seen how many of the men they met in town, and even Kazuko and Bill, stole glances at her. How when looking into the beauty of her face and eyes while talking to her, those men would become unaware there was anyone else in the conversation. Pinky's opinion of his own attractiveness was based on his experience. Women seemed unaware of him and, if anyone else was around, seldom acknowledged his presence. In terms of attractiveness, he and Emily Robin seemed an unlikely match.

And Pinky noticed how Emily Robin was aware of this gift of hers to charm men, turning it on and off at will. He wondered if she consciously turned it on for him but did not question her because if he was wrong, he might hurt her feelings by seeming to doubt her sincerity. And the risk of loss might not only be the withdrawal of her flirtation and friendly presence, which he suspiciously enjoyed, but might also mean the loss of Logan if she decided to leave the ranch. Losing Logan was a risk that Pinky would not take, so he chose not to question her motives. But he remained unconvinced that they should be lovers, so he also chose to be coy.

Every now and again, though, he considered how pleasant it could be to be the husband of Emily Robin. At such times he wondered if she might consider marriage to be a practical decision. If she did, that, in Pinky's mind, could be a sufficient reason for marriage.

SIXTEEN
SPRING 1954

Wilbur died that spring. Pinky found him in early afternoon curled up on the porch in a place he lay every day to catch the morning sun. No trauma was apparent. Pinky got a shovel from the shed and dug a deep hole beside the porch that, of all the places on the ranch, had been Wilbur's favorite.

It took him an hour, and every shovel-full he strained over felt like an honor given. When he was finished, he told Logan, who cried, and then Pinky told Emily Robin, who said, "Well, I guess that's life on the ranch."

Pinky agreed, and yet he knew that for a very long time he would feel the pangs of a good friend lost. Such a loss is not so much a remembrance of something that has moved away as it is a blank space held open by the memory of something beautiful, wonderful, intimate. The ranch would not be the same without Wilbur.

SEVENTEEN
SPRING 1954

The hills, covered in bright, new green grass, invited everyone outside. Emily Robin went discreetly to ask Kazuko to teach her to shoot a rifle. She said it was to prepare to go deer hunting with Pinky in the fall and was meant to be a surprise. Since Pinky was not to know, Kazuko suggested that they leave as though going to Bill's ranch, then drive up into the mountains for her lessons.

Kazuko told her that his .30-06 would have too much of a kick for her slight frame, so he borrowed a .32-20 from Bill. She seemed displeased that Bill knew, but Kazuko assured her that Bill would keep the secret.

It was an old gun, with a long hexagonal barrel and was hard for her to hold steady, so Kazuko taught her to shoot while resting the barrel on a fencepost. Then on a Wednesday in May he surprised her with a short barrel model that fit her perfectly. Kazuko insisted that it was a gift from him and Bill. Emily Robin gave him a hug while she told him how much she appreciated his help and attention. Kazuko told her what a great student she had been, which she was, having become an excellent shot in a very short time.

He meant to say more or to be more specific or to discuss further training or perhaps he had intended to show her how the new rifle operated, but he lost his train of thought as she pulled him close and talked.

Emily Robin felt him begin to react to her body, so she arched her back slightly and shifted her weight from foot to foot, lightly brushing back and forth upon him until she was sure of what she was feeling, and then she stepped back from him and feigned surprise. Looking back to his eyes, she said in her sweetest, breathy way, "Why, thank you for the compliment, Mr. Nakamura."

Feeling an odd combination of embarrassment and anger, Kazuko took in a deep breath and let it out slowly as he watched Emily Robin take the new rifle to their makeshift firing line and begin loading the magazine. He glanced upward toward the road, now becoming conscious that a car had passed by while he was preoccupied, and he wondered if they had been seen and thought not. However, Emily Robin had intentionally flirted with him, and he worried about his friend Pinky, who seemed quite involved with her. He would not be the one to tell him of her indiscretion and trusted that his friend would see what needed to be seen before he made any significant decisions.

As for his own intentions, Kazuko had none for Emily Robin. His heart was hopelessly, completely, and secretly bound to Mindy Wilson, Mrs. Buck Wilson.

———··———

Kazuko Nakamura was of the land, but while at university in Berkeley he came to enjoy the skylines of a vertical city and developed a taste for several of the arts: literature, ballet, opera, the classical music of a live symphony and the popular music of the many clubs. Literature was the most mobile, and after his return home he had access to books through Pinky's library and the library in Exeter. But he missed the bookstores of the Bay Area. And he missed the venues of the other arts.

While working the Eldridge farm, he asked Birdie to drive him to Exeter where he caught a bus to San Francisco. For three days he indulged himself. Spending all of his savings from working on the farm and some from his war bond stash, Kazuko purchased a charcoal grey suit, two white shirts, a dark blue tie, and tickets to the major theaters in Berkeley and San Francisco.

San Francisco hosted a large population of Japanese Americans and he never felt out of place.

On his third trip, during intermission at the ballet, Kazuko was approached by a startlingly attractive woman with long auburn hair she allowed to drape in wide curls past her shoulders. She looked somehow familiar. She wore an expensive-looking pale peach evening dress which complemented her complexion and accentuated her green eyes. "Are you Mr. Nakamura?" Her inquiry was cordial and not in the least timid.

"Yes. Have we met?"

"We both live near Exeter. I am Mrs. Wilson, Buck's wife." She extended her hand, which he accepted by the fingers and shook once lightly. With a sudden awareness, Kazuko looked around the theater. She smiled broadly and said, "Buck doesn't care for the arts."

"You come here alone?"

"It is a little difficult to find patrons of the arts from our area who are also willing to spend time this far from home. I stopped bothering some years ago. And since these were my haunts during my college years, I feel perfectly comfortable here."

Kazuko managed to say, "Me, too. Berkeley." That started a conversation, which at some time during the evening, perhaps over drinks at the Purple Onion while listening to the Kingston Trio, led to Kazuko and Mindy coordinating the dates of their next trip to San Francisco.

And so it went, even after Kazuko went to work for Pinky. They never traveled together, and Kazuko could not go as often as Mindy. No specific moral line was crossed during the following years, but a migration occurred, leaving the two mirrored souls eager for their time together and affectionate beyond the anticipation of either.

One night with the city shrouded in a muffling mist, Mindy took Kazuko's hand as they walked the pier and listened to the fog horns in the bay. Only their hands touched, nothing more, but Kazuko knew he would be in love if it were not impossible, which it was. Mindy moved as closely into the intimate space of friends as she could without their bodies touching, and Kazuko knew their impossible love was mutual.

Kazuko did not know one could bear such bracketed attraction for so many hours, so many months. Then months became years. He was happy but never without longing.

Other than during their trips, Kazuko and Mindy never saw each other. Their different worlds were kept distinctly separate. The line they drew together was invisible but uncrossable.

Kazuko discovered a part of his soul that, unknown to him, had always and unsuccessfully searched for an intelligent and discerning companion who could see into him and understand some hidden but clearly higher order of himself. He developed an unshakable sense of monogamy toward Mindy Wilson. And only he would know why Emily Robin's flirtation, though acknowledged by his impulsive nether regions, was not welcome.

EIGHTEEN
SPRING 1954

By May the new green of the grasses had darkened, the deep purple patches of Indian paintbrush had faded to a lovely pink, the orange of the poppies had deepened, and the buttercups in the swales had developed into the pale yellow of old linen. The mild weather and the soft beauty of the land forged a combination that encouraged feelings of affection, and Pinky was moved to accept Emily Robin's intentions as sincere.

Then Pinky noticed Emily Robin leaving with Kazuko in the mid-afternoon without saying goodbye. Each time, they drove in the direction of Bill's ranch, and at first he assumed they had yet to finish the rebuilding. But on a day when Pinky was working higher up in the foothills, he noticed Bill's truck winding its way up the valley toward the mountains and was close enough to the road to see that Kazuko was driving rather than Bill and that Emily Robin was with him. Pinky felt a stitch in his budding trust and wondered if this spring might end as one of the most beautiful he had known, or if it could end as a spring of disappointment. He felt a bit of shame at his feelings.

On a Wednesday when Logan arrived home from school with too much energy for him to handle and his mother nowhere around, Pinky decided to take him along to check if the roads in the high pastures needed any repair. On the "S" bend as the road dropped away from the top of the last grassy ridge before climbing into the brush and pines, a flash of sun on a windshield caught Pinky's attention, and he glimpsed a pickup parked down a dirt road. He felt a shock tighten his body, and his mind flashed and froze as the image he saw looped through his head with no way to understand it or to stop its recurrence. Beside the truck, Emily Robin was embracing Kazuko, their faces close.

Pinky was a quiet man with ever little to say about his feelings, so Logan did not notice the pain within Pinky's silence that afternoon. After seeing Emily Robin with Kazuko, Pinky was clear she had other interests, and he decided that he had no intention of buying into such a tentative relationship. When they returned, Pinky saddled up the little brown Morgan and rode uphill from the ranch without telling anyone where he was going.

———··———

The Morgan was Pinky's favorite horse, but he rode without pleasure. Pinky chose their general direction, and the Morgan went there while choosing her own path and footing. They plodded northward through the foothills and to the edge of the ranch, then under the light of the rising full moon made their way carefully east up into the scrub brush, pine and manzanita, and finally southwest on a route that brought them back without crossing the paved road to the last small hill before the ranch house. It was near midnight, and the full moon, overhead now, bathed the valley in heavily shadowed light.

Under the moonlight and with the Morgan's hooves plunking in the foothill soil and ringing against the ancient rock, it was a time for being with the land and a time for dreams. In the richness of the night air, Pinky allowed the dreams he had absorbed of a life with Emily Robin and Logan to wither and dry and then, with the stalwart intention of a Dust Bowl farmer, tilled them under the soil of his soul. And because it was Pinky's nature to go on about life when crops failed and when dreams were dashed, he opened himself to the eternal land and it opened to him, and he reached there and gathered alternate seeds of different, someday hopeful, dreams to be scattered in new fields.

Australia had been such a regular part of his dream life that it seemed the most obvious and inviting possibility as a land to begin new dreams. That night Pinky decided to go there. He started his ride out across the evening land thinking about disappointments and rode back through the early morning land with a plan for an adventure. This happened in one night on one ride through the valley where the Once Wide Creek flows.

———··———

Pinky had convinced Bill and Kaz that since it had been a long time since Buck had hassled him about selling his place, he was not the bad man they thought he was—a bully, yes, but too principled to harm a neighbor. Strangely, Emily Robin would not listen to any discussion of Buck, so he didn't know whether she agreed or not. No matter, Pinky was certain Buck would not be a problem in his absence.

He would ask Bill, with Kazuko's help, to manage his ranch while he was gone. Bill needed the income and as a ranch manager would make much more than he did doing odd jobs. Kazuko could continue in his current place as the permanent ranch hand and could be a foreman when other men were hired during the busy periods. Based on what he had seen, he expected that Emily Robin would also stick around, which would be good for Logan.

He would finish the inventory of the ranch in the coming weeks and then talk to Bill. Then, unless Bill thought of a damned good reason not to, Pinky would leave for Australia. He didn't know exactly how to get to Australia, but he knew the first leg of the trip was to San Francisco and then by ship the rest of the way.

Arriving in time for breakfast, Pinky ate quickly and wordlessly and took his coffee cup to the porch where, a few minutes later, Emily Robin found it half full on the railing. Pinky was nowhere to be seen.

———·——

Having made the decision and begun his preparations, the trip excited Pinky almost as much as Emily Robin and Kazuko had disappointed him. Though nothing could replace his desire to be Logan's father, the lure of the dreams of the vast Australian land was strong, and he was almost grateful to his two friends for releasing him to journey there, to be a stray in the midst of magic. He sensed a quality in his decision that was like the musty smell of rain on the way after a long dry time.

After a peaceful night of deep sleep, Pinky discovered how an expectant soul meets the morning. Even before his closed eyes noticed the darkness of the night sky giving in to a lighter way of being, Pinky knew it was going to be the kind of day that good things happened. Not sure what had awakened him, probably the last call of a night bird, Pinky blinked his eyes open and looked out through his window to see a dark array of popcorn clouds above the black mountain skyline. The unrisen sun was in the process of adding a layer of purple and a slash of orange to the undersides of their fluffy vapor bodies. What a view they must have, high above the magnificent granite crest of the Sierra Nevada, looking down into California and Nevada at the same moment.

Pinky felt rested. It had been a night undisturbed by the odd dreams he'd had for several months. He gazed sleepily across his valley at the brightening skyline. The clouds, those popcorn clouds, they were pure, undemanding enjoyment. From a contented place inside, he issued the simplest prayer: "Thank you."

Bill, Emily Robin and Logan were at Bill's ranch, and Kazuko had taken a day off to go fishing and was no doubt already on the banks of the Kaweah floating a worm down the rapids into a deep, rocky hole. So Pinky found himself doing all the before-breakfast chores — milking and feeding the cow and tossing scratch for the chickens. Enjoying the solitude and the avoidance of the communion of breakfast, Pinky tucked two end pieces of yesterday's bread into his shirt pockets and was cleaned up and out the door as the sun's first rays were streaming through the high mountain passes, painting streaks of light across the sky above him. In another few minutes the rays would creep down the hillside and light up the white clapboards of the farm house. They'd left the trees on the house's west side to provide summer shade, but, at Hazel's insistence, had cleared all the trees to the east down into the valley in order to get the morning sun and probably also for the view. The wisdom of Hazel's decision was particularly obvious on this grand morning.

On his drive around the ranch Pinky took the time to appreciate the wild mustard, poppies, lupine, Indian paintbrush and several other flowers whose names he did not know. He saw hawks and eagles and buzzards soaring overhead. He searched the sky, remembering condors, their wingspans easily five times that of the buzzards. They were graceful birds when in the air, riding thermals, changing direction by doing nothing but slightly altering the position of the finger-like feathers at their wing tips. He missed their presence. They were yet another being that died out when their place was taken from them.

When Pinky returned to the house to do his nightly chores, Emily Robin and Logan were still away, so he cleaned up and dished himself a bowl of soup from the pot on the stove.

After his supper, he decided to catch up on his reading. He went to his room, lit the kerosene lantern against the dusk and settled in to re-read the first few pages of Lord Byron's *Don Juan* from a ragged book titled *Literature Since the Renaissance, Volume II.* Pinky didn't know where it came from, and he didn't have Volume I, but when he was feeling particularly satisfied with the day's accomplishments, he would sit and read for a few minutes before turning in. This evening he enjoyed the strange rhyming pattern of the words and noticed a subtle tug inside himself around Don Juan's leaving home:

But Juan had got many things to leave,
 His mother, and a mistress, and no wife,
So that he had much better cause to grieve
 Than many persons more advanced in life;
And if we now and then a sigh must heave
 At quitting those we quit in strife,
No doubt we weep for those the heart endears —
 That is, till deeper griefs congeal our tears.

Pinky carefully placed the tattered, treasured volume on the bedside table, put out the lamp, and watched through his window as the midnight blue of the western sky dissolved into black.

That night Pinky dreamed an exciting, but unsettling dream about Don Juan leaving a good life, missing those he loved while traveling the world, and finding only a "deeper grief."

NINETEEN

SUMMER 1954

Pinky was in the midst of preparing the ranch for his absence, and there was one day left in June when he checked the cat's food, worried that it had gone untouched for several days. He hadn't heard the coyotes yipping over a kill recently — at least not close by. And looking around, there were no ragged patches of skin and hair that would suggest the cat might have been a meal for an owl or other predator. But Henry had not been seen, and Pinky was concerned.

Walking back from the barn to the house after a full day of knuckle-skinning work changing the clutch on his old pickup, Pinky wondered if the stray had simply decided to move on. Pinky could remember fairly well such events as plantings, harvests, heat waves and the like. But he couldn't remember for sure when the cat had arrived. He thought it might have been late in the fall, perhaps four, or was it five years? Searching the yard with his gaze as he walked, Pinky knew that whatever amount of time, it was enough to have become accustomed to the mangy critter's presence. Ah, hell, he thought, it was more than that. If Henry was dead, it was going to hurt. He was already hurting with the worry of it.

Kazuko and Emily Robin had been at Bill's place for two days. He didn't miss them in the evenings as much as before and was even a little uncomfortable when they were around. He could have used their hands today, but he knew his ranch wasn't the only one with work piling up, so he didn't begrudge Bill their help. On this evening there was much work to do, but they would have all the responsibility soon enough, and Pinky's fear for Henry overrode his concern for the work.

The sun was slipping toward the dense oak canopies on the hills to the west of the valley. Anxious hope was an expanding hollowness in his gut. He picked up the cat's feed sack from the back porch and went to check the pan on the corner rail of the corral fence. The pan was full. The hollowness in his stomach took on substance.

Pinky rattled the sack. No cat came running. He adjusted the brim of his hat against the low slant of the sun and looked to the west toward the house, letting his eyes move slowly through the shady area behind the porch lattice, the moist patch of green grass under the kitchen window where he threw the wash water, and under the lone shrubby rose at the south corner, places where a cat might nap, or merely sit and watch. With the same slow search, he turned his attention toward the barn and chicken coop, then up on the hillsides covered in the baked straw grass of summer. Rattling the sack again, he searched under the corral boards and rails and over by the stack of hay bales and in the dark spaces where the bales hadn't been stacked tight. There was no sign of the cat. Hope dissipated, and the anxiousness hardened and began to knot up.

First Wilbur, then Emily Robin, and now Henry. Pinky noticed how close together the losses had come, and his heart wondered to God why it should be.

As evening fell and the light went flat, Pinky removed the wire holding the pan to the rail and held the beat up tin pan in both hands like the preacher held the communion chalice on the first Sunday of the month. He studied the pan—the stained and dented grey metal with the nail hole in the rim, and the dirty crust of bread nested within the dry cat food. He stared at these items, which seemed to have outlasted their purpose, as though they were runes that if read carefully would illuminate some value or ethic, or something more basic, like... like.... Pinky didn't know what. And it bothered him that he didn't know. It had something to do with the hardness of life. But the hardness had a context that had to do with the passing of the seasons, and with the feeling of friendship, or perhaps even kinship, and with caring, and purpose, and place. Pinky sensed there was a vastness to these things that could dwarf the hardness, if he could only understand. Perhaps it had to do with love. He had never understood love. It made him sad that he lacked the wisdom to clearly see what he felt he was glimpsing.

Pinky wasn't aware how long he stood this way, but when he scattered the dry food across the ground for the hog, the light had faded and most of the world around him was barely brighter than a silhouette.

Pinky absently went to the well and picked up the washcloth from the wooden bench where it had dried in the summer wind and sun as stiff as if starched. Rhythmically pulling and pushing the pump handle up and down, he didn't hear the screech of metal on metal that always preceded the flow of water, and he didn't think about his movements as he soaped his hands and washed away the grease and removed his sweat-soaked but now dry and stinking shirt. He didn't feel the cold water that his hands splashed over his face, his head, his arms and his chest. Nor did he feel the rough washcloth as the coarse, nubby fabric half-sanded, half-washed the dried sweat-salt and ranch-dirt off his skin. He soaked the shirt and the washcloth in another vigorously pumped stream of water, wrung them out with a persistent twist of his calloused, rancher's hands and spread them on the porch rail to dry.

As he did these things, his heart and mind were scanning the silhouettes of his memories. In this vision, one silhouette was a crowd of people, milling, muttering. Not his family. Perhaps they were the people he ran into whenever he left the farm. They made him uneasy. Another was the church as a building with a steeple, and also as a congregation sitting in pews. He felt empty. Two people standing by an oak tree... they were familiar and comfortable, perhaps the Erlewines. A woman pointing into the darkness, looking over her shoulder at him as young boy. She was smiling. It was his mother. He was curious and confident.

The last silhouette was a black Sierra skyline against a charcoal sky, with a dark and empty valley in the foreground, the valley where Pinky's ranch would be if it could be seen in the grey formlessness.

Pinky blinked and was startled by the fact that the last silhouette he was mulling over was actually before him. He stood by the pump staring up the darkened valley toward the saw-toothed crest, backlit now by a pale light that flowed around his body and left him chilled. And he no longer felt as though he were home. Rather, he had an urge to go in search of a place to call home. But he didn't know if it was a place or a way of being.

Recalling his vision of the silhouette memories, Pinky felt that the people in the pews all seemed to be looking his way but did not see him. Pinky didn't like it. It wasn't about God. He was more comfortable with God than with church. Pinky thought he and God had a pretty good relationship as long as he didn't ask for too much. Pinky hadn't always dreaded church. But over the last few years it had come to that. The dread used to be sort of like a rash that was there all the time but could be ignored when there was work to do. But this past year the dread had grown stronger.

This evening, feeling a spiritual vertigo, the disappointment brought by Emily Robin, missing his dog, and missing the seldom grateful but never judgmental cat, Pinky felt tired. But there was more bothering Pinky this evening than he could put his finger on. Back home, in Oklahoma, when old Jake Stenquist was a young hell-raiser, he got drunk and fell asleep on the railroad tracks. The train that hauled cattle to market didn't kill him, but it did cut off his left foot. Jake said that for years he would sometimes feel an itch in his left big toe and want to scratch it. That was how Pinky felt about whatever it was that he was missing. It was some part of him that at one time, although he couldn't remember when, had made him whole, and it periodically itched, but wasn't there when he reached to scratch it. Something in the dreams he'd been having reminded him of this itch.

While his thoughts continued to flow by like a stream, Pinky's routine took him into the kitchen where he ate a hard biscuit and drank a cup of water for his supper. Wandering pensively through the house afterward, he noticed the book, *Literature Since the Renaissance, Volume II*, with its story of Don Juan, and remembered clearly his dream of Don Juan's travels ending in grief.

Finally, Pinky's routine took him to bed where he slipped into revealing sleep.

A cat he thought was Henry joined him in his nightscape. Henry sat beside him on a wide, rock strewn mountain trail, and in the way of cats, simply observed. Pinky trusted the cat to see what was important and, for the moment, suspended his own observations in favor of Henry's.

As though on a silent signal, the cat and Pinky started climbing up the steep trail, side by side. The cat was sure-footed and could see things Pinky could not. Pinky was bone tired in his body and anxious to the depths of his soul. But he believed the cat was taking him to a place, somewhere on the trail above, where he would cross over a line, such a definite crossing that he would see it and feel it and know he had passed over it. It would be as clear as topping a steep hill and going down the other side, where at once, at the crest of the hill, his regrets and failings would be left behind, no longer trouble him with guilt, and no longer intimidate him with doubt. He would be left to continue on in peace of mind and heart. He would know what needed to be done to get along in the world and would understand what it was that God wanted of him. He would go quietly and confidently about his daily life without the demanding or striving that had harried him all of his life.

As is often the way with dreams, the following morning Pinky didn't remember the specifics of what the cat had shown him, but he was left with a strange new sense of peace and confidence—as though he was moving easily on a downhill path and knew where he was going.

PART TWO

TWENTY
JULY 1954

"Excuse me, please," Orson said, rising from a hastily eaten dinner. "Mr. Hannigan gave us a buttload of geometry homework for Friday."

"Watch your mouth, Orson." Twyla stated the rebuke with little inflection and did not look up from the Dear Abby column in the Visalia Times Delta behind which she could see neither her son nor her husband. "Buttload" hardly made the bottom of the list of foul language issued regularly by Twyla's mouth, but it seemed appropriate for a mother to provide some guidance to her son.

"Homework. Homework. Homework," Orson said, sticking his tongue out in the direction of the newspaper. "The dirtiest word in the English language that's longer than four letters."

Twyla laughed, and Dave Wilson shook his head at the two and kept working on the double portion of apple crisp before him. "Show some respect for your mother. You're not too old for a spanking, you know."

"I was too old for a spanking when I got faster than you, Dad."

Dave didn't slow up on the apple crisp, but his eyebrows arched slightly as he said through a full mouth, "You want gas for your truck?"

"Sorry, Mom," Orson said quickly and insincerely, and then, still addressing the newspaper, "But if I'm going to the symphony with you tomorrow night, I've got a lot to do tonight."

When Orson had left the room, Twyla put the paper down and looked at her husband. "Have you had that talk with your brother?"

"Saw Buck this morning, as a matter of fact."

"I don't mean have you shoveled the shit with him. I mean have you had 'the talk'? The one about Orson. You know what I mean, which means you probably haven't."

"It's a hard conversation to start."

"How about I do it?"

"You stay out of this. I'm sure you haven't forgotten he isn't real fond of you. It would only make things harder."

"It's very simple, Mr. Big Shot Sheriff. Get some balls, for God's sake."

"We got time. Buck is a long way from dying."

"That's probably what they said about your father."

Dave's eyes narrowed and he pushed the empty bowl back and wiped his mouth with a cloth napkin. He hadn't used napkins at all before he met Twyla, and although as a public figure he now found them useful in maintaining a dignified look, he still thought using cloth napkins at home with the family to be snobbish. But there was nothing but the best for Twyla, which he knew was why she was so interested in getting Buck to change his will. The ranch was worth millions, and she wanted to make sure it was available to her if anything happened to Buck.

"That ranch is yours, Dave. I know your family tradition is that the ranch goes to the oldest boy, and that's Buck. But that ranch is yours as much as it is Buck's, and just because he doesn't have a kid doesn't mean it should go to someone else. The way he has it set up now is if he dies, it will go to you as trustee for Julie's kid, and when he grows up, he'll get it, and your family will be left out in the cold. That's not fair, and you know it isn't."

Dave had decided the comment about his father's tragic accident was over the line, and he was through with the conversation. He looked over at the family photograph on the wall. Julie, their sister, was standing between him and Buck. She had married a small time rancher down by Portersville with about a thousand acres and had lived a generally satisfying but rigorous and unprosperous life as a ranch wife. Dave could see why Buck wanted Julie's kid to take over the ranch. Denton, except for his sophisticated name, was so much like Buck at 17 that Dave sometimes wanted to call Denton Buck. The kid worked on his dad's ranch and enjoyed it, whereas Orson was bookish and more likely to be found dressed in the latest threads and running around Visalia in his shiny Ford pickup than up on the ranch getting dirt on himself and the new truck. But if Denton got the ranch, it would be the Nelson place, not the Wilson place, and Dave thought Twyla was right about one thing — the ranch really should be passed to a Wilson. Unfortunately, Buck didn't see it that way, and it would be near impossible to get him to change his mind.

Quietly, Dave got up from the table, grabbed his hat from its hook by the door and went out to his pickup, which was deliberately older than Orson's and therefore more acceptable to the average voter. There was probably a card game with a judge or two going on somewhere, and it wouldn't hurt his ability to function in Tulare County's justice system if he were to lose a few dollars to one or more of them.

———··———

"The kid's smart, Buck. He's ambitious. There's not a lazy bone in his body."

Three weeks had passed since Twyla's goading, which was enough time for Dave to feel like it was his idea to talk to his brother, enough to keep him from feeling pussy-whipped, a thing no man should have to worry about, much less the tri-county roping champ and the sheriff of Tulare County.

The two men sat on the front porch of the family ranch house where they had grown up, now Buck's place. They sipped lemonade that Buck's wife, Mindy, had supplied. As soon as Dave said what was on his mind, Mindy could see the two of them slipping into their roles as older brother and younger brother, so she announced that she had work inside and left them to slide down the alluvial fan of their childhood quarrels.

Buck was silent for so long that Dave didn't know if he was even going to respond. He knew that Buck didn't like to have his decisions questioned, especially by his little brother, no matter his station in life. When Buck spoke, he was firm and thoughtful.

"I know he's smart. And he's a go-getter. But that's not all it takes to run a ranch. I don't mean to just manage the damned thing, which is hard enough. Ever since we were kids, I've been saying I want this ranch to stay in the family and stay whole for 100 years. Hell, even 500 years. If somebody gets hold of it who doesn't give a damn for the place, that won't happen."

Dave laughed. "You know what's likely to happen is you'll live to be 90, and I'll be 85, and Orson will have been running it under our tutelage for 50 years. If that won't prepare a man, nothing will. Hell, by the time he gets it, he'll be so long in the tooth, he'll be ready to pass it off to his heir."

Buck didn't laugh. "If things happened that way, I could wait a few years to name an heir and see if Orson comes around. But the reason Twyla wants you to get me to change the will is in case things don't happen that way. If I die sooner and haven't seen fit to name Orson heir, our sister's kid gets everything, and Twyla doesn't get to live the rich life. No offense, little brother, but that woman is greedy. Everybody who knows her knows it."

Now Buck laughed, remembering the fun times he had enjoyed in high school with Twyla before she gave up gold digging him and went on to his brother. "You figured it out, too, as soon as you were married and started getting it often enough that you could see past her butt."

It was Dave's turn not to laugh. "Buck, I've never begrudged you getting the whole inheritance. It's what our family does. But if you die, that ranch ought to go to me, and you know it."

"But what then, Dave?" Buck looked Dave in the eye. "If Twyla and Orson get control of it, they'll start selling off pieces for the money. And you know it. They don't either one care about ranching, and they sure as hell don't care about the land." Buck stood, looking out across the ranch. "You never did see the land the way I do. You should spend more time out here." Buck paused and appeared thoughtful, something Dave knew he did only rarely, so he knew something of significance was about to be said.

Buck folded his arms over his chest and pointed out to the hills with his chin. "People drive through here in the spring and comment how 'beautiful' the place is. Sometimes they're taken with the rolling hills. Sometimes it's the oak forests. Sometimes they've seen the tall green grass bending in waves with the wind. There is a lot about this place that is pleasing to the eye, and that's a good thing. But open space, Dave, unbroken openness, is a quality all its own." As he spoke, Buck swept his gaze slowly from the foothill horizon to the north of the ranch, across the high Sierra Nevada, to the foothills of the southern horizon. "Land that goes on as far as the eye can see—without a covering of asphalt or concrete or building—is as good a thing as beauty. Maybe better." Buck looked again at Dave and waited until Dave returned his gaze. "This ranch has both of those things, Dave. But there's more. And it's a thing you can't know until you've spent some time in this valley, worked with it in every season, walked it, rode it on horseback, watched it give away and take back. When you've lived with it like that for a few years and see how the land bends itself around the seasons and keeps so much life going within it, you get a feeling like the place is almost alive, almost conscious. If a piece of land is too small, you don't have all of that. Here's the thing, Dave: A place has to be big enough to be itself. This place is and it should stay that way. It's more than just real estate."

Dumbfounded, Dave looked at his brother, waiting to see if there was more. Then he furrowed his brow and said, "Good God, Buck. When did you get back from Oz? I never thought I'd hear anything so bizarre come out of your mouth. What's got into you? It's a goddamned cattle ranch!"

"And it's going to stay that way! Passing on a legacy is a hell of a lot more than passing on the family name."

Buck had lost the thoughtful face, and Dave could see the muscles in Buck's jaw flex, so grew cautious. "So you're dead set against changing your will?"

There was a long silence while Buck looked out across the ranch and Dave watched his brother's face, curious at the intensity of his contemplation of a question he had thought would bring a quick and simple answer.

"Not exactly," Buck finally said. He turned again to Dave. Again making sure Dave saw him as well as heard him. "I don't know for sure yet how it might change things, but it seems I have a son."

Dave was stunned into silence and in the hush suddenly understood why Buck was so uncharacteristically reflective. He had always wanted a son, but he and Mindy hadn't had any children. If he really did have a son, then he would be looking at the future through the eyes of a personal heritage.

Dave slowly exhaled. "Who's the mother?"

"Don't matter."

"Well, you've screwed half the women in the county, so I guess one of 'em had to take. How long have you known?"

"A few months."

"How old is the kid?"

"Nine."

"You're sure the kid is yours, and this isn't some woman trying to get into your wallet?"

"Very sure." Buck stood up, looking into the foothills. "Sure enough to change my will if the boy seems to have promise."

"Well, son of a bitch, Buck."

———·———

"The hell he is! I'll pull the bastard's balls off first." Twyla was beside herself with rage, and spittle flew as she screamed. "I'll blow his fucking head off."

"For God's sake, quiet down. People can hear through these walls." Dave went to the door of his courthouse office and looked into the reception area. His secretary, Millie, had gone home, and the door from the reception area to the hallway was thankfully closed.

"You can't let him do this," Twyla sobbed. "That's our ranch."

"He hasn't done anything yet, but it's his ranch to do with as he pleases."

"We've got to stop him. You've got to stop him. Whether you have the guts to do what's right or not, there is no way in hell I'm going to let Buck's bastard kid take Orson's birthright from him."

"We don't know yet if that's going to happen."

"Do you propose we wait to find out? When did the big sheriff of Tulare County become a eunuch?"

Dave hesitantly went to his wife. She was never even-tempered, but he had never seen her berserk before. He put his hands on her shoulders, and spoke quietly. "Go home, honey. Take some of those pills Doc Winn gave you to help you sleep. I'll talk to Buck again, and we can decide then if we want to mount some kind of legal challenge."

"Fuck the legal system," Twyla hissed, batting his hands off. "This is a family matter, and you need to take care of it." She jumped up from the stuffed chair, knocking it backwards, and stomped to the door. "And if you don't, I will."

"Don't do anything stupid," Dave yelled after her, but with the deranged muttering, the slamming of two doors, and the stomping of cowboy boots in the granite hallway of the courthouse, he thought she probably didn't hear him. But he hoped she would go home and take the pills and sleep.

He had another poker game with the judges tonight, so he couldn't follow her home. If she was ill, he would have one of the deputies check up on her, but he didn't want any of them to see her like this. It would be best to call a friend, but unfortunately, Twyla didn't have friends. Perhaps he would ask Ruby Thomas. She had at least known Twyla since high school, might be willing to help and she wasn't a gossip.

Unable to reach Ruby by phone, Dave headed out of the courthouse to the judges' poker game, thinking Twyla would just have to be on her own for the evening and hoping she wouldn't do anything indiscreet.

TWENTY-ONE
JULY 25, 1954

Grasses, brambles and bushes grow thicker along the seams of the earth where water collects or comes to the surface. Farmers and ranchers take these thickets in stride, working around or through them. When these people of the land find that hard times have fallen upon them, it is as though the bad has grown up around them in a hateful thicket and, as is their nature, they ignore what might be ominous, shrug off the hindrance, and work their way through.

By the summer of '54, the bad in Buck Wilson's life had thickened into a dense undergrowth, but in his bullish way, he had not noticed how caught up in the brush he was until it was too late. And when he lost the quarrel with that thicket, many lives were rearranged.

———··———

Buck's blue chambray work shirt was dry and streaked white with salt. The summer was the hottest he could remember in his more than 40 years living in the foothills of the arid San Joaquin Valley. July had delivered a two-week string of blazingly hot days, and this day was the hottest by far. His clothes had been soaked with sweat only a half hour before, but once he stopped sweating, his dehydrated skin had taken on the dryness of sack paper, and his face gave off more heat than the summer sun was pounding down. Common sense waded through the heat waves in his mind to tell him in a harsh voice, not unlike his father's, that he was too hot for his own good. He wanted to set one more oak fencepost before resting, but knew he had to stop and drink. Working his ranch on this July afternoon, Buck wondered why his great-granddad hadn't settled in Oregon or Washington—or even Montana.

He raised the wooden handles of the posthole digger high in the air and jammed its shovels downward into the ground. With Buck's weight and strength behind them, the shovels sank four inches into the baked red earth. Leaving the digger standing as firm as a well-rooted tree, he swiped a calloused hand at the dried salt on his forehead and made his way across the hillside toward the shade of an oak. He felt woozy, which pissed him off, as any sign of weakness did.

Of the thousands of oaks on his ranch, this one demanded attention because of its sheer size. It was 90 or more feet high and the canopy was at least as wide. Buck could see four limbs that each would make a substantial tree and yield three or four cords of firewood. When he was 14 and had more ideas than experience, he made lumber from such a tree. Or tried. But he found the gnarly grain so insistent that the lumber warped even after being pressed and dried for a full year. The following winter his father had laughed about the fancy firewood every time they stoked the stove. It was one more bead in a lifelong string of beads that left him hating his father every time he fingered it. His father was dead, but the beads were still heavy around Buck's neck.

Two miles down the valley, visible between the oak canopies, Pinky Wollerman's house, a couple of sheds and a large weathered barn wavered in the heated air, galling and spiteful. Buck moved to the other side of the big oak so he couldn't see the damned things. The sight of those buildings on what should be his land filled him with disgust. It also reminded him of his stalled effort to reclaim the family land.

Absent the chunking and scraping sounds of his digging, Buck noticed the quiet. There was no rustling of leaves and grasses; even the bugs were on a heat-inspired siesta. Except for the throbbing of blood in his temples and chest, he heard no sound. Except for the shimmer of the distant oaks through the heat waves, nothing was moving across the entire scope of the valley. "My valley, damn it! My valley!" he shouted, breaking both the silence and his awareness of it.

In the shade of the big oak a gallon canteen hung by its strap over the stub of a rusted single-blade axe head nearly buried in the trunk. He had sunk the axe head into the trunk when he was 12 years old just to see how far in he could drive it with a single swing. It went deep into the gnarled wood, deeper than he expected, deeper than anyone would believe, and he never mentioned it to anyone, satisfied to keep the knowledge of his strength stored within himself, all the more powerful when someone didn't recognize who they were dealing with. He broke the axe handle off and left the blade in place, checking it every year or two to watch the progress of the bark. By the time he returned from the war, the bark had patiently swelled to engulf all but the last three inches of the head. Buck respected patience, knowing it was a character trait he lacked.

From under the oak's canopy, a small flat was visible with the rock remnants of an old foundation poking above the bleached summer grasses. The house of his great-grandfather had stood there from 1856 until 1926, when it was knocked skew-gee by a freak wind storm and had to be torn down. The storm also took down the water tower that his grandfather had added in the 1870s, as well as the three blue gum trees his father planted when he married Buck's mother in 1919. Only the barn, seemingly incapable of being overcome by the weather, had survived.

Buck had a nearly new Ford 2n tractor and a power train-driven posthole auger back at his barn, but when he worked this section of the ranch that was near the original home place, he liked to do things the way the old man would have when he built the place—with hand tools. And he did the work himself—no hired hand for this work. It was a kind of salute to the old guy's legacy of toughness that had put together a ranch covering nearly 40 square miles of foothill and valley land.

Buck had long ago stopped hitting things when he thought about how his father had lost one third of the original spread—more than 8,000 acres—the sweet core of the ranch. But the regret and the shame had never lightened, and he was dead set to be the one in the bloodline who brought the pieces back together.

Pinky Wollerman had the biggest piece: 8,000 acres along Once Wide Creek, three-quarters of a mile wide and nearly 17 miles long, following the creek from the lowland foothills up to the mid-mountain meadows.

Bill Jenkins had a pitiful, oddly shaped, 320-acre hardscrabble piece with volcanic rock scattered across half the place and no access to the creek. Nevertheless, Buck wanted it because when he saw the

Wilson ranch in his mind, it had no pieces missing. Ownership of any ranch in the Once Wide Valley that wasn't his was purely temporary.

Pinky Wollerman hadn't earned his place but had inherited it from the Erlewines, who weren't even relatives. Troy and Hazel Erlewine bought the place from the gambler who took it from Buck's father. Buck had gone to see them when he was 18, hat in hand, like a good neighbor, and told them he wanted that piece of land and would pay well for it. They had him in for a fried chicken dinner with fresh baked bread and a very pleasant Sunday afternoon of conversation. They seemed like nice people. But he found out when the Erlewines died that they'd ignored him and had left their place to that Okie runt in their will. Being ignored pissed Buck off as much as anything in the world.

Being away first for college, and then for the war, then being faced with rebuilding the ranch for a post-war economy had delayed Buck's efforts to consolidate the land. But when he came back from the service, he gave himself five years to reconnect the pieces. It was his obsession, and he was now overdue. He had tried to be patient, but that wasn't working. And now that he knew he had a son, his patience was stretched near the breaking point. Running a ranch this size was a bigger challenge than most men could handle. The boy was 9, and Buck would need several years with him to make sure he was up to the task and to make sure he understood the value of owning the whole watershed.

He knew ranchers who were all too quick to split up their places, first for the kids, then their kids, and so on, even selling a piece here and there during hard times to make ends meet, until the place was all torn up. The boy had to understand how that would destroy the place. His nephew Orson wouldn't understand it, not with his mother raising him. His sister's boy, Denton, had a rancher's way about him and would likely understand, but then it would be the Nelson Ranch rather than the Wilson Ranch, and it ought to keep the Wilson name.

Buck felt that he had done the right thing by changing his will. The best chance he had to make sure the ranch stayed whole for another generation was to adopt Logan and bring him up with the know-how and backbone to do what was needed. But he didn't want anyone to know he had already changed the will to leave the ranch to Logan. Not until he had the kid with him.

Buck knew the kid had a lot working against his success. He'd always be the bastard child, and no matter how proper the kid himself was, people have a tedious way of remembering such stuff as sordid. It also didn't help that his mother had raised him on the Poor Farm. The destitute were known to be destitute for a reason, usually related to a lack of character.

In the fall he would ask the lawyer who changed the will to figure out how to get custody of the kid. Emily Robin wouldn't like it, but given her situation, having very likely lied her way into the country, living on the Poor Farm, and not knowing any judges the way he did, she wouldn't have much sway in court. It would be best if he could get her deported. It wasn't that he didn't like the woman. She was a little wild-eyed at times, but she was a good-looking woman from a good family. But he wasn't going to give up Mindy for her. Mindy was special beyond good looks and fun. Mindy talked to him in a way that he could hear and understand. He didn't know exactly why, but Mindy was like no other person he knew, man or woman. So, when the war ended and his orders came to go to Japan, he'd had no problem leaving Emily Robin behind. He probably would have done the same if he'd known she was expecting, but he was glad he didn't have to decide.

Buck had never told Emily Robin exactly where he was from and wondered how she had landed so close to him. Maybe someone at the base had let it out. The Poor Farm was only a few miles southeast of his ranch, so if she knew he was here, why hadn't she contacted him? Buck didn't know what she must have been thinking, coming to the States — that he would marry her? Or support them? Did she want money to keep quiet?

Some of his questions had been answered when he saw her in the dry goods store. Emily Robin had remembered him, but she was her usual formal self and apparently not glad to see him. That part was just fine because lovesickness could be a pain in the butt. But when he told her he wanted Logan, she had threatened his life. It was an empty threat, but it made clear how much she wanted the boy, which meant he probably couldn't buy her off. He would have to get rid of her. He hadn't heard from her since then, most likely because she didn't know how to fight a legal battle with him and certainly didn't have the money.

What he wanted was an heir to the ranch—and to give the boy a better chance in life than she could give him. But he wanted nothing to do with her. The kid was born after she arrived in the States, so he was a citizen, which would make it easier to keep him here. Buck was pretty sure he could mold the kid into a rancher, but if he didn't work out, it would likely be easy enough to change his will again and "reunite" him with his mom in New Zealand.

Realizing he had been staring at the red stripe on the grey canvas cover of the gallon canteen, Buck shook his head to clear the murky blend of memories and thoughts, removed the strap of the canteen from the ax head, unscrewed the cap and drank almost half of it before pausing for breath. The canvas cover had dried since he hung it up that morning, and the water was warm but not yet hot. When it was 112 degrees out with no breeze, "not hot" was the best he could hope for. He knew the water would clear his mind in a few minutes, but as it landed in his stomach, it made him a little nauseous, which fed his anger. He had about one more hour of work to finish mending this section of barbed wire fence, and then he would go back to the barn and work the pump until the water came up cold from deep under the ground, stick his head under the stream, and return his heat-wracked body to normal.

Buck wondered about the runt, Pinky Wollerman. He was either stubborn or stupid because he didn't seem to be fazed by being pushed around. Mindy had seen Buck collar Pinky last year when he backed the little man up against the outside wall of the church and told him in hard and certain terms that he was going to buy his place. Mindy didn't like what she saw, said Buck was being un-Christian, and called him a bully. Buck didn't see it that way. His great-granddad had been a lot rougher. But Buck didn't like it when Mindy scolded him. Somehow her opinion of him counted in a way that no else's did. In some ways she felt like the mother other boys had, and he thought he might have had if his mother hadn't died when he was 5.

Buck had never cried for the loss of his mother, but he felt the absence in his insides left by that loss and knew it was one of several holes in his being that Mindy had filled in or covered over.

But Mindy was too often right, so he listened when Mindy lectured him about easing up on Pinky. She seemed certain she had the high moral ground. When she was finished with him, the back of his neck was splotchy and his jaw tight, but he never audibly disagreed.

Still, Buck thought Pinky was a miserly loner with a reputation of hanging to himself and not doing much of anything for his community. And he wasn't very bright either. So far he had responded to Buck's threats as though they were neighborly offers.

Mindy had more than once said she was his conscience, and he danged well better listen. Buck always smiled and hugged her gently because she honestly cared about his soul. He hoped she felt the same after he told her about Logan.

———··———

He walked back to plant another post, and the cooling sweat returned to his dehydrated skin. He felt less wobbly but also knew he wasn't out of the woods yet.

Buck was imagining the cold well water while pounding the red dirt tight around the base of a post with the blunt end of his digging bar when he heard a quiet engine on the paved road over the adjacent hill. Must be a car or pickup, he thought, too quiet for a truck. The engine noise ended so abruptly Buck wondered if the vehicle had gone out of hearing range or had been turned off. Curious, he glanced up occasionally, checking the top of the hill as he worked.

A few minutes passed, and then a grey hat came into view on the far side of the crest, wobbling in the heat waves like a rabbit in the grass. A shimmering figure emerged at the top of the hill, but the hat's brim kept the face in shadow, and Buck couldn't tell who it was. He could see that the stranger was short and slightly built, with a fluid, almost graceful gait. And damned if there wasn't a rifle cradled in the crook of the left arm. Buck frowned, leaned on his digging bar and watched as the silhouetted figure stopped and scanned the countryside, likely checking to see if anyone was around.

If this trespasser thought he was going to hunt on Buck's place, he had another think coming.

The figure stopped, facing him, so Buck assumed the guy saw him. He didn't wave at strangers, so to let the guy know he had been seen, he casually pointed a finger towards the figure on the hill, like little kids do when they pretend to have a pistol. But instead of coming down the hill, the stranger moved behind a dead oak where Buck couldn't see him as well. It appeared that the stranger was watching him over a dry, sun-bleached limb. The brim of the grey hat bumped against the trunk and was pushed to one side, which suggested the man was not used to wearing a brimmed hat or was in a big hurry. Buck took off his hat and held it above his face to better shade his eyes from the sun, hoping to see better, hoping to get his sun-addled brain around the senselessness of a trespasser with a rifle wandering around his place in mid-afternoon on one of the hottest days of the summer. Then he thought he saw the rifle barrel swing in his direction.

Before Buck could figure out what the stranger was up to, something hit the bones of his left shoulder with such force that his 250-pound body spun around, leaving him facing away from the stranger. As he spun, the report of the rifle covered the distance from the muzzle to his ears, and his mind recognized it as a light caliber, maybe a .32-20. He heard the slapping vibration of the digging bar he had dropped as it hit the ground and heard a faint metallic rattle from up on the hillside, a lever action seating another shell in the chamber. Before he could turn back, a second round from the stranger's rifle entered his back near the left shoulder blade, passing through and destroying his heart, knocking him face down, and sending him for a short slide down the hillside. His eyes and mouth collected red foothill earth, but he did not hurt.

Buck was busy inside turning his soul around—a thing that can happen in an instant. He chastised himself for not being quicker to take cover and for not being armed so he could shoot back, but at the same time he was a little pleased with himself that this one time in his life when he hadn't responded in anger was also, apparently, the time he was going to die. It was, of course, better not to die, but if he was going to, it seemed good to do it without anger. In his mind and in his heart, he was asking God to forgive him for anything he might have done that would be considered a sin. He was sincere, but he also wished Mindy could be with him right then to help him be more clear about what those sins might have been. He also wished that Mindy could know he had died talking to God and thinking of her.

And Buck wanted to cry but knew he didn't have the time or the tears. He would have cried for Mindy. He would have cried for Logan. He would have cried for the place around him, a place he thought was his, a place he should have made whole.

He felt grace flow through him, and even in the heat and the dirt and with the terrible explosive puncture through his chest, Buck Wilson died peacefully.

PART THREE

TWENTY-TWO
JULY 25, 1954

Back when the world was smaller, there were people for whom a new year began when barley ripened. In that world, barley might ripen over a two- or three-week period. But a year had to start on a specific day, so a holy man would decide on which exact day the barley had ripened so the year could begin with confident precision.

Pinky rolled out of bed and watched the dawn work its magic on the eastern sky above the granite crest of the high Sierra Nevada. In the increasing heat of July, this was the only time the air was cool. His thoughts tumbled through his mind like storm water through a steep creek.

Pinky decided that a new year could begin on any day a person wanted it to. In fact, a farmer might say it would make more sense to start the year, like the Chinese do, with the advent of spring rather than in the middle of winter. On that morning, Pinky reflected on the idea that time does not start over, but people can.

On Sunday morning Pinky's habit was to pull out Troy's old 8-by-12-inch mirror with the arched top that Pinky had inherited with the ranch. He would hang it on the wall in the kitchen, boil water on the woodstove and shave. There was a ritual to shaving, habits that made it go more smoothly. Part of the ritual was sliding the folding razor with the white, pearled handle back and forth on a leather strap to sharpen the blade. Another was running his hand over the stubble to acknowledge it had grown, and perhaps to warn it that it was time to go. After that he would soak a towel in hot water, and wrap it around his whiskers for a few minutes, allowing them to soften.

Then it was time to look in the mirror. Pinky had never liked looking in the mirror too long. To shave, he needed only to see the lower part of his face with the week's growth of pale stubble. He needed only to focus on the meeting of the razor's blade with the skin and whiskers. What he did not need or want to do was look too deeply into his own eyes.

If he looked himself in the eyes, he ran the risk of not just seeing pupils and pale blue irises, and whites, bloodshot from the wind and dust, but also something underneath, something behind. He ran the risk of seeing himself. When he saw himself, he couldn't hide behind the clean shaven face of a Sunday church-goer or the weathered face of a hard working rancher. When he honestly looked at himself, it was as though God was looking at him. Nothing could be hidden.

Pinky dipped the towel in the hot water, wrung it out in the grey-blue enameled cast iron sink, wrapped it around his face, and stood in front of the mirror. Pinky felt he had tried to do things right in his life, although "right" seemed to have shimmered a bit over the last few months—especially the last couple days. But today was the beginning of a new year, so Pinky looked himself in the eye, removed the towel and shaved.

Although it was Sunday, Pinky would not be going to the Once Wide Valley Methodist Church for worship services. He wasn't going to take Kool-Aid to the Methodist Women's Sunday potluck. And he wasn't going down the hill to do his weekly grocery shopping at the Exeter Safeway. Today Pinky was leaving for Australia.

July 25th would be the start of Pinky's new year.

Bill had enthusiastically agreed to take care of the ranch in Pinky's absence. Pinky would leave a letter for Logan telling of his anticipated adventures, asking him to help on the ranch and telling him he loved him. He had asked Bill to spend more time with Logan and to ask Kaz to do the same. Bill would tell the others of Pinky's trip after he was gone.

The only things Pinky would take with him were his black Ford pickup, a change of clothes, the $1,560 from under his mattress, a not-very-specific-plan for adventure, and the self he saw in the mirror. He would sell the pickup in San Francisco.

Pinky looked into the pale eyes in the mirror. They held an eagerness and a resolve he hadn't noticed before, and it made him smile. The face in the mirror smiled back.

The events of the first day of travel were inconsistent with the expectation of adventure Pinky felt coursing through his body upon departing Once Wide Valley.

Since leaving Oklahoma more than 20 years earlier, his ranch had been his home, his refuge and his greatest joy, but it had also kept him isolated and work-bound. The day Pinky left it in other people's hands was one of the biggest days of his life. But having anticipated this day so keenly, the day he left for Australia, he expected big things to happen — really big things. Tidying up the loose ends was far more difficult than he'd thought. There was a finality to it he hadn't anticipated. But after that, after he was on the road, nothing happened.

He drove miles and miles of highway bordered by cottonwood trees and seemingly enough farm land to feed the whole world. Pinky wondered where all this bounty had been during the Depression. He pulled into an 80-acre parcel of eucalyptus some farmer had planted during the war, intending to supply pulp for the paper mills. The market hadn't developed, and mostly the eucalyptus groves, too expensive to remove, had been abandoned, leaving good farm land unusable. But they made a good place for a traveler to camp, hidden and away from the main highway.

On his way to San Francisco, Pinky went north to Sacramento, just to see the California State Capitol. There, he stopped at a market and bought some bologna under a clearly well-worn sign that said "Today's Special." He thought it would be good to have some meat to go with the remaining bread he had brought from home. "Home," he thought aloud, as he often did when he and Wilbur sat on the front porch. "I wonder where home has moved on to?"

The grocer raised an eyebrow and looked at him, perhaps waiting for this man who talked to bologna to do something crazy. When it seemed Pinky was harmless, the grocer guided him to a cash register. Giving Pinky his change, the grocer said, "Home is where your family is, mister. Where's your family?"

"Either dead or gone," Pinky replied, picking up the bologna and heading towards the door. Then he paused and added, "I'm going to Australia."

"If you're going there for your family, mister, it sounds like they didn't go to heaven when they died."

What a curious thing to say, Pinky thought, noticing the grocer's serious face and wondering what the man knew about Australia. Not sure he wanted to hear, he turned and went to his pickup and made a bologna sandwich. As a rancher he had always eaten real meat and wondered if he should even be eating the blend of leftover scraps that went into bologna and became popular during the war when real meat was reserved for the boys in the military. But it filled his empty stomach, and he had learned long ago to be grateful.

Toward nightfall Pinky passed a pear orchard and came to a tiny roadside diner. He planned to buy a hot meal then drive out to the back of the orchard to camp for the night.

The diner had been a caboose for a train and was still the rusty red of the Santa Fe Railroad it had serviced for at least 30 years. The diner would hold a dozen people, if they were all friendly. The only patron sat straight-backed in a booth, facing a cup of coffee and a small plate that, judging from the crumbs, might have held pie a few minutes before. The man wore a grey felt fedora and a brown leather flight jacket above creased khakis and ankle-high dress shoes. He didn't look at Pinky when he came in but seemed to be staring out the window at Pinky's pickup.

As Pinky finished ordering meatloaf with mashed potatoes and gravy from a middle-aged waitress who sported a tall stylish stack of reddish hair and called him "Hon," the man in the fedora got up and moved toward his table. He was bigger than Pinky had first thought, maybe 6-foot-3-inches, and he moved gracefully, almost floating. Pinky looked up at the man towering over him. As was his custom, Pinky had removed his Stetson when he came inside and placed it on the bench seat beside him. A man wearing his hat while eating inside either had an unmannered upbringing or was in a big hurry.

Looking out the window, the fedora man said, "I'll give you $400 for your pickup."

Caught by surprise, Pinky motioned for the man to join him at his table. The man retrieved his heavy and once-white ceramic coffee cup, returned and sat across from Pinky, still studying the pickup. In the time it took the man to get seated, Pinky decided he didn't really need the pickup to get to San Francisco. He'd planned to sell it there but hadn't planned how. Making the sale here would be easier, but it was an odd request from a stranger, and he wanted to think about it for a minute.

"Name's Pinky."

"Frank," the tall man said with a nod.

In the way of men who work with their hands in the soil, Pinky did not offer a handshake, nor did Frank.

"Pleased to make your acquaintance, Frank."

Still looking out the window, Frank said, "I could use a good pickup."

"It's a good one," Pinky said, getting more interested in the new idea of selling the pickup now rather than later. "It'll get you where you want to go with no problems," he added.

"Got a sick aunt in up in Eureka."

Pinky noticed Frank raised his voice and turned his chin toward the waitress when he spoke, almost as though he wanted her to hear. "The Greyhound bus runs that way, don't it?"

"House is too far off the highway."

Having no idea what the old Ford was worth, Pinky countered Frank's offer, "Make it $450, and it's yours."

"Too much."

"OK, make it $425 and keep the camping gear in the back."

The man pulled a wad of bills out of his left front trouser pocket and counted out $425. He had one $5 bill in his hand when he finished counting. His hands looked strong but not calloused or sunburned. The knuckles on his right hand were skinned and swollen. Pinky didn't know what the man did for a living, but he couldn't leave him that short of cash, so he placed the pickup keys in the middle of the table and handed him back a $5 bill.

Frank's expressionless face did not change, nor did he say anything as he pulled another wad of bills from his right trouser pocket, added the $5 bill to it, and put it back. Pinky shook his head. He hated being taken when he tried to do the right thing.

Sitting at the table, holding a cup of coffee in a heavy ceramic mug, head turned sideways, looking handsome and expressionless out the window, Frank resembled the hero on a 1940s movie poster — the one of the man who had joined the Marines and in the adjacent poster would be in full uniform, wearing a helmet, holding a rifle with a bayonet, charging forward. But, Pinky thought, this was a different part of the world than he was used to, and he might not be able to count on things being quite the way they looked.

Still without looking directly at Pinky, Frank stood, scooped up the keys, touched the brim of his fedora, and left so quickly he appeared to Pinky to be fleeing.

Pinky scrambled for his wallet, threw $3 on the table, and ran to the door. "Hey!" he yelled. "How about a ride to the nearest bus stop?"

Frank pointed to a sign above a shed about a hundred feet from the diner. "Greyhound Bus Terminal," it read. Pinky looked back to wave acknowledgment, but the man was already in the pickup. He heard the engine come to life, then his pickup moved slowly out of the diner's parking lot, paused briefly a few feet from the edge of the black top, and then pulled out, turning east.

Pinky could hear the engine rev and a gear grind as Frank got the hang of the gear shift, then the tailgate of the old black Ford swiftly shrunk as Frank floored the gas pedal and wound the engine through second and third gear. Pinky winced at the overly revved engine, and then with a sigh, acknowledged that it was not his truck.

At first Frank didn't look like the shady type, but he appeared to be in a damn big hurry. He had suckered Pinky out of $5, and he had not turned toward Eureka. Standing in the gravel parking lot, Pinky had the feeling of being in a slightly off-kilter world that looked good but wasn't real, like the packing box labels showing broccoli in midnight green against a purple sky — very pretty colors, but nothing any real farmer had ever seen. It occurred to Pinky that his pickup might end up being used for something not exactly on the up and up.

Walking back to the diner, Pinky noticed that he held a bit of regret in his chest at the absence of the noisy, dirty old machine. It had served him well. Then he remembered his suitcase on the front seat of the truck and ran back toward the road, nearly tripping over the suitcase at the edge of the parking lot.

At the beginning of the summer Pinky had been running an 8,000-acre ranch with over 900 head of cattle, three horses, a dog, a cat, a farmhouse, a stock barn, a hay barn, and a mechanical barn with a combine, a tractor and a pickup—not to mention a 12-gauge shotgun and a prized little fly rod. And a .30-30 Winchester. All he had with him now were his newest pair of work clothes, which he was wearing, an oiled canvas slicker, and a small striped cardboard suitcase with his Sunday best, two changes of underwear, his shaving kit, a picture of his mother as a young woman, and a two-inch square sepia picture of him and Wilbur taken in a booth at the Lindsay Orange Blossom Festival.

But Pinky also had hope and a sense of adventure—and a decent enough bank account to take the adventure far—at least to Australia, and perhaps back if need be. He thought it was a fair trade.

Pinky wondered if Frank's shoes were the expensive, long-lasting kangaroo leather he had seen in the Sears catalog. Realizing he had the money now, he thought for a moment of buying such shoes but decided to wait until he got to the land of the kangaroos and see if he still wanted them. The thought of money reminded him that, with the addition of the $420 he still held in his hand, he had close to $2,000 on him, so even though he had seen no one else around except the waitress, he thought it best to rearrange his money in private.

Finding his mashed potatoes, meatloaf and gravy still on his table, he finished eating and then went to the diner's bathroom, put three $1 bills in his pocket, kept $33 in his wallet, put two $100 bills in each shoe, and the rest in a long pocket on the inside of his belt. He looked in the mirror, adjusted his grey Stetson, and then walked toward the bus terminal. There was a nearly new 1951 Chevy parked at the side of the terminal, but inside the terminal was dark, the front door was locked, and no one answered when he called out. So he went back to the diner, wondering if selling his truck had left him stranded.

The waitress was about to close up. "Do buses still come by here?" he asked.

"Next bus is at 7 a.m. tomorrow, headed towards Sacramento.

Bus after that is at noon, going over to Frisco."

"Noon, huh? Could I spend the night on your back porch? I won't be any bother, and I'll buy breakfast here."

Pinky's hopes fell when she shook her head, but what she said was, "No need for you to sleep outside, Hon. We'll move some cartons around in the storage shed out back, put some cardboard down for you to sleep on, and there's a packing blanket that should be enough cover for a night as mild as this."

"Thank you, ma'am." Pinky thought the woman seemed to know how to be kind to itinerants. She wasn't as pretty as Bessie, but she seemed to have the same friendly way of putting people at ease.

"Name's Alice." She pointed at a name tag pinned above an ample bosom.

"Thank you, Alice. What do you know about Frank?"

"Who?"

"Fella that was just here."

"Other than he seemed to want the world to know he had a sick aunt in Eureka, nothing."

Pinky nodded.

"Oh," she added, "and he left that shiny car he arrived in over by the bus stop."

———·———

The storage shed was far better than the worst place Pinky had ever slept — which was far better than the worst place he would sleep in the months ahead. While trying to fall asleep, he wondered again what use Frank might have for his old pickup. What an unusual man, he thought. He was well-dressed like a city man, but big as a steer and as light as a cat on his feet. Although he obviously was a man with someplace to go, wasn't much for words, and though he might be getting into some kind of trouble, Pinky wished, as he drifted off, that Frank had stayed to talk a bit.

The next morning after a late breakfast of pancakes, bacon, eggs and three cups of strong coffee, Pinky bid goodbye to Alice and went to the station where he boarded the bus to San Francisco, gateway to Australia, barely noticing what he was doing because his mind was pondering and re-pondering where the hell his pickup was now.

And the vision of midnight green broccoli floating in a purple sky didn't seem so odd to Pinky today.

TWENTY-THREE
JULY-SEPTEMBER 1954

Not everybody spent the end days of July with Pinky's awareness that a new day had dawned.

Deputy Sheriff John Dillard, who was on patrol in the Once Wide Valley the day Buck's body was found, was not aware that the outline of his future as a leading lawman had been scribbled in blood upon the sun-parched earth of the Sierra Nevada foothills.

And Sheriff Dave Wilson was not aware it was the beginning of his downhill slide.

———

The turmoil around Buck's death was far from sufficient for the very rocks to cry out. But the wind did move on. Slipping upslope through the pines, flowing over the granite passes, and spreading eastward down and across the desert beyond. The truant wind left behind nothing but an eerie stillness. And in that torpor the heat of summer settled without pity upon the Valley of the Once Wide Creek. Not a single blade of the dried summer grasses moved. Not a single leaf quivered in the slightest—not the oak, not the sycamore, not even the limp-stemmed quaking aspen. The entire flora of the valley, from its headwaters to its alluvial end, became as stock-still as the rocks of the land. It was as though the valley had exuded a long sigh and then held its breath.

If it was a lesson, if it had meaning, if it was a message of sorrow, an appropriate admonition, or a declaration of regret, it went unnoticed by the people drawn to the body. And though it was these things, it also was a line of demarcation, a border between worlds, for the people drawn to the body were people unaware of the land, people who could not connect the windless, motionless stench of death with the equally vile stench of greed and anger and self importance, who could not connect the four winds with the breath of life.

Still at the crime scene long after the sun went down, Deputy Dillard, by the dome light of the coroner's four-wheel drive pickup, wrote in his investigative calendar that the body of Buck Wilson was found approximately 10 miles by road from his ranch house, up a side canyon off Once Wide Creek, and that it was likely, given the decomposition and degradation of the body, that he had been shot approximately three days prior.

Standing in the headlights of the coroner's pickup, Sheriff Dave Wilson was telling Captain Clements, for the fourth time, to put every man they had on the case. Every time the order came, Clements would say, "We're on it, Dave," and then jerk his head aside and spit sweet-smelling tobacco juice on the ground. Sheriff Wilson, not normally one to chew, had temporarily adopted the habit as a way to take the edge off the foul smell smothering the area in the hot and windless night. The two maintained a syncopated cadence, alternately spitting and cursing. Deputy Dillard thought they looked like two wheels spinning in mud, gaining no traction but throwing crap everywhere. He shook his head and realized he felt both compassion and contempt.

Dillard wished Undersheriff Bertolli was on the scene, but he was away on leave. Bertolli was ugly as sin, which was why he would never be elected sheriff of Tulare County, but he was the best lawman in the whole office and would have taken charge and maintained order.

Dillard noted to himself that, as seemed to be the case more often than not, it wasn't so much that somebody was shot, it was more about *who* was shot that had everybody all stirred up. Not all lives were assigned the same worth, so not all deaths were assigned the same consternation.

The deputy refocused on writing his report and went over the afternoon's events in his mind. He had arrived at the scene in mid-afternoon and learned that a photographer from a San Francisco newspaper had stopped alongside the road to photograph of a flock of buzzards sitting across the hillside on jutting rocks and in dead trees. Normally the birds would be riding the rising heat thermals and soaring high above the valley floor. Deciding to investigate the unusual behavior of the birds, the photographer first noted the dead calm, and then over the first hill he found a bloated, smelly, decomposing, badly disfigured body. Many critters enjoy flesh — mice, rats, buzzards, raccoons, coyotes, possums and any number of insects. None of them have any respect for the difference between critter flesh and human flesh, so the body was sickeningly disfigured. The photographer had puked and then went back to his car to drive to the nearest telephone. On the way he had passed Deputy Dillard and nearly killed them both trying to wave him down.

Hearing the disturbed man's disturbing story, Dillard had driven to a spot where his police radio would work and called Sergeant Gordon who, eager to be in the field and do "real" police work, announced he was on his way.

The body was on land owned by Buck Wilson, so, not expecting Gordon to arrive in less than an hour, Dillard left the photographer on the road to meet Gordon and drove to Buck's ranch house to let him know of the grisly find. Neither Buck nor his wife, Mindy, were at home, so Dillard had driven back to the scene of the crime, arriving at the same time as damn near all the brass, from Sheriff Wilson on down, who having noted the good fortune of a newspaper photographer being at the scene of a dead body, had plans to get their pictures in the newspaper doing serious police work.

The coroner arrived slightly ahead of the mob, finished an initial investigation of the body, and was beginning a briefing of the brass and the press on his initial findings. He had stunned everyone with the announcement that the body was that of Buck Wilson, who apparently had died of a gunshot wound to the chest. And that's when the brass' sense of good fortune faded, discipline and confidence went south, and Sheriff Wilson started repeating himself.

The photographer jumped immediately into action, and with no apparent reverence for the gravity of the situation or sensitivity to the pain of death, began documenting the gruesome scene. Dillard figured the photographs shot in those moments were the pictures with the most human interest and would most likely be those printed in the newspapers. Dave Wilson seemed startled, anxious and even confused, but Dillard could see no evidence of the grief that might be expected upon the death of one's brother. He wondered why the coroner had been so insensitive as to not take Dave Wilson aside to give him the bad news in private.

John Dillard sat for a moment taking in the scene around him, noticing the indecency, the disrespect, the lack of common sense and discipline, and the reprehensible and soul-wrenching act of murder, and he felt a momentary shame for his species. As he thought these things, a breath of air moved a few stray strands of hair across his forehead. John Dillard shook his head, resumed his role as Deputy Dillard, and settled back into his task of documentation.

———··———

As this scene played out in the Valley of the Once Wide Creek, Pinky Wollerman was boarding a ship near San Francisco that would get under way for Australia at midnight, and Franklin Ventura was crouched behind Pinky's old truck on a gravel road near Lake Tahoe, waiting to ambush the FBI agent who was investigating an uncle to whom Franklin owed a debt.

———··———

Deputy Dillard was contacted by an old friend who suggested she might have firsthand information about the murder.

He fed the witness's words back to her, "You're sure it was a small man? And you don't know who it was?"

The feedback sounded confrontational, and Ruby Watkins did not want her statement questioned.

"Well, no self-respecting woman would be dressed in jeans, a work shirt and a damned Stetson hat, much less be carrying a rifle. Besides, whoever it was drove off in a pickup. How many women do you know who can drive a pickup? And he leaped over the barb wire fence like it was nothing. How many women you know can do that? And, no, he was too far away to see who it was, and the brim of his hat hid his face."

Ruby was satisfied that her delivery had communicated an adequate level of impatience with being challenged. In fact, Ruby liked John Dillard, which was why she had contacted him rather than someone else in the sheriff's office. But she would not have her story questioned. She sat back in her chair and stared tight-lipped at the handsome young man.

Deputy Sheriff John Dillard shrugged at Miss Watkins, his Sunday school teacher when he was 10 years old, and nodded. He was only stalling for time and hadn't meant to suggest that the suspect was a woman, but he wondered why Ruby had reacted so adamantly. In fact, he did know several women who would and could do some or all of the things mentioned, but this was Ruby Watkins, and she was nine years older than he and as lovely as when he fell in love with her when she walked into his Sunday School class and smiled. Red-faced, he nodded again, shifted his weight in the now-uncomfortable wooden chair, and regretted having aroused Miss Watkins' ire.

He politely asked her to go over the details again, listened attentively to her description of the man, then wrote in his report, "Miss Ruby Watkins of 1350 North Fifth Avenue, Lemon Cove, California, was on a Saturday drive in the foothills to visit her friend Mrs. Linda Carter, who lives near Clover Meadow, when she passed a black pickup parked beside the road very near where the body of Buck Wilson was found. Looking in the rearview mirror, she noticed a man walking across the hillside and stopped her car on a curve where she could clearly see through the side window. Miss Ruby saw a man with a rifle jump over the barbed wire fence at the bottom of the hill, get into the pickup, and drive toward Exeter. Miss Ruby said the suspect (whom she referred to as the murderer) was short and thin, but moved like he was comfortable in the mountains. Miss Watkins is a highly reputable woman with a clear head, making her a trustworthy eyewitness."

Deputy Dillard did not feel certain about what he wrote in his report, but it sounded fine when he read it. The first time Ruby told the story, she said the person "moved gracefully across the hillside" and "climbed over the barbed wire fence." The second time she told it, she said the suspect "moved like he was comfortable in the mountains" and "jumped the barbed wire fence." But Johnny Dillard wasn't going to go openly at odds with Ruby Watkins. He'd simply have to keep his mind open during the investigation.

Deputy Dillard drove back to his station in Exeter and handed the report of his interview to Sergeant Gordon. Gordon stopped reading before reaching the end, tapped the page with his finger, and said, "So, according to Ruby Watkins, we're looking for an agile man, smallish in stature, with a wiry build, dressed in denim trousers, a grey chambray work shirt and wearing a grey Stetson?" Dillard was about ready to suggest that it could have been a woman when Sergeant Gordon smiled and said, "I know a man of that description."

Gordon walked to the one window in his office and looked east toward the foothills.

"Pinky Wollerman," he said. "His ranch is right next to Buck's. He wears blue jeans and favors chambray work shirts, and he's small and wiry, with very pale blue eyes and white skin that always seems sunburned, so even in winter he's never without his Stetson hat. And he keeps a rifle in his pickup, and the pickup is black."

Deputy Dillard noted to himself that almost all the ranchers in this part of the country favored blue jeans and chambray work shirts and wore Stetsons and drove pickups, with black being the favorite color, and every one of them kept a rifle on a rack behind the seat. And, due to the kind of work they did day in and day out, most were fit and climbed fences on a regular basis. He figured the only thing they had gained from Ruby's testimony was that they were looking for somebody small, which narrowed the potential suspects down from almost everybody to more than a dozen men he could think of off the top of his head. More if it wasn't a local man. And, after thinking about Ruby's description, he still wasn't convinced the suspect wasn't a woman. Dillard opened his mouth to express these thoughts, but Gordon cut him off.

"A few weeks back, at a Sunday potluck, somebody said that Wollerman was leaving on some sort of trip to a faraway place. By itself you might think that's a rumor. But there's another thing that everybody seems to know for sure, and that's that for several months now Pinky and Buck have been at odds over something."

Sergeant Gordon folded his meaty arms over his chest, raised his right eyebrow, and confided to Deputy Dillard, "Not to jump the gun, but you know we may have to find out what Pinky Wollerman knows about all of this. He fits the description, lives in the area of the murder, and has an ongoing gripe with Buck Wilson." Gordon unfolded his arms and, staring up at the foothills in the distance, said, "And, he just left town without telling anyone where he was headed." Turning back to the young deputy and jabbing a finger toward him he added, "Get out to his ranch and find somebody that knows where he is."

When Deputy Dillard finished his assigned tasks, he reported to Sergeant Gordon that Pinky's hired hand, Kazuko Nakamura, said Pinky had been gone about three or four days but claimed he had no knowledge of his current whereabouts. Sergeant Gordon shook his head, muttered, "Very suspicious," went to the teletype machine and sent out an APB for Pinky Wollerman with the byline "Suspected in the murder of Buck Wilson."

Pinky's APB immediately became the primary topic of conversation in the foothill communities of Tulare County. Few who heard that Pinky was wanted for Buck Wilson's murder doubted in the least that he had something to do with it. Pinky was known to them as an odd loner they believed had come to California to escape the Dust Bowl, as had thousands of other shiftless Okies. And he had been pushed around by Buck in public. They also figured Buck had gotten his due. More than a couple of these conversations had an undercurrent of admiration for Pinky having taken care of the long-simmering problem of a man who walked all over anyone he thought was in his way.

————··————

When Undersheriff Bertolli returned to the office and was briefed, he thought that any fool would know that Dave shouldn't be involved in the investigation because he would be upset by his brother's death and might allow that to cloud his judgment. And every shred of evidence he touched would be suspect at the accused's trial. But Dave wasn't just any fool, he was Bertolli's boss, so with no indication of the contempt he felt, he suggested that they could avoid tainting the investigative conclusions by having someone other than Dave oversee the investigation. Dave agreed, so Bertolli appointed Captain Clements to coordinate the investigation into Buck's death, directing him to not discuss developments in the investigation with Sheriff Wilson.

Back in his office, Clements delegated the lead role. "Gordon! Get to work finding that asshole Pinky Wollerman, and do it now! And I don't want to hear any goddamned excuses!"

As Gordon left his office, Clements added, "And don't bother Sheriff Wilson while you're doing it." With the exception of the admonition to not bother Sheriff Wilson, Sergeant Gordon said something similar to Deputy Dillard, knowing full well that Dillard had been working the investigation since the day Buck's body was found.

Dillard nodded, then when Gordon left the room, shook his head and continued with the investigation.

Following up at Pinky Wollerman's bank, Dillard was told they did not hold a mortgage on Pinky's land and thought he owned it outright. He had made a small withdrawal a couple of days before Buck's death, but unlike a man expecting to run, had left a substantial sum behind. Even so, Dillard couldn't remove Pinky from the suspect list because Dillard knew that murder wasn't always part of a rational plan.

Dillard's second stop was the local fount of all of Exeter's public information and half of its confidential information—the barber, Ralph Watkins. Ralph mentioned four interesting things.

The first was that Bill Jenkins, in the confessional of the barber chair, told Ralph how a freak storm had flattened his house and he had lost almost all his livestock and equipment. While Bill was down and out, Buck skinned him good, buying his horse, saddle and tack for less than half their value. Ralph noted that Bill, normally an easygoing man, was pretty riled up about it and said some things that left Ralph thinking Bill could do harm to Buck if given the chance.

The second had to do with Kazuko Nakamura. Dillard knew that after the war Kazuko had been hired to help out on the Eldridge farm, previously his parents' farm. Ralph remembered that when Kazuko first moved back, Buck had bragged that when the war started and the Japanese were being herded into camps, he had made sure the relocation people knew that Kaz was a trained soldier and therefore, was a bigger threat than most of the Japanese. They sent Kaz to Tule Lake with the hard cases rather than to Manzanar with the more trusted internees. Kazuko's parents were sent to Manzanar and died during their first winter there. Ralph said that Buck had laughed about it. When asked, Ralph said that he'd never heard Kaz speak ill of Buck, but that if it was most men, they'd have a grudge to settle. On further questioning Ralph admitted that he did not know if Kazuko knew that Buck was responsible for his trip to Tule Lake.

The third interesting thing was that Buck had either stolen or borrowed a tractor, but in either version of the story it was in his possession without the permission of the owner, Arturo Hernandez. Arturo and his boys had gotten into a standoff with Buck. Arturo got his tractor back, but both Buck and Arturo were still pissed as hell over the incident, and everybody seemed to think those two were going to go head to head someday. Nobody gave Arturo much of a chance of winning that one with his fists, and Ralph speculated he might have a better chance by potting Buck from a distance.

Fourth, the minister who ran the Poor Farm south of Exeter had raged at Buck for impregnating one of his wards. When the young woman heard that Buck was dead, she hitched a ride south, some thought in search of an abortion. Hitchhiking and abortion were dangerous choices, and the minister feared for the young woman's safety. Ralph was appalled that the minister actually cursed Buck.

Of the four suspects, the minister and his ward were at the bottom of Deputy Dillard's growing list of suspects. He knew the other three men. Bill Jenkins was about 5-foot-10 with a lanky build and an experienced hunter who filled out his deer tags every season. Kazuko Nakamura was also a small man and had been a sharpshooter for the ROTC when he was in college at Berkeley. Arturo was a big man, more suited to steer wrestling than bull riding, but his oldest boy was short and slightly built. Any one of the three, or Pinky Wollerman, could have done the deed. But Deputy Dillard had acquired an additional suspect that he wasn't going to say anything about to anyone, unless something ironclad fell in his lap. You just don't go around investigating the county sheriff's wife — not if you wanted to keep your job. Hell, not even if you wanted to keep on living in the county. Besides, the source was an odd one.

Over the years, while waiting at the courthouse to testify on various cases, Dillard would sometimes play poker with a young attorney practicing with a prominent local firm. On one recent occasion the young attorney, in the strictest confidence of course, told Dillard that Buck Wilson, a client of their firm, had willed his ranch to his sister's kid, but had recently changed the named heir, and it wasn't his brother's kid. Nobody knew who the new heir was, though his personal guess was that Buck must have a kid of his own. Then he went on to confidentially explain that, under the original will, Dave was the designated trustee until his sister's kid came of age, which effectively put the ranch under his control, and therefore under Twyla's influence. He said that Dave's wife, Twyla, was quite upset about the change. With an emphatic nod he repeated the words "quite upset," and looked at Dillard to make sure his point had been heard. Twyla had gone screaming crazy, he said, when she heard that Buck had decided not to leave it to either one of his nephews.

That was apparently all the man had to say on the matter, and as though no discussion had occurred, went back to dealing cards while taunting Dillard about his measly bets.

Deputy Dillard knew he had heard more detail than would be professionally acceptable and wondered why. The young attorney's uncle had been a principal in the law firm that Buck had employed and had recently been appointed to a judgeship. As soon as the man assumed the autonomy of a judge, it became clear to everyone that he had no respect for Sheriff Wilson and, by extension, the sheriff's office, so Dillard thought he should be suspicious of the casually slipped information. But Dillard also knew that Dave's wife, Twyla, was a nut case—totally crazy when she was riled, which didn't take much. He didn't know if she was capable of murder, but all three of the murderers he had seen in his short law enforcement career had been so far above the suspicion of their neighbors and family that nobody thought they were capable of such a heinous crime. He decided not to say anything about Twyla to anyone, but he would keep his ear to the ground.

Deputy Dillard later called it an obfuscating event in the investigation. Sergeant Gordon's name for it sounded roughly the same. The event occurred when the El Dorado County Sheriff's Office called to say that they had recovered the pickup described in the APB for Pinky Wollerman. Thinking Pinky was in the vicinity of Lake Tahoe, Sergeant Gordon insisted that Deputy Dillard drive there and investigate. Given the tepid cooperation between an office that considered itself sophisticated and one they considered backwater, it took Dillard more than a day to ascertain that a Franklin Ventura had been killed in a failed attempt to kill an FBI agent, and that Ventura had been driving Wollerman's pickup. Wollerman had not been seen. Following up on a matchbook in Ventura's pocket, Dillard discovered a waitress at a diner west of Rio Vista who said that Ventura had purchased Wollerman's truck, and that Wollerman had caught the bus to San Francisco, saying he was bound for Australia. It took Dillard another two days to find that Wollerman had boarded a tramp steamer that very likely was bound for Sydney, Australia, but would undoubtedly stop in unspecified ports along the way, and that those stops could alter the order of landing in Australian ports.

Dillard realized that the red herring of finding the pickup in Lake Tahoe had given Pinky enough time to disappear on the ocean.

Dillard contacted all the major ports in Australia asking to be notified if the steamer, Eastern Song, should arrive. He received a call from Perth, Australia, at the end of September saying the Eastern Song had arrived the week before. No reason was given for the delay of the notification.

———··———

Sergeant Gordon stood in Dave Wilson's office. "I'll quit before I'll go down there, Dave." He had only the vaguest idea what Australia was like, but knew he didn't want to go.

Sheriff Dave Wilson laughed. He knew Sergeant Gordon wouldn't quit the best job he'd ever had, but he wasn't going to force the issue. "Then find someone who can do your job for you. And make it someone we can rely on to keep us informed."

With no idea why he had been summoned, Deputy Dillard stood cautiously at ease before Sergeant Gordon and Sheriff Wilson in the Sheriff's_P private office.

But when given the assignment to go to Australia after Wollerman, Dillard was stunned. He must have asked for how long because Sergeant Gordon was saying, "For however long it takes to find Wollerman."

Deputy Dillard didn't even know exactly where Australia was. He thought it was on the other side of China, which was on the opposite side of the world. "When do I have to leave?"

"You told me in your report yesterday that Wollerman arrived in Perth, Australia, a little over a week ago. I'm not sure how you get to Australia, but it shouldn't take more than a week. He'll only have a two-week head start on you when you get there, and while Australia is a big country, from what I've heard, there's not a lot of places that have people. A short American albino should be easy to trace, so you should be able to catch up to him within a month. Two at the most."

"You've got to get on Pinky's trail as soon as possible," Gordon said. "And think of all the world you're going to see."

Dave Wilson's political mind never rested. The next election was, as always, uppermost in his mind. He had noticed what a fine figure Deputy Dillard made in his uniform, which he kept tidier than most of the deputies. Dave was well-aware that his roping championship was a big reason he'd been elected sheriff. He wasn't as good with the rope as he was back then, so now he wasn't doing a damn thing on the rodeo circuit. He was afraid that someone who had a name might take him on and beat him—maybe someone like Dillard who had gone all the way to Australia to nab a murderer. There were more experienced deputies than Dillard, but he was tall, with broad shoulders and a ruggedly handsome face. And he was young, but old enough to have a look of authority. He also had a homespun way about him that convinced everyone within a couple of minutes that he had been their best friend for years. And he was smart, kept his head down and seemed to really enjoy police work. At present he was nothing more than a good deputy, but a few pictures in the newspaper could do wonders for a man's image—even make him look like a leader. Unfortunately, the paper ran a story about Dillard figuring out where Pinky had gone, so it was too late to fire him.

Dave didn't know why he hadn't thought of this opportunity earlier. It would be easy to bring back the Wollerman runt from Australia, and going halfway around the world to catch a murderer would make a great story in the press. If nothing exciting happened, it was far enough away that exciting things could be reported to have happened.

Sheriff Dave Wilson made a command decision. "Deputy Dillard, go back to work and forget this assignment. This one's too important to send the likes of you."

Both Dillard and Gordon stood open-mouthed looking at their boss. Gordon spread his hands and shrugged.

"I'm going to handle this personally," Dave said. Then he stood abruptly and ordered both men to get out of his office and get back to work.

As soon as the hallway door closed behind the two confused men, Sheriff Wilson called to his secretary, "Millie! Figure out how to get me to Perth, Australia, the quickest way possible."

Dave Wilson had no idea what that involved, but that was why he had Millie.

"And have Bertolli announce to the press that he's in charge of this investigation, not me."

Dave paused, trying to think what would sound good to the press.

"And have him say that since everyone in the office is currently overworked fighting crime here in Tulare County, he decided I was the most logical one to send for what is little more than a liaison effort.

"And that I'm only to act as a resource for the police organizations in Australia as they apprehend the suspect Pinky Wollerman."

Sheriff Wilson came out of his office, pacing back and forth as he talked.

"I'll, of course, escort him back to Tulare County, but purely in a custodial role, not as an investigator. Make sure to have him emphasize there is no reason to think I'll do anything but escort him back here so he can be questioned professionally by our investigative team and, if needed, properly tried in a court of law.

"Tomorrow will be soon enough for that announcement. He'll have the right words for all that."

Sheriff Wilson started back to his office, turned in the doorway and quietly added, "Oh, and Millie, let Mrs. Wilson know that I had to leave suddenly in the line of duty."

———·———

Millie, who had been undisturbed by the thought of figuring out how to get the sheriff to the other side of the world, suddenly felt terror-stricken. "I should probably wait until you're gone, Sheriff."

"That might be wise, Millie. Give me a three-hour head start."

Millie knew that Sheriff Dave Wilson had never understood the depth of the mental affliction of his wife. Millie had moved next door to Twyla's family when Twyla was 6. At first Millie thought she was seeing a spoiled child, but later she became certain there was a more serious problem submerged in the girl's emotional makeup. Over the years she had seen Twyla emotionally explode when the only issue was that she didn't get what she wanted—whether that was a dress when she was 12, or a car when she turned 16, or later on, a man she wanted to screw. As a young woman, Twyla gained greater control of herself, so the explosions seldom happened in the open, but Millie had seen the nastiness. Twyla always made sure the people who crossed her paid for it. Millie knew that Sheriff Wilson ought not to be simply irritated by Twyla's unstable moods. He ought to be seriously afraid.

Millie knew that any flight overseas started with a flight from Fresno to San Francisco, so she said, "Get someone to drive you to the Fresno airport, and I'll have your ticket waiting for you."

Millie didn't particularly like the idea of telling Bertolli what a stupid thing their sheriff had done, but the apprehension she felt for dealing with a pissed-off undersheriff was nothing compared to the apprehension she had for dealing with Twyla.

Two hours after Dave left, Bertolli, having been informed of Dave's departure by the deputy who was commandeered to take him to the Fresno airport, stormed silently through the office in the way only a large, muscular man of dark moods can. The only thing Bertolli said to Millie was, "Don't say anything to anyone about this until I tell you to."

Millie relayed to him the information Dave had asked to be released to the press and was amazed by how much a pulse in the temple could reveal about a man's anger. By Millie's count, 15 pulse beats passed before Bertolli, ever more cryptic as he was ever more angry, said only, "Nothing." After another five pulse beats he added, "Nobody." Millie was only too happy to oblige.

Then, as luck would have it, Twyla called the office to speak with her husband shortly before Millie was to call her, and Millie gave her an honest but abbreviated answer. "Sheriff Wilson is out of the office on an investigation." Millie always knew every detail of her boss's whereabouts, including when he went to the bathroom and for how long, but she never shared that information with Twyla. And it always pissed Twyla off, so it was not unexpected when she began cursing. At first Twyla's voice was low and strained, suggesting that her throat was constricted and she was perhaps not breathing, but she soon built up enough volume that Millie had to hold the phone away from her ear. After listening to Twyla rage blue for a couple of minutes, Millie suggested that Undersheriff Bertolli might be able to provide further information. Millie knew that Twyla despised Bertolli and expected the response; Twyla slammed the receiver into its cradle, and in the hum of the empty phone line Millie breathed a sigh of relief. The sigh dissolved into a chuckle as she imagined the contortions that must have been rippling across Twyla's face. From a distance it was funny — in a nervous sort of way.

———··———

The following afternoon, Millie mentioned to Bertolli that the grapevine was overworked and nearly every deputy in the department knew about Dave's travels.

Bertolli looked at her for a moment and said, "So?"

"Well," she said, "wouldn't you like to submit an announcement to the press before someone else in the office leaks something?"

She found Bertolli's response interesting. At first he gave his typical brief response, "No." Then, suggesting his anger had subsided, confided, "This is an opportunity, Millie. Seeing who slips what information to the press is our chance to see who's planning on running against Dave in the next election."

"While there's still time to discredit their careers?" Millie asked.

Bertolli looked at her blankly, then left without responding.

Millie was glad she was not responsible for the circus being played out. But Millie enjoyed a good circus. Dave's trip to Perth, due to the spare flight schedules and the uncoordinated scheduling of the three different airlines needed to get to and travel within Australia, was, with layovers, going to take nine days — if the Southern Hemisphere's winter weather cooperated. She smiled as she made plans to be unavailable for any explanation when Sheriff Wilson arrived at each of his stops.

Millie went home that night, fixed herself a double scotch, and toasted the entertainment value of the over-inflated ego.

A week after Sheriff Wilson left for Australia, Deputy Dillard decided to pursue his suspicion that a woman might have been involved in Buck's murder and decided to check in with Ruby again. On Sunday he followed her from the foyer of the Baptist Church and caught her as she reached her car.

"Morning, Ruby." Deputy Dillard sounded casual but his smile gave away his pleasure at seeing Ruby. "How are things going?"

"It's afternoon, Johnny." Ruby returned the smile. "Don't you carry a watch?"

Johnny Dillard, the boy who had grown up entranced and intimidated by Ruby Watkins, beamed. "Yes, ma'am. I guess the sermon was just so damned fine, I lost track of time."

Ruby laughed and gave him a look that told Deputy Dillard his charm wasn't wasted. About a half hour into their impromptu lunch date at the A&W Drive In, Dillard turned the casual talk to Sheriff Dave Wilson going away to Australia on business and followed that with a question: "Do you and Twyla still get together the way you used to?"

Ruby's smile crumpled like a time-lapse motion picture of mud drying. Then she began to cry. Johnny tossed a $5 bill on the counter and quickly escorted her out to her car. He gave her a long and gentle hug, and with real tenderness, asked her what was wrong and what he could do to help.

Ruby confided that both she and her friend Millie had noticed how Twyla had blown a fuse when she found out her husband had left for Australia and then had calmed down after she found out he was in pursuit of Pinky Wollerman who, the sheriff's office had decided, was the prime suspect in Buck's murder. Ruby said she thought she might know why Pinky's pursuit had such a calming effect. She had been worried about withholding information ever since her first interview with Johnny, but now she knew she had to tell him what she had seen.

"The person I saw climb the fence and drive away in a black pickup?"

"Yeah?" Johnny said, noticing the switch back from "jumped the fence" to "climbed the fence."

"I think it was somebody I know." Ruby was trying to catch her breath, trying to talk, trying to come clean. Johnny squeezed her hand, and she focused enough to say, "I think it was Twyla Wilson."

"Why do you think it was her?"

"Well, you know how you can tell someone at a distance just by their gait?"

Johnny nodded and raised his eyebrows in a look of concern.

"The graceful way that person moved... it sure reminded me of Twyla." Ruby paused and Johnny took both of her hands in his. "And the black pickup was sparkly clean or new," she said. "And Dave and Twyla bought a black Ford pickup for Orson to drive during his senior year. And Orson keeps it spotless."

Somewhere between the tears Ruby shed inside the A&W and her pronunciation of the word "spotless," Deputy Dillard made an irrational decision about their relationship. Perhaps the decision had been made when he was 10, and he was only now able to be aware of it and do something about it. He hoped that Ruby would know how he felt without his telling her because he did not know how to do that. He knew he was not going to ask Ruby why she hadn't told him these things at their first interview. That could spoil a thing far more valuable than the investigation. The thing to remember was that she was honest with him now.

Gently, while looking deeply into her eyes, he said, "Ruby?"

———··———

Ruby could feel the trust welling up in her for this now-grown man whom she had always known was going to make something of himself. She felt something else also, deep below her navel, and was surprised at herself given their history together and the seriousness of their discussion. She momentarily had trouble focusing on his words.

"Don't say anything to anyone," Deputy Dillard said. "I'm going to poke around a little, and I need for this information to remain totally confidential."

But Ruby had more to say. "It gets worse, Johnny. A couple of weeks before Buck was shot, I went over to Twyla's for coffee. She was in a real dither with her hair in a muss and pacing around the room, looking sort of wild-eyed and angry at the same time. She told me to come back some other time. I asked her what was wrong and she said 'that son-of-a-bitch Buck'—her words, and she was nearly screaming—had changed his will, and neither Dave nor Orson would ever have a chance for the ranch that was rightfully theirs. Then she pushed me toward the front door, and she was so distraught, I decided it might be a good idea to leave. The more I think about that day, the more worrisome it seems."

Deputy Dillard knew that investigating this lead could put him crossways with Sheriff Dave Wilson. But Dave was in Australia, and Dillard figured if he worked fast and maybe let someone else, perhaps the district attorney's office, draw any investigative conclusions, his job might not be in danger.

As he turned his options over in his mind, he realized that he had taken Ruby in his arms, and she was hugging him tightly. When the two released Ruby's cheeks were quite rosy and she said, "Call me later?"

"Count on it," he said and went, self-conscious but happily lightheaded, to his patrol car.

———··———

"Did you see Buck's obituary, Willie?"

Thomas O'Dell, former law firm associate and brother-in-law of Judge William Garrett sat in the judge's chambers. Tom knew his brother-in-law, having been appointed to a judgeship only one month ago, now hated being called by his childhood name, Willie, so Tom aired it out once in a while just to piss him off.

But for some reason the fledgling judge did not rise to the bait. Instead, he sat back in his overstuffed chair, closed his eyes, smiled and said, "Read it aloud to me, Tom. I think I might like to hear the sound of it."

"I'll tell you how it sounds, Willie. It doesn't sound like it's about Buck Wilson is how it sounds." Tom knew that using the familiar name twice would be pushing it, so he went on quickly. "It doesn't sound entirely like him anyway. Sounds more like they mixed in some other man's life story with Buck's."

Thomas O'Dell was curious about his brother-in-law's smile and why he was so interested in hearing an obituary read aloud, but he snapped out the folds of the weekly Exeter Gazette and prepared to read. Then, sensing he was being watched, he lowered it. The face he saw peering back at him was a judge's face rather than a brother-in-law's face, and the smile had faded. Tom looked down at the paper and waited.

When the judge finally spoke he said, "Tom, I told you not to call me Willie when we're at the courthouse."

"There's nobody here this late except the night janitor," Tom said and looked up. When he realized the judge's face was not going to dissolve into a brother-in-law's face, he added, "your honor." As soon as he said this, he realized that his sarcasm had shown through, so he braced himself and waited.

Judge Garrett cocked his head sideways and narrowed his eyes. "Thomas, someday you will regret your disrespectful sense of familiarity with me."

Tom looked back at the paper and started reading, hoping to conceal his hatred.

"Charles Anders Wilson, born September 4, 1920, and known as Buck since age 5 because of his large stature, was a fifth-generation cattle rancher in the Once Wide Valley of California."

Tom looked up to see that the judge's smile had returned and his eyes were closed, as though he were savoring the words. He wondered what his asshole brother-in-law was up to.

"Buck passed away unexpectedly while working on the ranch he loved and was laid to rest in the Wilson family cemetery in the Once Wide Valley. A graduate of Exeter High School, Mr. Wilson obtained a bachelor's degree in agricultural science from the University of California, Berkeley, and played fullback for four years with the Golden Bears football team. When the U.S. was invaded by Japan, Mr. Wilson joined the Marine Corps and served his country with distinguished recognition as a captain, first in New Zealand and then in Japan during the post-war occupation. He was honorably discharged in 1946 with numerous and various war medals. Mr. Wilson was an elder in his local Methodist Church. Over a lifetime of dedicated community service he held every leadership position of the Elbow Creek Grange, was a staunch supporter of the Exeter High School Monarchs booster club, selflessly provided much-needed materials and labor at the San Joaquin Poor Farm, and was a coordinator for the Tulare County Sheriff's Mountain Search and Rescue Team. Buck relished work and was there to help whenever his family or community needed him."

Tom glanced up at the judge who was leaning back in his chair with his hands resting on his ample stomach, fingers interlaced and eyes closed, and he still had that silly-ass smile on his face.

"He enjoyed hunting and fishing, rain or shine, and spent many happy times with his family at their cabin near the Mineral King Valley. His skills training pack animals are legendary, and his ranch supplied many of the strings of horses and mules used by the area's

National Forest and National Park services and by several Sierra pack stations.

"Mr. Wilson was preceded in death by his parents, Bradford and Sarah. He is survived by his true love, Mindy (nee Sawyer), whom he married upon graduation from high school; a son, Logan Wilson Macadam of Once Wide Valley; a sister, Linda Forrester, of Porterville and her husband, Tyler, and son, Denton; and a brother, David Wilson, Sheriff of Tulare County, his wife, Twyla, and their son, Orson. He is mourned by many friends throughout the foothill communities he so greatly cared for. The only consolation for Buck's loving family and friends in this tender time is the knowledge he is now walking with God, side by side with Jesus Christ."

Judge Garrett opened his eyes and turned his head toward his brother-in-law. "Sounds like a great man. What concerns did you have with his obituary?"

"What the hell's wrong with it is I grew up with Buck Wilson, and the man was a complete asshole." Tom held the paper aloft, pointed at the obituary, and growled, "This obituary makes him sound like a pillar of virtue."

Judge Garrett spoke evenly. "Buck Wilson was a pillar of the community, if not a pillar of virtue. Buck made things happen. Buck held things together. Buck was a leader. Not a loved leader, but a respected leader."

"People were afraid of him, if that's what you mean," Tom said shaking his head. "And from what I saw, with good reason." Tom threw the paper on the judge's desk and jabbed a finger at it, "And 'passed away unexpectedly,' my ass. The son-of-a-bitch took a bullet right through the heart. There's a murder investigation going on, for God's sake!" Tom lowered his voice, leaned in as though offering a confidence, and said, "I can think of more than a dozen people off the top of my head who at one time or another would've wanted to kill this virtuous community leader."

Tom stood up and paced the room, raising his voice again. "And what's this about a son, Logan Macadam? Considering how Buck was with the women, he probably had a lot of unaccounted-for kids, but nobody I know has ever heard of a son, which seems a little odd if the kid lives in Once Wide Valley. And what the hell kind of a name is Logan?" Tom opened his arms in exasperation. "And who writes this crap?"

Judge Garrett's eyes were small and very dark, which made it difficult even when his mood was pleasant to see exactly where he was looking, but at that moment they narrowed so intently that Tom could not even see the pupils. Nevertheless, Tom was quite certain he was the object of their focus. In the silence Tom noticed the hum of the air conditioner through the ceiling vent, the wetness of his underarms, and the accompanying smell of perspiration built up over the course of a long day of lawyering. When the voice came at him, it was a low rumble, landing upon his head like thunder from a dry summer storm.

"I did," the judge said.

After staring at his open-mouthed and dumbfounded brother-in-law for a while, the judge added, "And you're going to help your law firm make sure that nothing gets in the way of his son Logan inheriting that Once Wide Valley ranch." The judge stood and moved to the door of his office where he looked into the hallway before adding, "Nothing! Hear me? Not some jealous relative, and not some hack's interpretation of the will. We will fight them all for as long as it takes."

Tom realized he had just been told that Buck's wife, Mindy, would not inherit the ranch, but as a spouse she would be entitled to half of the assets, which meant that somewhere there was a big pile of stock or bonds or cash. But why would Willie be so concerned about the boy?

"Why worry so much about some unknown bastard kid?" he asked, his voice more feeble than he would have liked.

What the judge said was, "Because Charles Anders Wilson was a valued client of your law firm, and that is what he would have wanted us to do."

Tom knew that when the judge said "your" law firm, he meant the law firm he was a partner in before he became a judge, and the firm he still had some indirect associations with. And he suspected the unsaid response was something like, "Because the bigger and the longer drawn out the challenges, the bigger piece of the dead man's pie I get," but he said nothing. He also noted the judge had said "not some jealous relative," and wondered if he should move Twyla Wilson to the top of the suspect list alongside Pinky Wollerman.

'TWENTY-'FOUR
SEPTEMBER 1954

With the eyes of a first-timer Pinky walked down the gangplank of the steamer and into the city of Perth. He was in Australia, the country he had dreamed about, and he was full of expectation.

The incident with Frank had seriously distilled Pinky's possessions, which he had consolidated into a blue canvas rucksack. Without being aware of a reason or searching for one, Pinky pulled out the picture of his mother. It was a black and white picture, and she was a young woman standing beside an equally young Hazel Erlewine.

The women were dressed in identical shifts. Pinky remembered his mother's dress with the big pockets that, before the dry years won, always had something in them—clothespins on the way to the clothesline, an egg or two from the hen house, or a tomato from the garden. The dress was dotted with little spots that his mother told him were roses, a kind of flower, she had to explain, for in those days there were none in their world. The women stood in front of a squat wooden house gracelessly plumped in the dust of the barren land that Oklahoma had become. On the back of the photograph a message in the labored scrawl of a skill seldom applied said, "Me and Hazel in the good old days." Pinky's memories of his mother were all gentleness and caring, but the context of the place was all dust and drought and the Depression, and there had never been a father, and the years of his own struggles had taught Pinky how tough and resilient she really had been. Those were desperate times, and yet the two women smiled and wrote an inscription suggesting they had faced down the hardness around them. Pinky looked out toward Perth and knew that he had come far and liked that he had, and as he often did, gave silent thanks for the character and grit of the people who gave him the opportunity. He placed the picture back in its place and walked into Perth.

The road up to the town from the ship's landing was wide and lined with stately London plane trees. A gentle breeze at his back carried the scent of the ocean and provided a nice balance of balmy and cool that was so comfortable he would not have noticed except that it was not what he expected. Pinky was disturbed at the tranquil, comfortable, modern city before him. There were no basic frontier buildings as he had expected. Nor was there the heat, nor the dust nor the desolation he had been bracing himself for over the past months of reading and dreaming.

Perth was a fancier place than Pinky expected.

His mind's eye picture of Australia had been bleak, with mostly rock stretching to the horizon on all sides except where there might be red dust and sand. If there was any green at all, it would be in patches of grass as scarce as dust bunnies in a nunnery and even then the blades so widely scattered one could see a field of green only by lying flat and looking across the land at ground level. Other vegetation would be equally rare—desert oaks, one to the acre, and looking like worn out mops atop crooked handles, and scrubby little bushes splashed in passing with the remnant green of worn out chlorophyll. And he had anticipated he would find nothing more than this spare landscape for days upon days of travel by horse because there would be no roads.

But Perth was not this. Perth was white cottages and elegant homes surrounding a downtown of stone buildings serving as police station, town hall, and civic center. Perth had been clearly well-planned and laid out on an organized grid. Perth was not a cow town, but a first class business city supporting the area's rich mining industry. The latest cars drove by on streets that were paved, not dirt or even cobblestoned, and a clean and efficient streetcar system was crowded with well-dressed passengers.

Pinky was disappointed. Perth was not a place that he might find the adventure he had anticipated. Perth was civilized. Perth was pleasant.

TWENTY-FIVE
SEPTEMBER 1954

At the DA's office, Deputy Dillard asked the receptionist if he could meet with the DA himself, Lawrence M. Webster, Esq. After he was kept waiting long enough to emphasize the DA's importance and busy schedule, Dillard was escorted several paces into a spacious office with dark wood paneling and four stuffed leather chairs sitting in an arc before a massive oak desk with swirled tight dark grain—something Deputy Dillard thought might be called "tiger oak," something very expensive and meant to impress. Deputy Dillard was a country boy and did not notice the art on the walls, which was also rare and expensive and meant to impress. He did notice Mr. Webster's suit, which was shiny and probably expensive, but Dillard thought was ugly, so he wasn't impressed.

Webster sat, back straight and arms resting on his desk, and asked, "What can I do for you today, deputy?"

Dillard decided not to sit in one of the stuffed chairs. "Well, just between the two of us, I have a very strong suspect in the killing of Buck Wilson."

DA Lawrence M. Webster wondered why such news would be delivered to him by a mere deputy sheriff rather than by the undersheriff, but he was impressed, and he suddenly found a long break in his busy schedule.

After hearing the details of Deputy Dillard's investigation, concluding with a list of suspects, Larry Webster was almost certain that Dillard was right and that Twyla should be considered a prime suspect in the killing of Buck Wilson. But Webster also knew he wasn't going to prosecute Twyla.

For one thing, Ruby's story seemed a little imprecise, and a good defense attorney could make her sound unreliable. For another thing, Twyla was the Tulare County sheriff's wife.

But the clincher was that Larry Webster was forever in Twyla's debt.

Larry's marriage was a calculated business deal. His wife was a judge's daughter. It had been good for his career and good for her need for a husband with the promise of prestige. He did find her attractive and interesting, but love was not a primary concern. She married him because she thought he would be a good provider of the lifestyle she desired, and interesting, but not at all because she was attracted to him. After a few years, he was starting to feel like he was, in fact, as she saw him—a prestigious eunuch. Then, along came Twyla, working as a part-time clerk in the DA's office. She was young. She had a body that turned heads. There was something in the way she moved that was purely sensuous. And she seemed to delight in the prominence of the man she had an affair with. Their affair didn't last long, but it didn't take Twyla long to fully restore Larry's sense of manliness.

Larry used Twyla to heal his ego, and she did, so he would never see her go to jail. He would say there was not enough evidence to prosecute and go on the next big case. The fickle public would forget in a few months. And maybe Twyla would renew their old acquaintance. Underneath his slick-looking, expensive suit pants, Lawrence M. Webster, Esq., felt an expansion developing. It was an expansion he was proud of because of Twyla.

Larry considered three options. He had to get Dillard to stop digging, or to discredit whatever evidence he might pull together against Twyla, or make sure the evidence didn't see the light of day, or create a better suspect.

Webster decided the discussion with Dillard was over for the day, and stood, saying, "Keep up the good work, Dillard. As soon as you have a specific suspect, let me know, and if my office can help with the investigation, we will do what we can."

Dillard made no move for the door. "What do you think of Twyla as a suspect?"

"To my knowledge Twyla has no arrest record of any kind. In fact, she worked in this office at one time. She's the wife of the Tulare County sheriff and a model citizen. Of course, you should do what you need to do, Deputy Dillard. But use a great deal of discretion."

Dillard looked at Webster for a moment, then turned to leave, disappointed in Webster's response. Dillard realized that he would be on his own investigating the sheriff's wife.

When Dillard reached the door, Webster asked, "How's Sheriff Wilson's Australian vacation going?"

Dillard turned back, "It's no vacation. He's chasing down a fugitive."

Webster cocked his head to one side. "Not everyone will see it that way, Dillard."

"I guess it depends on who tells the story, Mr. Webster."

"Precisely."

Twyla answered her phone and heard Larry Webster's lilting voice. "It's me," he said and hummed a few bars of their favorite song, then added, "While the cat's away."

Twyla did not understand why, but she knew from previous experience what a calming effect her affairs had upon her. The ease with which she could manipulate prominent married men into having sex left her feeling stronger, more independent, more in control of the world. She needed that right now. "Where, when, and how long?"

"My office," he said, "Our favorite place." He paused. "Eight p.m. after work. Our favorite time." And with a comic's timing he added, "But you'll have to tell me how long it is."

"Almost too long," she lied, feeling better already.

TWENTY-SIX

Past the city center Pinky watched as a gentleman and a lady, dressed in their Sunday best, ambled across the street and passed in front of him. He touched the front brim of his hat as they passed, and the man returned the hello with a slight smile but did not stop.

It was Sunday and they were dressed well, so Pinky thought they might be headed for a church. The next intersection had a church with a pointed steeple and stained glass windows. In fact, there was a nearly identical such church on three of the four corners of the intersection.

Pinky nearly caught up to the couple, then stopped several steps back as they paused at the entrance to the church on the southeast corner. They met up with an apparently punctual but small and slow crowd, everyone greeting everyone by name but in no way acknowledging similar congregations in front of the other two churches. Pinky fell in behind the group and noticed none were children.

Inside the church Pinky became very aware he had been soaking in salt air for three weeks and chose a pew to himself off to the side and in the back.

Pinky stood when the congregation stood but did not sing when the congregation sang. They sang unaccompanied and well.

The next thing Pinky was aware of was the minister shaking his shoulder, and then he was aware of the emptiness of the church. He had fallen asleep, and the congregants were gone.

With the hospitality characteristic of a frontier people, Pinky was scooped up by the minister and his wife and taken to the parsonage for a bath and dinner. The Parson, as he wanted to be addressed, and Rae Lynn, were clearly not wealthy people, but they were as cheerful as anyone Pinky had ever met and smiled sincere smiles nearly all of the time. At the dinner table, while eating lamb stew and fresh cabbage and sipping hot tea, Pinky told his story and expressed his unmet expectation of finding a dry, hot, and wide-open frontier country. The couple assured him the Australia he had seen in magazines was inland a short distance from every major city and as vast as he expected. They also explained that he would find the hot and dry he was looking for as soon as spring advanced a bit and as soon as he left the cooler coastline. He asked about the customs of Australia and the possibility of work and let it be known that he preferred working a cattle ranch, or station, as they were called.

The Parson was unimpressed by the humble size of Pinky's 8,000-acre ranch, blurting out, "You call that a ranch?" and immediately wincing and apologizing as he saw Pinky's pained expression. He then explained to Pinky the size of a typical station in Australia. Pinky found it hard to believe, thinking the good-natured Aussie was pulling his leg. The numbers were astounding, averaging nearly 3,000 square miles, which at 640 acres to the square mile meant they were between 1 and 2 million acres, and contiguous acres at that. Pinky mentioned the XIT ranch in Texas, which he knew to be 3 million acres, but The Parson, smiling even broader, said that would only take third place in Western Australia and that Danna Creek, in South Australia, was twice that.

Though he didn't say it, Pinky brought some relief to his American pride by thinking that, from the pictures he had seen, it might take a thousand acres of Australian land to feed one steer.

The Parson was concerned Pinky had never been on a real cattle drive, but was impressed with his experience both working and running a cattle ranch, so he decided to help Pinky land a job on one of the stations. Prior to becoming a man of the cloth, The Parson had worked odd jobs on several stations and knew people and how to help.

———··———

The people The Parson knew were as handy to reach as anyone who lived and worked on a cattle station in Western Australia, which is to say that reaching them, if not by air, was at best a matter of several toilsome and exhausting days. Nevertheless, using a wireless, it took The Parson a little less than a month to arrange Pinky an introduction at a station near Sturt Creek and the promise of a tryout.

The day Pinky left, The Parson shook his hand and gave him the big smile Pinky had become accustomed to while telling him how much he enjoyed meeting him, and Rae Lynn smiled and hugged him and made him promise he would come see them again if he was anywhere within 100 miles of Perth. Faced with all that goodwill, Pinky happily agreed.

Pinky decided to go north on horseback via the legendary Canning Stock Route, a route so arduous and unpredictable it was barely safe for an experienced Outback drover or even a bush ranger, much less a lone Yankee just off the boat.

One who watched his eagerness for such danger said jokingly that he was either insane and thus incapable of making sensible decisions, or he had lived an unprincipled past and had no choice but to make a daring and dangerous escape. The joke first passed among the congregants of the helpful Parson's church but spread out through the pub regulars among the congregation, and by the time the telling passed through the fourth layer, the idea of a joke had been lost, and the two ideas of insanity and criminality had been combined into the seeds that would grow into Pinky's future reputation as a notorious outlaw.

Leaving Perth, Pinky caught a bus for Wiluna—a miserable trip with unpadded seats and a rough ride. He arrived in Wiluna as an estate sale of sorts was taking place. One of the nearby graziers had been bit by a mulga and, in spite of the large variety of deadly snakes, became one of hardly any each year who actually die of snakebite. His widow decided to move to Perth and was divesting herself of the station's assets, which included a nice-sized remuda of what she claimed to be Walers, a genetic hodgepodge of the world's horses with the greatest stamina, ability to haul a load, and to survive in a desert climate. Pinky bought a grulla and two sorrels, rugged looking animals, all smallish in the barrel. He outfitted the grulla as a mount, which gave him some pause because he was not familiar with the spare style of Australian saddles. He had asked a drover at the sale about the lack of a horn and was told they didn't rely on the rope, a fact that puzzled Pinky, for how might they hold the cattle for branding or vaccination? The two sorrels were outfitted as pack horses, and, if need be, could also be mounts. He then set out along the Canning Stock Route for the ranch. He chose the Canning because it was the most direct route to Halls Creek where the stockman's job awaited him, and the most direct route seemed the most sensible route.

It was with this foolhardy act that Pinky found the Australia of his imagination.

————·————

The Parson had provided Pinky with books and articles on the land he was about to enter, Western Australia, and the land beyond, the Northern Territory.

The words most often used by Australians to describe the place were: vast, empty, hot, waterless, barren and hopeless. It was, they said, a land of rivers with no water and towns with no people, a vague portion of earth, a world without time. The interior, it was said, had a reputation for swallowing both ambition and the ambitious. It wasn't just a different place. It was a different world.

Pinky was intrigued.

Ominously, one portion of the Canning Stock Route held an Aboriginal name that translated to "land of little water." The stock route originally was set up with 50 wells, but their initial construction had been such that the Aborigines could not access the water, and so the wooden infrastructures had been burned or torn apart. Even after reconstruction efforts and efforts at making the wells more useable by the locals, less than half the wells might have accessible potable water at any given time.

When Pinky left Wiluna, it was springtime in the Australian Outback, which is merely hot rather than hellishly hot. And, given that it was the third year of drought, very dry.

In the first two days on the trail Pinky passed only two wells, both dry, and used all the water he carried by the evening of the second day. On the third day he and the horses had become very thirsty, enough to cause Pinky to worry, and then they found water and Pinky found relief. And in seeing the great uncertainty of water, he also saw the foolhardiness of his choice. He hunkered down for a day, he and the horses drank their fill, and Pinky wondered whether to push on or return to Wiluna. In the evening light of his fourth day out he pulled a coin from his pocket, decided heads would mean heading on and tails would be to turn tail and go back. Looking away from the coin, he tossed it into the air, fearing the possibility of heads and regretting the possibility of tails.

In the instant of waiting for the coin to land, he heard a distant rumble, reminding him of a stampede. He swiveled his head in the direction of the sound, his ears alert, and heard the coin land in the sand. The rumbling sound was unquestionably a large number of hooves moving quickly. He stood, waiting and uneasy as his horses whinnied and stamped, ears pointed and staring at the skyline 300 yards away where the trail crested an outcropping of red sandstone. The sound grew closer, and Pinky felt elated at the sight of running horses streaming over the crest with the smooth and continuous flow of a flock of birds. Two riders skillfully cut across the path of the lead horses, changing their direction and turning the headlong rush into a circular, milling ring of horses. Pinky counted six riders in all, a small number to move what appeared to be upward of a hundred head of horses.

Four riders broke away and rode toward him, leaving two to keep the herd circling. Three men, two white and one black, went to the well and began the process of bringing up water. The fourth and largest rider pulled his horse up 20 feet in front of Pinky, silent, squinting and blinking, and shaking his head. Pinky, still in a state of wonder at the rapid and unexpected arrival of the large herd of horses, stared back for a minute, and then introduced himself.

"Name's Wollerman. Pinky Wollerman."

At that, the large man burst into laughter, dismounted, good-naturedly slapped Pinky on the back and said, "Wondering if you was real, mate. Name's Mills." Then, giving the area a quick scan asked, "Where's your mob?"

"Pardon me?" Pinky asked.

Mills squinted again, "You're not from around here, are you?"

"No. I'm from California."

"America?"

"Yessir."

"Well, what I was asking is where the rest of your drovers are and your cattle or horses or whatever you're shifting."

"I'm it."

The mystified look returned to Mills' face. "Alone?" the large man asked.

Pinky nodded, shrugged, and pointed to the tethered horses, saying, "I got three fine horses."

Mills laughed so loud the men at the well paused and looked their way. Mills' laugh ended abruptly and he said, "There's work to do," and led his horse toward the well.

Pinky picked up the coin, noticed it was heads and followed Mills. Two men were busy with the windless, so he helped the other install a hand pump. The men seemed to think nothing of it when he joined in.

As they worked, Mills pointed his chin at Pinky and announced, "This is Mr. Wollerman. Johnny Raw." The men glanced Pinky's way and nodded and then Mills added, "He's alone except for his three fine horses."

One man studied Pinky carefully and asked, "White ants in the billy?"

"Not sure," came the reply from Mills, waving a hand toward Pinky's horses and tack, and pointing to the neatly organized supplies near the pack saddles and adding, "Seems he's brought a fine plant." The men assessed Pinky's gear.

One man said, "Don't mean he's not crazy."

The black drover asked, "He's far away?"

"American." Mills nodded and swirled his hand to get them back to the work of pulling up water for the thirsty horses.

Pinky didn't understand all their words, but their expressions helped with the interpretation. It seemed they thought he was crazy to be alone in this hard place, a thought that had crossed his own mind.

Dining on tins of beef and white potatoes, Pinky found that Mills had worked with the legendary Wally Dowling and made nearly as many cattle drives on the Canning Stock Route as Wally had. But, he learned from the drovers, whereas Mills was the boss of this mob, it seemed that Wally was the boss on the Canning, rode barefoot, never smiled, always armed. Pinky was glad he'd met Mills and not Wally Dowling.

On Mills' last trip, six weeks past, he had delivered a herd of 600 cattle to Wiluna and had "picked up a mob of brumbies," which Pinky figured out meant a large group of wild horses, and which were mostly to be delivered to several stations in the Kimberley area. The remainder Mills meant to keep for his own string, and with a profusion of profanities he was adamant and clear that he would never again go droving down the Canning.

Whether Mills needed Pinky's help or thought him competent was not discussed, but, perhaps because he knew Pinky would be riding along anyway, offered him a job as a jackeroo. Pinky, mistakenly thinking the term equivalent to "buckaroo," rather than a beginner, and remembering that the coin had fallen heads up, accepted the job.

Though they had barely met, Pinky had no qualms about working for Mills. When Mills first rode in, he had flipped his reins ever so slightly, clicked his tongue softly, and the horse immediately stopped sideways to Pinky. Through the horse's reaction to this subtle movement and gentle sound, Pinky knew that this man and this horse knew each other well. Later he noticed the saddle was level on the horse's back, the sweat pattern was evenly distributed and balanced side to side, and there were no spots on the back or sides of the horse where the hair had worn away. All of this showed Pinky that Mills had taken great care to obtain a perfect-fitting saddle, which benefits the horse as much or more as it benefits the rider. Furthermore, Mills hadn't washed up or fixed his own meal until his horse had been watered, groomed and given oats from a wagon that followed well behind the arrival of the mob. After grooming the horse, Mills slapped him gently on the neck, and the horse pricked his ears and nickered, a special sound, Pinky knew for satisfaction or even affection.

Pinky believed he could tell a lot about another man by the way he treated his animals, and he was certain he would be treated fairly by Mills.

Twenty-one days after Pinky joined up with Mills, they rode past Hall's Creek and into the Sturt Creek Station where Mills introduced Pinky to the grazier, Boyle Humbert, who was sitting on the wooden porch of the government house. Humbert nodded to Mills but did not rise. Mills stayed mounted, saying, "Boyle Humbert. Pinky Wollerman."

Boyle squinted in Pinky's direction. "The Parson said you were coming."

Mills finished the introduction with, "He knows horses, and he knows cattle." Then he turned his horse, called over his shoulder, "I'll bring your brumbies in a week or two," and rode away.

Boyle said, "Good on ya, mate," but didn't watch Mills as he left, instead looking toward his barn he wondered aloud if he had enough feed on hand for another 20 horses and if he would need to bring in a drover from one of the other stations to break the brumbies. When he turned to Pinky, he asked, "Do you break horses?"

"Never was much of a peeler," Pinky replied.

Boyle cocked his head to one side as though unsure of Pinky's response, but then he took it as a "no," and asked, "You always do things the hard way?" Pinky looked puzzled, so he went on, "The Canning Stock Route. Fickle water. On horseback. Alone."

Pinky shrugged and Boyle shrugged.

Seeing a man leaving the barn, Boyle waved him over. While the man was walking over he said to Pinky, "You're lucky Mills found you."

Sturt Creek was one of three stations Boyle Humbert owned, and he could only be polite for a short time, so turned Pinky over to the tall, lanky man coming from the barn, the Station Manager, Andrew Fraser.

Andy told Pinky he would find the general hand out at the barn, a young blackfella who would take care of his horse. Pinky walked his horse there, relieved to be finished with the introductions. He was a few feet from the stables when his horse stopped short and blew through his nose. Pinky saw a young Aborigine dressed similarly to the drovers. He guessed the boy was the general hand. He appeared to be in his late teens and stepped out from the shadowed interior of the stables and advanced slowly to meet them. The horse nickered a hello in such a familiar way that Pinky wondered if the two had met before. Pinky watched as the stable hand smoothly approached, placed a hand on the horse's nose, and reached out for the reins. The horse's ears were forward and his eyes wide, but he nickered again and was calm. Pinky greeted the youngster with a soft hello, and the stable hand only nodded and flexed the fingers on the extended hand, waiting for the reins.

"My name is Roland," Pinky said, dismounting. "They call me Pinky."

Now that the Erlewines were dead, Pinky wasn't sure if anyone but his banker knew his given name. Without the slightest sense of why he used it with someone so far from home and appearing to be little more than a boy, he gave up the reins and wondered why he and his horse both had sensed a familiar spirit.

"What's your name?" Pinky asked. The stable hand almost looked at him and almost smiled, but stopped short of both, nodded, took the reins and led the horse through the barn door.

Pinky asked again, louder, "What's your name?" But he couldn't make out the response over the sound of the horse's snorting and hoofs plunking into the soft dirt.

"Nothing wrong with quiet," Pinky said. "Some talk too much." The stable hand did not respond, and Pinky did not know if he had been heard, so he shrugged and followed his horse and its new friend inside the barn.

Inside, the light was dim. Though Pinky could not see clearly, all of the sounds and smells were as familiar as any stable back home. He heard five distinct nickers from close by and a murmuring of several other horses from farther inside the barn. Teeth crunched on the wood of the low stable doors, an occasional hoof banged against the stalls' sideboards, and there was the smell of freshly thrown hay and manure and sweat, and the feel of straw underfoot. At a stall on the left Pinky could see the forms of the stable boy and his horse and hear a brush making quick passes over horse hair. As Pinky's eyes adjusted, he went to the stall, rested his arms on the top rail and watched.

After a while he said, "I been wanting to come to Australia for a long time." The boy did not look up, so Pinky went on. "I read about it in a magazine at the barbershop. It's a bigger place than I even thought." The boy seemed intent on his work and took only enough time for a glance in Pinky's direction. "Are you from around here?" Pinky asked, and heard a soft "yes" from the stall as the boy pointed with the brush, but, of course, Pinky had no idea what might lie in the direction the boy was pointing.

A few minutes later, having talked about his trip along the Canning Stock Route while he watched the boy finish up the brush-down and throw a can of oats into the feed trough, Pinky, feeling uneasy about not knowing how to address the boy, asked again, "What name do you go by here on the station?"

The stable hand stepped out of the stall and stopped directly in front of Pinky. "The drovers don't use my name. Even so, I know when they're addressing me because they only talk to me if they want something. Depending on what they want, I know if they're talking to me or one of the other general hands. The station boss does sometimes call me Treacle, or Stable Boy, or, sometimes, Spare Boy."

Pinky was taken by surprise at the sudden wealth of words coming from the boy. He spoke complete sentences as well or better than any of the drovers. "Where were you schooled?" he asked.

"My mother started me. The Station Master's wife—Andy's wife, Melinda—has many books and has continued my tutoring."

As the boy finished his work and they left the stable, Pinky felt a hand on his arm and turned, looking upward into the calm brown eyes and smooth face of the youngster.

"Truth is, other than Melinda, you are the first to ask."

"Ask what?"

"My name."

"What is your name?"

"My given name might be hard for you to pronounce," the boy said, offering nothing more.

Pinky thought the stable hand appeared to be a teenager, and was reminded of the Aboriginal man in his cat dreams who Pinky believed was called Bobbie and so he said, "I could call you Bobbie."

He paused and added, "If that's okay with you."

"I like the name Bobbie, and you can call me that, Mr. Wollerman."

"Then you better call me Pinky."

"Why are you called Pinky instead of Roland?"

Pinky rolled up his sleeve, exposing a part of his arm that never saw the sun. "White," he said.

Bobbie brought his fingers close to Pinky's very white arm and chuckled.

"I burn easily," Pinky said pointing to where the white ended. "So my hands and face are always sunburned and red."

Bobbie nodded and then asked, "Why did you choose the name Bobbie for me?"

Pinky looked at the boy and noticed again how much he looked like the man in his dream. They were both tall and thin, perhaps 5-feet-10-inches and around 150 pounds, but the dream Bobbie was likely twice as old as this Bobbie. And this Bobbie wasn't out roaming through the bush. This Bobbie was a spare boy, and from the look of his hands, a hard-working one at that.

"I dreamed it," Pinky said, and Bobbie broke into a broad smile that startled Pinky almost as much as the boy's sudden facility with words. The boy's smile made Pinky chuckle and reminded him of the gregarious minister and his wife, and he warmed even more to the boy. Pinky wondered what in the boy's childhood had led him to this mostly solitary life in the Outback as a drover.

Later when asked, Andy told Pinky that the boy had shown up on a Sunday five years back, walked into the stable and went to work. Andy said the kid must have had some good training somewhere because he seemed to know what needed to be done without asking or waiting to be told. He didn't ask for anything beyond being fed along with the drovers and being allowed to sleep in the stable. The boss said they didn't even know they needed help until Bobbie had been there a while, but it seemed a good deal to have someone like that around, so they'd offered him half pay.

"Of course," Andy said, "half pay for an Abo is less than half of half pay for the white drovers." Andy said he had no idea where Bobbie was from and offered no guesses. The important thing was his uncanny knowledge of horses and familiarity with the work of the station.

Pinky liked the way Bobbie was with the stock, careful and respectful, and clearly in charge with no sign of rough force. The horses were kept well-groomed, and the string was rotated around a balance of the demands of their work days and their condition, so there was always a mount to suit the drover that was healthy, rested and ready when needed, even if occasionally it wasn't the drover's own.

Most folks might not have appreciated it as much of a thing at all, but the good drovers saw it and appreciated it and knew they had something special without ever saying so to Bobbie or to one another. It wasn't that they weren't grateful men; it was that Bobbie had established a way of being that said that quiet was as good as words. And what needed to be done was done well, so the drovers treated Bobbie right and didn't bother to sing praises.

But after Pinky named him Bobbie, they appreciated having a name to use rather than "stable boy" or "spare boy." A name carried more respect, and in their opinion, respect was due.

TWENTY-SEVEN
MARCH–APRIL 1955

When Pinky had been at the station for four months, Bobbie bought a horse, and then unexpectedly began teaching a half-caste boy named Peter to take over the stable. Pinky was curious why Bobbie would do this, and then a few days later he learned that the grazier had agreed to gather his cattle with the cattle from two other stations and had contracted with Mills to shift them overland to Adelaide. Soon after the announcement, Bobbie told Pinky he was prepared to go, and Pinky wondered how a stable boy could know so far in advance as to have planned a replacement.

There was excitement among the drovers, curious who would be chosen to make the two-month trip. Pinky was chosen and told Bobbie, who showed no surprise. And then, without Andy or the stockmen feeling any need to question his actions, Bobbie outfitted himself for the drive.

On the day of their departure from the Sturt Creek Station, Bobbie fell in beside Pinky.

Pinky didn't know why Bobbie had adopted him, but Pinky was grateful for the company and saw the boy as no trouble. In fact, it was soon clear that Bobbie was not new to ringing cattle on the track and seemed to like it.

And, for reasons Pinky did not understand, Bobbie assumed the job of caring for him and for his favorite horse.

Bobbie would eat the morning and evening meals away from the group. When Pinky was ready to turn in, Bobbie would have Pinky's swag situated in the best spot to sleep — when there was a best spot. Pinky's canteen was always filled, even when there was little water available, though at times it tasted of vegetation and made Pinky wonder about the source. And whether Pinky was riding behind, ringing the herd, or rounding up strays, Bobbie would ride with him.

On occasion there was time to talk, and Bobbie asked many

questions. Some questions were about Pinky's bachelor status, which Pinky evaded because the recent and awkward ending to his one promising relationship had left him cynical. Some questions were about the recent war, but Pinky had been too old for the draft, and he had a large contract with the U.S. Army for beef, which everyone agreed was a better way for him to participate in the war than to serve on the front lines. So Pinky knew of the war only through newspapers, newsreels and the stories told by returning soldiers.

Most of Bobbie's questions were about Pinky's ranch and the land. Bobbie seemed particularly fascinated by the mountains that Pinky called the Sierra Nevada. He often asked Pinky to describe the way the arid San Joaquin Valley bumped up gently into rolling foothills of grass and giant oak trees, which then rose dramatically into mountains with pine forests, and ultimately into nearly vertical spires of white and grey granite along the spine of the range.

——————

Bobbie's mind compared the Sierra's 12,000- to 14,000-foot peaks to the highest mountain he had seen, which was a little over 4,000 feet. High, dramatic and rough sounded new, he thought. Time wears things down, even mountains. Judging from the flat and worn landscape around them, Bobbie thought the dream time, the origin of all that is, must have been a very, very long time past.

One day, watching the herd from a high ridge, as the cattle grazed slowly on a wide plane that sloped gently toward a ribbon of giant blue gums near a river bottom, grass shining brightly green under the morning sun, Bobbie said to Pinky, "There are different knowings among the clans of families. Some know that in the beginning there was land, but it was bare and flat. No animals, no birds, no trees or bushes, no sound of water, no light, no wind, no man, no woman. Then the Maker of Many Things brought the Dreamtime beings, the totemic ancestors, from under the ground. One of these was a vague form of human. Time began when the supernatural beings awoke and broke through the surface of the land. When the supernatural beings became exhausted and left the earth, man was left behind to wander the land."

"There is a Hebrew word for ground," Pinky said. "Adamah—which is much like the word for man, adam. And in my religious tradition there was a beginning, and in the beginning God formed a man from the dust of the ground."

Bobbie nodded, dismounted, knelt, and scooped up a handful of the dry, sandy soil, and as it sifted between his fingers, said, "Some know that Baiame walked on the earth he had made, among the plants and animals, and created man and woman. He fashioned them." Bobbie opened his hand to release the last of the soil, watching it fall, "from the dust of the ridges.

"Others know that when a wrong was done, the Maker of Many Things would rush down, consume the ancestors, and spit out their bones as rocks and hills." Bobbie offered his palm toward a field of giant boulders at the base of a nearby ridge.

"Still others know the making of a man was a great challenge, needing the powers of thought and reasoning. When at last Bunjil was ready, he prepared two sheets of bark, cutting them to the shape he envisaged as suited to such a noble purpose. Next he took soft clay, molding it to the shape of the bark, smoothing it with his hands into a man and a woman."

These stories were connected to Bobbie's inner heart, and it was an uncommon experience to share such intimacy. When Pinky listened so respectfully, Bobbie experienced a growing sense of affection for him.

One evening as the sun approached the horizon they sat their horses, side by side, watched the cattle drink from a small river and Bobbie said, "Pinky, it seems the whites use 'God' as the name of a thing. Do you believe in this God?"

"Yes," Pinky said quickly, and then paused awhile, looking into some empty distant place. "But I know God differently than many do. Some believe God is a being." Pinky spoke slowly, reverently. "I believe God is much more than any being because beings are limited by when and where." Then he looked at Bobbie. "But I can't tell you anything more about God than that." Pinky shrugged. "I don't know how to describe a God that is more than a being."

Pinky paused for a long while and Bobbie waited until Pinky said, "I only know that God *is*."

Bobbie watched as the shadow of darkness appeared in the eastern sky and crept to the west. Speaking deliberately, he said, "Language is important to knowing. I don't know 'God' the way you do, but I can use that word, which comes with your language, to talk to you about spiritual things. Our knowing of the Dreamtime is perhaps somewhat like your way of knowing God. Dreaming shows us where we came from and how we 'ought' to live.

"So here is what I want to know, Pinky." Bobbie, holding the reins in one hand, extended the other, swept the horizon and said, "God gave us this land." His arm still extended, palm up, he looked questioningly at Pinky and asked, "Did God not give the whites a land? Why did the whites come here to take this land?" Bobbie put one hand on the pommel, the other on the cantle, and twisted to face Pinky squarely. "Why do the Europeans destroy the song lines? Destroy the food? Tear up the soil from which we all have come? All of which is to destroy an entire people and their connections to each other and to their God."

Pinky did not even shrug. "I don't know" was not an answer. There was no answer. They settled again to watch the cattle, now little more than shadows, and remained quiet with their thoughts until they were relieved by two drovers, then rode to camp for their supper.

Pinky wondered at the education and the wisdom that could make a stable boy so fascinating. How could one so young have such questions about the world? And he became uneasy when Bobbie would sit with him as he talked, watching him so intently, laughing so heartily. He was uneasy with the intimacy he felt looking into the boy's eyes, and even more uneasy at how Bobbie's laugh had taken on a musical feeling, not only in his ears, but in his chest.

———··———

During the fourth week of the cattle drive, a squall with lightning and thunder settled in at dusk and continued into the night, the strikes coming closer and the claps louder until the land existed as though in a series of flashes of daylight under a booming that left the ears ringing.

Pinky slept roughly for a couple of hours. In his sleep the cat walked over and through his dreams of vast granite peaks viewed from the glide of condor wings. He flew through clusters of skybound white vapors that quickly morphed into a black and roiling mass that fired jagged, white hot streaks at the land and left a fearful rumbling rolling in from on high.

The rumble of the herd's pounding hoofs awakened Pinky. Even without knowing its origin, he knew it as a dangerous sound, entering the brain ahead of reason, demanding full and undivided attention, charging the body with fear and movement.

As he leapt from his swag and pulled on his boots, Bobbie arrived at his side, extending the reins of Pinky's saddled horse, making him one of the first to ride toward an inbound mob of terrified steers. Pinky managed to veer the stampede's leaders away from the encampment — no doubt saving the lives of some of the slower men.

But in the near darkness, there was no stopping the wild dispersion of cattle. The drovers quickly reassembled at the camp to get direction from Mills and wait for the dawn.

Under the clouds the morning light was slow in coming, and when sanity returned to the skies and the trails left by the cattle could be followed, Mills sent pairs of drovers in three directions to find the wayward cattle. Pinky was sent with Bobbie to the southwest.

The trail of the cattle was at first easily followed in the red dirt, but soon the land became gravelly and then rocky. If not for Bobbie's inherent understanding of how the features of this land were arranged and where cattle might think about running when scared out of their wits, they would have taken far longer to find them. The cattle had sensibly found an area to graze beside a pool of water with no apparent source flowing into it. The pool was surrounded on three sides by a few acres of grass surrounded by massive blue gum trees, sparkling white against the green of the grass. On the fourth side of the pool a spattering of orange boulders from the size of a cow to the size of a pickup led in an irregular line up to a small mesa of red earth covering a couple of acres and rising abruptly 40 feet to an unseen, but apparently flat, top.

Pinky and Bobbie rode slowly into the idyllic scene, Pinky marveling at the beauty of the colors and the temperate warmth of the late morning air. He took in a strikingly strange sky with a cobblestone pattern of cloud puffs neatly and completely paving the eastern half of the sky from meridian to horizon and seemingly unable to advance into the solid blue of the western half. Pinky stared in wonder at the half-and-half sky above the pastoral scene. It was as though east had met west without consummating their union, but creating a scene of peculiar beauty. As soon as he thought this, he was embarrassed and looked to see Bobbie looking toward the cattle. He was relieved the boy could not see his embarrassment.

"Well," he said, "that was quick and easy. I'll bet we'll be the first back to the herd."

Bobbie turned and looked at Pinky, "I know this place," he said.

"You've been here before?"

"No."

Pinky was no longer surprised at such from Bobbie, nor was he skeptical.

Bobbie rode around the cloud-covered side of the curious hill, dismounting and tying his horse to a mop-headed desert oak. Pinky followed and noticed they had stopped by a two-foot-wide crack in the rock wall. The floor of the crack was paved roughly with broken stones and climbed steeply, like a primitive stairway leading upward.

Bobbie raised his eyebrows, looked sideways at Pinky, and then started to climb. Pinky simply followed. It took them less than five minutes to scramble up through the crack to the top. The ascent ended on a small overlook where they could see the entire other world of the topside, a place of intimate beauty, separate entirely from the world below.

Pinky turned slowly, feeling such a sense of reverence he was unsure if he should walk farther, but he followed when Bobbie stepped down and walked toward the clear centerpiece of this hidden world, an oval pool approximately 50 feet long, lying like a mirror on a table, waiting since the land's beginning if only to reflect the day's half-and-half sky. The upper end of the pool ended at a nearly round rock, reminding Pinky of a pale but ripe peach the size of a shed. Crisscrossing arcs of white flowers and green grasses grew in cracks of the rough boulder creating a tapestry worthy of a museum painting. The background for the rock was the strange half-and-half sky. From where Pinky was standing, the dividing line between the deep blue half and the clouded half bisected the pool and the rock. Other than the end with the rock, the pool was surrounded by a ring of trees large enough to provide some shade but small enough not to be seen from below. The water was crystal clear with a smooth bottom of white stone.

"Garden of Eden," Pinky said with reverence.

"Perhaps," Bobbie responded, sitting near the pool and removing his boots. "Do you think they swam in the days of the Garden?"

Pinky realized the boy was removing his clothes, so in order to give him privacy, Pinky looked around the plateau, appreciating the beauty of the stone, a canvas of pastel orange and cream and black, curving sculptures carved beautifully by some ancient and relentless flow of water. Pinky also appreciated how the isolation of the place caused it to stand out. It was like a painting, artistically framed, and hung in the middle of a blank wall the size of a continent—suspended there for millions of years waiting to be seen and appreciated.

"Are you coming in?" Bobbie asked.

Pinky turned from the plateau and walked to the other side of the pool from Bobbie.

Bobbie, head only above the water, returned to Pinky the courtesy of privacy by studying the flowers in the crevices as he disrobed. When Pinky had entered the water, Bobbie turned to him.

"Everyone has secrets," Bobbie said and paused.

Stomach high in the water, Pinky noticed Bobbie staring at the brightness of his white arms and torso, which ended in weathered red at his wrists and neck.

Pinky cocked his head to one side, curious about the meaning of "secrets."

"Not all secrets are for shame." Bobbie spoke with confidence. "Some secrets are for safety. And for decency.

"My mother was separated from her parents and from the people and land of her birth when she was 7. She was educated to not be black, but to be like the whites. When she was 15 and she could read and write and speak well and could sing the Christian hymns, she was placed as a cook on a cattle station.

"When I was a child, I saw my mother taken regularly by the station owner. The thinking was that if blacks were bred through enough generations with the whites, the offspring would eventually be more intelligent and more civilized.

"Such education and placement as cooks and maids was a government-sponsored plan that had the quiet but strong support of the men who lived in remote places. It was a policy that seemed to evoke a sense of responsibility among many men.

"When my older sister came of age, the station owner, being a responsible man, began to mate with her also."

Pinky, disturbed by Bobbie's story, watched as he half walked, half swam, in the slow motion of being in water, and moved to within an arm's length of him.

"Pinky?"

Pinky looked toward Bobbie, brow furrowed, wondering what this mystifying boy would say now.

"My mother did not want me to be bred by the whites, unless it was my wish."

Now, thoroughly confused, Pinky shook his head.

"She raised me as a boy."

————··————

Bobbie stood slowly, exposing her neck and shoulders, pausing when the water barely veiled her nipples that had grown quite erect in the cool water. Then, sharing her secret kept since childhood, she stood tall and straight with her shoulders back and watched Pinky's face and his eyes as they fixed on her small but definitely feminine breasts and then fell to the submerged area below her waist. She knew he was wondering what was there and was not there. His mouth moved as if to speak, but there was no sound, not even the sound of breathing. A flock of magpies chattered as they passed by overhead, but neither Pinky nor Bobbie noticed. In the sky above them the puffy clouds began to dissipate, giving up more and more of the sky to the deep clear blue of the purest of days.

They stood quietly, each soaking in the sight of the other, standing so still that the surface of the pond became perfectly smooth, the clear water providing each with a view of the parts of the other's body that were submerged. Bobbie's was the first woman's body Pinky had ever seen in the flesh, and Bobbie, who had carefully and painstakingly avoided being seen by anyone at all since she left her mother, was pleased to see through the water to the expansion occurring below his stomach that told her he was pleased with what he saw — or at least his body was.

When she looked up, his head was tilted slightly, his mouth still in readiness to speak. She could not discern if the look on his face was curiosity or pain.

Pinky was stunned by the revelation that Bobbie was not a teenage boy, but a young woman. Then many things fell suddenly into place under this different light — the way Bobbie would eat and groom alone, the wisdom and learnedness that seemed to belie that of a teenage boy, the tenderness Bobbie had often shared with him. And then he felt curiously relieved, which for a moment puzzled him, and then he realized it was because he was now more comfortable with the affection for Bobbie that had been growing within him. And while he was thinking these things, his body reacted with pleasure toward her beauty. Noticing the feelings of affection and lust, some inner door opened, and Pinky's being was flooded with both. The lust gained strength rapidly, and left Pinky's mind fighting for control of his body — and so his countenance appeared as though in pain.

They moved toward each other, and Pinky reached out and stroked Bobbie's face, allowing the caress to trail down her shoulder, and she allowed her body to turn slightly so that his fingers stroked slowly downward across her breast, arriving at a firm nipple that he held lightly between finger and thumb. They stood this way for some time, the flashing sparks of possibility arising from within each one's eyes and being absorbed by the other's. Then Bobbie leaned in and kissed Pinky, and again they stood for some time with the gentle gravity of lips not allowing them to come apart. Bobbie wrapped her arms around Pinky's neck and aided by the buoyancy of the water, lifted herself to wrap her legs around his waist and then lowered herself slowly, the remainder of her secret finding him and working insistently and lovingly down upon him. Simultaneously they moaned and held each other tightly. Once he was fully enveloped within her secret, she rocked slowly upon him until, not long after, he came within her.

————·————

There is a time when and a place where the plainest and strangest among the peoples of the lands are found to be beautiful, one to the other. There is a day of magic for such as these, and for Bobbie, who had lived most of her life as a boy and more recently as a drover, and for Pinky, a slightly built Okie with the palest of skin, who had never found more than friendship in a woman's heart, their day came when they were sent to find the strays after the storm of the previous night, and the sun rose over the small red plateau holding a garden of first beginnings on its crown, and the sky was split between cobblestone clouds and clear blue—that was the day for Bobbie and Pinky. Their coupling in the pond, although a wonderful first for them both, was nothing more than the dawn of their first day.

————·————

They sat facing each other in the shade of a ghost gum at the edge of the pond, each clasping the other at the elbows and gazing slowly upward and downward from toes to crown with special searching looks for what might lie behind the eyes and casting appreciative looks for what had been the secret, the undiscovered and the unacknowledged places of their bodies. Few words were spoken, but both knew something very powerful had been released between them.

Neither of them could recognize what followed as either familiar or unusual for those in love because neither had any experience with unrestrained mutual love. But what followed during the rest of their day was extraordinarily uncommon.

While they sat, a force surged within Bobbie that had started as affection then built into an overwhelming love, and she tried to keep up with it, remain aware of its power, and when she could not, she accepted that it could grow and grow forever without limit, and with her acceptance, her love took on substance, a dense energy, and she was compelled to share this powerful matter with the man in front of her. So while she looked deeply into the world behind his eyes, she placed this loving energy before his mind to been seen and heard and within his heart to be felt; she filled his insides with it so he might taste it and breathe it, and she teased every inch of his skin with it. And then with strength and gentleness she filled his center with an eroticism he could never have imagined, and when he was to the point of bursting, she waited until he was within a single breath of orgasm and held him there for a very long time before allowing release.

Surprised by the substance, passion and strength of this consummation, Pinky felt respected and honored. He had received comfort for the child within him and a partnering for the man within him. He had received the eroticism of original creation.

Having learned of the existence of such energy, Pinky gave back the experience, filling Bobbie and teasing her and holding her in an erotic instant lasting many times longer than she thought she could stand, then releasing her to orgasm, only to repeat the cycle again and again.

Late in the afternoon they waded briefly and then lay resting, entangling their arms and legs, entangling their futures, untangling the pasts which brought them together, understanding they were enmeshed, distinct but swirling one within the other, caressing and braiding the threads of their language, their words, their culture, their male and female, their understanding and awareness of the world and of God, and deepening their relationship to the land that had given them their day—which is to say, on that day they had become one, as though a single fabric.

Neither felt any of the roughness of the land upon which they had lain, afterward wondering if they had been somehow physically suspended. And the next morning neither could remember the exact moment of falling asleep, for each moment of the day had been as though a dream. When they awoke, they could see the land around them more clearly than ever before. And this land was elder land, quiet and wise, as accepting of death as the old who have lived a full life, and as pleased as a grandmother in the joy of her descendants' coupling, invigorated by the joy of creation.

When the two lovers returned the wayward cattle, Pinky went to Mills and inquired how the collection of the stampede was going. Mills said it would take two or three more days to get the cattle back together and get them adequately grazed and watered before the next leg of the journey. Pinky nodded and without explanation said he would be back in three days. Mills did not question Pinky but remained aware of his movements, noticing when Pinky threw his horse in with the remuda, went to the wagon to eat, and when he walked north into the bush carrying only his slicker and a canteen. Mills also noticed later when Bobbie walked out on nearly the same path.

Soon after sundown on their first full day of wandering, Bobbie sat on the rock on the mountain they had walked toward since the dawn of that day had given it outline.

Pinky thought the mountain and the rock had been a simple marker for their direction of travel. Bobbie knew it to be an ancestor from the Dreaming when the world was brought up from the earth, the realization of the dream of dust to become aware and then return to dust. After a long day of walking she felt her body relax into the evening air and welcomed the return of the clarification of that which had once long ago been clear.

Clouds perched in a sky that was higher, wider, deeper and bluer than any in their memory.

Bobbie watched the land, remembering it as that from which her kin had become, and, although her people had no story of such, that from which Pinky's people also had become.

Pinky watched Bobbie, remembering her touch, her eyes, and how she had found a man, a being of stature, as yet undiscovered, unacknowledged, in a hidden place deep behind his eyes. And from this he knew Bobbie saw what he could not see, what no one he knew could see, and he wondered what world, beyond the red ridges, beyond the ghost gums on the plains, behind the blue gums in the river bottoms, beneath the streak of popcorn-topped clouds receding to the horizons, wondered what world she was taking in with her eyes, her body, her soul.

Pinky's curiosity wrestled with his respect for the quiet and won, and he asked, "What do you see?'

"The Dreaming," she replied.

Pinky knew somewhat of the Dreamtime, though far less than he could imagine, and asked, using words he had heard but had not understood, "Of the beginning? The Dreaming when the world was made?"

Bobbie was still for a long while, Pinky wondering if he had spoken too softly, she searching through that which she knew, that which she was within as they had walked, that which they were within as they sat, that from which her people had come, sifting around through the whole of it for words, needing words with enough power, words with enough meaning, enough clarity for Pinky to know a way of being he had never known. And finally, trying to stay within what was real and yet pass words of meaning and truth, pass the light through the window that had opened between her and this man she had come to love, she said, "Though it seems we are in the middle, we are also in the beginning. There was not a 'Dreamtime,' but there is only the Dreaming. It was before and is still." She paused, again a long while, and Pinky remained silent, knowing he was hearing truth if only he could understand.

"This," she waved her hand slowly across the valley, across the sky, and across the mountains. "This is what we are. We are the land, the soil... we are the soil still becoming. And, thankfully, Pinky, we have been given words to discuss and describe our awareness to one another so that we do not need to walk through the land alone, but we can walk with stories and songs."

Pinky heard what Bobbie said, and they were not alone and they knew they were not alone, knew they never had been and never would be, and they did not touch, but they held each other for a long while, from their dawn until the dawn of the land and sky.

And then they walked on.

They walked through the morning of the second day, buoyed by the knowledge of having already arrived. Pinky enjoyed the effortless energy of walking about upon the land, walking with the ancestors, walking with Bobbie, and walking with their descendents. And his awareness of the latter stirred his loins with the vigor of life.

Bobbie knew this and stopped him and held him as lightly and as firmly as he had ever been held so that he was within Bobbie's dream and she within his.

And afterward they walked on, surprised by how late the day had become and by how little it mattered.

As they wandered, they came to a nearly round boulder the size of a barn, and climbed up and sat high on its shoulder looking out over a great valley bathed in the light of what, in a few more hours, would be a harvest moon passing over the Once Wide Valley.

The world above, in front and below him sank into Pinky's inner being. He felt it swirling around within his body and meant to tell Bobbie what he saw. "The moon is bright," he said, meaning to notice the awe in the scene before him, but lacking the words to do the beauty justice.

"The sun casts a light on what is, but the moon illuminates the mystery of the land," Bobbie replied. "And the moon's light is sufficient to move through this mystery, but only with faith."

Pinky noticed Bobbie's form next to him, remembering the curve of her bottom and her slender, muscular legs, her thin torso and the terse mounds of her breasts, tipped a reddish black.

Bobbie knew his thoughts and smiled.

Pinky felt the smile and said, "Some days we need faith to move even in the daylight."

They kissed and again entangled themselves in their love.

———··———

On the third day they returned to the herd, secured their mounts, and came back to the routine of the lives they had chosen, back to the need for hard work and the demands of cattle and horses and bosses, back to being with drovers, back to the need for secrets.

Pinky and Bobbie talked often after those days of awakening and found ways to be alone though they could not find an entire day nor could they find the mystical aura of that first time.

———··———

Again, Bobbie asked Pinky, "Why did 'God' give the Europeans and the Aborigines each a land of heritage and then put them together on one land?"

Pinky had been thinking about this question since Bobbie asked the first time, and this time he had an answer.

"Many peoples, not only the European whites, twist God's justice to their own benefit. They believe God gave them their land and all the lands of the earth. They put their words in God's mouth to be sure God tells them what they want to hear: that the world was made for them, and it is up to them to go and take it."

———··———

On a day with no clouds, and as a hot wind blew away all moisture and left their faces feeling as dry as cracking leather, Bobbie said, "The first thing taken was the land. The land was our way of life. Without a way of life we knew we could choose to fight or to become dependent on the whites. Those who fought, died. Those who live on without land live with dead roots.

"The next thing taken was the children. The whites assume their way of life is better than the way of life God gave those who have been here since the beginning of time, so they took the children and placed them in schools.

"In the schools they took our language and our memory. To lose our language is to lose our way of thinking of the world. To lose our memory is to lose our history, including our knowledge of 'God.'

"And, Pinky, then they took our blood. They believed if they could breed our blackness from us they could breed out our way of life and breed in the European way of life. The children who had lost their language and the memory of their ancestors, were given to whites to teach them to be useful. 'Useful' is different than good and different from happy. The blacks were known by the whites to not be useful until they were re-made in the European image. The boys were placed on stations to learn to be stockmen ringing cattle on the track, but never to be station managers, never the boss. The girls were placed in station houses to be water carriers, tend the garden, do the laundry and work in the kitchen—and to be bred by the graziers and station managers—in the interest of having children who would be more 'useful.'

"The Europeans say I am half-caste, Pinky. My mother was Alyawarra. My father was station manager at a cattle station I will not name because I have chosen to have it not remembered. My mother did not want me to have my bloodline further diluted so she raised me as a boy, something my slender body and small breasts allowed me to keep doing into and beyond my teenage years.

"Pinky, it seems to me that you have drifted here on the wind of God's reason. Perhaps the Dreaming is not over and we are still becoming. Perhaps we will have a child."

Pinky's eyebrows rose and he smiled. "We will have a child?"

Bobbie thought for a while, and both were quiet, then she said, "The Dreaming is not over. Nor are the ancestors of the Dreaming dead. What appears as barren country is a living, exciting map of life. It is a part of us, us a part of it. Pinky, we have been the barren country, but no more. We hold the seed within the soil that will continue the Dreaming."

The herd, unsettled by the sound of dingos howling, demanded the attention of the drovers, and as the two reined their horses toward the milling cattle, Bobbie handed Pinky a piece of folded paper and said, "Read this at another time."

—·—

For the rest of the day Pinky was elated as he went about his work, and that night he slept with the paper under his head, but he was afraid something might happen to it, and he would never know what his love had wanted to say to him. So in the early morning light he opened it and read.

I am only the dust on my Lover's path
and from dust I will rise and turn into a flower.
Rumi

Pinky read it four times. The first time he felt the love within the words roll through his body like waves in from the ocean. The second time he remembered how they both believed it was the land that had somehow brought them together, and their love had risen from the land in the same way a flower arises from the land. The third time he paused to relish the extent to which flowers had become more beautiful since their love flowered. And the fourth to ensure the words were committed to memory. Then he folded the paper back as it was and placed it in his saddle bag, safely toward the bottom.

It was about that time that Pinky asked Mills if he had paper and pencil. It was perhaps the oddest question Mills received on the entire trip, perhaps on any drive he had ever been on, and he wasn't sure what to say. He could deal with stampedes and poisonings and drought and flood and foot-blistering heat, but a request for pen and paper by one of his best drovers confounded him. So he looked away from Pinky at a tree, several miles away on the horizon, and then he turned his horse and rode away, and Pinky went back to the herd.

But later Mills asked Terry, the wagoneer and cook, if he could ask a silly question, and then asked Terry if he had a pencil and paper. Terry looked a little surprised, and said, "I didn't know you could spell." But when Mills did not laugh, Terry went to the wagon and came back with a three-inch remnant of a lead pencil and six pages of bills of lading, with printing only on one side. "Will this do?" he asked. And Mills took the paper and pencil and looked at Terry for a minute without saying a thing. So Terry said, "Well, I better check on something," and went on his way.

During quiet moments Mills noticed Pinky thinking and writing. Mostly thinking. And Mills didn't bother Pinky during these times because, Mills figured, to write something down right in the middle of a cattle drive meant it must be rather important.

During supper one evening Bobbie took her meal away from the others and sat on a rock overlooking a wide river valley, and Pinky sat eating with Mills.

"Why does Bobbie eat alone?" Mills asked.

"She just likes it that way," Pinky said without noticing his mistake. Mills was quiet and when Pinky looked up, he saw Mills was looking at Bobbie's silhouette above the camp.

"You said 'she'," Mills said.

Pinky stopped chewing for a moment. "I meant 'he'."

Mills was still watching Bobbie's form as she moved about, laying out Pinky's swag. "That would explain a few things," he said thoughtfully.

And Pinky knew Mills was running through the same checklist he had used himself on the day of Bobbie's unveiling—too wise and educated for a teenage stable boy, curiously aloof, and so on. So he accepted that Mills had uncovered Bobbie's secret and said, "She's got her reasons, Mills. Best to let her keep what she needs to keep."

Mills watched Bobbie a moment longer, then looked at Pinky. "Right, mate. No need to change things. But be careful, Pinky. She belongs here in a way you never can. And, man or woman, Bobbie has a good heart, and I'd hate to see even the slightest crack in it."

Pinky had stopped eating, his eyes on Bobbie. "I'm in love with her, Mills. I've never said that before in my life. But it's true. I'm in love with her."

Mills wondered about paper and pencil and love on a cattle drive. Fleetingly he wondered if Pinky might have been writing poetry. He had seen men in love do strange things.

Then Mills felt a twang of homesickness for a place he had never been and thought how lucky two people were to find each other and how seldom it happened. And when it did happen, how little it mattered if they were from opposite ends of the earth or if the world around them saw them as strange, unlikely and bound to fail. And Mills wanted them to know that he thought it all to be very fine, but he couldn't find the words to say that without sounding silly.

So in the way of men who are good at doing but not at feeling or at saying how they feel, he took off his hat, nodded, and looked intently at Pinky and pointed at Pinky's chest with the hat and he said, "Tell her that I know, Pinky. And tell her that if either of you ever need anything, anything at all, come get me. I'll help."

If Pinky had not been so absorbed in his newfound love, he might have noticed how far Mills had strayed from the beaten path of his own feelings to make such an offer, and he might have given

Mills some acknowledgment. Or, if Pinky had known that he was wanted for murder and was being pursued across the Outback by Dave Wilson, or if he had known Bobbie would be accused of cattle thievery and chased into the bush, he might have said much more than he did. But he said only, "Thanks, Mills. I think the best you can help us with is to keep her secret."

TWENTY-EIGHT
MAY 1955

When the drive passed near Alice Springs, two young and inexperienced drovers in training—called "spare boys" because they cared for the spare horses—were added to the roster to replace two drovers who had decided they could be of more use back on their home stations.

One boy was 14 and, given his inexperience, justifiably uncertain and quiet. The other was 15, unjustifiably sure of himself and loud. Though with the herd for a week, the boys stayed to themselves, met only the foreman and the cook and a couple of drovers. They had seen, though not met, most of the other men, but had not seen Bobbie, who, on one unfortunate day, went off to collect water for herself and Pinky.

———·———

The quiet spare boy, assigned the task of collecting stragglers on the back side of the drive, came upon a scene he could not at first fathom. A young blackfella, appearing not much older than he, and dressed as a drover, was standing in front of a downed steer holding the head of the steer in his hands. Behind him a few yards stood two older blackfellas, who, judging by their appearance, were bushmen.

As the quiet spare boy watched, and the bushmen waited, the hind legs of the steer kicked hard a couple of times and relaxed into death.

One of the bushmen waved a spear he had been holding low, warning the young blackfella to leave. The young blackfella was tall and thin, obviously, the quiet spare boy thought, no match for either of the stout-looking men facing him. The young blackfella dropped the head of the steer, and backed away.

The quiet-boy decided a cattle theft was taking place, and shot his pistol in the air. Before his blinking eyes had opened, the two bushmen were gone, and the young blackfella was looking directly at him.

Not knowing what to do next and not relishing the thought of shooting a man, even if he was a blackfella killing cattle, the quiet-boy turned and rode away. He had traveled no more than 200 yards when he encountered the other spare boy and told him quickly how a young blackfella had killed a steer and would have given it to two bushmen, but he'd scared them off with a pistol shot.

The other spare boy, being sure of himself, knew exactly what to do and urged his mate to lead him to the scene of the crime. Arriving there, he saw a young blackfella, curiously dressed as any other drover rather than a bushman, but nevertheless identified as a cattle killer, so he quickly drew his pistol, which was a signal for the young blackfella to begin a run for his life downhill and very fast. As the young blackfella leaped into a dry gulch, the sure-boy snapped off a shot that hit inches above the young blackfella's ducking head, scattering gravel but missing the target. Believing the running blackfella would stay in the cover of the gulch and run downhill, the sure-boy urged his horse toward a point where the gulch curved back on itself and he could intersect the fleeing thief. His companion followed, and this young, uncertain drover, who a moment earlier felt that he could not shoot a person, was caught up in the chase. And leaving his unmolded sense of morality with the sweat that fell from his horse to the red dust, he gave a whoop and a loud warbling laugh and rode swiftly on his way, intent to kill.

———·———

Bobbie soared downward 10 feet, landed hard, and collapsed into the sandy bottom. Hearing the hoofbeats pass at a distance on their way downhill, she changed direction and, in a crouch, walked up the gulch to the cover of a massive cottonwood and sat.

The sound of the whooping and the insane laughter subsided for a moment. Then she could hear the horses returning and, though most of the yelling was indistinct, clearly heard "thieving bastard" among their rhetoric. Knowing her assailants would try to find tracks and that she had very little time before they returned, Bobbie climbed from the gulch, and grateful she was barefoot, which left more indistinct tracks than boots, doubled back on the drovers' trail, running hard for a mile and then slowing to a ground-covering lope that she knew she could maintain for hours. In two hours, Bobbie arrived upon a great plateau of rock where no footprint could be seen and changed direction toward Alice Springs and the hope of obtaining a horse, then following Pinky and the herd toward Adelaide.

Running along a rock outcrop, Bobbie passed beside a bush and, expecting firm ground underfoot, found only air. She fell sideways, grabbing a branch as she went down. Swinging on the pendulum of the branch, she crashed into a rock wall, smashing her shin, then falling at least her height to the rock floor below. Her head hit a glancing blow on a branch near the bottom, likely saving her life, but knocking her unconscious.

As she lay hurt, Bobbie periodically became vaguely conscious. On one occasion it was daylight with the sun overhead, and on another it was evening with the most beautiful sunset colors she could remember. Then it was night with stars, brilliant in the deep darkness of the sky, and then it was morning again. In her more lucid moments, Bobbie knew she needed water but she could not stand and could not stay awake.

Toward the end of the second day an old man happened by. Not by chance. In a dream he saw himself come upon a young half-caste who was injured. The figure in the dream was murky, but the place in the dream was clear and he knew it well, so went there and found a boy dressed as a drover. His hair was matted into a cut on the back of his scalp, and his shin was bloody.

The old man washed the drover's wounds and spoke a song of healing. Then he set up a brush shelter and foraged for bush tucker and water. He went away at daylight and returned in the evening. He saw that the drover slept most of the time, but on the second day was awake and was alert, so the old man stayed for a while, asking questions about his origins and the origins of his kin. The answers were often no more than a shrug, so the old man said, "Words create a path for the mind to follow. With only the words of the whites you think as the whites and see the world as they see the world. Knowing only the words of the whites, you are lost. Now you must know the words of the people. With the words of the people, you will know the people and the land and how the world was formed."

With that he began telling stories and songs every boy should know.

———··———

On a morning with wind and the promise of heat, Bobbie awoke feeling strong, and after searching for the old man decided it was time to leave. She went to the top of a hill to gain her sense of direction. The old man was there waiting. He pointed in the direction of Adelaide, and Bobbie chose to go there rather than to Alice. Then the old man stepped over a hide water bag and a few steps into the bush could no longer be seen.

Bobbie picked up the water bag and struck out for Adelaide, thinking of Pinky Wollerman and feeling empty and lonely for the first time in her life.

———··———

On the day of the dead steer, Pinky was with Mills moving a dozen of the more recalcitrant steers across the Myrtle River. They heard a gunshot, but it sounded to be a far distance to the east of the drive, and the balking steers needed all the attention the men could give them. When in the middle of the herd, the cattle had traveled for days, crossing rivers as easily as pastures. But now, in this small group they had become stupid and would sometimes shy away from the banks of the river, sometimes stop at the bank and refuse to step into the water, and sometimes even turn around mid-river to go back to the shore they had come from. When all were across but for one firmly disagreeable steer that would not set one hoof in the water, Mills fashioned a breaststrap for his horse from a saddle blanket and rope, lassoed the steer around the horns, and pulled him across, nearly drowning him in the process and, by that time, hardly caring. As days went on the track, this was a bad day, and Mills was in a foul mood.

When they arrived in camp that afternoon, the sure-boy was telling the tale of the steer-killing blackfella they had shot and wounded and had chased out of the country. When they described the complete scene, Mills asked for a description of the blackfella standing over the dying steer, and when the boys had completed their description, Mills looked over at Pinky, who was watching the eastern horizon. Then Mills asked the boys where this happened, and the two pointed in the same direction. The quiet one said, "A couple hours ride over there. On the side of the only mountain between the folded country and the flat country." Mills had never heard the place described in those words, but the description fit a place he knew. He nodded and told the two boys to mount up and lead him to the scene of the crime. Before they left the camp, Mills told the boys to bring their swags with them, and they assumed he meant to send them to track down the blackfella. By the time the boys were ready, Pinky had already ridden out.

When they found the steer, the dingos had begun to tear at the body, but the carcass was whole enough for Mills to see that the cause of death was an infected leg, possibly from a snake bite. "You say the boy was giving the bushmen the steer?" he asked.

"Yessir," the quiet one said. "He'd killed it, but they threatened him, and he backed away. They'd have taken it if I hadn't shot in the air."

Mills turned to Pinky. "Bobbie knows we often leave a bullock leg for the desert bushmen and probably didn't figure it was worth fighting over. Especially with that poisoned leg."

Pinky nodded.

"Who's Bobbie?" the quiet one asked.

"One of us," Pinky replied. "How badly did you wound him?"

The quiet-boy looked at the sure-boy, and when the sure-boy didn't speak the quiet-boy said, "Walt lied. Couldn't tell if the shot hit or missed. He got away clean."

Pinky said nothing, but tears streaked slowly down through the dust on his cheeks.

"You boys can go on now," Mills said.

The two boys looked at each other and the sure one asked, "Where to?"

"The Alice." Mills said, pausing long enough for the boys to look at him, then in the direction of the herd, and then at each other, and then toward Alice Springs.

"You know the way 'cause we just came by there. And a thousand head of cattle leaves a trail that can't be missed." Mills tossed a small but heavy cotton sack to the quiet-boy and said, "There's enough food in here to get you back if you don't dawdle. And you know where the water is, but some of it is fickle, so make sure you tank up when you can and carry as much as you have canteens for."

"I won't leave without my pay," the sure-boy said, trying to sound sure.

"Shut up, Walt," the quiet-boy said.

"Pay's in the tucker bag," Mills said to the quiet-boy, who looked out at the horizon looming between him and Alice Springs. Mills addressed him. "You want to amount to anything, you best pay attention to who your friends are." Then Mills turned his horse back toward the herd, and Pinky followed, leaving the two spare boys on their own.

"Something's wrong, or she'd be back at the herd by now," Pinky said.

"Getting shot at spooks a person," Mills replied.

"Where would she go from here?"

"Her mum, Daisy Green, works at a station over by Blenheim Creek. That's closer than Sturt Creek Station and seems a likely place to run to, if you think you're being chased."

"Maybe she went back to Alice Springs?"

"The Alice would be my second guess, Pinky. But with family at Blenheim she could get outfitted for the trip to catch up with the herd on the way to Adelaide. But it's damned hard to guess how she might think. She might even be heading to Adelaide on foot."

"I'll start with Blenheim then. Can you point me, Mills?"

Mills shook his head slowly. "I know better than to try to talk you out of it, Pinky, and blind-stabbing it to Blenheim Creek may not be as foolhardy as you setting out on the Canning Stock Route by yourself, but it's damned foolhardy."

Pinky said nothing, so Mills went on. "It's about two days from here on horseback if you know where you're going. It will take you three. Or more. Come on back to the herd and pick up a spare horse. And pack a tucker bag and some extra water canteens. I'll give you the best of my memory."

Within a half hour Pinky was packed. Mills watched him ride out with little more than a direction pointed to guide him. It was hard country to traverse alone, and he wondered if he would ever again see Pinky or Bobbie.

----··----

Bobbie left the old man on a day that darkened into a moonless night, and she spent the night in a dry camp and dreamed. In her dream she came upon the herd, but it was far away. She sat atop a ridge and watched as the procession slowly approached, and she wondered about Pinky.

Then, in the way of dreams, a cat appeared beside her. The cat was not there and she did not hear him come, but then he was there and said clearly, "My name is Henry."

The cat, a brindle mix of black and tan and grey, leapt gracefully up onto a boulder. "Henry" seemed a strangely plain name for such a fellow, but Bobbie nodded and with the deep-seated caution of the years, presented herself as the boy drover.

Henry offered Bobbie water from a canteen that appeared before her. She accepted the canteen and drank.

"Are you following the herd?"

"No," she said, thinking the cat sounded more like an American than an Australian. Henry's coat was smooth, and he seemed well-fed. Bobbie thought the cat was not from anywhere close by and had not been in the Outback for long.

"You've been watching them for some time now."

Bobbie felt the indifference of many years come over her, and she did not respond in any way. And as Henry watched her, she believed her body to be invisible. And yet she feared her thoughts, her feelings, her motivations even down to that which she knew to be her "self" — were transparent to this cat named Henry.

They sat together and looked out at the land, watched the herd move through the valley, watched the clouds float slowly over, and Henry said, "He's a good man."

"Who is?" Bobbie lied, and immediately knew that Henry could feel a lie pass through the air like others feel a dry wind.

Still watching the cattle, Henry said, "Mr. Wollerman."

A moment later he said, "Roland. A name few know."

Henry looked at her, and she was sure he smiled. "Most call him Pinky. Only you have seen his whiteness that burns without tanning."

Suddenly, Henry's face, covered in worry, expanded to fill her field of vision, and he said, "He is also known across the Outback as the bush ranger, the Yankee Ghost."

Bobbie knew the first three names were right, and so she wondered if the fourth was also. Then, with some urgency, Bobbie felt the need to relieve herself and reached to remove Henry from her shoulder. But Henry was gone and she awoke, troubled, and wondering what the dream meant. She felt a chill pass through the warmth of the morning. Then as she realized the need to relieve herself was real, she thought perhaps the whole dream had been initiated by that simple physical anxiety. She could not reconcile anything she had known of Pinky with the claim that he was an outlaw. Nor had she heard of an outlaw called the Yankee Ghost.

When Bobbie picked up her things to begin the day's journey, she was surprised to find the canteen full, though she could not remember when she filled it. The dream stayed with her as she walked toward Adelaide, loping when she could, hoping to overtake the herd before it arrived there.

———··———

Pinky's ride to Daisy's Station by Blenheim Creek took four days, and he was starting to worry that he might be lost when he happened upon two half-caste drovers eager for information from anywhere, who guided him to the station house. The drovers, in countenance and stature looked exactly alike, sitting in the saddle with the same slouch, holding the reins slightly aloft in their left hands, and cocking their heads in the same direction and same angle as they listened or talked. Their saddles were black and identically worn, and their horses were the same size, but one was a red roan and the other a blue roan. The man sitting the red wore a red shirt, and the one on the blue wore a blue shirt. When Pinky asked about Daisy, the two men looked at each other, as though communicating, but neither spoke. Pinky told them he was hoping to meet Daisy's daughter, the stable hand and drover he had worked with at the Sturt Creek Station. Again the two men looked at each other without speaking. Pinky allowed the quiet to sit unnoticed for a time, and then one of the men said Daisy had a son who was a drover, but not a daughter. Pinky described Bobbie's physical appearance and her life as a drover and the love between them that had allowed her to acknowledge she was a woman. The two men brightened, for they knew Daisy and Bobbie's secret, and although they knew Bobbie by a different name, they were eager to talk to her after so many years away. But, Red Shirt said, they did not know when Bobbie might return, and Blue Shirt said that Daisy had gone away for a while.

"Walkabout?" Pinky asked.

The two drovers shook their heads in unison.

"No," Red Shirt said. "She is ill and wanted to be with her daughter in Wiluna."

Blue Shirt frowned and said, "Women don't go walkabout."

––––––

At Daisy's station, unable to sit and wait, Pinky approached the station master and offered to pitch in for no pay. He worked the stable and helped with the remuda. The station master and his wife were a kindly, well-educated and curious couple, and Pinky enjoyed the distraction of their conversation over dinner. Like Andy and Melinda Fraser at Sturt Creek, they were more concerned about the welfare of the Aboriginals who worked for them or lived in the area than some station owners were.

On the second day the two drovers asked him to help dip a small herd of cattle recently purchased from a bush drover who rounded up and sold unbranded strays for a living. Pinky went with them, hoping every moment of those two days that Bobbie or Daisy would be there when he returned. But they were not, and his fear that Bobbie had gone to Alice began to crystallize. He realized she could have reached Alice in the week he had wasted on this trip to Blenheim Creek.

That evening Pinky filled his canteens, put three bullies and some bread in his saddle bags, and announced his intention to find Bobbie in the Alice.

"Adelaide," both drovers said to him in unison, pointing in that direction.

But Pinky believed, as Mills had, that the second most likely place Bobbie would have gone was back to the Alice. The drover look-a-likes shrugged and wished him well.

———·———

In Alice, Pinky stopped at the first livery he came to, left his horse there with a stable boy who was not Bobbie, and asked that his horse be well cared for. He walked the streets of Alice in search of Bobbie. He walked through the alleys and skirted the camps of the blacks in the blue gums down by the creek, asking everyone he met about a boy, about this high, slender, with an easy face. He did not find Bobbie nor anyone who had seen such a drover, so on second thought, he went to the diners and bars and hotels, not expecting to see Bobbie as a patron but perhaps to see her in the kitchen with dishes or sweeping up or scrubbing littered floors or stained tables.

Every time he saw Bobbie's face, she was at a distance and her face was always that of someone else when he came close.

On the morning of the second day, fearing that Bobbie must have doubled back on the path of the cattle drive and headed back to Sturt Creek, Pinky went to the livery stable, paid up his bill, and asked that his horse be ready after he had his breakfast. Then he strolled through the town again, for one last hopeful but unpromising look.

After seeing many disappointing faces, some more than twice, Pinky thought he recognized a face through the window of the Red Dingo Diner. His spirit soared, but the boy left through the back door before he could be certain. Pinky hastily backtracked from the window to the diner's entrance, only to run headlong into a short but rather stout man leaving the diner.

"Oops, sorry, mate," Pinky said, standing back to allow the man to descend the steps to the street. The man was dressed somewhat like a drover and smelled strongly of many days in the Outback.

"No worries, mate. But the food's not worth such haste." The man tipped a finger to the front of his well-worn leather hat and hurried into the nearly vacant street.

"Gooday, mate," Pinky said stepping into the doorway.

"Name's Darcy," the man called over his shoulder.

Standing in the doorway to the diner, Pinky waved and yelled at the man's receding back, "Wollerman. Pinky Wollerman. Thanks for the tip, Mr. Darcy,"

When Pinky stepped into the diner, Bobbie was nowhere to be seen. The cooking area and dining area were part of one large room. Pinky could see only an outhouse through the open back door of the diner. He ran to the doorway and looked out. An old Aboriginal man sat on his heels in the red dirt a few feet from the back door, and the man said he had seen no one pass by. Pinky ran to the outhouse and knocked on the outside, "Bobbie? Bobbie! You in there?" The old man watched and shook his head.

Going back inside, Pinky found the diner vacant. He tried to remember what he had seen on his way to the back door. He was sure there was a man standing somewhere near the stove with his arms stretched upward in what might have been a greeting — or might have been.

Pinky heard the commotion long before the loud footfall of running men and the cursing of angry men burst through the front entrance. He understood little of the excited Australian-accented discussion between a man with an apron and a man with a drawn pistol. But certain words registered, such as "thief" and "robber," and Pinky perfectly understood the message of the pistol as it was brandished in his direction by a wild-eyed, screaming man. So without waiting for a chance to discuss the man's concerns, Pinky bolted for the back door.

As he approached the doorway, someone yelled, "Duck!" And as Pinky did, he heard the pistol boom and, a few feet in front of him, saw the old black man falling forward off his heels and splinters flying from the outhouse wall. In his haste, Pinky's right shoulder slammed into the door frame, the momentum spinning him into an unbalanced right turn. And the only way to maintain his footing was to run faster, which seemed like a good idea anyway and was a fortunate choice because the man with the gun burst out the diner's back door and tripped over his unintended casualty, who was cursing the crazy whitefellas and holding his left ear. Before the gun-wielding crazy man could stand again, Pinky was five buildings away from the horribly inaccurate pistol and approaching the livery stable where his horse stood saddled and readied.

It passed through Pinky's mind that he was lucky to have already squared his bill because he would not want to leave with a debt unpaid. He leaped upon the wide-eyed horse and urged him into an immediate gallop toward the back side of the buildings across the street. In the shadows he glimpsed a figure who looked like Bobbie, but he did not think it a good idea to stop. So he rode out of the small huddle of buildings called Alice Springs and down past the camp of the Aborigines in the river bottom. His horse kicked plumes of sand and rock in a series of quick S-turns around the stands of massive old eucalyptus trees, and Pinky could hear shouts of encouragement—"Ride, mate, ride!" and "Go, bush ranger!" and "Bugger the constable!"

Pinky followed a well-trampled cattle trail out into the bush and could hear the crazy man's yells growing fainter behind him. "Stop in the name of the law, you thieving bastard!"

The man again fired his pistol, but he could no longer see Pinky and had the gun pointed high in the air so as to incur no more bystander casualties, which he knew would cause a great deal of consternation in the community.

Pinky knew he would come back to Alice someday and clear up whatever misunderstanding had occurred, but he also knew this was not the day, so he rode the grulla hard until he could no longer hear the sounds of pursuit. Then he slowed the horse to a walk, staying in the dry river bottom where there were many tracks to confuse his own.

———·———

Upon recounting the day's events, Constable Richardson noted that Mr. Byron Tilden, the owner of the Red Dingo Diner, had sought Richardson's assistance to apprehend two thieves who had stolen

$2, three tins of beef and an expensive meal. The first man's name was overheard to be Darcy, and hearing the man's description, the constable had no doubt he was the notorious bushranger Melvin Darcy. The second man was dressed like a drover and smelled like one, according to eyewitnesses, who seemed to grow in number as the constable investigated. But all who heard him agreed that the man sounded foreign, probably American.

Judging from the enthusiasm of the blacks in the river bottom camps, it would seem that the second man was a member of the Darcy mob. According to the constable's recounting of the incident, Darcy's accomplice, who he named "the Yankee," shot an innocent old man as he escaped. The stable boy said the Yankee had called upon the stable earlier in the day to ensure that his horse would be saddled and readied upon his return. The constable saw this as clear evidence of a well-planned robbery perpetrated by dangerous men. Furthermore, Darcy had too much of a head start, and the Yankee, with the skills particular to outlaws, easily concealed the route of his escape so that no immediate chase was possible. And, he said, looking perplexed, the Yankee rode a strange, winding route among the big blue gums in the river bottom and then faded away like smoke in the wind. The constable knew it wasn't exactly like that, but people were asking him why he hadn't given chase, and this explained why and fit neatly with the story that the blacks in the river bottom were telling.

Their version of the incident was what the old black man told — the shot that took off the top of his ear had come from behind the fleeing drover, and the bullet had passed through the drover without causing harm. It was, he said, as though the Yankee was a spirit. No thought was given as to why a spirit might have to flee, and when the men in the river bottom camp heard the story, they remembered the stealthy drover, how easily he had passed through their camp, touching nothing, and evaporating into the bush as to make them wonder if it was a man or a ghost that had ridden through.

Constable Richardson's conclusion that the Yankee was part of the Darcy mob was confirmed when a week later he was visited by Dave Wilson, a lawman who had traveled all the way from California in the United States to apprehend the murderer Pinky Wollerman, who exactly fit the description of the Yankee. Constable Richardson made sure his confirmed assessment was communicated to every lawman and newspaper from Perth to Sydney and from Darwin to Adelaide.

In fact, it was Constable Richardson's insistence on making his routing of the Darcy mob known throughout Australia that gave the American cowboy known as the Yankee his legendary status among European Australians, many of whom already had a historically ingrained disrespect for law enforcement.

The second version of the incident in Alice became the story of the Yankee Ghost and was passed from the encampment in the river bottom and through the Aboriginal communities. The river bottom version took a little longer than the constable's version to make its way through the Outback, but not much.

Of course, the two stories together made an even better story, and eventually they were woven together by Australian newspapers.

———·——

Pinky left the Alice knowing there had been a terrible misunderstanding, but knowing nothing of his growing criminal reputation.

TWENTY-NINE
JUNE 1955

Judge Garrett knew things. He knew the people living in the suburbs wanted a mix of city convenience and country seclusion. From his local and state political connections, he knew a freeway would be built within a few years that would bring the Buck Wilson ranch, with its idyllic combination of rolling foothills, shady oaks and grass lands, into an acceptable driving distance from the city. Developing the area, starting with perhaps 20 houses and expanding to 10 or 20 times that as the area grew in popularity and value, could make many millions of dollars.

Judge Garrett was not a patient man. He had held his Tulare County judgeship for only a few months, but, he thought, what's the good of holding power if you don't make it pay off? And the real payoff in Buck Wilson's death was in managing the trust for Logan's inheritance of Buck's ranch. Managing it for Logan's wealth — and the wealth of the boy's investment partners — partners already identified by Judge Garrett and his associates.

The boy was a minor, so for several years after the inheritance, his mother, Emily Robin Macadam, would have responsibility for the affairs of the ranch, a task for which she had no preparation. She could be easily convinced to hire Judge Garrett's former law firm to manage the trust, making it easy to steer towards the development project. But what if she turned out to be the killer? In that event, Dave Wilson, as Logan's uncle, would likely become the trustee, and Dave was fully capable of managing the trust.

But Judge Garrett had an idea. It wouldn't be hard to pull off if he had the assistance of the sheriff's office and the district attorney's office, which he was certain he could finesse, and all of the necessary players were waiting for him in his chambers.

———·——

Judge Garrett walked into his chambers without looking at the three men he'd called together. Each of them had a different way of thinking about the Buck Wilson murder investigation.

Deputy Dillard was the only one he hadn't known before Buck's murder. The man seemed smart and competent, presented the image of a leader and was ambitious. And his ambition, Garrett noticed, surfaced only below the radar of his superiors. All were good qualities for what he had in mind.

District Attorney Webster was extremely sharp, politically ambitious, and morally corrupt. Everyone except Sheriff Dave Wilson knew that he'd had an affair with Dave's wife, Twyla. And it was clear as soon as Garrett had his first golf course discussion with Webster that Webster's only interest in this murder case was making sure Twyla didn't get hung for the murder. District Attorney Webster would also fit nicely into the plan.

Judge Garrett had watched over the years as Sergeant Gordon had appeared in court as an arresting officer. He clearly had slipped into being a bureaucratic lackey, mostly interested in hanging on until retirement. But Gordon seemed to know the most about Dave Wilson's activities in Australia, so he had to be included in this meeting.

———·———

Judge Garrett had the attention of the three men but rapped his knuckles on his desk anyway and opened the meeting with, "It seems the murder investigation of Buck Wilson is going nowhere." Judge Garrett continued immediately because he knew there would be no argument. He was a judge, and it didn't really matter if his assertion was accurate. "Let me be clear that I intend to recuse myself from this case, so you can talk openly with me with no conflict of interest." The three men's faces showed neither comprehension nor disagreement, so he said, "Let's jump in. Deputy Dillard, who are the suspects?"

Judge Garrett expected that Deputy Dillard recognized the impropriety of a judge inserting himself in the case, but his supervisor, Sergeant Gordon, was sitting right next to him, so he probably wouldn't balk if Gordon didn't, and Gordon wasn't the kind of man to disagree with the power structure.

As Judge Garrett expected, Deputy Dillard, before answering, looked to Sergeant Gordon, who remained quiet.

Deputy Dillard turned back to the judge and began. "It is quite a list, your honor. Turns out Buck pissed off a lot of folks."

Judge Garrett nodded. "Okay. List the names first and then we'll talk about them."

"Well, we all know Sheriff Wilson is in Australia chasing down Pinky Wollerman, and that puts Wollerman at the beginning of the list."

Everyone nodded.

"As I did some checking, I added Emily Robin Macadam, Bill Jenkins, and Kazuko Nakamura. Arturo Hernandez's name came up, but I've ruled him out."

"Is that all?" Judge Garrett asked.

"No, sir."

Judge Garrett saw Deputy Dillard glance at District Attorney Webster. It was clear the deputy wasn't anxious to name the next suspect. It was probably Twyla Wilson, and the deputy, like everyone else, knew about Webster's hard on for Twyla.

"I think we might have to include Sheriff Wilson's wife, Twyla, as a serious suspect."

"Does Dave know?" Judge Garrett asked quickly.

Sergeant Gordon waved Dillard off and took the question. "Sheriff Wilson has been in some remote places lately and hasn't had regular communication with this office. But who knows? He didn't get to be sheriff for two terms without good contacts."

During the sergeant's response Judge Garrett didn't take his eyes off Deputy Dillard. "Why is Kazuko Nakamura on the list?"

"When the war with Japan started, Buck made accusations that landed Kaz in an internment camp up north while his parents got sent over to Lone Pine. Manzanar. His parents were old. They got sick and died in the camp. Kaz figures he could have helped them if he'd been with them."

"And Bill Jenkins?" Judge Garrett asked.

"Same problem Buck had with Pinky. Bill owns a piece of land that once belonged to the Wilson family, and Buck wanted it back. It's a marginal place and Bill was having a tough go of it, and Buck did everything he could to starve Bill out."

Judge Garrett nodded. "Is losing a worthless farm enough reason to kill a man?"

"It is if all you got in the world is that piece of land, worthless or not. Besides, I stopped a long time ago trying to decide what's reason enough to kill a man."

Judge Garrett sat quiet and poker-faced, so Dillard went on. "Emily Robin Macadam followed Buck here from New Zealand after the war. Seems that Buck had knocked her up and abandoned her there."

Judge Garrett immediately saw this infidelity as motive for Buck's wife, but decided that whatever reason Dillard had for not including Mindy Wilson as a suspect was a good reason, even if it was because Dillard hadn't thought of it. So he did not interrupt Dillard's report on Emily Robin.

"It's been quite a few years," Dillard was saying, "and Emily Robin seems like a proper lady, and, as far as we know, there'd been no contact between her and Buck. Recently she's been living on Pinky's place, and word is that she's taken with the little man, or at least his place, so it seems unlikely she'd want to shoot Buck and mess that up. But she's got strong motive."

"Isn't her son, Logan, Buck's heir?"

"I've heard that, your honor. But not from a source I can quote."

Judge Garrett knew he had dropped a bombshell and could see Deputy Dillard tense up, but Garrett went on as though he'd said nothing unusual. "I think I heard about Arturo. Seems there was a tractor belonging to Arturo that Buck said he'd borrowed and Arturo said Buck had stolen."

Deputy Dillard looked relieved at the change of subject. "That's the short version, your honor. But, whatever it was that happened, Arturo has a priest that says he was at an all-day wedding celebration on the day of Buck's death. Him and all his boys. A priest's word is a pretty good alibi. And Arturo's built more for calf roping than hopping fences. Anyway, I think we can count Arturo out."

"And Twyla?" Judge Garrett asked.

Deputy Dillard took a deep breath. "Buck inherited the ranch when his daddy died because he was the oldest boy, and that was their family custom. Dave accepted his position as younger brother and didn't quibble. But it was a sore point with Twyla from the day she married Dave. As time went on and they didn't have kids, Twyla assumed he would name either Dave or her and Dave's boy as heir. Twyla was publicly and vocally both certain and eager. But Buck didn't do that. When he found out he had a son by Emily Robin, he named Logan as heir. Twyla was pissed off that a bastard son was spoiling her plans. Pissed to the point of raving. The night janitor at the courthouse told me he heard her shouting at Dave one night, threatening to kill Buck. Two weeks later Buck was killed, and a witness saw someone who looked and moved like Twyla in the vicinity of the murder, driving a truck that looked like one the Wilsons have. I'm afraid she is as strong a suspect as Pinky Wollerman." Deputy Dillard looked again toward District Attorney Webster who was scowling at the ceiling lights. "Maybe stronger."

Judge Garrett remained poker-faced. "What's happened with Wollerman?"

"Well," Sergeant Gordon jumped in, "Pinky's been the most promising suspect from the git go. Everybody knows Buck wanted Pinky's place, and pushed him around in public. And Pinky took off the same damned day Buck was shot.

"What's more, I traded wires a couple days ago with a constable near Alice Springs, smack dab in the middle of Australia. Seems Pinky may have thrown in his lot with a famous outlaw, or 'bush ranger' as they call them. The two are alleged to have held up an eatery of some kind.

"But then, strange as it sounds, he got clean away. Just disappeared. Like a ghost, the constable said. He's managed to stay a step ahead of Sheriff Wilson and few people have actually laid eyes on Pinky. Lots of them have seen where he's been and heard what he's done. But neither Wilson nor the Australian lawmen can find him. The constable says folks down there enjoy a good outlaw, and they haven't had one in a while, and so Pinky has become kind of a hero. A ghost hero, he said. Constable said the Outback is a harsh place and he thinks the man is most likely dead by now, but even if he isn't, he don't think anyone will ever find him."

Judge Garrett decided it was time to put the pieces of his plan together. "Deputy Dillard, you ever think about running for sheriff?"

Sergeant Gordon sat bolt upright and scowled at Dillard.

Dillard kept his eyes on the judge and answered evenly, "No, sir. I have not."

Judge Garrett didn't believe him.

"You have any suspects to add to Dillard's list?" Judge Garrett asked Sergeant Gordon. Gordon shook his head, so Judge Garrett went on to the second leg of the plan. "You know what we have here? Unless something unforeseen and substantial falls in our laps, it seems to me we have so many suspects with so much circumstantial evidence that none of your suspects can be convicted."

Judge Garrett saw District Attorney Webster brighten and knew he had just recognized how this line of thought could address his interest in not having Twyla investigated too closely.

Webster spoke hurriedly. "No matter who we prosecute, they'll point the finger at one or two other suspects with at least as damning a case against them, and we'll be chasing our tails."

Judge Garrett smiled inwardly at how easy it had been to co-opt District Attorney Webster. He thought Deputy Dillard was on board also, but wasn't sure yet. "Who's in charge in Sheriff Wilson's absence?"

"Undersheriff Bertolli," Gordon answered. "But he appointed Captain Clements to be in charge of the investigation."

Judge Garrett, remembering the bullish common sense of Bertolli, said, "Let's get Captain Clements over here and make some decisions about this case. We can brief Bertolli later. If you boys need a piss break, this is the time. Judges' bathroom is down the hall on the left, and contrary to what you may have heard, it don't get any more crap than any other."

Sergeant Gordon and Deputy Dillard stood to go, and Judge Garrett said, "It's a one-holer, so unless you two are more friendly than it seems, you might want to take turns."

Sergeant Gordon went for the door, leaving Deputy Dillard behind.

"Rank has its privileges," Judge Garrett said. Then, when Sergeant

Gordon was well down the hall, said, "Listen up, Dillard. You clearly have the smarts to do police work, but you've also got what's known as command presence. And, given the right endorsements, you could also have voter appeal. Dave Wilson isn't going to withstand the negative press of having chased the wrong man to the other side of the world at taxpayer expense. There are a number of people who will happily make sure of that. As a judge, I need an effective sheriff leading that office. As a man with an eye for talent, I recognize you could be that man." He paused. "Could be."

Deputy Dillard cocked his head to the side.

Judge Garrett was waiting for Dillard to digest what he'd offered when District Attorney Webster showed the judge that *he* knew what "could be" meant when he said, "Could be that it depends on how this investigation shakes out, Deputy Dillard. Judgment and discretion are often more apparent in vague situations such as this."

Judge Garrett nodded.

Deputy John Dillard knew his ship had come in, and he didn't want to run it aground. He thought there might be more to be learned on this case—for instance, what about Buck's slighted wife, Mindy Wilson. She was reputed to have been in San Francisco at the time of the murder, but he hadn't confirmed that. But he didn't consider her a strong suspect, and his investigative results had been inconclusive even for the strong suspects. Deputy Dillard thought Judge Garrett and District Attorney Webster clearly had some reason for ousting Sheriff Wilson, maybe not the same reason, but Dillard had the confidence in his talent and intuition that he would someday figure it out, and he thought the two men might even have good and honorable reasons. And finally, Dillard recognized that both of them, again maybe for different reasons, wanted the investigation to stop, which Dillard could accomplish by putting the investigation into operational limbo. He could see the two men's assertion that the case would be difficult to prosecute as reason enough to make that happen. It wasn't ironclad logic, but it could be worked into a convincing story, if anyone were ever to inquire.

So, with no more time to think, Deputy Dillard said, "Why don't you let me take the lead with Captain Clements? He knows good police work and appreciates how I've handled this one. I'll suggest we take everyone off the case but me, and I'll spend some time finding out more about that mysterious black pickup. When Sheriff Wilson brings Wollerman back—if he brings Wollerman back—we'll interrogate him if the case hasn't taken another turn by then."

Two wrongs don't make a right, Dillard thought, smiling, but sometimes four or five do.

Judge Garrett and District Attorney Webster were also smiling.

When Sergeant Gordon returned, the judge asked him if he had summoned Captain Clements. But when Sergeant Gordon shook his head and picked up the phone, Judge Garrett took the phone from his hand, returned it to the cradle, and said, "That call is no longer necessary."

———·———

Gordon noticed that no one else rose to go to the restroom, and from the satisfied looks on all their faces knew he'd missed something important and would be left on his own to figure out what it was.

———·———

The morning after Judge Garrett's summit meeting, a document titled "Preliminary Closing Report of the Charles Anders Wilson Murder Investigation" arrived simultaneously on the desks of Judge Garrett, Undersheriff Bertolli, District Attorney Webster, Captain Clements and Sergeant Gordon.

Undersheriff Bertolli shook his head and knew from the simultaneous distribution that he was witnessing checkmate in a game of chess that he had not been invited to play.

The conclusion of the report was that, at the time, there was insufficient evidence to consider Pinky Wollerman, Emily Robin Macadam, Kazuko Nakamura, Bill Jenkins, or Twyla Wilson as viable suspects. The report stated the killer could have been an unknown person who drove the black pickup.

An addendum to the report noted that Buck Wilson was an

extremely possessive property owner who was known to physically confront trespassers, especially hunters. In just the past year two hunters had filed complaints, one saying that Buck had shot near him, the other saying he had been struck in the face and knocked down by Mr. Wilson. Both dropped their charges after hearing they could be counter-charged with trespassing. And so, the report said, the possibility the killer was a trespasser who might have become enraged during a confrontation with Mr. Wilson was as likely a conclusion as any other.

———·———

The day after the report was distributed, District Attorney Webster made sure the press knew the generalities of the report's conclusions and, in terms of highest praise and admiration, told the story of the dedication of an incredibly talented lawman named John Dillard, who had searched out the truth and cleared several local and innocent residents of the County of Tulare. He noted that a good law man was as concerned for the good name of the innocent as he was in catching the guilty, and he was certain the guilty would eventually be caught by Mr. Dillard.

After the official press conference, District Attorney Webster managed to conversationally mention Sheriff Wilson's "wild goose chase, now spanning many weeks" to capture an innocent man, who was, in fact, a respected rancher and a good neighbor of Buck Wilson. Gaining righteous indignation as he spoke, the District Attorney also noted that Sheriff Wilson was pursuing this ill-conceived, taxpayer-financed trip to an exotic location while his wife, Twyla, was left behind to undergo the arduous ordeal of being falsely named as a suspect.

PART FOUR

THIRTY

JUNE 1955

On the way to Adelaide, Bobbie was met on the trail by the bush ranger who called himself Darcy, and who, being rather proud of his reputation, told of his latest exploit — the story of the Alice diner and the polite American drover. Bobbie, tipping her hat before the man finished his story, turned toward Alice.

In Alice, Bobbie asked the whereabouts of Constable Richardson and found him with an American sheriff named Dave Wilson in a bar talking to two young drovers, one quiet and one loud. The loud one bragged that he shot the Yankee Ghost off his horse in the middle of the Gibson Desert and, though he fled into the twilight and disappeared, the young man was certain the Yankee was wounded so badly he could not have survived the remoteness of the desert and a large pack of dingos they saw in the area. Upon questioning by a doubtful constable, the young men gave a detailed description of the wanted man. Dave Wilson verified the accuracy of their description, and still the lawmen were skeptical. When learning no reward had been offered, the braggarts moved on to a mob of drunk drovers at the other end of the bar.

Hearing that they had worked for Mills, Bobbie wondered if they were the two drovers who had shot at her, so she moved outside the bar and listened discreetly through a window. The quiet young drover seemed amused by the mob who hung on his partner's every word. Then upon being offered drinks for his version of events, he became nearly as boisterous as his loud partner, telling a story of danger and bravery, which, he assured the crowd, was a true story.

Bobbie heard the braggadocio and bull-dust within the telling and was less willing than the bar crowd to accept the boys' story as true. If Pinky was still healthy and on the run, he most likely would go to the Sturt Creek Station, so she set out for there.

On the way Bobbie saw the Old Man in the distance and, hoping he might have some knowledge of Pinky, tried to catch up to him, but the Old Man avoided her.

Bobbie did not find Pinky at Sturt Creek Station, but knew he would return there when he could, so she waited.

THIRTY-ONE
JUNE 1955

Pinky knew he had done nothing wrong, but finding Bobbie was far more important than his reputation in Alice Springs, so he decided he would not return to Alice until after he found Bobbie and, he hoped, when clearer heads prevailed.

Pinky remembered that Mills had promised them help if it was ever needed. Perhaps Bobbie was going to take him up on the offer, in which case she would be following the herd toward Adelaide.

Pinky could not remember for certain if he had or had not told the stable boy he was with the Sturt Creek bunch, but if he had, the crazy constable might be headed that direction, and if he was found there his search would be over. Following the path of the herd toward Adelaide was clearly his best option.

Two nights out Pinky noticed an Aboriginal man on a distant skyline and wondered if he was being watched or followed. On the third sighting Pinky waved to the man and turned his horse toward him. The man disappeared from the skyline, but after following a dry gulch a quarter-mile into the bush, Pinky came to a small billabong, a water hole left from the recent flood. The man, with a balloon of greying curly hair atop sorrowful features, tall for an Aborigine and naked, sat on his heels, watching Pinky approach.

Pinky opened a bully of beef and offered to share with the old man, who reached out his hand to accept, but remained squatting. After they had eaten, Pinky filled his canteen and decided to ask the old man if he had seen the herd or Bobbie. The old man remained on his heels, staring without focus toward the skyline, and did not respond to anything Pinky said. Pinky wondered if he was being understood, but continued because it felt good to talk to someone. He described Bobbie as precisely as he could, and when he said that Bobbie was living as a drover boy but was in reality a woman, the old man suddenly stood and faced away from Pinky and appeared to talk to someone for several minutes. Pinky did not understand the language, but the old man was clearly agitated.

When the old man finished his conversation, he stood, looking into the evening sky for quite a long time, and Pinky respected his silence.

———·———

Thinking that Bobbie was a boy, the old man had passed on knowledge meant only for men. He was not sure what happened to people who told what they should not, or to people who knew what they should not, but he thought the error could be corrected, and in the way of certain old men, decided whatever ill would come of the error would be upon the woman. He mulled this over several times in his mind before deciding it was right. Then, knowing that with spirit matters speaking a thing can make it happen, he chose to speak to the whitefella.

———·———

When the old man finally turned to Pinky, the evening had progressed to the point that Pinky could barely see his features. The old man stared at him a while, turned to the darkness in the east, and spoke the words he believed would right the wrong:

"She is dead."

The old man spoke English well, and Pinky heard the words clearly, but they made no sense, so he asked the old man to repeat himself.

The old man's words scraped across the dry evening air like fingernails on a chalk board. "She is dead. The drover girl that lived as a boy. She was here. She fell and was hurt."

The old man looked into the darkness and thought, but did not say, that the drover girl knew the whitefella words but not the words of her people, the words that make the world as it is. He did not tell Pinky he thought she was a boy and taught her words only men should know. Nor did he say that a woman who hears these words through deceit has sealed her own fate. These thoughts reached into the origins of the people, into the ancient ways, and gave him the power of speaking what must be. And again, but more softly because he knew it was already done, he said, "She is dead."

————·————

As quickly as sound hits the ear, as quickly as a dreadful word can soak through the dry sand of the mind and chill the soul, that quickly Pinky was left behind by the world of the living. His heart and lungs, those parts that are kept engaged by a different will, kept pumping and kept him from the world of the dead, but life had moved on and he had not. He was left standing in the twilight land between — not in the land of either/or but in the land of neither/nor.

If Mills or Bill Jenkins had been there, men he respected, they might have said something that might have helped. They would acknowledge her death but not use the words "die" or "dead." "She was far too young to be gone," or, "She was one of the good ones and it will not be the same out here without her," and eventually, "I know that you loved her, Pinky, and it was plain to see that she loved you as well," and then, "The only way to work out a pain this deep is to keep moving."

And whether or not Pinky's heart or soul could find meaning in their words, the fact that a friend spoke them caringly would provide him with a tether, a dreadfully thin tether, but nevertheless a connection to the world of the living, and it might have pulled Pinky along and eventually pulled him back. But the men were not there, and Pinky fell behind, disconnected from life.

Pinky fell to his knees in the sand next to the billabong, and the anguish sparked by the three final words formed around him, crushing him within a force he could not bear. But he could not cry. When he looked up, the old man was not to be seen. The stars were out, and Pinky tried to see as far into them as he could, but he could see only the emptiness of the nothing that had taken over all of what had been. He had nothing to say, no question, no cry of torment, no prayer. He could find no words because he was in a place where there were none, nor could there be any, because in a place without meaning, words were a useless, ragged sound.

Pinky had nothing to say to God.

If he could have moved, he could have wanted to find a place of relief, but his will had been replaced by the emptiness. And there was no place of comfort to move to.

Throughout that night, the heart, the soul, the whole of the self of Pinky Wollerman remained numb and lifeless, infused with and surrounded by absence.

Then, in the pale light of dawn, long before the sun would rise, Pinky's body suggested that he drink from the pool, and he moved there and drank from his hand, the water tasting foul. But it was a start, and afterward he began to recover himself. Words returned to him, but still he could not pray. He was too angry to address a god without kindness, without compassion, without grace.

As the sun rose and his awareness of the outside world began to function, Pinky saw the thin clouds smeared across the morning sky as empty promises, dead to the thirst of the pleading life below. He now knew the purpose of rock and gravel and dust strewn across the land. It was left by God to impede anyone who would advance, to frustrate, to quell any sense of ease, to make any crossing a thing of great effort.

Pinky had returned to the world, but the beauty of the world was as absent as if it never had been.

The sound of his horse nickering brought back Pinky's humanity. When Pinky looked up, he realized the poor animal had spent the night with his saddle on, and worse yet, with the bit in his mouth. Pinky rose quickly and removed the gear. He stood on stiff legs and watched the horse graze. And in doing these things he was aware that he had regained the ability to feel pain and movement, and, perhaps more importantly, to feel sympathy and remorse.

He looked to the horizons, hoping to see the old man. He wanted to know where Bobbie's body had been laid to rest. He wanted to make certain it was adequately covered and lastingly marked. He wanted to heap love upon that site. And so he called out for the man and climbed to high places to look for him. But the old man was gone.

For three days, Pinky poured his grief and his love across the red earth, and on the morning of the fourth day, when the sun was still well below the horizon, he set out for Perth. Australia now was only a place of sorrow. He was on his way home to the Once Wide Valley. It crossed his mind to write to Andy at Sturt Creek to apologize, but through his grief, apologies seemed worthless to him. He knew he would never contact Andy or Mills or anyone in Australia again.

But Pinky did not know exactly how to get to Perth—he only knew the general direction—so he wandered through the bush, which did not bother him because he needed to be alone. He found bush tucker in the way Bobbie had taught him. He never felt disoriented because he cared so little about how long the trip might be. With help from no one, because he avoided all human contact, turning away from station houses or herds of any kind, Pinky made his way toward the coast.

On one evening he noticed the beauty of a full moon rising and a red sun setting, and he was surprised that he noticed.

A morning came when, having walked through the night by the light of a half moon, Pinky sat on a rock and watched himself as he made his way effortlessly to the top of a low, grassy hill at the edge of a wave of hills where he could see from horizon to horizon. The vast dome of the sky that stretched above it all was stippled with clouds, grey-tinged white stamps upon the pale blue, and their presence left the land speckled with slow moving shadows the size of barns.

Two days after the week of hard rain, the land was green, a thing Pinky had not seen since his arrival in the Outback. Upon receiving water, grass that was ankle high had grown higher than his head. He heard the rush of water in the canyon off to one side and watched as the valley below slowly filled to become a large lake.

When he awoke, the land was dry, and he was very thirsty, so he stood and walked on.

On another day in mid-afternoon Pinky felt a chill cover him but could see no sign of a breeze. Looking around, he saw a series of large, round rocks scattered haphazardly across the landscape for several miles. They were rough-textured and mottled in the colors of rust and silver, ranging in size from that of a freight wagon to that of a large stock barn. Farther on, he stopped by a unique formation of red earth rising vertically from the desert floor. It was a mile long and a quarter-mile wide. The shape reminded Pinky of a burial mound, and it crossed his mind that it could be the burial site of an ancient giant, or perhaps the giant himself turned to stone and deteriorating for time unimaginable. Pinky felt his senses expand to fill the land and sky from horizon to horizon, and he recognized this as the awe of open space and eons.

Pinky heard a familiar sound, and, looking to his right toward a ghost gum growing above him on the hillside, there was a wavering of vision, like the heat waves common to mirages in the great deserts of the world. In this wavering Pinky saw a cat. The cat was not Henry. He was grey and different in other ways. At first he was tall and then taller. Then he transformed into an old man wearing a robe of indigo blue. The old man held a staff in his right hand, made from the limb of a ghost gum tree, worn smooth from years of handling and fissured in the way of wood long dead. He had a foot-long white beard that had trouble keeping up with the movement of his head as he scoured the landscape, as if expecting to find danger. And with another waver, the old man was again a cat, but now he looked a bit like Henry, the mangy cat Pinky first saw out by the barn in Once Wide Valley. But the possibility of Henry evaporated, and the large grey cat was back by the ghost gum.

Pinky knew that what he had seen was not real, and he looked again at the massive red mound. He was now certain it was a burial mound and he shivered — for it was the land itself that was buried here.

———••———

Pinky was on his way to Perth but had passed over the mountain of a different place, so when the cat spoke, Pinky did not find it unusual in the least. In fact, he found comfort in the musings of a stray he had befriended in the other world.

"The land is old and has slipped over the mountain."

The cat spoke slowly and stopped when Pinky stopped, but often moved on before Pinky was ready. Many times it was nothing more than Pinky's curiosity of what else the cat had to say that kept his feet moving through the gibberstone desert, through the spinefex shards, through the red sands in the heat of day, and across the rocky flats under the light of a moon that during his journey made a complete cycle from full to new to full again.

"The volcanoes have cooled and cracked, their cones have lost their angular stance, been worn down to hills, and those hills, once pert and young and feminine, have given up even their structure and not so much collapsed as settled sluggishly into the defeat of near flat, undisturbed by uselessness."

Pinky was surprised by the eloquence of the cat. He remembered how he had also been surprised by Bobbie's speech, and vowed to never again underestimate the potential for the intelligent expression of any being.

"The tectonic plates below have grown bored with their eons-long quest for a neighborly fit," the cat continued.

"It is tired land where there was once wind and the wind became reluctant to move even the lightest of dust, a land without crickets, without grass, without sky, no trees by churches, no churches, no grace, no love, no friends. Now there is only a dead calm sea of dust, absent even a ripple. Calm without irony, justice or despair. Languishing without humility or pride. A place not only without complexity but without even the simple click of duality.

"A place without a sense of place. A place without image.

"A place that waited for inertia and welcomed it without reflection.

"An exhausted land so grown over, so swamped in the murk of the infinite, that it sloughed into sameness and without a whimper, became the dead place, the place with no mystery."

At sundown, seven days after the cat appeared, he leapt up on an outcropping a few feet in front of Pinky, turned to him, made sure their eyes met, and finished his story of the other land with what Pinky took as a warning. "There is no happy ending for the land situated beyond the mountain, for given the chance of life, the chance to dream, the chance to become, this land nourished only the knack for dying."

Pinky recognized his heart in the cat's description of desolate land, and, looking across the dry, dust-covered desert within, found himself praying for rain. He closed his eyes and prayed as he had not since Bobbie's death. He called upon God, upon the Maker, upon the Creator, upon the Intention he believed to be a part of all living beings. He called out for them to share their stories with him. And when he heard nothing, he opened his eyes to ask the cat, but the old cat was gone. But beyond where he had stood on the rock outcropping was a stone structure, possibly a barn or a church. Though probably a vision, Pinky thought he should go there, but he could no longer stand, felt as though he was floating when he fell and felt only comfort when he landed on his side on the hard rock.

Pinky curled up with his head on his arm, and even as his body relaxed into the comfort of stone, his soul knew there was hope, knew that Pinky Wollerman's story was not finished, knew there was more for him to become.

And in the morning he was aroused by the whinny of his horse, and he stood again and walked.

———·——

The path given the spirit of Pinky Wollerman had been a nearly continuous uphill climb through thick brush without a clear compass reading, and there had been damned few places to rest and hear the words "well done" from a God that, by the standard of a satisfied heart, seemed to favor some over others.

There might have been another way to crest the ridge, perhaps an easier way, but this was the one given Pinky Wollerman, and he did not complain, for it had been a long time coming, and a long way around to get here. And, if Pinky were prone to understanding the journeys of others, he would have known that few ever hold the question that leads to the quest, and fewer still ever find their way.

At any given moment Pinky Wollerman could recall more of the good times than the bad times, and he had made it through hungry times and painful times with neither a sense of being sorry for himself nor a sense of pride. Given where he was in the hardscrabble landscape of the Outback, the valuable result of the life he had lived was that every difficult day had layered a thin film of confidence that had built up like 10,000 coats of good paint upon his bone and sinew and muscle fiber, so that now, with his mind a scatter, his body stood and led the way entirely on its own.

Then precisely at sundown, as the third full moon of his wandering rose, there was a green flash, and Pinky became an observer within his own being, finding himself on the crest of the hill his spirit had longed for throughout his life.

As though taking in a vast mural in a single glance, with no preconceived notion of what to focus upon, and no assessment of distance or effort, without the context of early or late, and without a judgment of any kind, Pinky, the observer, walked into the world of which he was now aware. And as an observer he was aware that he was so woven into the fabric of the world that the cloth would not exist without the splash of color and speck of fiber he, Pinky Wollerman, brought to the thing.

Pinky rejected the dead world described by the odd cat, and with a different mind he walked on.

Pinky's soul found peace, and his body walked on.

When he arrived at the vision of the stone building, he could see no human sign, but Henry was there waiting, and Pinky knew he had arrived, and he lay down and slept under the full moon.

———•———

When Pinky awoke in the early morning darkness, Henry was gone, but he could see the lights of a city, and he went to mount his horse and saw that he was ragged and thin, so he walked, leading the horse, into the city of Mandurah. For the first time in many days he spoke with another person, his voice cracking as he inquired about Perth and found it to be 50 or so miles up the coast.

In Perth someone might have recognized Pinky, but in Mandurah he was unknown.

At the edge of Mandurah he passed by a neighborhood of grand houses each set in the middle of an acre of gardens. A young man, apparently a gardener, stood in front of one such house watching Pinky, and, after the boy was assured that Pinky was simply ragged from the trail and would do him no harm, Pinky gave him $25 and his trust to take his horse and gear to The Parson in Perth. After spending some time saying goodbye to the horse, Pinky bought clothes to replace what had become rags hanging from his bony frame and bought a hat made of rabbit fur felt, which the haberdasher told him was the only good to ever come from rabbits. He secured a room with a bath, attempting to scrub and soak away his journey. The old woman at the boarding house directed him toward the harbor, and Pinky went there and asked about ships going out—he did not care where—and found a tramp steamer leaving within the hour.

The steamer had room for five passengers, and Pinky booked passage and boarded with the clothes on his back, the picture of his mother in Oklahoma, the oiled canvas slicker he had upon his arrival in Australia, and his belt, still holding a little over $1,000. It occurred to him that neither Andy nor Mills had paid him his drover wages and realized that meant nothing to him because the work itself had been sufficient pay, and he knew he would work for free forever if he could be with Bobbie.

Looking out to the empty horizon, Pinky wondered if anything would matter to him, really deep down matter, ever again. A faint part of him replied that it would.

Australia was through with Roland Washington Wollerman. The dust, the soil, the rock and all that sprang from it, walked upon it or soared above it—all of Australia was through with him. So he turned his back to it in favor of the open sea, a place lacking the joy he had found in Australia, but also lacking the pain and the grief, a place where the seed of hope, a seed that needed time and great distance, could germinate, however slowly.

The last people to see Pinky who knew him were the people in Alice Springs. As far as anyone knew, his absence meant that he had met his demise somewhere in the Outback. And when the gardener boy from Mandurah arrived at The Parson's house in Perth, The Parson was not at home. So, having arrived with the delivery and not knowing any better, the boy tied the horse to the porch railing and made his way back home to the grand houses needing his services. The Parson, rather than knowing Pinky was alive, was only perplexed by the anonymous gift of a bony horse he had never seen in his life.

THIRTY-TWO
JULY 1955

A story ran in the Visalia Times Delta exposing Sheriff Wilson's irresponsible spending of taxpayer money. The reporter received tips and information from a respected source within Tulare County's justice system.

Additionally, a source at a newspaper in Perth provided a wealth of stories about Pinky Wollerman's adventures in Australia. Pinky, the man said, had started his run from the law by going to Australia and then hiding in plain sight by moving in with a parson in Perth. He then set out on the Canning Stock Route, a place too dangerous to be followed. Then again he hid in the open, working as a drover on a remote cattle station. In Alice he undeservedly ran afoul of a restaurateur. He was fired upon at point blank range, but not hit, and Major-Mitchelling through the river bottom camps of the blacks, had disappeared so quickly and quietly into the bush he could not be followed. After that, the source said, the stories were less reliable, but widespread—told around every soak and humpy from the top end to the Simpson—stories told of a bush ranger called the Yankee Ghost, a maamu, a spirit. The Constable from Alice said the man was dead, but the stories of the Yankee Ghost said he could not be killed.

The Times Delta reporter, overwhelmed by the variety of stories passed to him, not entirely proficient in the slang of the Aussie English, and perhaps feeling some influence from the source who tipped him to the story in the first place, made a decision to tell those stories as he understood them, describing Pinky as the elusive Yankee Ghost. He mixed Aboriginal "rumors" and drover "reports" in a way that did not conclude either the guilt or the demise of Pinky with any certainty, but in a way that suggested he was innocent and still out there. One story expressed the serious doubts of the Australian public (who were represented by the assertions of two drovers from the Blenheim Creek area) that Pinky could ever be captured by the

American sheriff who had only been able to follow some days behind Pinky as he roamed across Northern and Western Australia, but could never come close enough to see the fellow's dust.

The final story in the series expressed the inferred conclusions of reports from within the sheriff's office and the district attorney's office, that evidence of Pinky's guilt in both countries was, at best, inconclusive.

The Times Delta articles circulated widely throughout Tulare County, and when Sheriff Wilson returned home with news of Pinky's demise, expecting a hero's welcome, he found an electorate that did not believe his story, a career heading for ruin, and an unstable and contentious wife.

THIRTY-THREE
1956-1979

Bobbie's wait for Pinky at Sturt Creek Station started with optimism. As the days passed and he did not return and did not contact anyone she knew, her confidence faded to hope, then months passed, and her hope faded to wishes. When their son was born, Bobbie knew Pinky would have been there if he were alive, so her wishes turned to despair.

Melinda Fraser, the station master's wife, worried that Bobbie's desolate heart was responsible for the indolent spirit of her 2-month-old son, Roland, and urged her to heal herself for his sake. Bobbie knew she would adapt to the boy's needs in time, but she also knew she could not wait. She asked Melinda to care for Roland for a short time, and walked into the past that deserts hold, seeking the wisdom of untold generations. The land she trod was ancient. The footsteps she walked in were hundreds of thousands of years old.

As with many open lands, modernity came to Australia unevenly, spotting the coast with cities as modern as any in the world, and leaving the vast interior behind. The foliage of the landscape was forever changed by such introductions as the rabbit, but the interior was left wild. A few scattered open-pit mines changed the land itself, but even those of gigantic proportions were lost in the vastness of the Australian interior. It was easy in the 1950s to see a land skipped over by time, and it was such a land that Bobbie walked into at the beginning of her last spring.

Bobbie's journey could not be called a walkabout. It was her grief and loss that drove Bobbie to go on foot into the desert beyond Halls Creek. Few people find love of the depth she had experienced with Pinky Wollerman. She grieved the loss of that love, and she called out to any God that might respond, seeking some understanding of the fleeting nature of something so profoundly beautiful, so complete in its promise, so peaceful for a soul in continual strife since childhood.

When Bobbie had traveled for many days, sometimes walking

in a trance, sometimes loping to work her grief through the sieve of the movement of muscle and sinew and bone, the skipping stone of time landed squarely upon that part of the Outback where Bobbie lay fitfully sleeping.

Bobbie awakened in pre-dawn to a scratching near the mouth of the small cave where she had taken shelter in the evening before. A small creature, its form indistinct in the grey rubble but with the fluid movement of a cat, darted into the outside world. She rolled over on the soft earthen floor, pulled herself into a fetal curl with her face nearly touching the sandstone wall, and in the way she had started every day since she accepted Pinky's death, she cried.

When she had cried sufficiently, Bobbie squeezed her eyes tightly, forcing out the remaining tears and hoping for a fresh world where Pinky and love were still present, and in that moment the inside of the cave became visible to her in a reddish hue. She was startled by the light, but hopeful. As the vision began to fade, Bobbie opened her eyes to a world of daylight that slowly faded back into the usual dun of dawn. Then the ancient world met the atomic world with a rush of wind and dust surging first outward, then pausing and then backward, and Bobbie's moment of hope was snapped up and swallowed within a nightmare of destruction.

Hours after the winds calmed and the earth cooled, Bobbie came from the cave into a world she scarcely recognized, and she set out for the station that might still be called home.

At a place between the cave and home she awoke after a night of fitful sleep to a rapidly increasing sense of nausea and weakness. She staggered as far as she could for two days, then improved and made better time. But after a week, when she was still far from home, she noticed bleeding from her mouth and splotchy spots on the skin of her legs and arms. A couple of days later her hair began to fall out.

After three weeks and with help from two drovers from a sheep ranch, Bobbie arrived at the Sturt Creek Station. Feeling herself near death and void of hope, she commissioned Andrew and Melinda Fraser to care for Roland. As Bobbie had developed into a young woman, Melinda had given her loving care and made sure she was not just well-educated, but extensively educated. Melinda had no children of her own and enjoyed baby Roland, so she readily agreed.

Four days later, comforted that her baby was in good care, and confident her spirit would blend within Pinky's love, Bobbie died.

———·———

In 1957, a year after Bobbie died, the Frasers adopted her baby, who became Roland Wollerman Fraser.

Melinda, the only mother Roland remembered, died when he was 16. Roland helped Andy on the station, but Andy insisted the boy attend college, so in 1974 Roland traveled to the United States and enrolled in an agricultural curriculum at California Polytechnic College in San Luis Obispo.

Roland knew that his mother, Bobbie, had loved a man named Wollerman and had taken the name as hers. He knew the man who fathered him was dead, but knew nothing else of him.

Boyle Humbert passed away in 1976, and Andy Fraser purchased over half of Sturt Creek Station from Mrs. Humbert.

Roland returned to Sturt Creek Station in his 22nd year, having graduated with honors, a double degree in agriculture and cultural anthropology, and a strong desire to be in the spaciousness of distant horizons offered by his home land.

Andy Fraser passed away in 1979, and Roland inherited a 35,000-hector cattle station, small by Australian standards, vast by any other standard, and rich in diversity of range land and sources of water.

———·———

During a time of nuclear bluster a test was conducted to prepare for war. Or perhaps it was a demonstration intended to intimidate against war. By either intention, it took place some distance to the northeast of the station in what was called empty desert. But, of course, as Roland knew, land is never empty, and Bobbie, the mother he never knew, following the paths of her ancestors, had found herself standing in old land, but in the midst of a terrible future.

Since returning to Sturt Creek Station, Roland had held a persistent but niggling thought to create a monument for his mother.

Then, as October of 1979 arrived and advanced, he felt this intention sweep outward, as though a living thing, roam through the timeless consciousness of the vast Australian Outback, and return to him as a charge too compelling to be ignored.

So, on the border of the desert closest to the nuclear test range where his mother was exposed to the radiation that killed her, Roland and several of his men searched out a large, oblong stone. They carved the name Bobbie Wollerman on the flattest surface and stood the 12-foot-long stone on end.

When the stone was inscribed and standing, Roland was greeted by an inner quiet. And he felt a promise, a promise that someday he would also be greeted by understanding.

Standing by the stone and scanning westward from the land at his feet to the horizon and beyond, it dawned on him what he'd just been given and he smiled at the land and said, "You promised." Still smiling, he shook his finger in a friendly manner at the land and repeated, "You promised."

ᴛHIRTY-ᖴOUR

On the oceans Pinky's sense of the passage of seasons slurred, and he knew only that the steamer had stopped at many of the world's ports before arriving in San Francisco Bay. Pinky asked a longshoreman and was told it was 1959, near the end of July. He had been at sea for nearly four years. For no reason other than the proximity of memories, he decided to go home, and with that decision felt the long-awaited germination of the seed of hope. He disembarked and called Bill Jenkins asking for a ride home.

Bill met Pinky with a nod outside of the customs office and carried Pinky's duffle to a brand new Dodge panel wagon. Once they were out of the maze of the port, Bill, showing nothing of the curiosity he'd lived with for years, said, "Good to see you, Pinky."

"You, too, Bill."

With that they rode in silence toward Sacramento, and Pinky appreciated that Bill was giving him time to feel at home before pelting him with questions. He was happy to sit and watch as the capital city disappeared and they rolled past the lush farm lands along Highway 99.

When they came to Highway 198 and turned east, Pinky asked about the ranch, then about the people—Kazuko, Emily Robin and Logan.

"The ranch is doing well," Bill said. "There was a couple of dry years, but nothing like the drought that ended in '47.

Pinky saw that Visalia had grown far beyond anything he might have expected.

"Your collection of strays is also doing well. Kazuko bought the Eldridge farm southeast of Exeter where he worked after his internment, and he's planted a small peach orchard and a couple of acres of strawberries and blackberries. He spends his winters in San Francisco."

Pinky looked over at Bill, puzzled that Kazuko would winter in San Francisco, but Bill continued before he could be questioned.

"Emily Robin and Logan are living in the valley and doing well."

Pinky felt slow with his words and wondered if perhaps he had lost the art of spontaneous conversation.

"Things have been a lot quieter in the valley since Buck died," Bill said matter-of-factly.

Pinky's head jerked toward Bill. "Buck's dead?"

Bill glanced at Pinky, smiled, and continued with more feeling, "I knew you probably didn't know anything about it! Yeah, Buck's dead. Nobody knows for sure, but everybody thinks his sister-in-law shot him for cutting her family out of the inheritance. She's not in jail because they couldn't prove anything, but Twyla was the likely killer. At first most folks thought it was you."

"Me?" Pinky's brow was furrowed in disbelief. "Any particular reason?"

Bill laughed. "Well, for one thing, you left town about the same time Buck was shot through the heart."

Pinky shrugged, following the countryside with his eyes.

"Trouble is, Pinky, not many people knew you that well. But a deputy sheriff named Dillard—you'll see his 'vote for me' posters plastered around the whole county—was the one who decided it wasn't you. You probably ought to vote for the guy."

"What happened to Dave Wilson?"

"Well, he chased you down to Australia..."

"He did what? I never saw him!"

"Dave Wilson thought you were the guilty one, so he followed you to Australia and ended up having quite an adventure. Those Aussies are a cantankerous bunch. Especially when it comes to the law chasing a man down. He chased fake leads for several months, then gave up. And, from what we read in the paper here, you had quite a reputation down there. And that's a day's story by itself, so I'll show you your clippings when we get back to the ranch.

"By the time Dave came back to the states, your name had been cleared, but he tried to tell everyone that you were dead. Most of us didn't buy it. And those that weren't sure got pissed off that an innocent man might have died because of Dave's blundering around Australia hounding the man."

Bill paused to see if Pinky was following the importance of what happened while he was gone, but couldn't tell because Pinky was looking out the window, so Bill went on.

"The district attorney wouldn't prosecute Twyla because he said there wasn't enough evidence, but everyone thought it was more likely because she was Sheriff Wilson's wife, and they didn't like that, so Dave has been pretty useless as a sheriff since then, and for sure, he won't get re-elected. The district attorney probably won't either."

———·———

Pinky shook his head, trying to reanimate the petrified memories formed before his leaving. Trying to grasp the roiling surges that had been real life.

"How's Mindy Wilson holding up?"

"She moved to San Francisco right after Buck's funeral. Hasn't been seen here in a while."

"What about the ranch?"

"Buck left that to Logan. When I said Logan and Emily Robin were living in the valley, I meant living in Buck's old place. The law firm that handled the will wanted to manage Logan's trust and the ranch, but me and Kaz and Emily Robin were up to that challenge. In fact we managed both places, yours and Logan's."

"That's quite a job, Bill."

"Its been fun, Pinky. Maybe not fun. But a satisfying challenge."

"Shouldn't Mindy have gotten some of the ranch?"

"Buck apparently left something of equal value for Mindy and she moved out right away. Seems she only stayed on the ranch because she loved Buck and was more than happy to see it go to Logan."

Pinky nodded. "She was a good woman."

"Kaz apparently thinks so."

Again, Pinky was puzzled. "What?"

"They got a lot in common. Seems his wintering in San Francisco includes quite a lot of time with Mindy. Some say full time."

Pinky sat silent for a few moments, watching the countryside sliding by, remembering how he met Kazuko and smiling. "Kaz is a good man," he said.

"Mindy apparently thinks so."

——··——

When they reached the Highway 65 turnoff toward Exeter, Pinky asked Bill to take that way home so they could go up over Rocky Hill on the way into the Once Wide Valley.

When they topped Rocky Hill, Bill pulled off the road. Pinky let himself out of the truck and climbed up on a rock outcropping where he could see the whole valley. His home-thirsty soul drank in every square inch of the land and he was so engrossed in his memories that he did not notice when an old black pickup pulled over beside Bill's truck. Pinky couldn't take his eyes off the valley, shimmering and magic in the summer heat, and was startled a moment later by a gentle hand on his arm.

"Hello, Pinky." It was Emily Robin's voice. "Welcome home, pilgrim."

As Pinky turned toward her, she wrapped her arms around him, buried her face in his neck, and held him for an uncomfortably long time. Pinky was surprised by the affection and wondered why it was given him.

"Good to see you, Emily Robin," Pinky said, putting her at arm's length. "I hear you've been helping to manage two ranches and that Logan is doing fine." Pinky knew it sounded awkward, but it was the best he could do.

Bill started talking, and Pinky, grateful for the reason for escape, excused himself and moved to where Bill stood and asked him to start over, feigning that he had not heard. Bill was talking about the land, and, as he spoke, Pinky noticed that Bill had developed a new vocabulary.

"You know how long a million years is, Pinky?" Bill asked. Then, without waiting for an answer, he opened his arms to encompass the entire mountain range in front of them. "These mountains used to be a sea bed. They were pushed up over 50 million years ago. The Once Wide Valley was cut out of them by glaciers that came and went three or four times. The last glacier left here 10,000 years ago. But, Pinky, it took that glacier 100,000 years to do its work."

Bill paused to give Pinky a chance to take in the magnitude of the time frame he was describing.

Pinky used the pause to interrupt, "You talk funny, Bill. What's happened to you?"

"Oh," Bill said, "I been doing a lot of reading. Emily Robin—" He pointed to where she now stood on the rock outcropping. "Emily Robin and Kaz got me going to the library and reading about stuff I didn't even know existed, like geology and the history of the earth. Scientists have learned a lot about this land we live on. Not that they know everything, but they got me to thinking, so I read a lot and came to think differently about the land around us, which requires a different vocabulary."

Pinky remembered learning much from Bobbie about vocabulary and ways of thinking.

"And even a different way of seeing time," Bill said. "When you think differently, you need different words, Pinky. Do you know what I mean?"

"I believe I do, Bill," Pinky said. But Pinky was thinking about Bobbie and the Aborigine way of being in the world.

"But, the thing is," Bill went on, "when you think about how long the land has been at work, it is clear we're merely visitors. And you and me are for sure not the first visitors. We're just the ones that managed to change the land in a way it never has been. And when you think about what work the land has been doing, you start to see that the land will take care of itself. So all that stuff you see—the blacktopped roads, the cuts through the mountainsides for the roads, the buildings, the dams, the leveling of the prairie pastures—given the timeframe the land lives in—all of that is purely temporary."

Again, Bill opened his arms up toward the mountains, raising and lowering them and waving his hands to punctuate each point. "Someday these mountains will sink to sea beds, and sea beds will rise to be mountains. In between there will be fires and earthquakes and floods, and the land will burn itself clean, shake off what it can, and wash the residue away."

"Sounds like the apocalypse," Pinky said, eyebrows furrowed.

"No," Bill said, "Just Mother Earth doing her housecleaning. And she will. She'll clean up the whole mess. It's hers, not ours. We're only borrowing the place for a time. A brief time." Bill looked across the valley for a moment, then added, "Makes ownership seem like a pretty arrogant concept, don't you think?"

Both men were silent for a moment, thinking about the valley, thinking about time. Then Bill nodded toward Emily Robin. "She's in love with you."

Bill paused, thinking he probably had asked Pinky to fathom something far more puzzling to him than how long a million years is.

"We should have seen it before you left. But it was real plain after you were gone. We all missed you, but she was beside herself. Every time someone mentioned your name, she looked lost. She would go out at odd times to just stand and look down toward the road."

"Are you sure it was because she missed me?" Pinky asked, remembering how flirtatious Emily Robin had been. He wondered if anyone had considered that she might have taken revenge on Buck Wilson, and what they thought was pining over lost affection was really nervousness and guilt. It was a terrible thought, and Pinky felt ashamed and shook it away.

"You don't know much about women, Pinky."

"Probably not, Bill."

———·———

But Pinky remembered Bobbie's eyes and remembered the sensation of flight he had felt when he looked into them and with that sensation felt he might know something about time so immense that it could easily engulf a million years. He also remembered how much he loved the boy, Logan, and knew that Emily Robin and Logan were a package.

Pinky turned away from the Once Wide Valley, his focus far beyond the distant western horizon. "I probably don't know much about women, Bill." He paused a moment, thinking, remembering, giving up the past for the future. "And I probably ought at least talk to Emily Robin." He dropped his gaze to the rocky earth at his feet, and, with quiet resignation, said, "Maybe I'll learn something."

THIRTY-FIVE
FEBRUARY 1960

On a cloudy, rain-threatened day, Pinky parked his pickup on the narrow paved country road where the grasslands rise into the elevation band of manzanita and scrub brush. He guided a young Morgan from the horse trailer, led the horse through a wire gate and scanned the hillside to the north.

Five years had passed, and he still would look upon a thing of beauty and describe it in his mind for Bobbie, or encounter a problem and ask Bobbie how to look at it. He would wonder about things for her, show her what he saw, question and ask her for answers, feel and tell her how he felt, and in all this he would see her face and hear her voice.

Pinky loved being home, loved the narrow country roads with their uneven blacktop bleached grey by years of summer suns, roads that reliably led to places such as this, places not marked on the maps given out at the gasoline filling stations, places scratched in the species memory of the wild things who made the valley home, places marked only by the crisscross tramping of those who worked the land.

The two things country roads have in common, Bobbie had said, is first a sense of being only slightly evolved from a dirt track, and second, an ancient memory buried deep under them within the soil, of having once been a trail defined by the subtle bent of the grass. What Bobbie also taught him was that not all of the appealing country roads are in one's own country.

Such was the trail through the bush of Australia's Northwest Territory that Pinky and Bobbie followed to its end and beyond on the morning of their awakening, which was the same morning the land awoke and the sky yawned itself from slumber, blinking sleepily in the bright of day break after a long night of gentle starlight.

It seemed to the two lovers that God had watched.

God had watched all through the night and into the morning and used all of creation to smile upon them. They were as sure of that as they were of the rocks beneath their feet.

Riding the sure-footed Morgan across the upland pasture, Pinky sought within himself for the memory of that day and its conversations, and it came, willingly, whole and fresh, for it was a part of him.

Pinky remembered that it was a morning made for the senses. A morning when they saw the land rolling away to every horizon, splashed in a thousand shades each of orange and black and green, sensed the endlessness within the blue above, felt the absence of boundaries, and, as though standing before a gateway to the infinite were stricken with awe. They felt their hearts expand to fill every canyon, crack, and crevice across the earth all that is between the earth and the farthest stars.

Pinky remembered that day, and then he pulled a handwritten letter from the inside pocket of his coat, the page meant to send his heart to her, words of tenderness and excitement and promise, scribbled on the back of a bill of lading.

But she had died, and after he learned of her death, he had shredded the first page—shredded it with the need to cover as much of the landscape as possible, shredded it and thrown it to the up-canyon wind beside a massive uplifting of rock on his pilgrimage to Mandurah.

And now, Pinky rode with the second page, borrowed paper with precious words, moistened by a fast moving and unexpected shower that freshened the Sycamore Spring where it ran into Alder Creek a half-mile above the Once Wide. There he dropped the second page and the remainder of his heart. He felt them dissolve and flow down-canyon, and he knew they would someday soon seep back into the land.

Pinky was lost for a time in his memories, and when his focus returned to the flow of Alder Creek, his eyes searched downstream, but the letter for Bobbie had sunk within the gentle current and remained now only as a memory among memories.

Pinky had felt the surge of love, had been moved by the power of love, had been in the center of the promise of love. And his experience was so powerful that he was certain he knew what love was.

But Pinky was stuck at the peak of his own experience, an experience with a gravitational field far too powerful for him to escape. He never knew there was more about love, never knew the peaceful maturity of love. And not knowing what he did not know, he carried the power of certainty that often accompanies ignorance, and it was a certainty that would keep him from loving a woman ever again.

Yet four months later Pinky married Emily Robin.

THIRTY-SIX
1961–1979

For a few years the Wollermans were a stable family, well-integrated into the foothill communities around the Once Wide Valley. Pinky and Emily Robin were friends, and Pinky was neither surprised nor particularly hurt when she engaged in discreet dalliances. He, after all, engaged every day, in his heart and mind, with his own true love.

When Logan went away to college, Emily Robin traveled to New Zealand for a visit that she ambiguously extended for so long it was no surprise when she acknowledged she had no plan to return. Through the years Logan visited her occasionally. Pinky did not. Pinky was, again, neither surprised nor particularly hurt when he received a letter from Emily Robin requesting a divorce. When he sought an attorney, Pinky was surprised that divorce had become so common; there were law firms that specialized in divorce law.

Logan returned from Berkeley married to an English professor, Vivian Stanley. Vivian continued to teach, commuting to Berkeley, and Logan worked closely with Pinky, slowly taking over the operation of the ranch, and feeling a part of a working partnership.

Then, as 1978 reached its zenith, Pinky Wollerman's body finally gave out. Pinky saw it coming—the winding down of his body and mind. His spirit was still strong. And before he was too far gone, Pinky told Logan he had spent his whole life fighting the natural tendency of things to go wild when he should have been fighting the possibility of things going to rest. But that's what farmers and ranchers do, he said, organize the wild things, if only for a season.

And then Pinky made that pursed lip smile of his and slightly flipped his right hand. "There's a season for everything," he said, "and they're all good." Words that had carried him through the Depression, the Dust Bowl, the loss of his family, and the loss of the one love of his life.

Logan thought Pinky was fortunate to finish the way he did.

Everybody loses it all in the end. The self arrives naked and then builds and adds and gains and becomes. And then people start dropping pieces of themselves along the way toward the finish. The lucky ones keep most of themselves nearly to the end, as Pinky did. In his 76th year, though his mind remained relatively clear, his body ceased to carry him upright.

Over the years Pinky would periodically look Logan in the eye and tell him something that the ranch had taught him, and as he weakened he did so more frequently.

On a brisk October morning Pinky suddenly shucked off his quilt and asked Logan to take him out on the back porch.

Logan helped Pinky into his favorite chair—a simple faded, blue wooden chair from a long-ago kitchen.

Pinky sat for a while, looking out at the foothill ranch he had willed to Logan. "It's yours now, Logan. All of it." The rattle in his chest was louder. "I hope you..."

The pause was long enough to cause Logan to want to complete Pinky's thoughts for him, so he asked, "Make something of it?"

"You could whitewash the Mona Lisa and use it for a grocery list or a for sale sign and that would make something of it. But what I hope is that you simply leave it whole. You've got Buck's place, soon you'll have my place and when Bill dies, you'll have his. The whole Once Wide Valley will be one place again. Keep it that way, Logan. That's when it's at its best."

His eyes, poor as they were, seemed to see all the way across and up the valley, and he looked over and caught Logan's eye, and then he scanned the whole scene again. And when he looked back at Logan, Pinky's chin was shaking, and his pale blue eyes were fierce under a light cover of tears. He had big hands for such a small man, and he flung his hand out and swept the whole of the scene and looked again at Logan, who could see in Pinky's eyes how serious he was in the presence of the land. Logan nodded, and when he did, Pinky also nodded and relaxed a little and almost smiled.

Logan put an arm over Pinky's thin shoulders as he spent his last minutes seeing the land beyond his porch, seeing what Logan knew he had yet to find the wisdom to see. Then Pinky said, "Dust that dreams." Logan questioned him with his eyes, and Pinky added, "That's all we are, son. We come from dust and we go to dust. And in the middle, we dream."

Pinky smiled. "The lucky among us dream in open places. Dreams of love."

———.———

The summer after Pinky's death started by showing a strong preference for heat and drought, but October's weather, fickle as a well-fed cat, slipped in a short but wild thunderstorm that scattered cattle and washed out fences. Logan liked weather because the changing of the seasons put different faces upon the land. Underfoot the ranch was all rock and dirt and dust, but somehow, working with open space and weather, working with rolling hills, a slow creek, and the covering sky, the place could put together a presence that made a soul feel at home.

In this dry year the high meadow grasses were grazed dangerously low, and any sprouts drawn from the ground by the recent storm would shrivel in the pending frost. Lacking sufficient pasture the cattle would begin to forage on shrubs, some of which, like poison oak, were toxic, and they could die. Logan needed to bring them in before the grass was gone.

Coming to the shoulder of a wide ridge high above Once Wide Creek, Logan sat his horse and enjoyed the view of the rolling foothills forming the valley below. One Eyed Jack, the ranch's old border collie, ran ahead of Logan to a shelf of granite nearly covered by centuries of decomposing oak leaves and twigs. Coarse lichen, baked hard by many summers of relentless sun into a varnish of black and pale jade and persimmon, covered the boulders that rose above the duff and debris. Jack sniffed and pawed and whined and looked from the ground to Logan and back again in deliberate repetition.

Knowing the find must be of keen interest to keep Jack from his cattle, Logan pulled his horse up beside a dead oak, swung his leg over the saddle horn and dropped to the ground. He found the dog nose to nose with a small grey lizard half as long as his snout. "Oh, Jack. Growing old and easily entertained, are you?" But the lizard dropped into a hole in the rock, and when Logan kicked aside the leaf litter, he found the hole to be the size of a grapefruit with smooth sides and rounded bottom. Clearing more of the area while Jack conveyed an "I told you so" attitude by sitting nearby but not watching, Logan found the stone shelf covered with holes of various sizes and found three oblong stone pestles with round, smooth ends.

"People once lived here, Jack." Logan stood and looked down the valley to the west and scanned back toward the high ground to the east. Jack stopped panting, intently watching Logan speak. "This was their kitchen."

Jack woofed softly, as though he understood, and the two scanned the area, Logan imagining a day some hundreds or perhaps thousands of years ago. A day in early summer with children in the thicket down in the creek bottom picking blackberries into woven grass baskets and a clutch of women, crushing acorns or buckeyes in the stone mortars, smoke curling skyward in the still air and the rusty-hinge squawk of a jay on the ridge above announcing someone's arrival.

Had they, Logan wondered, and their generations of ancestors, ground away the rock? Or had they found it already in place, a relic of an even earlier people?

As an act of respect for the people of the past, Logan scattered the duff, leaves and twigs back across the work bench, and noticing the dog's attention, said "I wonder, Jack. How many different peoples have lived on this land? Is it even the same land? With the same kinds of trees growing in the same places? Were the winters colder or the summers hotter, the canyons deeper or the creek wider?

"How long, Jack, does it take for a place to not be the same place?"

Jack whined, and Logan turned to see him lying belly flat on the ground, his eye on the ancient kitchen.

Logan wished he could have this talk with Pinky, but the dog would have to do, so he answered the dog's questioning eye.

"I don't know why they are gone, Jack. Most of the time we don't even know the what of their daily lives. And when we do we only know a smattering through bits and pieces, relics and artifacts. But they are long gone."

Logan mounted his horse and sat looking at the place a community once lived. "And the why of it will never be more than a guess," he said and looked back at Jack, but the dog had decided there had been enough rumination in the middle of a work day and was running again, up and across the hill, intent to find some remnant of the scattered herd.

Logan laughed and yelled after him, "You shouldn't have asked if you didn't want to hear." But Jack ignored him, so Logan pointed his horse toward the dog and gave him his head.

Upon entering a sparse grove of old oaks on the hillside above the ledge, the horse whinnied and stopped and shook his head, and Logan thought he heard a voice calling quietly. He turned in the saddle and looked back toward the abandoned rock kitchen. For a moment and for no good reason he was unsure if the ancients had gone on.

But there was only the land. And the quiet.

ACKNOWLEDGEMENTS

I am grateful to Jan Haag and Katie McCleary for providing the forum in which the character of Pinky Wollerman came to life, their encouragement and guidance as Pinky's story became a book, and finally, for their decision to publish *The Love Story of Pinky Wollerman*. Other than my children, Jessica Kasparian and Samuel Cole, and my partner, Cheryl Fuller, it is the most delightful gift of my life.

A special thanks to Krista Minard for bringing her amazing talent and professionalism as an editor to this project. A special thanks to the wonderful artist Angela Tannehill for visually interpreting Pinky's character and story in a single beautiful collage that became the cover art.

During the years of uncovering Pinky's story, I was blessed with working with some of Sacramento's finest writers in my Saturday Writing Group and in my Novel Writing Support Group. My heartfelt thanks to all of them for allowing me to observe and learn from their talent in the craft of writing, for their enthusiasm that kept the joy in my writing, and for their feedback that helped turn a series of vignettes into a novel.

Love and great appreciation to the best of parents, George and Vessie Cole, who supported and encouraged my love of the outside and for making me comfortable in the wild places where nature's beauty, mystery, and stubborn endurance are an inspiration for life and love.

And finally, I am grateful for the laws and acts that preserve the wild places, to those ranchers who keep open spaces open, and to the people of the Pacific Crest Trail Association and other such organizations for protecting vast stretches of wild and scenic lands.